TEXAS DIVIDED

LONE STAR REDEMPTION
BOOK TWO

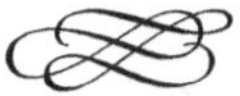

SHERRY SHINDELAR

*This book is dedicated to my husband, who is my biggest fan.
And to the Lord, who picked me up every time I couldn't find my way
in this book and pointed me to how to turn the next corner.*

CHAPTER 1

NOVEMBER 1863
COLORADO COUNTY, EASTERN TEXAS

orning Fawn "Beth Logan" did not want to be here. She sucked in a breath and blew it out hard. Despite the chill in the air, sweat dampened her palms. All around her, families, mostly mothers and their children, stopped to greet each other as they headed into the double doors of the weathered church. Black, gray, and deep purple, the colors of mourning and half-mourning, reigned amongst their apparel. Too many deaths from this war, but these were not her people, and it was not her war.

A few elms and scattered oak trees dotted the pebbled yard. Above their heads, the bell clanged in its wooden tower. Empty of welcome for her, the sound scraped her nerves.

She looked up, placing a hand to her straw hat to keep it from falling off. Aunt Judith had wanted her to wear a proper bonnet, just as she'd wanted her to wear a hoop beneath her dress. Morning Fawn had silently placed the straw hat on her head, tied the ribbons under her chin, and walked out to the waiting four-seat landau with her skirt flat against a single petticoat and chemise.

On the way to church, Cousin Thea had prattled on and on about her visit to Robson's castle the day before. Who cared about a limestone monstrosity in the middle of the prairie where all the folks who considered themselves high society could go to put on airs? Morning Fawn had escaped the stuffy carriage as soon as they arrived at the church.

"Beth, hurry along." Aunt Judith adjusted her fox stole across her shoulders as she turned toward the clapboard building. Her broad-rimmed bonnet with lace trim did little to hide her displeasure. "We're going to be late."

"Never mind her." Cousin Thea smoothed her flounced taffeta skirt after its crunch through the narrow carriage door. "If Beth wants to stay out here with the servants and the drivers, let her."

"She'll do no such thing." Aunt Judith extended her gloved hand. Morning Fawn grimaced and stepped to her aunt's side, avoiding her clasp. The woman's touch was as far from comfort as a prickly pear.

Nothing like Morning Fawn's *pia*, her adopted Comanche mother. Would she ever see her again? For nine years, Morning Fawn had lived with the Comanche only to be ripped from her home and family by two-bit ruffians her uncle had hired to kidnap her. *Rescued.* That's what they called it. Destroying her life was more like it.

Thea tossed her head with a familiar scowl marring her otherwise pale, smooth complexion. Ringlets of auburn hair jiggled beneath her high-brim bonnet. "Cousin Beth has the manners of a fishmonger," she muttered and waved to the middle-aged man at the hitching post. "Mr. Henry?"

Mr. Henry handed his reins to his slave and tipped his stovepipe hat, revealing graying temples and a receding hairline. "Good morning, Miss LeBeau, Mrs. Lebeau...Miss Logan."

Morning Fawn turned away as Thea curled a hand around the portly man's bulging arm. Let her cousin set her cap at a man twice her age. There was no light in their eyes when they looked at each other. Nothing like the glow between Morning Fawn's sister, Eyes-Like-Sky, and Dancing Eagle. That was love, regardless of her sister's marriage to a soldier after Dancing Eagle's death. A love she, herself, had never known.

Thea gushed as Mr. Henry guided her past. "Thank goodness, there's still a few men around these parts to look after us womenfolk."

Any man worth his snuff was out fighting. Not that Morning Fawn agreed with these Texans and their Confederacy, but if there was fighting to be done, a man did it. He didn't hide behind his servants and his acres of cotton. And he didn't ruin someone's life for three hundred dollars, like the blue-eyed, dark-haired weasel warrior who had helped kidnap her from the Comanche and thwarted her best escape attempt. She clenched her hands.

"Please try to behave yourself," her aunt whispered at her side.

"Don't I always?"

"Most certainly not. We're going to Cedar Crest plantation after church. Mrs. Brown has invited us for tea and dinner." Worry lines across her brow and at the corners of her mouth deepened. "Try not to slurp your tea, and if you're not for sure which fork to use, follow my lead. A young lady is judged by her manners."

Morning Fawn rolled her eyes. "In East Texas, women are judged by nothing that matters." She jutted out her chin. "I can ride faster and hunt better than any woman in this county."

"You're not on the frontier anymore. Hunting won't—"

"I wish I was."

"Excuse me, young lady." Aunt Judith bit off her words.

"You interrupted me. I was about to say that hunting won't get you a husband. That you need—"

"Last thing I need." Beth gathered her bothersome skirt and marched ahead, sidestepping two little boys playing jacks in the middle of the pathway.

She wanted nothing to do with citified men. Besides, she'd had more than her share of lectures from her aunt on proper behavior. Better to sit in church and hear the preacher than to listen to another dose of her aunt's disapproval.

Despite the wool stockings, her rock-hard leather shoes pinched her feet, rubbing her big toe raw. She was going to find a way to go hunting, kill a deer, and make her a pair of moccasins and leggings. She'd learned to pick the lock on her door. It was just a matter of getting access to a shotgun.

But it'd be simpler to persuade Mr. Nicholas Moyer, the administrator in charge of the cotton warehouse in Alleyton, to take her hunting. She'd seen the way he looked at her, and the way her uncle's jaw had clenched when she'd flirted openly with the man at dinner the other night. There was more than one way to show her uncle he couldn't control her.

Flirting was one thing. Finding a way to use Moyer's resources for an escape was another. Seventeen months since her kidnapping, and she'd failed to make it back to her Nokoni Comanche home. Even if she found a way to return, it would never be the same. She wasn't the same. What if she didn't belong anymore?

Head down, as though buffeting a wind, she clomped up the wooden steps and past an elderly gentleman at the door. The whispers and stares of the congregants, muted now compared to the roar they had been months earlier, trailed behind her.

"'Amazing grace, how sweet the sound...'" played from the piano as Morning Fawn walked down the aisle, past the pews of families of storekeepers, tradesmen, and overseers. Only a couple able-bodied men under fifty sat among them. She slowed near the front row of padded seats where the planter-class families sat and entered the LeBeau pew. As if one needed a special pew or four stuffy walls to worship the Creator. It was show, all show, except for the way the preacher's eyes lit up when he spoke, and a few of the voices from the back which usually sang out with gusto.

"'Amazing grace...'" It had been her settler mother's favorite song. How did she know that? She couldn't remember her mother's face aside from the portrait in LeBeau's library, but she recalled the song. Her throat tightened as she shuffled to the far end of the pew. She would not think of her mother.

Face frozen in a scold, Aunt Judith pulled in alongside her, taking a seat almost a foot away. Cousin Thea, Mr. Henry, and Aunt Clarey followed close by, leaving Morning Fawn hemmed in between them and the wall on the other side of her. Stupid mistake to bolt ahead and be the first one in. Her heartbeat thrummed in her head.

Dressed in a dark suit and a white cravat, the slender preacher with spectacles stepped up to the pulpit. The music stopped. Thank God. Hungry for air, Beth trained her eyes ahead and swished her fan. Couldn't they open a window in this place?

The preacher's voice rose and fell as he read a few verses. *God help me.* Did He listen? Did He care? A portly woman whose girth dominated the piano bench struck the chords of a hymn on the ivory keys.

The congregation stood. Beth followed suit, gripping the back of the pew in front of her. Then came "Amazing Grace." The first time had only been the prelude. They'd sing all the verses this time. "'I once was lost...'"

A snippet of memory. Her mother brushing her hair. Morning Fawn squeezed her eyes shut and tried to swallow, but the acid stuck in her throat. Her mother. *Oh, Lord...*

The spells, which had started shortly after she'd come to the Comanche and often struck at night, had dissipated after a couple of years. Shortness of breath, shivers, waking dreams. Her Comanche pia had wrapped Morning Fawn in her arms and held her until the terrors faded. However, they'd returned full force since her arrival at the LeBeau plantation, the last home her family had stayed at before they'd headed for the Texas frontier and their deaths—except now, there was no one to hold her.

"'I once was blind, but now I see...'"

She had to think of something else. The bronze and golden leaves of the pecan and cottonwood trees along the creek on the way here. Had she finished peeling the apples in the basket this morning on the back porch? How many apples were there? But when she started to count them in her head, they turned red, red like blood.

The song finished, and the congregation sat. She did not. Her aunt nudged her arm with a knuckle, nodding toward the pew.

Sweat beaded on Morning Fawn's temples. Sitting with her mama by the campfire, the last calm moment before the night exploded with nerve-piercing howls, warriors charging, and shrieks. Blood red. The fire and screams. The neighing of horses. Too many horses. She mumbled, "I need to be excused" and squeezed out past half a dozen legs, trampling a shoe in the process.

Mr. Henry jumped to his feet to make room. Heads turned.

Morning Fawn kept going. Couldn't she go to the privy without causing a commotion? But the privy wasn't what she was aiming for. Out the door and down the steps, she willed her legs to take one step at a time until she'd made it around the front to the side of the church, away from the curious eyes of the drivers by the hitching posts.

Her head pounded. She had to get away. From the past. From everything.

Stumbling on a root, she bent down and yanked the deplorable shoes off of her feet. Ahead, Mr. Franklin's chestnut Thoroughbred nibbled on grass, no owner in sight. She'd heard rumors it could beat any horse in the county.

A thought sizzled through her. Freedom. She broke into a run, her skirt flapping against her legs. Pebbles dug into her stocking feet. No walls. No people. Escape. She yanked the lead rope from the rail and grabbed the reins.

The horse snorted as Morning Fawn latched on to the pommel, stuck a foot in the stirrup, and heaved herself onto the saddle.

"Miss Logan—" A man came around the corner.

Morning Fawn snapped the reins and pressed her calves to the horse's side. The chestnut quickened from a trot to a lope past the weathered fence and down the hill. Horse hooves tore through dried grass and onto the packed-dirt road.

Wind whipped the hat from her head, and her hair unfurled as they galloped past stubby brown picked-over fields, empty of cotton. The blood red faded, along with the screams.

Someone yelled behind her in the distance.

No. She would not, could not stop. She'd never get free. If they caught her, they'd lock her up.

When she'd first arrived at her uncle's plantation, they'd promised to let her eat once she took off her buckskin garments. She'd gone hungry instead. When they'd finally offered food, she should have suspected something. Instead, she'd gobbled down the dinner and promptly fell into a deep sleep, drugged. Her Comanche clothes were gone when she awoke, along with everything she owned.

She'd been livid. If she'd had her knife, she would have sliced LeBeau. Instead, he'd had his men carry her to the attic, throw her on a mattress, and lock the door on their way out.

She'd spent a month there. And he'd threatened to send her to an asylum if she tried to run away again or refused to listen to their lessons on how to be civilized. Her uncle wanted a porcelain doll, not a niece with a mind of her own.

The stink of manure assaulted her nose as she rode past a hog farm.

The horse's muscles churned beneath Morning Fawn. She tightened her grip on the reins, digging her nails into her palms.

A slave boy, fishing pole across his shoulder, jumped out of her way as she swerved her mount around a corner. Trees. She needed the cover of trees. A jerk of reins, and her mount left the road, pounding down the hill toward the creek. Scatterings of cottonwood, pecan, and mesquite populated the banks.

They plunged through the gurgling water and up the other side. She dodged a limb and bent down over the horse's withers, her nose inches from the tousled mane. It didn't matter where she was going. Anywhere was better than here. After her third failed attempt, she'd played it safe too long, waiting for a perfect plan. No more.

CHAPTER 2

Stepping through knee-high sedge grass, First Texas U.S. Cavalryman Lieutenant Devon Reynolds hooked his small shovel on his saddle horn and smacked his gloves together. His shoulders and neck muscles ached as if he'd just finished digging a grave. If they found his buried Federal uniform and his cache of weapons beneath the gnarled roots of the giant elm tree, it'd be his own final resting place.

He swiped his butternut-colored sleeve across his sweated brow. Leave it to East Texas to be warm even in late November. Tonight, he'd camp beneath the stars miles from here. Somewhere by a creek so he could bathe and clean up. Tomorrow, he'd find Robert LeBeau's plantation near Columbus, and the act would begin. He'd have to play up his position as a stepson of a planter-class gentleman, even if his slave-owning stepfather was the last man on earth he wanted to emulate. He needed LeBeau to view him as an equal and introduce him as such to the other well-to-do men of Colorado County, not just as the scout he'd hired seventeen months ago to track down his niece and help kidnap her from the Comanche.

Morning Fawn. How had she fared since she'd been taken

to her uncle's? What would it be like to see her again? For all he knew, she'd managed to escape and return to *her* people.

Stubborn. Defiant. During the journey to Fort Belknap, she'd grabbed a gun from one of the younger hands, and Devon had to wrestle her to the ground to get it away from her. Mostly, he'd kept his distance.

Her eyes haunted him still.

Had he ruined her life or saved her? He prayed to God it was the latter.

He should have never taken the job. And he shouldn't be here now, but a man with any conscience couldn't stay out of the war forever. He could have remained in Brownsville with the rest of the Federal invasion force, but Captain Jeremy Carson had convinced him that as a Texan, he could better serve as a spy and saboteur.

The Rebs would have to shift the cotton trade now that Brownsville had fallen. It was his job to discover the new routes and disrupt the flow to Mexico, and LeBeau's plantation lay in the county that housed the most significant cotton warehouse west of the Mississippi.

A leather patch scraped against the thin pinkish scar that ran from his cheekbone just beneath his left eye to the bridge of his nose, the result of a knife fight with a disgruntled Reb. The injury had missed his eye, but a stranger looking at the patch would assume differently. Perfect excuse for being away from his supposed Reb regiment.

He exhaled and willed his hands to leave the stiff patch be.

Instead, he wedged a finger beneath his yellow-trimmed collar. A thin silver chain and locket which had once adorned his wife's neck now lay cool against his skin. A heavy sigh rattled through him. He had failed her. He'd asked God for forgiveness. Forgiving himself was a different matter.

A far-off yell. Overhead, a handful of crows took flight.

A shiver ran down his backbone. Anyone within shouting

distance was too close. Knife drawn, he whacked off a nearby juniper branch and swished it across the freshly covered spot beneath the elm.

Another shout, almost discernable.

He hurried to his horse. The last thing he wanted was to be seen near this location. Foot in the stirrup, he nudged his light bay mare forward before he'd settled in the saddle. Up the incline from the creek, he headed for the road, dropping the branch by a cluster of trees.

Hard, quick clomps, and a horse and rider galloped around the bend, a girl with honey-colored hair flowing in the wind.

"Stop her." A fellow in a red shirt goaded his mount at full throttle, beating his way toward the girl's dust. "Thief."

Another rider followed close behind him.

A thief? Devon swung his mount toward her as the girl charged past on a Thoroughbred. She couldn't have picked a finer horse to steal. With a snap of the reins and the pressure of his calves, he drove his horse to its limit to match her speed, squinting against the stirred-up sand whirling in the air.

Green plaid dress and no side saddle, she rode as if she were being chased by a herd of buffalo. The butt of a carbine bobbed along in a sling. What kind of girl was this?

"Wait." He charged up alongside her.

Both horses snorted with the effort. Hooves tore through the withered grass.

His heart pounded.

The rider whipped the loose end of her reins against his hand like a matchstick striking kindling. "Get away from me!"

He would not be beaten and outrun by a girl, especially not a thieving one. Pressing the balls of his feet against the stirrups, he raised himself in the saddle and drove his horse onward.

Hair flying, she veered her animal toward the road. Devon kept pace.

Her stirrup dangled within inches of his. *Wham.* She rammed her foot into his.

Blasted left eye. He should have approached on the other side. Enough. He wrapped the end of the reins around his hand.

Her foot came again. His horse flinched.

Now was the moment. He leaned half out of the saddle, grabbed her, his left arm around her back, and pulled with all of his might.

Her upper body shifted to his lap.

She dug her nails into his thighs. Trying to hold her was worse than wrestling a wildcat. Did she want to get them both killed?

He pressed his weight against her and gave one final yank. Her foot slipped free of her stirrup.

Goggle-eyed, the Thoroughbred slacked its pace and veered away.

"Whoa." Devon pulled back on his reins.

An elbow jammed into his gut as his mare slowed. "Unhh."

His grip loosened, and the woman jumped.

He yanked his horse to a full stop and hopped off.

Scratched and dirty and dress torn, she rolled to her feet and jerked her head toward the sound of hooves.

She looked familiar. No. It couldn't be—

"Keep her there," the man in the red shirt yelled as he charged toward them.

She spun toward Devon with eyes blazing. Morning Fawn. With honey-blond hair, not dark brown.

His mouth dropped.

Recognition dawned across her face. "You're one of them." Her face contorted. "You. Ruined. Everything." She screeched, hitched her skirts, and ran at him.

The impact almost knocked him off his feet. Her fists struck him in the chest, the shoulders. Devon gripped her wrists.

Their gazes locked. Specks of gold in a sea of brown-green glared at him, as fiery as a branding iron. A spark sizzled through him and buried deep, awaiting ignition.

She shoved him. Both of them toppled to the ground. He fought to escape her fists and feet. Rolling on top of her, he pushed himself up on all fours and pinned her down.

"Get your hands off me." She spit out the words, clear English, not the Spanish and Comanche she'd been confined to when they'd snatched her last year.

It's good to see you. He pressed his lips shut against the idiotic pleasantry, but other words bubbled out. "What happened to your hair?"

She scowled at him. "What are you talking about?"

"It used to be dark—"

"You're destroying my life"—Morning Fawn's breaths came in short huffs like a steam engine—"and you're worried about my hair?"

"I—"

A horse drew up to within a few feet of them, saving him from further stupidity.

Devon blinked at the spray of dust.

"Let me help." The red-shirt man swung down off his mount and hitched his trousers. "Mighty obliged to you. We can take it from here."

"I can handle her." Devon moved off her legs and shifted his body weight to the ground without letting go of her hands. He scoured the man with his gaze. "Why are you chasing her? What'd she do?"

"I did nothing." Morning Fawn squirmed beneath his hold. "You animals—"

"Ran away. Stole the finest horse in Colorado County." The man bent down and aimed his thick hand at Morning Fawn's arm.

"I said I've got her." Horse thieving could be a hanging

offense. Devon grabbed her and pulled her back against his chest, away from the hefty man's reach. Her mussed hair brushed his chin.

She stiffened.

He'd best make sure she didn't slam her head into his jaw.

The second rider, a tall black man wearing a patched jacket, frowned as he slid out of his saddle.

"What are you doing, George?" The red-shirt man jabbed his finger at the new arrival. "Get back on your horse and round up Mr. Franklin's Thoroughbred."

"Yes, sir." George pivoted and mounted.

The boss narrowed his eyes at Devon and rested his hand on his holster. "And who might you be? Don't let that pretty face fool you. She's a real wildcat."

Devon tightened his grip on Morning Fawn's wrist and drew her to her feet as he stood. "I recognize her. I helped rescue her from the Comanches."

"Rescue?" She lunged against his hold. "Kidnapped."

The fellow blinked wide and nudged his battered brown hat up a notch off his forehead, revealing a receding hairline. "You're Reynolds?"

Morning Fawn blew out a breath. "You two should have a lot to talk about." Lace trim hung loose from one of her sleeves, probably torn in the scuffle. Dirt marred her green plaid dress. "Both of you are money-grubbers willing to do anything for a dollar."

The man stuck out his chest, stretching his worn suspenders. "I heard tell you did fine work, but I also heard you got yourself in trouble at Fort Belknap. Escaped from the provost marshal and went on the run. What'd they do? Force you to enlist?" He nodded toward Devon's uniform.

"You heard wrong about the provost marshal. Just a bunch of trumped-up charges from a colonel who had a personal grudge. And no one forced me. I volunteered. Mister?"

"Owens." He swiped his neckerchief over his brow. "Mr. LeBeau's overseer. It's my duty to get this girl back to her uncle." That explained the whip on the pommel of his saddle.

"I was on my way to visit Mr. LeBeau when I saw this girl galloping by and you behind her yelling 'thief.' I'd be pleased to—"

Morning Fawn pivoted and shot her hand toward Devon's holster.

Devon clamped his fingers over hers on the leather flap. "You're unbelievable."

"And you're the same weasel warrior you were last year."

The nerve of her. Devon's jaw clenched. *You have no idea what I am.* "I gave my word to your uncle last year that I'd bring you home, and I kept it." He met her glare.

She looked at him as if he were a vulture hovering over a wounded deer. "Your word is about as good as dirt." She scrunched up her mouth and spat on the ground, barely missing a spider. "Let me go. I can walk to a horse and ride back without help from the likes of any of you."

"You ain't walking nowhere." Owens grabbed a hemp rope from his saddle horn.

Devon stiffened. "You don't need to tie her."

"Are you insane? I don't aim to have to chase her again today. This is Sunday. Time for a man to have a rest, not go gallivanting all over the country."

"I'll tie her." Without letting go of Morning Fawn, Devon snatched the coil from Owens. He wasn't about to allow this oaf to put his hands on her.

"You take a mighty keen interest in the girl, Lieutenant Reynolds." Owens threw back his shoulders and swatted at a mosquito. "There's no reward for bringing her back if that's what you're after."

A tinge of heat burned Devon's cheeks as he avoided Morning Fawn's prying gaze and grabbed her other wrist. "I'm not after payment, Mr. Owens, just a job until my eye heals up enough for me to return east to my regiment." He squeezed both of her hands in his one and cinched the piece of hemp tight for Owens's sake, flinching right along with her as the frayed edges bit into her skin.

"You know what they're going to do to me?" Morning Fawn lowered her voice for his ears only. "Lock me in the attic. Like when I first arrived. You know what they did then? Poured laudanum down my throat anytime I wouldn't behave. That's what you and your men are responsible for."

Like a knife to his gut. Did she know that? He held his expression impassive and fought to steel his voice. "They weren't my men. But I'm sorry for my part."

"I bet you are."

Owens shouldered his way between them. "Let me check those ropes." He tugged on the loose ends of the knots, cinching them further.

George trotted up with the Thoroughbred in tow.

"I'll put her on her horse." Devon took her by the arm.

"Not hers. That's the point. She's not going near Mr. Franklin's animal again. That man will sue Mr. LeBeau if there's even a new scratch on the hoof." Owens hooked his thumbs around his suspenders. "She'll ride my horse. I'll ride Mr. Franklin's."

Morning Fawn grimaced as Devon helped her into the saddle. Her torn, bloodied stockings showed beneath her skirt hem.

He shook his head. "You set out on a four- to five-hundred-mile trip without even a pair of shoes?"

"I have nothing else to say to a weasel warrior like you. You probably ran off from your regiment, afraid to fight." She slammed her heel into his gut.

He gritted his teeth and gripped the bridle. He had half a mind to step away. Wash his hands of her. Let Owens take her back. LeBeau wasn't the only aristocratic Reb around who'd be willing to welcome a wounded Confederate officer. But a glance at her disheveled clothes told him he wasn't going anywhere. It'd be like leaving a two-thirds-grown cougar cub with its paw in a trap. A fellow with any heart couldn't abandon the creature, even if it was liable to bite his hand off. "You try running away, and I'll catch you again. Hog tie you and throw you across the saddle on your belly, Miss Logan."

"Morning Fawn."

"That's the problem. You still see yourself as Comanche." Jaw clenched, he wound her lead rope around his gloved hand and led Owens's horse over to his own, without venturing another look in her direction.

Best keep his head on straight and cauterize his sympathy. He had a mission to complete, and if this woman caught wind of it, he'd end up swinging from a noose. She'd turn him in quicker than an arrow springs from a bow.

~

*M*orning Fawn sat rigid with her hands tied to the saddle horn of Owens's horse. Not much of a horseman, Owens struggled with reining in the Thoroughbred as George followed behind. On her left, Captain Devon Reynolds rode close enough to smell. The odors of wood smoke, horse, and sweat drifted her way. From the looks of him, he must have been on the road for a week or more. Dust and red dirt coated his yellow-piped Confederate shell jacket and trousers. Thick stubble covered the lower half of his tanned face, forming a thin, dark beard. He clenched her lead rope in his gloved hand.

What had happened to his eye? There'd been no patch summer before last when he'd helped ruin her life. The pinkish scar across the bridge of his nose looked fresher than that. And the way he'd glared at her when she'd remarked about him being a coward? His scowl could have flayed her.

If he hadn't butted his nose in where it didn't belong and spoiled her escape plan—

Plan? There hadn't been any, other than riding as fast and as far as she could toward the western horizon and Comancheria. She could have made it. Maybe not to Comancheria, but somewhere away from here.

Clouds drifted over the sun, sucking away the warmth.

Tension knotted her stomach as she cantered past too-familiar fields. Withered brown leavings from the cotton harvest littered the hardened rows, rows trodden by hundreds of feet. Her grip on the saddle horn tightened.

A hawk soared overhead, gliding over the fields. Free.

Reynolds glanced her way, his lips set in a firm line. Beneath his slouch hat, a lock of chestnut-brown hair dipped over his forehead. One smoky turquoise eye studied her. "It was never my intention to do you harm."

She exhaled. "You took me from my family and my home. My way of life. Did you expect me to thank you for that?"

"Not exactly." He hesitated. "But I figure I probably rescued you from working like a slave sun-up to past sun-down at the mercy of some warrior. And from being part of a tribe hunted by soldiers, Texas Rangers, and any settler with a gun and grudge. As a matter of fact, I might have saved your life."

"I was no slave. And it'd be better to work hard at the side of a man I love than sell my heart to the man with the most cotton." She jutted her chin. "And as for being safe, you don't strike me as a man who goes out of his way to be safe."

"Were you...did you have a beau?" His brow furrowed.

That's no concern of yours. She rolled her eyes, giving his impertinence the response it deserved. "Now's a little late for you to be asking, don't you think? After you destroyed every-thing. I could have had a husband for all you know."

He blinked wide.

Did he feel guilty? Might there be a chance? She leaned toward his mount, keeping her voice low. "It's not too late. You could…" She lifted her tied hands. "And let go of the lead rope."

"Absolutely not, Miss Logan."

"You're no better than the rest of them." She ground her teeth.

A chilly breeze rippled through her hair and seeped beneath her dress.

A chaw of tobacco tucked in his cheek, Owens veered down the lane to the right, and Reynolds followed. Morning Fawn's chest tightened as she rode through the wrought-iron gate of Sweetbriar. Trees lined this part of the pebbled lane. Overhanging branches of oak and elm dangled yellow and red leaves overhead.

Owens slowed and cast her a sneer. "See, Miss Logan, we got you home safe and sound."

She scowled at him, tempted to spit on his boot.

A dog barked. Old Blue Belle, Uncle Robert's hound, ran up, took a sniff, and settled into pace alongside them.

Morning Fawn's shoulders slumped as the main house came into view. Its majestic white columns extended from the wide porch to the gabled roof. Dark green shutters accented the tall windows. The upper branches of the twin cottonwoods stretched toward the attic. No surprise, they'd nailed the attic windows shut temporarily when she'd first arrived here.

Hoopskirt swishing through the doorway, Aunt Judith stepped onto the porch. A deep frown pinched her pale face as she called into the hallway behind her. "Robert, come quick. They've caught her." She unfurled her flowered fan and flapped it in front of her face as she stepped across the porch. "You worried us sick, Beth, dear. Why, I almost swooned when I heard you'd taken a horse and run off."

Worried about her or what the gossips would say?

Silver-tipped walking stick in hand, her uncle came through the door as Owens dismounted. A crimson cravat encircled his neck. His lip curled as his icy-blue eyes scoured her from head to toe. "What'd you do, Mr. Owens? My niece looks as if you wrestled her to the ground. There'd better not be a scratch on Mr. Franklin's horse."

Mr. Owens smacked his dusty gloves together. "Miss Logan's a wild one, Mr. LeBeau."

Reynolds drew up alongside her and tipped his slouch hat up to fully reveal his face. "Afternoon, Mr. LeBeau, sir." His Texas drawl twanged deep as he dismounted.

"Reynolds? And in uniform? I'd wondered what had become of you after you delivered my niece." Uncle Robert's eyebrows arched toward his peppered, pomade-tamed hairline. "What in the devil are you doing here?" His shiny leather boots clicked on the steps as he descended. "You played a part in all of this?"

"Just the rescue, sir." Reynolds tied the bay mustang to the hitching post and stepped forward. His jacket fit snug over his muscular form. "I'm on leave from the Third Texas Cavalry. Just passing through the area."

Mr. Owens hitched his trousers. "Lieutenant Reynolds here had to yank the girl off her horse to keep her from riding clear to Dallas."

"I apologize." Reynolds stepped forward. "I didn't intend to rough-handle your niece. Thought she was a horse thief. I had no idea it was Miss Logan until I'd grabbed hold of her."

"Not a thief. Just a troubled young lady liable to do herself harm. Obliged to you, Mr.—or should I say Lieutenant—Reynolds, for your assistance. Glad to see you've joined the service." Uncle Robert shook his hand. "Lucky you showed up at the right moment. My niece hasn't attempted an escape in over six months."

Morning Fawn fidgeted in the saddle. Six months too

long. Every day these people whittled away at who she was. She wouldn't even be fit to return home by the time she got there.

"Happy to be of service." Reynolds snagged her bridle in his hands as if he were concerned she might try to take off again. "I had been thinking of stopping by to see you...and then your niece—"

"Any man serving the Confederacy is welcome in my home, especially one who has rescued a member of my family not once, but twice. You must dine with us this evening and give us news of the front."

What she wouldn't give to bury her foot in the belly of this two-bit lieutenant. Any more help from him, and she'd be in chains.

"I'd be much obliged, sir." Reynolds's lips flickered upward in a shadow of a smile. "My news might be a bit rusty, but I'll be happy to share what I know."

Uncle Robert motioned across the withered lawn to the scattered outbuildings—a smokehouse, spring house, black-smith's shop, barn, and much more. "George can show you to the stables and help you look after your horse."

Lock the horse in the stable. Her in the attic. Owned like his horse. Only less important. They had another thought coming if they believed they could hold her forever.

Reynolds pivoted and extended his hand toward her as if he were a gentleman helping a lady. His blue eyes were similar to her uncle's, except his were more like a lake at sunset than ice, but it might as well be a frozen lake for the warmth he displayed toward her.

"You forgot something." She held up her bound hands.

"Sorry about that." He quickly undid the ropes, and tossing the hemp aside, he held his hand out to her.

She turned up her nose and swung down from the saddle on the other side. "I need nothing from you," she muttered and marched past her uncle into the house, not about to give any of them a chance to touch her.

Warm air struck her as she blinked in the foyer's dim light. Her bruised feet scraped against the woven grass rug and then cooled on the tile beyond.

Thea stood in the parlor doorway twirling a spool of lace around her finger. Her dour expression contrasted with the cheerful light-green wallpaper printed with bright red berry brambles which lined the walls behind her. The curtains on the front parlor window billowed. She'd been listening. "Enjoy your ride, cousin, dear?"

Morning Fawn bit back a rebuttal. Best keep her mouth shut and get upstairs.

"After that scene at church today, there won't be anybody in the whole county who doesn't think you're out of your head." Thea smoothed her palms over her lavender skirt. "Keep this up, and you'll be headed for the asylum."

Morning Fawn's pulse throbbed. "A better place than you're headed for the way you hang off Mr. Henry's arm."

"At least I'm not being tackled to the ground by strange men and looking as though I just crawled out of a trough."

Morning Fawn smacked a stray strand of hair from her face. Her torn sleeve hung loose on her shoulder. "A strange man wouldn't waste his time with you."

Thea tossed her head. "I wouldn't get myself so worked up if I was you, or they'll shovel a double dose of laudanum down your throat."

"Thea, hush." Uncle Robert rapped his cane against the door jamb and crossed the floor, Aunt Judith at his elbow. "Beth, get upstairs to your room. If you weren't under my protection, Mr. Franklin would have sent the sheriff after you for stealing his horse. The man will still probably show up demanding restitution." He jabbed his pale finger toward her. "You have lost our trust."

"I never had your trust."

"Watch your mouth, young lady. By the time you get to come out of your room, you'll realize how much freedom you had and threw away." His silk waistcoat stretched against his puffed-out chest. "My men have work to do. I can't send them chasing after you every time you have a fit."

Her hands balled into fists. The memory of the lock clicking on the attic door resonated in her head. A cage, that's what it was. She glanced at the back hallway, its door leading outside to the kitchen.

"You take off running, and you'll spend a month up there." His voice cut through her indecision.

"I don't have fits. And I never asked for your help or wanted it." Spittle wet her lips. "I'm not my mother, and I'll never be the lady you want me to be. So why don't you let me go?" Her words echoed off the walls.

Her aunt drew back. "What are we supposed to do with her, Robert? She's an impossible girl. One minute, she's calm. Then she explodes. You never know what she's planning."

Eyes narrowed, her uncle marched over to Morning Fawn, toe to toe. "You should be thankful I don't listen to you and let you leave." A vein bulged in his forehead. "You'd be in the gutter somewhere or in a saloon. Some man's kept woman. The Comanches you're so fond of are hundreds of miles away. And if there was a brave you were thinking of sharing a tipi with, he's probably taken a wife by now, maybe two or three. There is nothing and no one waiting for you out West."

Aunt Judith flinched. "Robert. Don't—"

"I bet my mother ran away from you and her father." Morning Fawn's voice shook. "Probably tried to control her just like you do—"

His hand fell hard across her face.

Morning Fawn dropped back. A metallic taste pooled in her mouth.

"I've had enough of your sass. You have no right to speak of things you know nothing about. Now go." Her uncle jutted the walking stick toward the stairs.

Aunt Judith wrung her hands.

No wonder her mother and father had braved the frontier rather than live under this roof and off this man's mercy. A memory flashed. Her mother's gentle hands brushing Morning Fawn's hair, her sweet voice telling a story. The same woman who'd shoved her under a wagon the night of the attack and then ran in the opposite direction in an attempt to lure the attackers away. Trembling, Morning Fawn had covered her head and her eyes, but her mother's screams had pierced to her soul. They still did.

Fighting back tears, Morning Fawn rubbed her cheek and pivoted toward the stairs. She would not cry in front of these people. They would not defeat her.

If only her mother was here now. Or her pia, her sweet Comanche pia who'd gone hungry herself in order to give her food. Someone who cared.

CHAPTER 3

Devon sliced into the quarter of roasted chicken on his plate. Since leaving his regiment at Brownsville, his meals on the road had included little more than hardtack and salted pork. His mouth watered at the abundant fare before him—rice, tomatoes, squash, and freshly made bread, even butter. The lower half of Eastern Texas was making do with scraps and wondering how they were going to get through the winter, and these people ate like they'd never heard of a war or a drought. Maybe it was because he was a guest, maybe not. But he knew one thing for sure—the folks down in the slave cabins on the backside of the plantation weren't eating like this.

His stomach twinged as he glanced at the ceiling. Morning Fawn was somewhere upstairs. A prisoner of her uncle's once again. Because of Devon. But what was he supposed to do? Let her run off to the city or some cow town with a stolen horse and gun, without a penny to her name, not even a pair of shoes? Besides, he hadn't known it was her. Better he stop her than a posse. Did the girl even stop to think?

Across the table from him, Miss Thea LeBeau's silk dress rustled as she shifted forward. "Mr. Reynolds, I'd love to hear about your battles. We receive so little news here." Her auburn hair fell in ringlets along the sides of her pale skin. Despite her Grecian nose, she was fairly attractive, but the way she'd waltzed into the dining room like royalty was enough to make him look the other way.

"Thea, darling, give the man a chance to eat his dinner." Mrs. Judith LeBeau dabbed her mouth, her own hair a duller shade of auburn with gray streaks. "A soldier doesn't always like to speak of such things."

LeBeau leaned back in his seat while a servant girl scooped gravy onto his chicken breast. "But we must hear the lieutenant's story, Judith." He tugged on his striped waistcoat. "Last I heard, Reynolds, you planned to use your three hundred dollar reward for rescuing my niece to pay your substitution fee and avoid conscription. Did you have a change of heart, or was it that trouble you ran into up at Fort Belknap?"

"The trouble at Belknap was nothing. Just a disgruntled colonel with a grudge over a parcel of land. He refused to take my word that I was on my way to pay my fee—"

"You considered paying someone to go in your place?" Thea fluttered her fingers against the lace fichu which covered her bosom. "Most of the young men of my acquaintance welcomed the chance to become a soldier and serve the Confederacy."

"I didn't have to dream of being a soldier. I was one." Devon pressed his lips together. He'd been a fine soldier once, but he had no intention of fighting for a Rebel fiefdom. "I was in the U.S. cavalry before the war, ma'am. Left the service when Texas seceded."

"Bravo. You did well to wash your hands of the Yankees." Her eyes lit. "But why didn't you enlist in the Cause immediately?"

"I've been curious about that myself." LeBeau carved a slice of meat.

Devon studied his plate. He couldn't afford to have his

loyalty questioned. The best lies were often half truths. "It is due to my late wife." His voice dipped, and he reached for his water. He'd say this once and be done with it.

"I'm so sorry. I didn't realize you'd been married." Mrs. LeBeau frowned.

"She passed... It's been three years." He swallowed. Three years and the mention of her death still felt like a punch in the gut. "On her deathbed, she asked me to give up soldiering." Not exactly the truth, but how was he to explain that soldiering had become so entwined with his sorrow and guilt, he couldn't bear it anymore? "So when secession hit, I followed her wishes. I did my part for Texas through various scouting missions and frontier defense. I even hauled cotton."

"A man who still loves his wife." Thea smiled. "How romantic."

Devon fought to smother his scowl. There was nothing romantic about death and grieving. This girl was as shallow as a slipper. "But eventually, I determined that a man of any conscience couldn't stay out of this war forever." That part was true. "I figured that if Isabella were still alive, she'd understand."

"Oh, I'm sure she would." Mrs. LeBeau moved her jeweled hand across the lace tablecloth as if she might actually touch him but stopped short.

Devon shifted in his chair. Too much talk of Isabella. Too many raw emotions. "After Belknap, I decided that if I was going to fight, I was going to do it on my own terms." Devon picked up his knife. "I evaded the colonel's clutches and made my way east. A few months later, I enlisted in the Third Texas Cavalry from Marshall." He stabbed his fork in a slice of chicken and prayed they didn't have friends or family anywhere near Marshall. "Like too many others, I thought we'd whip the Yankees in a few more months."

LeBeau puffed out his chest. "If the generals had done right by our men, we'd have whipped those factory-boy bluecoats in less than a year." His voice rose. "But with leaders like Pemberton, handing over Vicksburg without a full fight, it's no wonder we haven't defeated them yet."

"You weren't at Vicksburg, were you, Lieutenant?" Thea batted her eyelashes.

Flickering light from the chandelier cast shadows on the cherry-bramble wallpaper.

"No, Miss LeBeau. But I saw some of those men. Nothing more than scarecrows after the siege." Or so he'd heard. "I was wounded in a fight around Jackson, Mississippi, shortly after that." He tapped a finger to his eyepatch. Best paint a quick picture for them before they had a chance to ask too many questions. He had no idea how complete the information was from the deserter-turned-Yankee he'd questioned in Brownsville. "I got left behind when the Yanks retook the city. Managed to get a parole by the time I was well enough to leave the hospital. Reckon they didn't want to bother shipping me north. Probably doubted I'd be fit for service."

"You poor man." Thea opened her fan and fluttered it in front of her face.

Devon's cheeks heated.

"So you came back home to Texas?" Mrs. LeBeau scooped a spoonful of squash.

"Yes, ma'am. Until I could recover. Had a hankering to see my sister in Brownsville. But the Yankees invaded before I got within fifty miles of the city. Been drifting north since then."

LeBeau held up his brandy snifter toward a butler who stood at attention by the walnut sideboard. "What about your family? Doesn't your father have a plantation up north near the Trinity River?"

"Stepfather." An edge crept into Devon's voice.

LeBeau's eyebrows arched.

Devon swiped a napkin over his mouth. "He and I don't

exactly see eye to eye. I'm in no hurry to visit him. I was hoping you might need a hand, or perhaps you could be a reference for me in Columbus or Alleyton. I'm looking for a temporary position before I head back across the Mississippi to find my regiment—"

"Papa you need all kinds of help." Thea leaned forward, elbows on the table. "Owens can't manage anything right. You said so—"

"Not a topic for the ladies." LeBeau swished his newly poured brandy in his snifter and gave Thea a stare that managed to shut even her mouth. "We'll discuss it after dinner, Reynolds. I'm sure something can be arranged."

Thea beamed in Devon's direction.

He shifted his gaze back to her father. "Thank you, sir." His skin itched beneath the eyepatch. Too many more looks from Thea, and he'd feel as if he'd just bathed in a patch of poison ivy. But wars weren't won by bullets alone. He pressed his hands on the table.

"You must tell us about your plantation." Thea wrapped an auburn curl around her index finger. "I'd love to hear about your home."

River Place was no home of his. Devon sat back in the fine cherry straight-back chair. What kind of dinner was Morning Fawn having? Did they bother sending a tray up to her? Surely, they wouldn't really lock her in the attic and dose her with laudanum. "Will Miss Logan be joining us for dessert?"

Thea snorted.

LeBeau's fork clunked on the table. "I'm afraid she won't be down for meals for a few days. Once she gets herself worked up into one of her tirades, it can take a while to settle her down."

Worked up? Morning Fawn had been calm enough as she'd marched into the house. Silently fuming, no doubt. Most likely ready to break away at the first opportunity. But to keep her upstairs for days? Like keeping a cougar in a barn. "I apologize once again if I did her any injury when I pulled her from her horse.”

“We should be apologizing to you, Lieutenant.” Thea’s thin lips didn’t quite hide the traces of her sneer. “I’m surprised she didn’t try to claw your face. You should have seen her the times she tried to escape when she was first brought here. She’s rather tame now compared to then.”

“Thea.” Mrs. LeBeau fidgeted with her napkin. “You’ll have our guest thinking Beth is uncivilized.”

“Isn’t she?” She gave her mother a pointed look. “I’m only—”

“You ladies forget. Lieutenant Reynolds helped rescue Beth from the Comanches.” LeBeau fingered his watch fob.

“Oh, I bet you could tell us stories, Lieutenant.” Thea squirmed in her chair, probably salivating at the possibility. “What was it like when you first grabbed her? Did you have to use a gun? Did you kill any Comanches?”

Devon cleared his throat. “Miss Thea, I wouldn’t want to disturb your refined nature with such rough discussion.” He almost choked on the word *refined*. That’d be the day.

“But I must know about my cousin. So that I can be aware of any dangers, or so that I might find ways to comfort her.”

Even her mother had to smother a hiccup over that one.

Devon arched his eyebrows. “Gentleman do not tell tales on ladies. My lips are sealed regarding Miss Logan.”

“Surely, you’re not implying that my cousin is a lady?” She gaped.

He held up his wine glass toward LeBeau. “With an uncle like your father, how could she not be?”

Thea rolled her eyes.

But LeBeau threw back his shoulders. “We still have a substantial bit of polishing to do, but underneath, she’s a LeBeau.” His brow darkened. “Living with those savages would be enough to derange anyone’s mind.” His voice contorted with emotion. "I loved my sister dearly, and I will not give up on her daughter."

Spoken like a Good Samaritan. The man probably felt he was caring well for his slaves, too, when he sent them out to the cotton fields from dawn to dusk likely dressed in raggedy homespun, feeding them on rough corn and bits of pork, separating families, laying the whip on them when they disobeyed. Shaped in the same mold as Devon's stepfather.

LeBeau pushed his chair out. "Let's talk of you, Reynolds. You mentioned you're looking for a position. I have something in mind, but we'll discuss it over cigars. We won't bore the ladies with business. They can join afterwards for dessert in the parlor."

"Papa, you mustn't send him off on some far-flung mission. We have so few gentleman callers of class with the war on. We need his protection right here at Sweetbriar."

Devon gritted his teeth. What if the success of his mission and his access to Morning Fawn hinged on his ability to feign interest in Thea LeBeau?

CHAPTER 4

How had she been so stupid to take off like that? Morning Fawn jabbed her arms together and paced from the closed window to the locked door. Thank goodness, it was late November, not July. The rough attic floor stung her scraped feet as she paced. Daylight had faded into darkness except for the flickering of the oil lamp. Shadowed rafters loomed overhead.

For months after her early failed attempts, she'd been biding her time, learning and preparing for the right opportunity. And today she'd given into temptation and run off without thought, throwing away every scrap of trust she'd managed to accumulate. How stupid.

They'd re-nailed both windows shut. Trapped. And her uncle had threatened to leave her up here for days—weeks, even. She dug her fingernails into the flesh of her arms. Someday she'd like to lock that man in a room and throw away the key.

Jaw clenched, she grabbed at the loose lace on her torn sleeve and yanked. The seams ripped free of the wool. She wadded the despicable material and tossed it. They'd taken her sewing basket. Another punishment? Or were they afraid she'd stab herself with a needle? Her improvised pick for the door had been buried in the swatches of cloth.

Thank goodness they hadn't found her journal. At least, she'd had sense enough to return it to its hiding place on the far side of the bed, wedged in tight between the ropes and the mattress.

Her stomach growled as the delicious smell of baked chicken and buttered squash drifted her way, but her supper sat untouched on the silver tray. She knew better than to eat it after Thea's comment about the laudanum. It wouldn't be the first time they'd laced her food with the mind-numbing sedative after an incident. And if they figured out she hadn't eaten, they'd try to get it in her another way. If she had a fireplace, she'd toss her uneaten meal in there and let it burn, but the chimney that ran up along the outer wall was solid brick, no opening in her room. The chamber pot would work if Lucy was the one who came to empty it in the morning. But sometimes they sent a different servant.

Sweat broke out on the back of her neck. Locked in. No escape. Her breath came short and quick. She had to think about something else before panic consumed her.

Morning Fawn paused at the small mirror over the washstand and hugged herself. Honey-blonde and light-skinned, she no longer looked Comanche. The mesquite dye used to darken her hair had faded to such a pitiful brown that she'd cut off the ends where the color remained. Her weather-beaten tan of nine years in the making had retreated in the seventeen months of heavy, bothersome clothing and stifling confinement where stepping outdoors was a privilege to be earned. If she made it back to Comancheria, would she be welcomed by anyone other than her pia and her *ahpu*, who had adopted her and loved her as their own?

Since the first days of her life in the village, she'd devoted herself to blending in, to being the best Comanche she could be. The other girls had years of practice and experience over her, but by the time she was eighteen, she could ride, tan a hide, tear down and erect a tipi, and use a bow and arrow better than most. She'd caught the eye of a warrior named Two Feathers. But admiration of her skill didn't equal love.

Stands-His-Ground had taken notice, as well. A strong warrior and good provider who'd lost his first wife, the man was twice her age. But her parents, concerned about her future, insisted she seriously consider his offer of marriage. Marriage to him would have given her standing in the tribe and respect she'd only dreamed of. Reynolds and his cohorts had torn her away from the village before she'd given her answer.

And here she was. Without a place in the world. Her head pounded. She needed to get her pick back. The security of knowing she could open the door, even if she didn't, would ease the tension that gripped her chest—

Heavy footsteps sounded on the staircase. Someone was coming to check on her.

Dashing to the dinner tray, she grabbed the plate and dropped to her knees by the bed. Mouthwatering food, but she couldn't take the chance. She grabbed the chamber pot, yanked off the lid, and dropped the chicken in.

The door lock clicked.

Not enough time. She jumped to her feet and shoved the pot back under the bed, the half-empty plate still clutched in her hand.

The squash slid sideways on the porcelain and onto her rumpled green skirt as the heavy door opened.

Her uncle stood in the entrance, shadowed by Owens, LeBeau's face as welcoming as a stone. "What have you been up to?" His gaze traveled from the spilled food to the bed.

She cringed. How could she have forgotten to flip the bedcover back down over the side?

Lebeau jutted his finger at Owens. "Look under the bed." A spoon and a small bottle dangled from his other hand. "I might have known she was too riled up to behave."

"I've done nothing wrong." Her voice cracked, even as she stiffened.

Half tempted to kick him, she stepped aside as Owens knelt and dragged out the pot. Did they think they could get the laudanum down her throat without a fight?

Owens lifted the lid. "Up to her old tricks."

She opened her hand. The plate clunked on the hardwood floor and chipped.

Jaw clenched and eyes narrowed, her uncle moved toward her. "You'll have to hold her, Mr. Owens."

Owens pulled himself up to a stand and cracked his knuckles. "My pleasure."

They couldn't give her the laudanum if there wasn't any. Morning Fawn lunged for the bottle. Her nails dug into LeBeau's pampered hand. The spoon clattered to the floor, and her fingers closed around the maple-colored glass.

Owens grabbed her from behind and jerked her away from Uncle Robert. The brute's arms cinched around her as he hauled her backward, squeezing the air from her lungs.

Her uncle reached for her hand.

She flung the laudanum and rammed her heel into the leg of the man behind her.

"Yeow." Owens yelped but held firm.

Gasping for breath, she kicked at her uncle as he dove for the bottle—

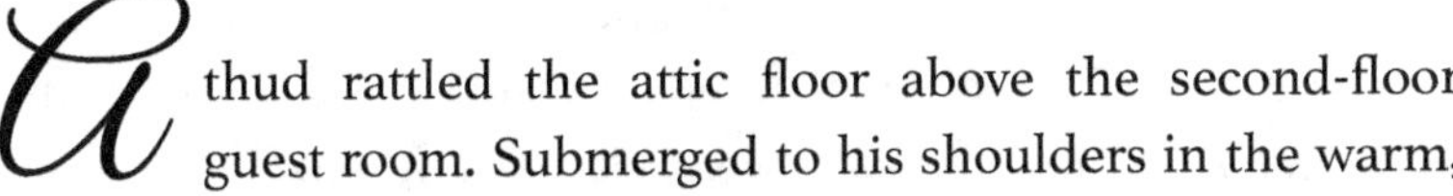

A thud rattled the attic floor above the second-floor guest room. Submerged to his shoulders in the warm, bubbly water of the copper tub, Devon glanced upward and frowned. Morning Fawn?

Hurried feet thumped somewhere above—not over him directly, but nearby.

As Devon sat up and reached for the towel, water sloshed over the sides onto the carpet.

A scuffle followed by raised voices and another thud. It sounded like a fight. Morning Fawn and who? Were they trying to tie her or dose her with some concoction? He hopped out of the most luxurious bath he'd had in his entire life, leaving the dust and grime of weeks on the road behind. Water and suds streamed off of him as he dashed the towel across his body.

A muffled female yell wafted from the thick ceiling, followed by raised voices and more scuffling.

He had to get up there. Damp hair fell across his forehead as he grabbed his pants. No time to put on his drawers or undershirt. He pulled his shirt on and headed for the door, halting in midstride. His eyepatch. Couldn't forget that. He snatched it from the bureau and tightened it around his head before charging into the lamp-lit hallway, barefoot, suspenders dangling from his sides.

George, the second rider from the afternoon, stood at the bottom of the ascending stairs conversing with the maid from dinner in a barrage of whispers.

They fell silent as Devon approached.

The young maid, dressed in a simple black dress, clutched her hands. A web of concern clouded her face.

George crossed his arms over his worn coat with its frayed cuffs. "Sorry, Massar. Mr. LeBeau sends his apologies if the noise disturbed ya."

"Stand aside." Devon moved to push past the man.

"Sorry, sir." George planted himself dead center and stretched his arms across. "Orders. No one goes up."

"You've got to be joking." Devon blew out a breath. "What in the devil are they doing to her up there?"

George pressed his lips flat and shrugged.

More rumbling sounded through the floor.

"You tell me, or I'm going to see for myself." Devon jabbed his finger toward the man who matched his height and likely his strength.

"It's her medicine." The girl knotted her apron in her hands. "They's giving Miss Logan her medicine."

"Her medicine? Sounds like they're wrestling her to the floor." He spit out the words. His body trembled with unspent fire. He was ready to bolt up those stairs and yank LeBeau and whoever else away from Morning Fawn. He could do it. Then, what? His hands curled into fists. If he got himself kicked out of the house, he'd have no way to help Morning Fawn in the long run. And he'd destroy any hope he had of obtaining a reference and jeopardize his mission.

"They's won't hurt her, Massar." The big, brown-eyed girl pleaded with him. Her gaze landed on his chin. "Just hold her down. Give her the medicine."

Devon scowled at her and George. "They do this every night?"

Uneasy quiet pervaded overhead.

"No, sir." She held out her callused hands. "Hasn't happened for months. Please, sir, go back to your room."

The truth or an appeasement for him?

An angry screech echoed from above.

"Sounds like they finished." The girl lowered her gaze.

Devon squeezed his eyes shut. He'd brought Morning Fawn back to this house. Put her here in the first place. "*Estupida.*" He hit his fist against the wall and muttered in Isabelle's mother tongue. "*Brutos. Me gustaria retorcerles el cuello.*" *I'd like to wring their necks.*

A door opened above. The sound of crying drifted down the stairway.

Dear God. A flash of memory sliced through him. Isabella, on her deathbed, crying over their lost infant. He shuddered. Nausea filled his stomach.

Footsteps sounded overhead.

"Please, Massar. Your going up there won't do any good." The girl swiped her cheek. A tear?

Mute, George stuffed his hands into his pockets and shifted closer to the banister.

Devon could not, would not put up with Morning Fawn being treated like this. He clenched his jaw and pivoted away. If he laid eyes on that cane-wielding puff-shirt right now, he was liable to throttle the man.

By the time he returned to Brownsville, Morning Fawn would be out of this house.

~

Two hours later, Devon crept up the forbidden stairs, mindful of every creak. He couldn't sleep until he made sure Morning Fawn was all right. His palms throbbed from slamming his fists into them. Better his palms than LeBeau's face. Too bad he hadn't had a cord of wood to chop.

With no light in the attic foyer, he felt along the wall until he bumped the door handle. He had his pick in his pocket, but first, he traced the doorframe with his fingers. Along the top jamb, he struck metal.

Sweat dampened the armpits of his cotton undershirt as he inserted the key in the lock and turned. Morning Fawn might scream and wake up the whole house. Worse yet, she could be unconscious. He was hoping for somewhere in between.

A quiet hum drifted through the opening. A song he couldn't quite place.

An orangeish glow emanated from the oil lamp, casting shadows across the plaster walls and wide oak rafters. His swallow stuck in his throat as his glance skittered from an over-turned cane-bottom chair to the bed.

Eyelids sagging heavily, Morning Fawn rested on her side, half covered by a disheveled mess of bedclothes. She hugged a blanket to her chest, but she'd kicked her lower legs free of covering. The hem of her rumpled dress gathered just below her knees. A torn stocking hung on the bedpost. Her honey-blond hair splayed across a pillow.

Alive. Beautiful. Subdued against her will.

His thoughts scattered. He shouldn't be in here alone with her. But he couldn't turn and leave without checking on her.

His foot struck something cool and squishy. Squash oozed into his stocking. He grimaced and reached for a towel on the washstand, bumping against a plate. *Thump, thump.* It rattled across the floorboards. He froze. What if someone came upstairs to check on the noise?

Morning Fawn raised her head an inch and squinted at him through her lashes. "What're you doing here, Mr. Trouble?"

His skin prickled beneath her gaze. The door. He pivoted and closed it behind him without a whisper of a click. He yanked off his stocking and grabbed the towel.

"Everything. Today. Your fault." She gnawed her lip as he bent to clean the floor. "You stay away." Words slurred, her voice had lost its hard edge.

Nothing like the fighter he'd encountered on horseback today. No wonder she'd tried to run away. His stomach dropped.

"I wanted to see how you were doing, Morning Fawn." He stood and righted the chair, placing it three or four feet from the head of the bed. He didn't deserve to sit.

"Using my name will do you no good." Eyes open to half mast now, she cuddled the blanket, nuzzling her chin against the white wool. "If you come too close, I've got a fork." She poked metal tips out from beneath her covering.

The corner of his mouth twitched upward at the threat of the weapon, even as her lopsided smile sank his heart. LeBeau's methods robbed her of her dignity. This wasn't who she was, and she'd likely hate him for seeing her like this.

"Poor eye." She pointed at his patch.

"It'll heal. I hope." His fingers twitched on the back of the chair.

A small desk sat beneath the window, supplemented by a cedar chest at the foot of the bed, a washstand with its jumbled items in the opposite corner, a tumbled stool, and a small bedside table and lamp. Hardly anything to show that this was someone's room and not just an extra bed tucked in the attic. "Where are all your belongings?"

"My belongings?" She frowned.

"You know, the things that make this room yours. Treasures, knickknacks, maybe a drawing—"

Her sharp exhale fluttered a strand that had fallen across her forehead. "Women who live in an attic don't get things, Mr. Trouble." She shoved her hair from her face. "You know I read a story about a woman in the attic a few weeks ago. *Jane Eyre*, that's what it was called. Every once in a while, they allow me a book. I had to start with ABC's and a *McGruffy Duffy Reader*, or something like that. Thea thought she was so smart. Looked down on me like I was a six-year-old. But I showed her. My reading came back to me in a matter of months." Her face glowed in the lamplight. "Sometimes when I'm downstairs, I sneak a book. But when they saw me with *Jane Eyre,* they took it away, and I found out why too. It's about a woman in the attic. She's insane. Locked away up there, hidden. Finally, burns the house down, but you know what my question is?" She raised up on both elbows and leaned toward him, so dangerously close to the edge of the bed, he had to stop himself from scurrying over to make sure she didn't fall off.

"What is your question?" He waved his hand toward her as if that might give her a clue to move back.

"Question?" She squinted. "Oh, yes. Was she out of her mind before they locked her in the attic? I don't think so. I think it was that husband of hers, Mr. Rochester, sealing her up there 'cause he couldn't control her, couldn't make her behave. He stuck her up there, nailed the windows shut, and threw away the key." She lifted her chin. "I think it's my uncle's favorite book. Except the part about the house burning down."

His glance flickered to the sealed chimney.

Her eyes lit with amusement. "You're worried? So are they."

Was it just the laudanum talking? "I haven't read the story. But it's fiction, and it's not you."

She wagged a finger at him. "How many women do you have locked up in your attic?"

He crossed his arms. "I don't lock women in attics."

"But you take money for it. Three hundred dollars each. My uncle told me. You could make a lot of money if you have a big enough attic."

He sank into the chair. Would to God he could throw the money in LeBeau's face and take back any part he had in the matter. But if it hadn't been him, LeBeau would have hired someone else. "I'm sorry I took you from your home."

She blinked at him, her eyelids drooping. Would she remember any of this tomorrow? "Your fault." She stuck out her lip. "They try to rob me. Take my mind."

He leaned down, elbows on his knees. What if she became dependent on the medicine? Conviction steeled his words. "I'm not going to let them continue to treat you like this."

"What are you going to do about it?" She rolled onto her back and spread her arm across the bed. "All you care about is your money."

He looked away. "Which servant do you trust the most?" If he was going to do something about the laudanum, he'd need help.

"Hmmm. Lucy." She wove her hand through the air. A giggle escaped her lips as she returned to her side and pulled the covers up. "I saw you looking at my ankles."

"I...wasn't." But the heat that rushed up his neck contradicted his words.

"I don't believe you." She arched her eyebrows, but they only rose halfway. "They try to steal my breath too. Won't even let me open my windows."

"Windows?"

"I told you how they nailed them shut."

"That was in the book."

"Well, it's here too. Trying to suffocate me." Her eyes filled with unshed tears. "I used to ride toward the sunset as far and as fast as I could. You took the sunset. Now I have nothing."

She might as well fill his boots with lead and throw him into the Brazos River.

"I don't want you here, Mr. Trouble." She nestled her head in the pillow and sniffled. Big, wet eyes, pools he could drown in, held him transfixed. "What if there's no home for me left when I get back to my village?"

Enough. He jumped to his feet. He had to do something. "I'll fix your window."

"Really?"

He tiptoed over to the sash and fished his pick out of his pocket.

The forest-green drapes hung off to the sides, revealing a moonlit night through the half-barren branches of the cottonwood.

Morning Fawn plodded over.

He grimaced at the sound of her feet. If anyone below was awake listening—

"It's there." She stumbled up beside him and planted her finger over a dent in the window rail. "See."

He sucked in a breath. The heat of her seemed to permeate his sleeve even though at least an inch separated her arm from his. Tensing, he kept his gaze trained on the window. "Move your finger."

The scent of lavender mixed with a sickly sweet smell stung his nose. The brute had probably spilled some of the medicine on her dress.

Her hand dropped, and she swayed against the wall, head tilted against the sash. Oh my goodness. The last time he'd been alone with a woman this close, he'd been a married man.

Isabelle.

Did Morning Fawn think she was the only one who'd lost their sunset? Isabelle's locket pressed against his sternum. He'd lost everything.

Best get his work done and get out of here. He moved his hand over the wood. Sure enough, a nail, and another one on the other side. Hammered in at an angle, a slim edge of each cap protruded. "I found them. You go lay down, and I'll take care of it."

"My people used to dance beneath a moon like that." She rolled her eyes toward the pane. "Huge bonfire. Drums—"

"You need to go to bed."

"I'm too tired to move." Foreign words, Comanche, drifted across her lips as she wove a quiet melody beyond his comprehension.

He exhaled and pressed his lips together. The nail was snug. Someone had done their job well. Devon wedged his thin, pinky-length pick in at the nail's edge and pried into the wood beneath the cap. A few splinters and a mashed finger later, he managed to wedge it free.

"You got it. Let me have it." She leaned against his arm.

Sweat broke out along his hairline. "You don't need it. You

stay put there." He nudged her back with his elbow and jammed his pick beneath the rim of the second nail.

His jabs left a mess of scratches. Hopefully, no one would look too close. He blew off the shavings and turned to her.

Although she attempted to steady her upper body against the wall, her feet slid out a foot or more. Like molasses, she was slowly inching her way down to the floor.

"Morning Fawn," he whispered.

Her eyes flew open. "Yes?"

He held up the two nails.

A muffled squeal. "You did—"

"Shshsh." He leaned down to meet her gaze. "If you wake them or tell them...they'll put the nails back and kick me out of the house. Maybe out of the whole county."

With a smile, she pinched her lips as if applying a clothespin. "Not a word, Mr. Trouble."

"You need to go to bed, and I've got to leave."

"I don't think I can make it. My legs are like jelly." She slipped another inch.

He groaned. There was no getting around it. He bent and scooped one arm beneath her knees and one behind her back.

Her eyes widened. "I've got a fork, you know." But her head lolled back, and her shoulder-blade-length hair cascaded against his arm as he lifted.

Lilacs and heat and too much softness overwhelmed his senses, barely held intact by the stink of laudanum and the smell of horse.

Cheeks burning, he carried her to the bed and lowered her to the rumpled covers.

The movement roused her. She locked her fingers around his neck. "You're breathing on me."

"I'm trying to leave." He arched against her hold, to the full length of her outstretched arms.

Her hands slipped loose, but before he could move, she

latched onto the top button of his shirt, sending his pulse throbbing in his throat. "You took away my moon. How am I supposed to live without the moon?" A childlike tone crept into her voice.

His gaze sank into gold-speckled hazel, and he swallowed hard.

He could not leave her without hope. His voice was barely a whisper. "I'm going to get you out of here someday, Morning Fawn. The moon will be yours for the taking."

She smiled as her eyes closed, and her hand dropped to her side. "I think you're a fancy liar, Mr. Trouble."

"We'll see about that." He stood and stepped toward the door, refusing to allow himself one more look. Tomorrow, she'd probably hate him. Then, again, she might not even remember tonight.

But he had no clue how he'd scrub the memory of her touch from his skin. And those eyes of hers went deeper still, piercing through cobwebs and dust to the dungeon door of his heart.

<h1 style="text-align:center">CHAPTER 5</h1>

$\mathcal{M}$orning Fawn ran her fingers through her tangled hair. Half the morning was gone, and here she was in bed. She squinted at the bright sunlight pouring in through the windowpane. Her head felt as if it were stuffed with cotton, and her mouth was so dry, her tongue stuck to its roof.

How dare they do this to her? She crammed the pillow to her mouth and screeched into the down. Her fingers dug into the fluff. She should have never touched that horse yesterday. That's the message they wanted to get across. If only she could scour every trace of poison from her, inside and out.

Throwing the pillow aside, she tossed off the covers and swung her legs over the edge. The leftover whisperings of the laudanum would likely sap the strength from her muscles for another half day, and from her heart, even longer. An enemy more insidious than a rattler.

Her hand brushed the fork, and she threw it on the floor. What she wouldn't give to skewer her uncle.

A food tray sat on the side table and fresh water in the washbasin. Lucy or someone had already been here this morning, and she'd slept right through it. Eggs and toast. Her stomach rumbled. Was it safe to eat? They usually saved the poison for the night. Now that she'd misbehaved, in their opinion, they'd likely try it several nights in a row.

She glanced at the door and the window. What if she rammed the chair leg through the pane? What would they do then? The chair—

An image of Devon Reynolds sitting there flickered through her mind. Had she dreamed he'd been here last night? His deep voice barely above a whisper, he'd rested his elbows on his knees and studied her with that all-seeing gaze of his, a frown shadowing his face. He'd look mighty fine with his white shirt contrasting with his tan and his black suspenders stretching taut against his muscles.

No. Nothing but a figment of her imagination. The laudanum did things like that. She moved to the washbasin and splashed her face, avoiding the mirror. No doubt, dark circles underscored her eyes.

Her hand shook as she picked up the water pitcher and drank from it directly. She closed her eyes as the sweet liquid traveled down her throat. The bed called. Another couple hours of sleep would help mute the effects.

A tree branch scratched against the pane. Morning Fawn stilled. Another image. Reynolds at the window pulling out a nail.

Water sloshed out of the pitcher as she clunked it down. It was a dream. Wasn't it? Why would he come here in the middle of the night? How would he have gotten in? Her uncle would never have allowed it. He'd be more likely to skin Reynolds alive.

Pivoting, she strode to the window sash. An empty hole. Goose bumps spread over her arms. No nail. She rubbed her fingertip over the scratched wood. A second hole.

It was no dream.

I'm going to get you out of here someday... That's what he'd said.

Her knees wobbled. He'd leaned over her. What in the devil had happened after that? What had she...what had he done? She sagged against the wall. Her fingers had been linked around his neck, pulling him down to the bed. *Dear God.* Surely, she'd imagined at least that part.

With trembling fingers, she examined her underclothes. Nothing out of order. *Thank God.* She smoothed her skirt. But how much had happened? There'd been something about a fork and Reynolds locking women in the attic.

She buried her face in her hands as the jumble of slurred memories assaulted her. What kind of man was this Devon Reynolds? He snuck into her room, likely aware she'd been force-fed laudanum. How could anyone in the house have missed that whole struggle?

A knock rattled the door.

She jumped. "Who is it?"

"Lucy, Miss Beth." The door handle clicked, and the maid entered, her long, dark hair pulled back in a chignon. A white apron covered the front of her black dress. "Thought you might need help cleaning up this morning." She offered a tentative smile and curtseyed.

Morning Fawn ran a hand over her hair. "Thank you, but I can look after myself. If you could just empty the pot."

"You've had a rough night." Lucy closed the door. "And I'm in no hurry to get to Miss Thea's room or Mrs. LeBeau's either." She strode over to the trunk, picking up a discarded stocking as she went. "I'll help you find something pretty."

"What's it matter?" Morning Fawn grabbed her brush from the washstand. Half of her brain felt as if it were still asleep. "No one's going to see it."

"Sometimes it's good to look pretty for yourself, Miss." Lucy pulled out a petticoat, followed by a blue floral-print dress.

"I'm not up to flowers, Lucy." She brushed through her tangled ends. Cacti would be more of her style, far from here.

As usual, Lucy didn't listen. She never did when it was just the two of them. "You get that dirty one off, and I'll take it down with me to the sewing room when I finish here."

Morning Fawn blew out a breath and picked up the water pitcher for another drink.

"I could pour you a cup of water, you know." Lucy laid the clean clothing over the back of the cane-bottom chair and stepped behind her. "I'll help you with the top buttons."

Their gazes met in the mirror. Lucy's eyes said it all. She felt sorry for Morning Fawn.

I don't need your pity. Morning Fawn bristled but held her tongue. She couldn't afford to lose the closest person she had to a friend this side of the frontier. Outside this room, she couldn't even carry on a decent conversation with Lucy, not if any of the LeBeaus or Owens were within earshot.

The dress slipped off of her shoulders, and she shimmied out of the remains of a day she longed to forget. "Did you see Lieutenant Reynolds this morning?"

The maid exhaled and scooped up the discarded garment with long, slender fingers. A triangle-shaped scar marred the back of her hand. "I saw everyone at breakfast." But the way she gnawed her lip hinted there was more.

"And?"

She dodged Morning Fawn's gaze. "You've got bruises, Miss Beth." She pointed to a dark black-and-blue mark on Morning Fawn's upper arm.

The way her hip felt, there was probably one there, too, and her ribs. No surprise. Jumping from a horse. Scuffling with Reynolds. Then, being manhandled by Owens. No wonder her body told her she should be in bed.

"It'll heal." Morning Fawn rubbed her arm. "But I want to know about the lieutenant. What are you not saying?"

Lucy wet a washcloth in the basin and gently touched it to the bruise. "He showed up at the hen house when I was there. Claiming he likes eggs and wanted to inspect the hens. But that's just what he said."

"What was the real reason?" Morning Fawn took the washcloth and skimmed it over her face.

"To ask questions about you." Lucy unbuttoned the petticoat at Morning Fawn's waist and let it fall to the ground. "And I tries to say as little as possible."

"About me? What kind of questions?"

"About your medicine, mostly."

"And why's he so almighty concerned about that?"

"Didn't say." Lucy's brow furrowed. "But he wouldn't let it be until he had some answers. I was a bundle of nerves, him being a white man and all and us being alone." She handed Morning Fawn a clean chemise and drawers and turned toward the bed. "I told him it was the first time in months they'd given you laudanum, and they usually put it in your food. That it only comes to what it did last night when they figure out you haven't taken it."

The soft linen hung loose in Morning Fawn's hands. Her humiliation a matter of conversation. It was none of this man's business. "What did he say to that?"

"Nothing." Lucy shrugged and yanked the blankets off the bed. "Looked real serious as if he was studying on something, then thanked me and left."

What was he up to? Maybe he hoped for a repeat of last night. Or an even friendlier reception. He'd live to regret it if he dared come near her again. If Reynolds had any decency or honor, he wouldn't have snuck into her room. But what should she expect from a man who traded her for money as if her freedom could be measured in coin? Last night, he'd seemed almost...kind. A delusion of her laudanum-soaked brain.

She yanked the rest of her garments off and scrubbed.

"What should I do next time?" Lucy removed a sweat-stained sheet.

"Next time?" Morning Fawn hurried to replace her drawers while Lucy still had her back turned.

"If he asks me more questions. And what if he tells the master?"

Tell him I might twist his nose off if he keeps putting it in my business. Morning Fawn bit her lip and tugged her chemise over her head. "Tell him as little as possible. Then, let me know every word he says. If he's sneaking around asking questions, I doubt he'll be gossiping to my uncle about it."

"I reckon." Lucy nodded. "And he did look concerned about you last night."

"He did?" She gaped. Had Lucy seen him come to her room? "When?"

"While they was giving you the medicine. Came out of his room as if he planned to march up them stairs and tell your uncle what's what. Me and George had to plead with him to stay put."

Concerned about her? Probably just guilt. Maybe that's why he'd removed the nails.

Lucy snapped a sheet wide and waved it over the straw-stuffed tick. "I've got a feeling that man is going to stir up trouble."

Mr. Trouble. Morning Fawn covered her eyes. Had she really called him that? She'd probably sounded like some scarlet woman at a saloon.

"Miss Thea hasn't wasted any time." Lucy tucked in the corners.

"What's that supposed to mean?"

"Batting her eyes, twirling her fan, trying to act as sweet as if she were born in a honeycomb. Weaseled her way into riding with the lieutenant and the massa. Your uncle's showing off the plantation, but that ain't what Miss Thea's showing off. She done set her cap for Reynolds."

Morning Fawn jabbed a hand to her hip. No surprise there. Thea would chase after anyone in pants as long as they owned a cotton field or had money. And Reynolds? His concern wasn't worth spit. Going riding with that woman a few hours after he'd snuck into Morning Fawn's room?

That man was a downright scoundrel in so many ways she couldn't count them. Serve him right if he were to get caught in Thea's web. And if he'd gossiped to that plantation princess about what he'd seen last night? Morning Fawn gritted her teeth and jabbed her arms into her dress. Those two deserved each other.

CHAPTER 6

*D*evon picked up the gunpowder flask from the top of the weathered fencepost and measured a load. This was his chance to talk to LeBeau about Morning Fawn. Helping her without sabotaging his welcome and his mission was as easy as walking between bullets.

Thank goodness, Mrs. LeBeau insisted that Thea accompany her on a visit to a neighboring plantation. A morning of feigning mild interest had grated on his nerves worse than clanging pots.

A cotton field with its stubbled leavings stretched before him and LeBeau. A murder of crows hopped along the hardened rows pecking. Seventy-five yards out, a board swung from an extended branch of a post oak. Yellow leaves dangled above the bull's eye George had used coal to scrawl on the target.

LeBeau held out his revolver and rotated it from side to side. "You ever seen one of these, Reynolds?"

"No, sir. Looks mighty fine." Devon admired the iron barrel and wood grip with its brass trigger guard. Steel was hard to come by these days with the Union blockade of the entire Southern coastline and control of the Mississippi.

LeBeau rubbed his thumb over the polished walnut. "Dance and Brothers Company. Made here in Texas." He pulled his powder flask from the pocket of his buckskin hunting coat.

Might as well have been playing dressup for the frontier. The hypocrite probably wouldn't last two days in Palo Duro Canyon. If Morning Fawn attempted to don anything that came off a deer, her uncle would undoubtedly have a fit.

LeBeau stuck out his chest. "We'll see how this beauty fares against that Northern-made Colt of yours."

"Colts have served me well." Devon poured a load in the fifth chamber and dug wadding out of a pouch on his belt.

"1860 Army model?" LeBeau arched his eyebrows. "That make is hard to come by in this neck of the woods."

"I ran across a dead Yank in Louisiana. He had no further need of it. That's where I got these boots too." Devon scuffed the heel of his knee-high cavalry boots against a clump of shriveled grass.

LeBeau's lips twitched upward as he finished his loads. "You ever put a bullet in one of them blue-bellies?"

Devon's stomach turned.

A breeze rippled across his face and tugged at the corners of the brown frock coat LeBeau had loaned him until his uniform could be washed. Tailor-fitted for LeBeau's son, Arthur, doctor in the Confederate army, the wool stretched against Devon's muscles, limiting his range of motion.

"I've killed a man before." He answered without looking up. "More than one. Only, I don't care to talk about it, sir." He rolled a soft lead ball between his fingers and dropped it into the first chamber.

A ripple of sound erupted overhead. *Honk. Honk.* A V of geese flapped toward Mexico.

"Blast. I should have brought my shotgun." LeBeau smacked his palm against his hip. "George," he hollered to the slave who leaned against the fence about fifty yards down the line. "Hurry back to the house and get my shotgun."

"Yes, Massa." George waved and trotted off.

Devon rammed the loading lever into the fifth chamber and glanced toward the distant house, where only the roof above the smattering of trees could be seen at this distance beyond the rolling fields. Was Morning Fawn at her window? If she was smart, she'd crack it open a couple of inches, no more, so that it wouldn't be noticed from the ground. Would she recall he'd done that for her?

If only she could remember that and forget some of the fool things he'd said. He'd give her the moon? Had that really come out of his mouth? What had gotten into him?

"Care to wager?" LeBeau threw back his shoulders, adjusted the brim of his brown top hat, and lifted his revolver toward the target.

Betting? He'd done his share of playing cards and gambling. A skill he'd picked up evenings along the scouting trail after he'd run off at age seventeen. A skill that had earned him the scar on his nose in New Orleans as a newly enlisted Federal officer. "I'll pass. I'm a bit short on funds at the moment."

"I'd accept an I.O.U. After all, you're going to manage my cotton shipment."

Devon added caps to the chamber nipples and clicked the cylinder back into place. Maybe this was his opportunity. Did he dare ask? With most able-bodied men off fighting in the war, LeBeau was more than eager for his services. Maybe that'd buy him a bit of grace if he overstepped boundaries. "Suppose we wager for something other than money?"

"And what might that be?" LeBeau shifted his revolver in his gloved palm.

Devon exhaled. The mission had to come first. He should keep his mouth shut. Sabotaging the cotton warehouse in

Alleyton had the potential to cripple the Trans-Mississippi Confederacy's ability to buy arms for months.

His throat tightened. If he didn't do something to intervene on Morning Fawn's behalf, and they tried to shove that trash down her throat again tonight, he might run up those stairs and wring her uncle's neck. Devon had brought her to this house. The responsibility lay on his shoulders like a yoke. Surely, there was a way to protect her and complete his mission. He swallowed hard and jumped into the muddy waters of risk. "If more of my shots come closer to the bull's eye than yours, Miss Beth gets to join us for dinner."

LeBeau pivoted toward him, mouth ajar. Piercing blue eyes scoured Devon as if he were a page in an accounting ledger. "You have an interest in my niece, Lieutenant Reynolds?"

Sweat broke out on the back of Devon's neck. How should he play this? Interested beau? But there was Thea to contend with. He couldn't slight the man's daughter. And Morning Fawn would welcome his attentions about as much as a momma cougar would allow a stranger near her kittens. He shrugged. "I feel bad about treating her so roughly yesterday. She reminds me of my sister." Mostly a lie. But he had to find some way to intervene without criticizing the man who held the reins of authority. "My younger sister is a wonderful girl, but she can be a bit strong-willed and stubborn."

"Your sister... I see." LeBeau smoothed his thumb and forefinger over his mustache. "And how does your stepfather deal with the young lady?"

"By trial and error."

"Hmmm." LeBeau squinted his left eye shut, inhaled, and fired.

The target rattled.

LeBeau blew the smoke away from his barrel. "If I win, you'll act as my factor overseeing the selling and transportation of this year's crop for free."

Devon nudged his slouch hat off his forehead. "You drive a hard bargain, sir, but you have a deal."

"A real gambler for a lady's hand." LeBeau eyed him as if measuring his response.

"Mercy for a sister."

"So you say." LeBeau squinted, stilled, and fired again.

Footsteps crunched on the graveled walkway.

LeBeau held up his hand toward George. "Stay put." He fired again. Five times in total, the board rattled each time. 'Leave the shotgun by the fence and go check my hits. Use the charcoal to mark the spots."

Should he trust the man's slave? Devon itched to follow after George and see for himself. But he planted his feet firm and flexed his fingers. Gentlemen didn't question each other's honor without reason.

George's footfalls churned across the field, scaring off a rabbit.

LeBeau swiped his brow with a handkerchief and dug his brandy flask from his pocket. "So, Reynolds, tell me more about your sister."

An opportunity to bring in his idea regarding Morning Fawn. "My stepfather discovered she cooperated more fully when she earned a reward for doing so."

"Sounds like a way to spoil a child." LeBeau took a swig.

Is that what he'd done with Thea? Devon swallowed his smirk. "In some cases, perhaps. But not in my sister's, and maybe not in Miss Beth's either. A spirited young woman needs something to work toward, a goal."

"Do you consider yourself an expert on the fairer sex, Lieutenant?" LeBeau handed the flask his way.

"No, thank you, sir. I still have shots to fire. And no on the second account, as well. I'm no expert. Just on my sister."

"You had a wife."

Sure way to rattle his concentration, ten times worse than

the brandy. "My wife was a different sort. Sweet, demure..." He rubbed his palms on his trouser legs and slipped his revolver from his holster. "But you asked about my sister. My stepfather persuaded her with new dresses, a trip to New Orleans—" Drew her into the planter culture so tight, Devon hardly recognized the young woman she became. "And a horse." The horse. That was the only gift worth having, the one in which he could still see the girl she had been.

"A horse is the last thing my niece needs." LeBeau chuckled. "But dresses, a trip after the war—"

"All of those fancy frills wouldn't mean a thing to Miss Beth. But a horse would be a different story."

Lebeau's eyebrows cocked. "Are you insane? Give her a horse, and she'd run off the first time our backs are turned."

"Well, then, something more permanent, something that'd give her a reason to not escape."

George ran up to them, grabbing his battered slouch hat to keep it from slipping off his head. "Mighty fine shootin', Massar. Three in that there bull's eye."

LeBeau grinned. "Better get to it, Reynolds." He nodded toward the target and slapped Devon on the shoulder. "If you want to give up now, I'll only have you work three days without pay."

Devon ran his finger along his steel barrel and spun the chamber. It'd be prudent to allow his host to win. But he wasn't going to leave Morning Fawn up there another night to a dinner of laudanum. If the LeBeaus could see her at the table behaving like a reasonable person, they'd be less likely to force-feed her that poison. Could Morning Fawn behave herself? The question rolled around in his head as he lifted his revolver, steadied his right hand with his left, and inhaled.

He squinted through the sight.

A mockingbird whistled from the field.

Devon cocked the hammer, squeezed the trigger, and fired.

Morning Fawn dragged her feet on the stairs as she followed behind Jim the butler and Lucy. Were they supposed to be her guards and stop her if she did something wild and insane like bolt for the front door and steal another horse? Her uncle had some nerve sending a message that she had one hour to make herself presentable and meet him in his office. As if he were a king. She ground her teeth and stuck a loose strand behind her ear. Lucy had tried to talk her into pulling her hair back in a chignon, but a simple ribbon had been Morning Fawn's limit of cooperation.

Still, the summons to leave the attic was unexpected.

As they reached the painted-tile foyer, Jim, with LeBeau's hand-me-down suit hanging off his pole-bean figure, pivoted and lumbered toward Uncle Robert's office door.

Lucy hung back and sidled up to her. "Reynolds had something to do with your uncle sending for you."

"He did?"

"Yup. The lieutenant met me on the second-floor landing as I headed up to your room. Wanted me to tell you to please behave."

"He said what?" Morning Fawn stopped walking, barely keeping her voice to a whisper.

"For your own sake. That's what he said." Lucy gnawed her lip. "And I think he's right."

Morning Fawn shot her a glare. "Don't you dare go agreeing with that man." She stomped ahead past the closed parlor door. Reynolds had a lot of gall. Telling her what to do as if she didn't have any sense.

He'd seen her under the influence of laudanum. No wonder he thought her incompetent. But why should he care what happened to her?

He'd taken the nails out for her. Why?

Jim opened the brass-handled door, and Morning Fawn followed.

Her uncle stood by the expansive window which looked out upon the shrubs and the dormant garden, Aunt Judith's glory when it was in full bloom. His smooth, pale hands rested on the top of his cane. From what Morning Fawn had seen, it was more like a scepter she'd read about in the stories on his shelves than an aid for walking.

"Jim, you can wait in the hall." Uncle Robert clicked his watch lid shut and nudged it into the pocket of his gray silk waistcoat. "And tell Lucy to help Flora in the kitchen."

"Yes, Massa." Jim's Adam's apple bobbled.

The door clicked.

Back stiff, Morning Fawn stepped to the center of the room which acted as both library and office and clasped her hands. Jane Eyre wasn't the only one in an attic. The fairytales told of princesses locked in towers. If her uncle could play king, she could play princess. A Comanche princess. Only, she'd be gray-haired and old, craving every drop of laudanum she could scour if she waited for a warrior in shining armor to come along and rescue her.

The fading light of almost-sunset illuminated the dark-stained walnut of the bookshelves and side table. LeBeau's mahogany desk, with its closed ledgers and cigar box, stood at the side of the second window providing a view of both the garden and the door.

Her mother's youthful portrait hung on the far wall. Wavy, dark hair, pale blue eyes. Sweetness and hope shone from her face. Morning Fawn had battled with that painted gaze more than once, yearning for the woman whose image had been captured in oil yet wanting to block it from her mind as if that might erase the soul-deep ache.

Her uncle pivoted toward her, silencing her ponderings. Brow furrowed, he scrutinized her from head to toe. "Mr. Franklin was highly displeased with your absconding with his Thoroughbred. He was ready to turn you over to the sheriff and have you hauled off to the jail in Columbus. I've agreed to loan him my best stable hand, Cole, for a month to shut him up."

Absconding? Probably some fancy word for stealing. Morning Fawn lowered her gaze to the red-and-green floral carpet. She hadn't intended to keep the horse. She only wanted to get away, but she would not apologize to the man who lorded over her like an ogre.

"If you weren't a LeBeau, I'd send you to work in my stable to replace Cole's lost labor. Though I'd probably have to chain you there. Lord knows, I couldn't trust you to stay put."

She lifted her chin. "I'm told my name is Logan, not LeBeau." *Thank goodness.* "But I'd be happy to work with the horses. Chainless."

"You're going nowhere near my horses." He thudded his silver-tipped cane on the floor. "And as for the Logan name, your grandfather is your only saving grace. It was painfully obvious your father didn't have any sense. Turned his back on his inheritance and family. Might as well have called himself an abolitionist. But you're here because of your LeBeau blood."

Too bad she couldn't wash her veins free of the connection.

No wonder her sister had run off with a Yankee rather than live under the shackles of this man's hospitality. "You've persuaded me. I regret not taking better care of Mr. Franklin's horse. I'd be willing to work in the stable, chained." Anything to end the scolding.

He narrowed his gaze. "Your impertinence is going to get you sent back up those stairs for the next week if you don't watch your mouth."

Impertinence? She didn't need a dictionary to decipher the gist of his rebuke. She pressed her lips shut and simmered. The mantel clock chimed five times.

He crossed the room, leaned his cane against the desk, and uncapped the decanter. "Lieutenant Reynolds believes you can be reasoned with."

She blinked wide. "Reynolds said that?"

"I'm far from convinced." Her uncle poured a half inch of brandy into a glass and swallowed it. The glass clunked against the wood as he set it down. "But I'm a flexible man, and in the spirit of generosity, I'm willing to give it a try."

Generous? That's probably what the king said before he banged his scepter and yelled, *Off with their heads*. "Give what a try?" She held her breath.

He strutted to the back of the desk and sank onto the padded leather seat. His handlebar mustache twitched like the tips of a fox's tail. "You have two choices, Beth. You can continue with your hysterics and fits, trying to run off every time you have a whim—"

"I'm not hysterical, and I don't have fits. All I want is to—"

He struck the desk with his palm. "I didn't come here to argue, young woman. After your incident at church a couple days ago and escapade with Franklin's horse, I have half a mind to send you off to an asylum. If you have a fit like that again, that's exactly where you'll be headed. I'm done coddling you." LeBeau leaned forward, jutting a finger in her direction, his tone as flexible as an arrowhead. "I'm offering one chance to earn your way out of the attic."

Her eyebrows edged upward. "Earn my way out?" Scale a tower? Apologize a dozen times? Be Thea's maid?

He pinned her with his gaze. "Prove to me you can conduct yourself as a proper young lady of class and represent your family in a dignified manner."

Was that all? Be something she'd never been and had no desire to be? If this was Reynolds's suggestion, he might as well have boarded up her windows and thrown away the key to her room. "I prefer the stable job." She crossed her arms.

LeBeau glowered and steepled his fingers. "You're already working on proving Reynolds wrong. I should have bet the man."

I'd like to kick the man. She dug her nails into bell sleeves and rolled her eyes. "So how am I supposed to prove I'm a lady?" If that's what Thea was, she wanted nothing to do with it.

"Marry."

"What?" Her arms fell to her sides.

"Earn the affection of a respectable Confederate gentleman, win his proposal, and wed him." His voice practically purred.

"You can't be serious." This was what Reynolds was up to? Was he thinking of her for himself? Her legs wobbled. What *had* happened last night? Nonsense. A man like that wouldn't propose just because he'd bedded her. But he hadn't, had he? Her clothes had been intact.

"I mean what I say." His voice cracked like a whip. "Your aunt is anxious for you to pursue a husband."

"From the little I know about being a lady, it isn't the lady who does the pursuing."

"That may be, but a lady needs to open herself up to the possibility and welcome the attention of respectable gentle-men. But I'm not going to sit here and explain the nuances of flirting to my niece. I'll leave that to my—"

"I have no idea what a nuance is."

"Young woman." His voice rose. "Before you sound off and turn your nose up at the only opportunity you have for a decent life, you should wait until you hear about the gift you'll receive on your wedding day."

"I'm not interested." No one was going to force her to marry.

He puffed out his chest. "Land."

"Land?" Goosebumps tingled up her arms.

"Two hundred acres just inside the settlement line in Parker County, the northwestern frontier. It's where your parents were headed when the savages attacked them. Your mother used her inheritance, the little bit that my father had given her to protect her against the whims of that fool husband of hers, to help your father purchase it. Upon her death, the land went to me. I'm offering it to you as a wedding present, upon your marriage to a Confederate gentleman of means and from a good family."

Her head swam. She turned away from her uncle's prying, icy gaze and drifted to the window. Her parents' land. At the edge of the frontier. Hers to keep. Freedom. Not exactly free. There'd be a husband. Someone to tell her what to do. Someone who'd expect her to sit around the parlor gossiping and fanning herself. Someone trying to tell her how to behave. Reynolds? She gripped the window sill. The lieutenant was out of his mind if he thought he could make her marry him or obey. But her uncle didn't say it had to be him.

Land. A home. A place to call her own, where she didn't have to worry about whether or not she fit in. But to marry for it and give up all hope of love? All hope of a man looking at her the way Dancing Eagle had gazed at Eyes-Like-Sky. Maybe there'd be someone who fit LeBeau's stipulations and also captured her heart, but what were the chances of that? Especially with her heart feeling like a dried-out water pouch left in the sun so long it'd cracked beyond use. Her stomach knotted.

"Two hundred acres on the frontier. You want to throw it all away and run off to live in a tipi after you're married, it'll be your choice." His voice blended with the growing shadows of the room calling to her, like the Pied Piper she'd read about. She'd need time to consider it. What in the world made her think her uncle was a man to be trusted?

"You said a Confederate of means and family. You didn't name a name." Her blasted voice shook.

"I don't intend to dictate your specific choice of a husband."

She coughed back a snort. How could he say that with a straight face?

A real home. Maybe she could bring her pia there. Offer refuge. Ideas swirled in her head. Playing along with LeBeau's offer would buy her time to decide and unlock the attic door. Had she ever really been foolish enough to think she'd marry for love? That she deserved happiness? "In that case, Uncle, could you please invite Mr. Nicholas Moyer, the new cotton warehouse supervisor, to dinner next Saturday evening?"

<h1 style="text-align:center">CHAPTER 8</h1>

*D*evon stood in the parlor doorway, hands stuffed into his trouser pockets, supposedly listening to Thea plunk notes on the piano, but his gaze drifted toward the stairs. He'd beaten LeBeau by a single notch. If anything, the patch over his left eye had proved a help, not a hindrance for target shooting. Much different than the battlefield, where it would take away half of his peripheral vision and leave him open to attack. His battle yesterday had been to win by the smallest margin possible.

LeBeau had begged off from having Morning Fawn join them for dinner last night. In fact, it'd been a small, informal meal, with Mrs. LeBeau and Thea away at Cedar Ridge plantation overnight. There had been no scuffles or screams upstairs. Hopefully, that meant no laudanum.

Tonight, Morning Fawn would join them. His chest swelled at the thought he'd won this for her. LeBeau had slapped him on the shoulder and informed him he'd decided to try out Devon's stepfather's advice, but the rest of the conversation had centered around cotton. No clue as to what reward he'd offered Morning Fawn in hopes of gaining compliance.

Thankfully, Devon had escaped everyone's company today by volunteering to exercise and groom the horses.

As the music played, LeBeau lounged in a parlor chair, its thick cushions covered in cherry-bramble patterned velvet, a match to the wallpaper. Mrs. LeBeau sat at the edge of a wine-colored low-back sofa, her gaze fluttering between her husband, Thea, and the door.

Thea banged out a grand finale note to a Chopin piece Devon couldn't name. Her parents clapped, and he willed his hands to comply. But his heartbeat picked up a notch as a pitter-pat sounded on the stairs, followed by a tromp.

Eyes downcast, Lucy hurried off the last step and halted in the foyer.

Morning Fawn followed. Head held high, she'd used a ribbon to draw her hair away from her face, but silky honey strands fell across the shoulders of her dark green dress. The same dress she'd worn the day he'd yanked her off the horse and tumbled her to the ground. But it'd been mended without a tear and adorned with white bell undersleeves and black lace trim.

"What's going on?" Thea hopped off the piano stool, but he ignored her.

"I granted Beth permission to come to dinner." LeBeau stood and tugged on his sack coat lapels.

He hadn't told his daughter?

Another explosion from Thea, but the words escaped Devon.

Morning Fawn clomped off the last step and marched straight for him. Color enlivened her face, so much better than the unhealthy pale of his midnight visit two nights before.

Eyes narrowed and chin jutted, she whispered, "I'm not going to choose you."

"Choose me for what?" His brow furrowed, even as a hint of

rosewater tickled his nose. What the devil was she talking about?

"As if you didn't know."

"I-I don't." He sputtered, but she'd lifted her skirts and headed down the hall.

"What did she say to you?" Thea sidled up to him and curled her fingers around the crook of his arm.

Take your hands off me. He coughed down the words before they could erupt. "I have no idea."

Mrs. LeBeau rescued him, came up on the other side of Thea and touched her elbow. "We must be charitable with your cousin, dear. Your father has decided to give her one more chance to prove she can learn to behave like a lady."

Thea scoffed. "That'll be the day." Her fingers loosened.

He slipped free and hurried ahead.

Carrying herself like a princess, Morning Fawn opened the dining room door and entered, without waiting for the servants or LeBeau.

Thea latched on to Devon as his foot crossed the threshold. "You'll sit by me, of course."

"I'll leave that for your father to decide."

Lucy and two more servants he couldn't name hurried to the sideboard where silver-plated serving dishes awaited. A fire crackled in the small hearth.

Morning Fawn shot him a look as if he were beneath contempt and pulled out a chair to the left of Mrs. LeBeau's seat. "I don't need any help."

Mrs. LeBeau *tsk*ed as she arrived at her own seat. "Ladies wait for gentlemen to pull out their chair."

Morning Fawn pressed her lips together as Mr. LeBeau strode up and helped his wife.

Thea sashayed over to the seat by her father's end of the table and rustled her skirts as if she need remind Devon of her presence. He seated her and sat between her and Mrs. LeBeau.

His gaze fell to the empty chair beside Morning Fawn. They were one gentleman short, or more likely, one lady too many, the extra one being on his side of the table.

They bowed their heads as Mrs. LeBeau said the Lord's Prayer. From what he'd seen, it was a nightly custom. He whispered his own in silence, thanksgiving that Morning Fawn was out of the attic and safe for the moment, and a petition that she'd stay that way.

As they raised their heads, hazel eyes lit with determination and something less than friendly met his as the first dish was served. Obviously, his removal of the nails and his part in getting her invited to dinner were insufficient penitence for prior offenses. And who knew if LeBeau had mentioned Devon's role in her reprieve from the attic?

Steam drifted up from the potato soup, and the scent of freshly baked bread caused his stomach to rumble.

Morning Fawn broke eye contact and inhaled. Her spoon was in her mouth in seconds. Had she been afraid to eat in the attic, concerned her food might still be tainted?

Thea touched his hand. "Lieutenant, you must tell us more about your adventures."

Her father cleared his throat. Over the touch?

Morning Fawn clinked her silverware against her china bowl.

Devon scooted his hand free and reached for his glass of water. "I'd rather hear something about Morning—Beth's travel."

Everyone but Thea stopped chewing. Not a good topic?

Thea splayed her fingers across her fichu-covered cleavage. "I'm sure it'd be very informative to learn how to coat one's self and hair in bear grease and how to properly skin a buffalo. However, I don't believe recalling such details would aid in the civilizing of Cousin Beth."

Morning Fawn flipped her hair off her shoulder. "I'm sure

you'd rather burn to a rosy crisp beneath the sun on the plains. The only question would be whether you'd die from the heat or starvation first."

"I wouldn't be fool enough to be stranded in such a predicament. Unlike some—"

"One could only wish." Morning Fawn sliced a chunk of bread from the loaf near her and took a bite.

"At least I know how to conduct myself with lady-like deportment and demeanor." Thea lifted her nose. "Should I fetch the dictionary for you—"

"Girls." Mrs. LeBeau snapped her napkin. "Thea, why don't you tell the lieutenant about Robson's Castle? I'm sure he's never heard of such a wonder in Texas."

"Castle?" His eyebrows quirked up. Anything to avoid a fight at the table.

"Oh, you'd be amazed." Thea glowed. "Colonel Robson is from Scotland. I believe he's a duke or lord, or something like that. He came to America in search of adventure and found his way to Texas, of all places. He built a castle on the shores of the Colorado River in Columbus. Three stories of granite. You should see it."

"Limestone." LeBeau waved a servant over.

"A real castle?" Devon shifted in his seat.

Morning Fawn slurped her soup and glowered.

Thea smirked across the table. "It has a moat and a drawbridge. A rooftop garden. And the ballroom with its chandeliers and the carpets, and champagne dinners... Why, I feel as if I'm visiting the Queen of Scotland when I go there."

"I read that they chopped off her head." Morning Fawn's voice rang with a touch of amusement.

"Speaking of heads..." LeBeau drew his carving knife through the ham the servant had given him. "I heard news today that the Yankees have moved farther up the coast. They took Mustang Island, and it's rumored they'll try for Matagorda Island next."

Mrs. LeBeau gasped. "That means there's nothing between them and Corpus Christi."

"I'm sure Amy is on her way to Austin, Judith." LeBeau exhaled and handed Thea a plate with a thick slice of ham. "Harris wrote that he'd made all of the arrangements." He nodded to Devon. "Amy is our oldest daughter. Her husband is a major serving at the capital."

Mrs. LeBeau gripped the table edge. "I will not rest assured until I receive a letter confirming she's there safe and sound. Why didn't you tell me this earlier, Robert?"

"I didn't want to worry you." LeBeau dug his knife into the thick, juicy meat again. "Amy should have plenty of time to escape. The Yanks won't waste their forces on the city when they need every man they can muster if they plan to head for Fort Esperanza.

"Remember Sabine Pass? Forty-two Confederates held off a fleet of Yankee gunboats and troop transports. Did you hear about that battle, Reynolds? It was something."

"Forty-two Confederates?" Devon choked on his peas. That wasn't the way he'd heard it, but the troops who had drug themselves off the transports back into New Orleans had been in no mood to talk. Thankfully, he wasn't part of the mission. There'd been no fleet of gunboats. That much he knew. Reb newspapers had probably filled the citizens' heads with propaganda.

LeBeau showered them all with the glorious details as the servants added stewed tomatoes and buttered squash to the ham-laden plates.

Thea pressed her palms together at the end of the rendition. "Papa, maybe we should evacuate and head to Austin too. You know that's where our men will hole up. I've heard the horrors of New Orleans. General Butler threatened to treat respectable ladies as women of the street plying their trade. I swear he must have horns under his hat."

Devon dropped his gaze to his food to hide the roll of his eyes.

A murmur from Morning Fawn snapped him to attention. Had she noticed his disapproval, or was she merely voicing her own?

LeBeau puffed out his chest. "Daughter, I have no intention of fleeing. Cotton is the blood of this Confederacy. If the Yanks dare set foot in Colorado County, I'll stand my ground. This is our land, our cotton."

Devon rubbed his thumb over his fork handle. If the Rebels made a stand in Colorado County, he'd be expected to help. What a conundrum that'd be. He glanced up from his plate to catch Morning Fawn staring at him.

She played with her spoon. "It sounds like the army needs every man it can get."

Meaning him? She might as well come out and say it. His hand twitched upward to his eyepatch. "If the enemy heads this way, Miss Logan, I imagine even you would be relieved that not all of the men are in the middle of a swamp somewhere defending the coast or marching through cacti to defend the cotton."

She plunked her forearms on the table. "Seventeen months ago, when you sneaked into my village and paid someone to lure me to the creek so *you* could kidnap me, *you* were the one I needed to be protected from. I'd rather take my chances with the Yankees."

His food turned to sawdust in his mouth.

"Young lady, you will be respectful to our guests or go to your room." LeBeau clenched his fork.

"It's all right, sir." Devon waved his hand toward his host. He deserved her wrath.

Morning Fawn flicked a strand of hair from her forehead.

"Don't worry, Uncle. I'm done pining away for what was. You've made me an offer, and I'll accept it."

"What kind of offer?" Thea perked up.

LeBeau pinched the bridge of his nose. "I might as well say it and be done with the fussing here and now." He tossed his napkin on the table. "I've agreed, if certain stipulations are met, to give Beth the plot of land in Parker County that belonged to her parents."

Land? Not a horse. Amazing.

"Land?" Thea's voice crescendoed. "You're going to give her land? What about me? You promised the plantation to my brother Arthur—"

"Parker County is on the frontier. Dry, scruffy land with little protection from Indian raids. Nothing you'd want, daughter. As for your inheritance, we'll discuss that at another time."

Thea gaped. "She has a fit and steals a horse, and you're rewarding her?"

"Watch how you speak to your father." Mrs. LeBeau firmed her voice.

Brow furrowed, LeBeau fingered the silver fob that dangled from the pocket of his waistcoat. "I did say there are stipulations. Conditions that must be met."

"And pray tell me what?" Thea bristled out of the chair.

LeBeau's glower lowered Thea to a sit. "The land will be a gift upon her marriage to a respectable Confederate of good family."

Marry? Devon blinked wide. LeBeau was going to force Morning Fawn to marry to get her freedom? What kind of freedom was that?

Thea sputtered. "Beth? Marry a man of class?" She slapped her hand to her chest and coughed for effect. "That will be the day."

"You'll see." Morning Fawn narrowed her gaze at her

cousin. "I haven't made my mind up who. Only who it will not be." Hazel eyes zeroed in on Devon like a gun sight.

What in the world made her think he was interested? What had her uncle told her?

Thea leaned toward her cousin. "As if any man this side of a saloon would have—"

"Silence." LeBeau clinked his wine goblet against his plate.

Cross-armed, Thea smoldered.

Morning Fawn's hands dropped to her lap, her lips pressed together, and Mrs. LeBeau fumbled with her emerald necklace.

LeBeau touched his midsection. "This family is enough to give me indigestion at times." He heaved a sigh. "Judith, I'd like for you to accompany Beth to Columbus and help her pick out material for a couple of dresses."

Thea gaped at him. "Dresses? Lucy's hand-me-downs should fit her—"

LeBeau held up his hand. "Next week, you may travel to Columbus, as well, on a separate trip with your mother, but I'll not have the two of you going together."

"Beth might still be in Columbus when I travel there. It wouldn't surprise me if she didn't find a way to get herself thrown in jail." Thea snickered.

"Perhaps you're right. That's why I'm asking Lieutenant Reynolds to accompany them. Besides, I'd never send two women on the road unprotected."

Devon almost choked on his saliva. LeBeau might as well have fired a cannonball right into the middle of the table.

Thea was beyond words. She shot out of her chair and shoved it against the table.

Mrs. LeBeau handled the announcement with a measure of decorum. She dabbed her mouth with her napkin. "If you say so, Robert, and if the lieutenant is willing."

"My dresses are fine as is." Morning Fawn gnawed her lip.

"You're excused from the table, niece." LeBeau snapped his

fingers at a servant and pointed to a wine bottle on the side-board. "Take the rest of your dinner with you. Lucy will escort you. I've had enough commotion this evening."

Her gaze flickered over Devon as she stood, her expression unreadable. Did she believe he'd orchestrated this? Was this the reason for her whispered outburst when she'd come down the stairs?

Probably already plotting how she was going to run away from him tomorrow. But the thought of sitting beside her on a wagon seat or riding alongside of her perked him up more than a cup of good, dark coffee.

As the door closed behind her and Mrs. LeBeau, Devon braced himself. It didn't make any sense. Was this man targeting him as a potential husband for his niece? LeBeau had said a loyal Confederate from a good family. That's exactly what the man believed him to be. Only. he wasn't.

"Forgive me for not talking to you ahead of time, Reynolds." LeBeau swirled his wine.

"Excuse me, sir?" What was this man up to?

LeBeau waved the other two servants from the room and settled back in his chair.

"I see the way Thea looks at you. You're a good man, but I have someone else in mind for my daughter, a fellow planter named Major Leander Thomas. They courted before the war. He only needs a little more persuading, but Thea is impatient. She thinks she has to grab a husband before they're all gone." LeBeau swallowed more wine. "Thomas comes from one of the finest families in the county and has a thousand acres of good bottomland. I'm not opposed to your keeping company with my daughter for a stroll or a dance, as long as you know where she's intended."

Second rate? Not good enough for his daughter? Thank God. He'd welcome the insult if it saved him from Thea. But what about the man's niece? What was expected there? His pulse strummed at the base of his neck. Foolish. He had no intentions toward Morning Fawn, other than making amends for past wrongs. Had her uncle mistaken kindness for something else?

Devon deflated his voice, doing his best to present a token of regret. "I understand and respect your decision, sir." He tugged his coat sleeve to his wrist. The sooner he got into his own clothes, the better, but that wasn't going to happen until the mission was over. Destroying as much cotton as he could—that was the mission. Not looking after a girl who speared him with her eyes every chance she got. "But what about your cotton? Shouldn't I work on arranging the shipment instead of escorting the ladies?"

"All in due time, Reynolds. With the uncertainty of the invasion forces on the coast, I'm not ready to move it yet. Waiting might also give me a chance to avoid the government getting their grubby fingers in a portion of the profit. But you'll have a chance to make connections in Columbus while the ladies shop. I'll write you a couple of references."

Devon rubbed the back of his neck and chose his words carefully. "Since you've been upfront with me, sir" —the man had hardly done any such thing—"I'll return the favor. I'm not looking to marry. My wife was very dear to me. My heart is not open to new love."

The corner of LeBeau's mouth quirked up. "Love isn't a requirement for marriage. But thank you for clarifying your position."

What kind of dismissal was that? "I will very likely never remarry."

"I understand." LeBeau tapped his fingers together. "I'm simply asking you to look after Beth and my wife tomorrow. I have confidence you can restrain my niece. And I'd greatly appreciate it if you'd stick around for the time being. With all the unrest on the coast, we'll need every gun we can get if worse comes to worst." His host's voice took on a wistful note. "Beth reminds me of her mother, not in features necessarily, but in heart. I cannot and will not allow her to throw herself away on some rebellious adventure. If giving her the land buys her a settled, respectable life, so be it."

Could land really buy all of that? What about love? Not his concern. But a flash of memory sent his heart thudding. Hazel eyes, her fingers around his neck, a dreamy voice... Stupid. He'd better get ahold of himself by tomorrow, or he'd be chasing her halfway to Dallas.

Tension seeped from Morning Fawn's shoulders as she fingered the empty hole on the window sash. The moon shimmered through the scantily clad branches of the cottonwood. She inhaled as a cool breeze drifted beneath the window where she'd raised it an inch. A smidgen of freedom, courtesy of Devon Reynolds, and proof she wasn't trapped despite the locked attic door. Obviously, her uncle wasn't ready to trust her yet. But the fact that she was going to be allowed to journey to town tomorrow was nothing short of a miracle.

Was Reynolds responsible for all of this? The splintered gouge scraped her skin as she rubbed the spot where the nail had been. Reynolds wasn't a kind man. Of that, she was almost certain. Yet she couldn't squelch the trace of warmth that spread through her chest, defying the depths of her skepticism.

Morning Fawn cupped her elbows. The man didn't deserve her gratitude. Two days ago, he'd dragged her back here. Seventeen months ago, he bribed someone in her tribe to lure her to a nearby canyon. She'd stuck her knife into the side of the man who sneaked up behind and grabbed her. A steel grip had yanked her off the wounded scoundrel and thrown her to the ground.

The new attacker had shoved her face first into the pebbled sand, his knee boring into her back. Strong, muscular hands had wrenched her arms backward, grinding a rope around her wrists as if she were some calf to be tied.

He'd bent down, his breath hot against her ear. Spanish, the trade language of the frontier from the high prairies to Mexico, had poured from his lips. "I don't want to hurt you. But I'm not going to let you kill him, and I'm not going to let you warn your tribe."

That was Devon Reynolds. And if his hard blue eyes had softened a bit since then, she shouldn't let it fool her. He cared more about money and his own interests than the people he hurt. It didn't matter that he'd freed her from the attic cage for dinner and saved her from another dose of laudanum. She couldn't trust him. She had no idea of what scheme he might be up to. Maybe he wanted the land in Parker County, and this was his way to get it. Or perhaps he felt guilty for ruining her life for three hundred dollars and was trying to make amends. Either way, she wanted nothing to do with him.

Now, marriage was the price to be paid for land and freedom—the choice of a groom narrowed to only those who fit her uncle's specifications. What kind of freedom was that?

She pressed her forehead to the pane and closed her eyes. *God of my mother, where are You?* Was her imprisonment on this plantation a punishment? She'd fallen short so many times. *Don't leave me alone. Please.*

A shiver ran through her as she straightened. Two nights ago, she'd stood here with Reynolds. Well, not really *stood*, as she'd been sliding down the wall. He'd carried her to the bed. And then? Left like a gentleman. At least that seemed to be what happened. It was all a bit blurry. *"I'll give you the moon."* The words trailed across her memory, the residue from a dream-soaked whisper, too vapory to grasp. Had Reynolds really said that?

~

*M*orning Fawn peeked out the porch window. A heavy sheen of early-morning dew coated the courtyard. Breakfast had been a quick affair in her room. Fine by her. No Thea, no uncle, no critique of her manners.

A steady murmur of wheels and hoofs sounded on the gravel drive as Reynolds drove up in the new Victoria—a one-bench, open-front carriage with a raised driver's seat. He'd donned his butternut-colored uniform again. One of the servants must have finished scrubbing the dirt and sand out of it. Odd, how the shell jacket fit him snugly, hugging his muscular arms. One would have thought after all those weeks in an enemy hospital and tramping about the country making his way to Texas and halfway up the state that the wool would have hung loose on his limbs.

He secured the brake and climbed down. A frown settled on his face as he glanced at the carriage. She didn't blame him there. She'd much rather have a horse and saddle beneath her and ride in the open air than to be shuttered inside on cushioned seats, elbow to elbow with her aunt.

A flock of geese honked overhead.

Removing his tan slouch hat, Reynolds raked his fingers through his thick brown hair, sweeping a couple of wayward strands from his forehead. No pomade. The man wasn't a dandy. Any man who could travel to her village beyond the Palo Duro and make it out alive again with a captive knew how to live rough and survive on little.

He glanced her way.

She ducked behind the curtain.

Hurried footfalls sounded on the stairs. Her aunt reached

the landing and strode toward her, with a blue wool bonnet in hand. "Here, wear this. A perfect match for your dress."

Morning Fawn pressed her lips together as she accepted it.

"Have Lucy fetch you a cloak." Aunt Judith buttoned her own heavy garment of pink-and-brown silk and draped it over the folds of her deep-purple skirt and blouse. "I've already asked her to bring out a quilt. There's a chill in the air today."

"I'm coming, missus," Lucy called from above, but Aunt Judith was already heading out the door.

Morning Fawn turned toward the hall mirror by the coat rack and gingerly set the bonnet on her head. Not her. Not at all. The royal-blue dress with its rose-patterned print was more than enough. She yanked the dainty hat from her head.

"The missus won't be pleased." Lucy *tsk*ed as she walked up with a red wool cloak on one arm and a quilt on the other.

"I need my straw hat."

"I ain't going to help you get in trouble."

"You don't have to." Morning Fawn reached around the backside of the rack and retrieved the hat from beneath the coattails of her uncle's hunting coat where she'd hidden it.

Lucy blew out a breath and draped the cloak over Morning Fawn's shoulders. "Maybe all your gumption will catch the lieutenant's fancy." She'd lowered her voice to a whisper.

"I could care less about what he thinks."

Lucy smiled. "If I was you, I'd find me some mud puddle to trip over and have him rescue me."

"That man isn't to be trusted." She narrowed her gaze at her friend. "He stole me and sold me."

Lucy shook her head. "Begging your pardon, but you don't know much about being sold." The doom of the auction block weighted her tone.

"I'm sorry. You're right." Morning Fawn touched her friend's arm. "Maybe once I have my land, I can ask my uncle to give you to me, and then I can set you free."

Lucy blew out a breath. "You'll have your husband, and he'll be the one doing the deciding."

"I'll find a way. Or who knows? The Yankees might win this war."

Lucy gnawed her lip, her expression flat, and handed her the quilt. "You'd best find your way out to the carriage before your aunt comes to fetch you."

Morning Fawn would show her there was hope. Until yesterday, she hadn't believed in it herself. She turned and hurried outside.

A mockingbird trilled from a nearby tree.

Her aunt peeked from beneath the carriage top. "I told you to wear the bonnet."

"It didn't suit me." Morning Fawn pattered down the steps.

Reynolds's mouth quirked upward as he stood at the carriage step ready to assist.

"Mr. Nicholas Moyer prefers bonnets." Her aunt waved her finger.

"He can take me as I am." The shoes were already pinching her feet. What she wouldn't give for a pair of rabbit fur-lined moccasins.

"What do you mean, take—" Reynolds cut himself short.

Morning Fawn glared at him. Moyer was none of his concern.

No softness in those lake-blue eyes today.

Aunt Judith scooted her skirts over to her side of the seat. "If we have time after shopping, I'm thinking we'll drive over to Alleyton to ask Mr. Moyer to supper later this week."

Reynolds glanced at the sky with its trace of clouds. "I doubt we'll have time. I think the weather might turn."

"We'll leave it up to your discretion, Lieutenant." Aunt Judith folded her cloak around her. "We can always send a note if we don't go in person."

We will not leave it up to you, Lieutenant. Morning Fawn

jutted her chin and lifted her cumbersome skirts, which hung about her like weeds.

Reynolds held out his gloved hand. Work gloves, not fancy ones like her uncle and not the gauntlets of real cavalry who were out doing their duty.

She merely stared at it as she placed her foot on the carriage step. Her gaze skimmed his uniform. "I see you're a lieutenant again."

With a smirk, he whispered, "I see you're still Miss Trouble."

She blinked. A reference to the night he'd sneaked into her room? Heat spread across her cheeks. The nerve of the man. She bristled into the carriage and settled herself next to her aunt. This was going to be a long ride.

Reynolds climbed into the driver's seat, not nearly far enough away. He clicked the reins, and they trotted down the tree-lined path, past stubbled fields and the distant slave quarters. She'd heard tell that eighty men, women, and children lived in those shacks. Lucy was one of the fortunate ones, spared from the fields. At least when Morning Fawn had been captured by the Comanche, she'd been taken in by a family who came to love her and eventually treat her as an equal.

Eyes-Like-Sky had not been so fortunate.

Morning Fawn clenched her hands in her lap, resisting the urge to yank the straw hat off her head and stomp it. Instead, she pressed her lips together as Aunt Judith chatted on about lace, and silk, and linens, and how a proper young lady should drop her handkerchief or wave her fan to discretely catch a gentleman's eye.

Morning Fawn shut her eyes, but the memory erupted. Eyes-Like-Sky in a dirty, worn buckskin, scabs from half-healed wounds on her arms, gathering firewood in the brush for her master. Trembling, Morning Fawn crouched behind a tree with a cake of pemmican in her hand and tears streaming down her cheeks. She longed to take the food to her sister and hug her, but she was afraid. Afraid of being seen with her, afraid that the people in the village would recognize how she belonged right there with Eyes-Like-Sky, beaten and enslaved, with no pia or ahpu, no one, not even a little sister, brave enough to stand up for her. She ran, shoved the pemmican in Eyes-Like-Sky's hand, and fled. No wonder the Lord shut his ears to her prayers.

"Have you listened to a word I've said?" Aunt Judith spread the star-patterned quilt across both of their laps.

Morning Fawn shuddered and sat forward, glancing beneath the side canopy. Off to the right, withered grass and caked mud banks led to the narrowed Colorado River. Rain had been scarce all summer and fall.

"Beth?" Her aunt nudged her arm.

"I've been listening enough to wonder how a young lady with all of the hankie dropping, eyelash fluttering, and flattery can ever hope to secure a man of any worth."

Reynolds snorted.

Morning Fawn rolled her eyes. Didn't the man have anything better to do than eavesdrop?

"Keep your ears on the road, Lieutenant." Aunt Julia pointed a finger at his back.

Morning Fawn unbuttoned the cloak at her throat. Too warm. Too confining. Sweat beaded on the back of her neck. She had to get her mind off the past before she had another panic fit.

Aunt Judith lowered her voice. "A young woman of character doesn't make up falsities about the man in question. She merely searches her mind for compliments, accentuating the gentleman's good qualities."

Accentuating? She wouldn't bother to ask the meaning.

Aunt Judith tilted her chin. "A pleasant smile and a little fluttering are means of showing you're agreeable and discreetly conveying your interest."

Discreet? From what she knew of that word, it had never entered into Thea's vocabulary. "In my village, if a warrior was interested in a maiden—"

"That was a world away from here." Aunt Judith wiggled her ruby ring. "You must focus on the present and show the gentlemen of this county that you are a civilized young woman capable of running their household and being an asset to them in the community. That you're not a wild horse in danger of breaking down the fence and fleeing to kingdom come at the drop of a feather. Forever chomping at the bit."

"I don't care for bits," Morning Fawn muttered and pushed the quilt to her aunt's side of the carriage.

The lieutenant's shoulders twitched. Was he listening? He was the exact type of man who'd think he could bridle a woman and have her trot or canter at his command. He'd best go find himself a little mouse who didn't know how to squeak.

Traffic picked up as they neared town. Morning Fawn had only been to Columbus once in the year and a half since she'd come to live with her uncle. Outside her aunt's window, wagons and buggies passed in the other lane. People strode by. The women wore wide hoops and bonnets. Most of the men were either boys, old, or in uniform.

Morning Fawn's shoulders tensed. Too many people. Too many buildings, one wooden structure after another.

Reynolds pulled up to the iron horse-head hitching post in front of Gilbert's with its freshly cleaned windows reflecting the late-morning sun.

To her aunt's chagrin, Morning Fawn hurried out of the carriage before Reynolds had a chance to offer assistance, but he beat her to the mercantile door and opened it wide.

"Thank you, Lieutenant." Her aunt entered the store, a parasol on her arm, as if she might need such a thing inside.

Morning Fawn glared at him as he waited for her to pass through, as well. "Don't you have something else to do? Or do you plan to neglect the poor horses?"

He smirked. "I'm a cavalryman, Miss Logan. My horses eat

before I eat. But since my top priority is guarding you, I plan to see you safely inside. Then I'll drive the carriage down to the livery stable and have one of the boys look after the animals."

"I have no intention of running off." She tossed her hair back over her shoulder. "And I'm not 'Miss Logan' to you."

Their gazes met. Light flickered across his blue iris, outshining the dull brown patch which shaded half his world.

He moistened his lips. "I trust you about as far as I can throw you. Morning Fawn." His voice dipped as he spoke her name, sending a tinge of warmth down her neck and into her chest.

She should have left it at *Miss Logan*. What was she thinking? She hurried into the cool dark of the mercantile and halted. A menagerie of trade goods lay before her. Barrels of brooms and ax handles stood next to a woodstove. Other barrels brimmed with apples, potatoes, and onions. A glass-fronted counter stretched along the right side of the store with a multitude of jars of pickled edibles, everything from eggs to beets. Tin plates and cups, iron pots, and oil lamps filled the shelves alongside hats, shoes, and boxes marked *lace* and buttons and more, above rows of drawers.

She'd been to the trading rendezvous with her tribe, but that was in the open at the convergence of hunting and raiding trails in Palo Duro, Tecovas Springs, and other campsites. The Comancheros displayed their goods on blankets and in carts, eager to trade for the buffalo hides and horses acquired by her people. A time of celebration and excitement. The rendezvous five springs ago was the last time she'd seen her sister. A life time ago in a different world. Morning Fawn's heart drooped.

A man with suspenders and black armbands bustled from behind the counter. "Mrs. LeBeau, so good to see you. You couldn't have picked a better time. We just received a shipment all the way from Matamoros. The teamsters had to switch routes and come by way of San Antonio to avoid the Yankee invaders, but not directly through San Antonio. They didn't want to risk having the military confiscate the goods." His waxed mustached wiggled as he spoke. "If the governor listened to General Magruder, there wouldn't be a sack of flour or cornmeal left for us civilians."

"We have to make sacrifices for our boys, Mr. Garner." Aunt Judith loosened her bonnet strings and smiled. "But I'm thankful for your resourceful suppliers."

As Mr. Garner led her aunt to a display table, Morning Fawn walked over to the counter. Amongst the feast of goods, a jar of white-and-red-striped sticks called to her. A shadow of a memory flickered. She touched the lid.

Reynolds came up alongside her and laid his gloves on the counter. His gaze traveled over her face. "You never been in a store before?"

"It's been a long while." Before the Comanche. Scents drifted her way—coffee, wood polish, leather, apples, and sugar.

Reynolds lifted the lid on the jar. "Would you like one?"

She shrugged. "No."

True to his nature, he didn't listen. Pulled a stick out, dug in his pocket, and laid a penny on the counter.

He handed her the treasure. "It's peppermint candy. Smell it."

Gingerly, she touched the powdered surface.

She didn't need it. But the whiff of mint tickled her nose. Her father had given her something like this. An image flashed through her mind. Her father bending down, rain dripping off his felt hat and wool coat, crinkles around his eyes but a smile lighting his face. He'd been away. She was so excited to see him.

A shiver ran through her as she took the stick from Reynolds and brought it to the tip of her tongue for a taste. Her dear, sweet papa. He'd loved her. Loved their whole family. He hadn't deserved to die defending his family on the prairie.

Her hand trembled as she shoved the candy back toward Reynolds. "No, thank you." She pivoted, almost colliding with a barrel of brooms, and made her way over to the bolts of cloth.

Her aunt *tsk*ed as she fingered a fold of blue linen. "Three bolts of cloth. If you don't count the brown wool. Before the war and the blockade, there would have been ten or fifteen different choices."

The owner shoved his fingers through his well-oiled hair, loosening a lock in the process. "Before the shipment yesterday, madam, all we had was the wool. It's the Yankees' fault, I tell you. But let me assure you, the linen is from the finest mill in Manchester, and then, there's the taffeta—"

"It's beautiful." Morning Fawn stroked the wine-colored material. "But I hardly need a new dress, Aunt Judith. I could make do with hand-me-downs."

"'Aunt'? B-but..." The man fumbled over his words. "This is Mr. LeBeau's captive niece?" He stared at her as if she wore a placard.

Aunt Judith arched her eyebrows. "We'll take eight yards of the taffeta, Mr. Garner."

"Why, of course, Mrs. LeBeau." Mr. Garner snuck a pencil from behind his ear. "Happy to oblige you. Every young lady needs a fine gown." He picked up the bolt. "The cost will be a little more considering all of the difficulties in getting the ship—"

"You may put it on our tab." Aunt Judith lifted her chin. "My husband will settle his account once his cotton reaches San Antonio."

"Your credit is always good here." Mr. Garner hustled over to the counter to measure the cloth.

"Aunt, you needn't go to so much trouble for me." Morning Fawn clasped her hands against her waist. She had no desire to be indebted to anyone, especially a LeBeau.

"You should have at least one new dress. Then we'll have

the seamstress refurbish one of mine, change the waistline and sleeves, and bring it up to date in fashion." Aunt Judith made her way to the display case with its shelves of gloves, hair combs, and more.

Morning Fawn scanned the store. Reynolds must have headed over to the livery stables.

Wine-colored taffeta, soft to the touch, shimmery to the eye. What would Reynolds think of such a dress? She gasped. What in the world was she thinking? That man's opinions didn't matter a scrap.

Only, it'd be mighty fine to show him she wasn't some pitiful weakling in need of help, like she had been the night he'd come to her room. She'd show him she could be as fine of a lady as any in the county. And that she had no interest in whatever scheme he had of winning her hand through the land deal, or was it winning the land through her hand?

Nicholas Moyer would like the dress. The very thought of him was enough to make her want to tug her neckline upward. Earlier in the month when he'd come to speak with her uncle on business and stayed for dinner, he'd hardly noticed Thea was in the room. Instead, he'd offered to take Morning Fawn riding and even hunting, a measure of freedom. But still, an agreement with him would be like trying to outsmart a coyote.

She drifted to the other end of the counter, away from Aunt Judith and the lace. Pocket watches, straight-blade razors, and combs vied for space alongside percussion caps and a well-used revolver. The gun would be of more use than any fancy garment. She was willing to bet she could master it quicker than she'd learned how to conduct herself properly at the LeBeaus' elegant dinners. Navigating all those utensils, saucers, and bowls was enough to boggle her mind.

What she needed was a man who didn't care about the marriage, who'd wed her for half the land. How easy would it be to undo a marriage? How could she be certain her uncle would keep his part of the agreement with no hidden tricks buried in the paperwork? Still, her best option was to play along for now and bide her time. Land close to the frontier. Hers. If only there could be a place where she could truly belong.

Three ladies entered the store, their skirts wide, their bonnets stiff, and their noses too long from the way they looked her up and down.

Morning Fawn tensed. She'd had her fill of these walls and smells and too many shelves. Aunt Judith was still talking with Mr. Garner and looking over spools of ribbon. Morning Fawn blew out a breath and slipped toward the door, side-stepping the three busybodies.

Fresh, cool air struck her as she walked outside. Almost as sweet as the breeze through the open window in her room. Relief. She closed her eyes for a moment as the sun peeked around a cloud and warmed her face, her whole body.

"What do you think you're doing?" Reynolds crossed the street, hustling out of the path of a four-mule wagon. Plumes of dust floated up from their hooves.

Morning Fawn jabbed a hand to her hip as he hurried over to her. "Do you have a rule against breathing?"

He frowned beneath his slouch hat, his slim, dark beard contrasting with the deep blue of his eye. "No, just against ladies who don't stay put."

She chuckled. "Well, you'd better go play nursemaid to my aunt, then. She's an expert at that."

His lips quirked upward. "It's the troublesome ones who need to be kept within an arm's reach. That's why I'm taking you with me on the rest of my errands."

"What errands?"

A breeze lifted the rim of her straw hat, whipping the ribbon against her cheek.

"The saddle and harness shop, for one." He held his elbow

out toward her as if she might consent to place her hand around the crook of his arm.

She rolled her eyes and stepped back. "Lead the way."

"First…" He held up a finger. "I have to tell your aunt. Don't move a step." He stuck his head inside the mercantile and called to Aunt Judith.

Morning Fawn scooted over a foot just for spite.

"Just full of contrariness, aren't you?" Reynolds smirked as he pointed the way forward.

A young boy in knickers tugged on his momma's arm as they strolled past. "Is she the one who stole the horse? She doesn't look Indian."

"Hush." The stout lady with the flower-covered bonnet yanked him along.

Morning Fawn picked up her step.

Reynolds glanced over his shoulder. "Should I have said something?"

"Not a word."

The smell of leather washed over her as they walked into the dimly lit store. Harnesses, horse collars, bridles, and their various parts hung on pegs along the barn-like walls. Saddles straddled narrow benches, and strips of leather, both wide and narrow, lay haphazardly on a long table with a draw knife on the end.

The owner, canvas apron smeared and sleeves rolled up to his elbows, spit tobacco juice in a spittoon and greeted Reynolds with a howdy.

Morning Fawn glanced around as they spoke about a harness her uncle had ordered, and then, of course, the man wanted to know about the war. Reynolds asked about the cotton shipments as if he were eager to drive a load down to Mexico himself. Such a trip would be six to eight weeks each way.

Reynolds seemed intent on taking his time returning to his

regiment. Come to think of it, he'd taken his time on enlisting in the first place, too busy with minor details like ruining her life for three hundred dollars. And now this whole marriage-for-land scheme? She'd better figure out exactly what he was up to.

A striped cat with a bent ear scurried out from beneath a bench as she approached. It pattered over to the corner, shaking its paws in the scattering of sawdust and discarded scraps of leather.

Morning Fawn smoothed her hand over the seat of a saddle, rounded and not as hard as the rectangular-shaped, rawhide-covered wood of a Comanche woman's saddle.

"You miss riding?"

She jumped, startled to find Reynolds two feet from her elbow, studying her. She lifted her chin. "I used to almost live on horseback until a certain party came along and forced an invitation on me to leave the only home I knew."

He flinched. "Maybe it's not as wonderful as you remember." He swatted a fly. "From the little I've seen of Comanche culture, you probably spent most of your time scraping and curing buffalo hides, setting up a tipi, or carrying water for some brave."

She rolled her eyes. "You don't believe in work, Mr. Reynolds? Not all of us can lounge about as you do until you have another kidnapping."

"It's Lieutenant Reynolds, or Devon, to you."

"It'll never be Devon." She crossed her arms.

"Makes no difference to me." He rubbed his thumb over a rope coil on the bench. "But as for the work part, I left home when I was seventeen. Been working or fighting ever since. I earn my way. I don't live off the labor of oth—"

He halted mid-word and glanced back at the owner, who was busy talking to a new customer. To see if they'd overheard?

She tossed a strand of hair over her shoulder. "What about

your stepfather? From what I hear, he has a fancy plantation, and you've spent your life living off the labor of others." Though he sure didn't look like it. Muscular, tanned, more like a man you'd find around a campfire on the trail than standing around a parlor.

"I have never." He glowered at her, his voice more hushed than it had been before. "My stepfather and I don't see eye to eye."

She blinked at him and pivoted toward the harnesses. Was he against slavery, maybe even an abolitionist? A crime in these parts. Enough to get a man hated, or even tarred and feathered. Maybe that was why he was after a piece of land any way he could get it. Maybe he'd lost or declined his inheritance.

"I'm curious, Lieutenant." She kept her voice low. "Why did you volunteer for the Confederate Army if you're against slavery?"

"I never said I was." Jaw firm, he placed his hand on the wall. "But regardless of what sympathies I may or may not have, I'm loyal to Texas, and I'm willing to risk my life to defend her."

She nudged her straw hat farther back on her head and searched his walled expression for truth. The glance didn't give her anything but a flutter in her belly. She turned, almost stepping into a blasted spittoon. The nasty things were everywhere, it seemed.

Reynolds hooked his thumb over his cartridge belt. "What I was trying to say before you got snippety was that if you missed riding, perhaps I could ask your uncle for permission to take you on a ride sometime. I wouldn't mind exploring more of the county."

A genuine invitation? Her pulse quickened, but she shrugged and meandered toward the bridles. "I heard you already took Thea riding the day after you got here."

"Thea tagged along. Her choice, not mine."

"Well, I'm sure she'd be happy to keep you company.

Besides, my uncle will likely remind you that I already went riding a few days ago, and it ended with some off-duty soldier yanking me off Mr. Franklin's Thoroughbred." Why did her stupid voice rise and fall like a leaf on a breeze? As if she were a maiden greeting a favored warrior by the creek. Maybe the laudanum had finally soaked her brain to the core too deep to ever dry out.

He tugged on a harness ring, testing the strength of the leather. "You can't run off like that, with no supplies and no plan. Especially on a stolen horse." His breath smelled like mint. Had he taken one of the peppermint sticks for himself?

"When should I run off, then?"

"You shouldn't."

"Stay at my uncle's forever and be his china doll on a shelf?"

"I didn't say that either."

"Oh, you mean take my uncle up on his deal."

He pressed his lips together.

Of course, that's what he'd recommend. Marry him. She'd be free of her uncle. Stuck with a man who cared more about money and land than her. She knew every bit of the cold logic, yet the tug was as real as if Devon Reynolds had looped a pair of reins around her heart.

The cat jumped up on a nearby bench and swished her tail.

"I don't like bridles." Morning Fawn reached for one that hung near his shoulder, inhaling soap and horse and bay rum as she did so. He'd used cologne? "My aunt seems to think marriage is about bits." She ran her finger along the edge of the shiny metal, almost as sparkly as a ring. "What do you think, Lieutenant?"

Reynolds's eyebrows arched toward his hairline.

Her cheeks heated. What a stupid question. Didn't she have any sense? "Forget it."

He exhaled and brushed his thumb over the headpiece of the bridle.

She turned to move away.

"If you really want to know, Morning Fawn..." He whispered her given name. "Marriage has nothing to do with bits. And it shouldn't have anything to do with land. It's about love and commitment. And choosing to honor God and the other person before yourself."

She gaped at him as a lake-blue eye met hers. Her stomach wobbled, and so did her knees as his words penetrated her core. "Then why did you come up with the whole marry-for-land scheme?"

"I didn't. That was your uncle's doing. My idea was that he give you a horse." He rubbed his nose. "He thought that was too risky."

"A horse? You expected me to sign my life away for a horse?"

"No. My suggestion had nothing to do with marriage." He scrubbed his hand over his jaw. "Your uncle added that part on. I was only trying to save you from the laudanum."

She blinked at him. "Save me?" As though she was some charity case. He wasn't interested in marrying her. Why not? Not that she wanted anything to do with him, anyway. But what about all of that sweet talk about giving her the moon? Maybe he'd been drinking that night. Or felt sorry for her and wanted to ease his conscience. "I don't need your help, Lieutenant." She clunked the bit against another. Gathering her skirts, she marched for the door. She'd show him and her uncle too.

CHAPTER 11

$\mathcal{A}$s Devon watched her go, he scuffed his boot against the worn oak floor, careful to avoid the patch of dried tobacco. He'd thought it'd help matters once he'd dispelled the notion he had concocted a scheme to win her hand. But he should have kept his mouth shut. She wasn't one to take kindly to someone offering help.

And who was he to talk about marriage? *Honor the other person before yourself?* He'd gotten that one right, not being there when Isabelle needed him most. His jaw tightened. But he'd told Morning Fawn the truth. Marriage had nothing to do with bits or property or any of a half dozen other things people sold their hearts for.

Isabelle... Their wedding had been the happiest day of his life. Her smile. Her quiet demeanor. She could say more with a look than someone else could with a hundred words. And she'd fit so smoothly in his arms, as if they were two parts of a whole. They'd had their entire lives before them.

He shuddered and slung the bridle he'd been fingering back against the wall.

Morning Fawn didn't know the first thing about marriage.

She was the most noncompliant girl he'd ever met. You'd think a captive would want to be rescued, but obviously, not her. And who was this Moyer fellow? Whether Morning Fawn wanted help or not, Devon wasn't about to allow her to go throwing herself at some dandy for a piece of land.

He stomped out the door and watched her march down the plank sidewalk toward the mercantile. The way her shoes clomped on the boards and the stiff set of her back, she'd be riled up all the way back to Sweet Briar. Did the girl ever smile?

Her aunt stood in the doorway and quick-stepped to meet her.

Devon turned to finish his errands.

Half an hour later, he met them in front of the bank. The hard set of Morning Fawn's jaw and glare left no doubt he hadn't finished paying for his earlier comment.

Mrs. LeBeau handed him a note. "The milliner is finishing up a bonnet I ordered. While we wait, I'd like for you to deliver this invitation to Mr. Nicholas Moyer. Beth and I will have a bite to eat at Miller's Hotel."

He stared at the lady. Did she think he was her lackey or something? Giving Morning Fawn a ride to town and running a couple of errands for Mr. LeBeau was one thing—after all, he was working on earning the man's good graces—but hand delivering notes to the front runner in the wed-for-land scheme was another.

He glanced toward the sky with its fast-moving puffs. The white had given way to heavyset gray. "There's dark clouds to the north and a cool breeze. I'm willing to bet there's a storm brewing. I say we have the restaurant pack us up a meal and head back now."

Mrs. LeBeau pursed her lips. Her rose-print reticule swung from her wrist. "I'm sure an extra hour or so in town wouldn't hurt, Lieutenant. Besides, I need the new bonnet for church on Sunday. You can take the ferry across the river to Alleyton.

You'll find Mr. Moyer at either the cotton warehouse or the quartermaster's depot."

"The cotton station?" Exactly where he needed to be. "Moyer works there?"

"He manages the warehouse." Morning Fawn narrowed her eyes at him. "But I don't need an errand boy to deliver my invitation. I can go myself."

"You'll do no such thing." He got the words out two seconds before her aunt did.

Devon hooked his thumbs around his cartridge belt. *Errand boy?* The same one who'd caught up to her on her stolen Thoroughbred and saved her from wandering the prairie, ill-prepared, hungry, and in danger of attack. "It's my duty to guard you and bring you home safely." The woman had probably never made a plan in her life beyond sunset.

"I have no intention of running—"

"You'll wait here for the lieutenant." Mrs. LeBeau tugged her lace cuffs past her wrists.

"Sounds fine to me." He tipped his hat.

"I'm going, with or without the errand boy." Morning Fawn snatched the note from his hand.

He scowled. It'd be just like her to take off once he got out of sight and latch onto the nearest conveyance possible as if it were her own. And he'd be blamed.

Mrs. LeBeau gnawed her lip. "It wouldn't be proper for the two of you—"

"Let's go." Enough of the bickering. Devon grabbed Morning Fawn's arm. "You can't go on your own, and I can't leave you here." He couldn't pass up a chance to scout out the depot and warehouses facilities and estimate troop strength in the area. Maybe while he was there, he could even conjure up an ailment, an excuse to seek out Dr. Schramm, his contact.

Morning Fawn stiffened beneath his grip.

Mrs. LeBeau exhaled. "Then I'll have to come."

Devon glanced over his shoulder. "I wouldn't want to put you to all of that trouble, Mrs. LeBeau. We'll ride the horses. They've been unhitched from the carriage for a rest. We'll rent a couple of saddles from the livery. Be back in an hour or so."

As they parted ways from her aunt, Morning Fawn's molasses-feet picked up speed, almost outpacing him. "I don't need a sidesaddle. I can ride—"

"Don't you get any notions." He tightened his grip on her elbow. "I'm bringing you home to your uncle's tonight. You can count on it."

She tossed her hair. "I wouldn't have it any other way. After all, I certainly must be there when Mr. Moyer comes to dinner on Saturday."

"What makes you so certain he'll accept the invite?"

"He'll accept." Her hard-soled shoes clicked on the boards. "If he has plans, we'll simply adjust the date."

Half an hour later with lead rope in hand, Devon guided his mare down the ferry plank, keeping pace with Morning Fawn. The quarter horse's hooves clomped on the damp boards. Devon had suggested they walk the horses through the shallow Colorado River. Morning Fawn had seemed tempted at first but then insisted on the ferry because she didn't want to ride up to the depot with the bottom half of her skirts muddied and wet. As if she needed to impress this Moyer character.

Withered Indian grass lined the clay banks as they mounted and ascended onto the Columbus Road. Pin oak, pecan, and mesquite flanked the rutted lane where a wagon rattled by. Only a few leaves clung to their branches. Were they victims of the shortfall of rain, or did the trees around here shed their leaves by the end of fall as those did farther north?

Morning Fawn slowed her horse as they neared a field of white tents, some planter's dormant land turned into a Confederate camp. Thank goodness, he'd donned his butternut-colored uniform. Showing up in civilian clothes might have earned him a forced trip to the provost marshal's office to explain how he'd evaded the draft.

"Howdy, miss." Two scruffy privates ambled by, hands stuffed in their pockets, no rifles, just their revolvers stuck in their holsters. Cavalry, if that was yellow piping beneath the dirt on their trousers.

Morning Fawn nodded. No word. No smile.

Devon pulled up alongside her. "Good. Best not to be too friendly."

"Don't worry about me." She tossed her head. "I don't believe in talking to men I don't know."

"Wise plan."

Her gaze drifted back to the encampment, and his followed. Stumps stood where trees had once thrived. Soldiers meandered about. An occasional trail of smoke drifted upward from cookfires. Farther across the field, horses stirred in a wooden corral. Eighty, maybe a hundred tents. Two hundred men, at least. Maybe half that many horses. Good information to pass on to Captain Carson when they met up in a couple weeks.

He and Morning Fawn passed more men, more wagons. She drew her shoulders inward as if to put more distance between her and the passersby. Was it the number of people or the fact they were soldiers that bothered her?

The town came into view—an odd collection of one- and two-story wooden buildings, thrown together in a haphazard manner like logs in a jam. A runoff ditch with its murky water ran alongside the pock-marked road. A stink rose from the drainage.

Devon veered to the right. On the other side of the lane, a six-mule team pulled a long wagon loaded with ten bulging cotton bales. Two more wagonloads and teams trudged along behind. Soldiers on horseback caught up to the wagons at a steady clip and passed with only a nod. They were likely along for the ride, guarding the cotton all the way to San Antonio and beyond. Too bad there wasn't a Federal raiding party waiting down the way to take the cotton off their hands. Pay these Rebs back for the way they'd kicked U.S. troops out of the state and forced civilians to take up arms for a cause some of them didn't believe in.

The road ended in a mass of buildings. A train depot, with the tracks and roundhouse behind, stood next to the loading docks where burlap-wrapped cotton towered three bales high —around five hundred pounds each if they were according to standard. Nearby, troops guarded the quartermaster depot. What Devon wouldn't give to light that place up with a torch some night. From what he heard, thousands of pounds of gunpowder traveled through its doors bound to the Rebs in Louisiana and points east. Between the quartermaster's and the train depot lay a wooden structure half a block long—the cotton station, according to Mrs. LeBeau's directions.

Soldiers patrolled the entire area thick as a work party of ants, Confederate infantry and Texas militia alike. The Rebs weren't about to make his mission easy. He rubbed his thumb back and forth across the reins as he moseyed his horse forward, studying the layout.

Morning Fawn's interest in this Moyer fellow could be a definite asset. By all rights, he should encourage the attach-ment and tag along as a chaperone, get access to the inner workings of this place. He could stomach that about as much as filling his canteen in the drainage ditch.

As they reached the hitching post, Morning Fawn blew out a breath. "You can wait outside."

He narrowed his eyes at her. "You and your aunt need to get one thing straight. I'm not at your beck and call. I do my work the way I see fit."

"Have it your way." She dismounted and marched on ahead of him, straightening her skirts as she went, her stride as strin-gent as an officer on his way to reprimand a private.

"Whoa." Devon swung off his stallion and caught up to her. He blocked her path. "You're not going to hurry in to Moyer as if you can't wait to see him. This isn't a horse race."

"Are you trying to tell me I don't know how to behave?" She crossed her arms.

The breeze rippled the rim of her straw hat and tossed a tendril across her brow. She swatted it away.

His gaze fell to her hazel eyes. Like a river current, they swept his thoughts away. He blinked himself free and glanced at the rest of her face and dress. Beautiful and unpolished. No hoop. No bonnet. Maybe this Moyer fellow wouldn't even respect her as a lady, or maybe he'd think her a country bumpkin and easy to trick.

He stuck his right elbow out. "Take my arm. You're going to show Mr. Moyer you could care less if he accepts the invitation."

He braced himself for her to turn up her nose and cut around him. But she didn't. He sucked in a breath as she latched on to the crook of his arm, her fingers sinking into the butternut-colored wool.

Inside, a clerk showed them down a hallway to a glass-doored office.

Morning Fawn hesitated at the threshold.

A man with dark, tonic-smoothed hair and a thin sliver of a mustache looked up from a ledger. "Miss Logan." His eyes lit a second before his smile. A shadow twitched across his face as his gaze shifted to Devon. "And who is your escort today?"

She stepped in. "This is Lieutenant Reynolds."

Lips pressed tight, Devon nodded.

Morning Fawn exhaled. "My uncle felt I needed a chaperone. After—"

"Oh, the Thoroughbred race." Chuckling, Moyer stood and moved from behind his solid oak desk. The man was around thirty, maybe a little more. Not in uniform. Probably talked some judge into giving him an exemption. "I heard about your ride. I'm thankful to see you're not injured."

Devon clamped his hand down on Morning Fawn's before she could slip it free. "Mr. and Mrs. LeBeau asked us to extend their invitation to you for dinner at Sweet Briar this coming Saturday evening if you are free."

"Us?" Moyer tugged on the lapels of his gray-striped frock coat.

"He means my family." Morning Fawn squirmed.

Moyer extended his hand, his slender white fingers unscarred by physical labor. "Pleasure to meet you, Lieutenant."

Slow to respond, Devon released Morning Fawn and accepted the handshake. "Quite an operation you have here, Mr. Moyer."

"Just doing my part for the Confederacy. You've heard of the Shenandoah Valley being the breadbasket of our new nation? Well, the Alleyton Depot is the bank. Cotton will pave the way to victory." Moyer stuck out his broad chest. "But tell me, Reynolds, what brings you to our fair town? Part of the troops stationed here? An acquaintance of the LeBeaus?"

"Not stationed here. Paroled. I was a prisoner of the Yankees. I'm back in Texas to recuperate before making my way to my regiment, the Third Cavalry. I'm helping Mr. LeBeau for the next few weeks. Business."

"Business? Hired pirate," Morning Fawn muttered under her breath.

Moyer latched onto the military part. "Third Texas? Part of Van Dorn's division? My cousin was in his brigade. Helped them hit the Union supply depot at Holly Springs, Mississippi."

Devon pursed his lips. His informant had given him details of the attack. But how trustworthy was the word of a deserter, even if he did claim to be a Unionist? "We hit 'em hard." He forced a smile.

"Easy prey, I heard." Moyer smoothed his mustache. "Were the Yanks asleep or just incompetent?"

"I don't know about the infantry boys, but the cavalry were in the middle of a drill."

"Captured enough supplies to outfit an army?"

"Four train loads."

"I heard it was three." Moyer's brow crinkled.

"Maybe it was." Devon shrugged, but his voice hitched. "But with all of the whooping and hollering from our boys, and me busy rounding up prisoners, I didn't stop to count. All I knew was that my men had their bellies full, new rifles in their hands, and the Yanks looking more whipped than hound dogs left out in the rain."

Moyer chuckled and offered him a cigar. "And what about the raid into Tennessee?"

"Some other time." Devon twirled the cigar in his fingers. Best stick the thing in his mouth and endure the taste. "We don't want to bore Miss Logan with war stories. She might prefer a tour."

"Of cotton bales?" She blinked.

Devon reached for her arm, but Moyer was quicker. His hand closed around her elbow. "I'd be delighted to show the lady how we serve the Confederacy. If you prefer to rest in the outer office, Lieutenant, my clerk could supply you with a glass of brandy recently arrived from London."

Wait in the outer office with the potential of finding an excuse and a few moments in Moyer's office unobserved? An unexpected opportunity. Exactly what he should choose.

But Morning Fawn glanced at the man's hand as if a dog had latched onto her sleeve.

"I'd enjoy a tour myself." Devon hooked his thumb over his cartridge belt, resisting the urge to grab her other arm. He'd not stoop to playing tug of war. After all, Devon was the one leaving with the lady.

CHAPTER 12

Out front an hour later, Morning Fawn firmed her mouth as Nicholas Moyer bent over her hand and brushed his lips across her knuckles. She cringed at the tickle of his mustache but held her peace.

Devon clamped his jaw shut, looking as if he were fit to be tied.

She smiled. Now she knew how to show the pirate she wasn't some desperate damsel in need of saving.

Moyer straightened, giving her hand one last squeeze before he released it. "Till Saturday evening, my lovely lady." Fire sparked in his deep-brown eyes.

"I shall look forward to it." She batted her eyelashes as she'd seen Thea do a hundred times, trying not to wince.

"Your aunt's waiting for us." Devon grabbed her arm, not quite gently, and tugged her toward the horses. "Probably in a panic."

"If you need to go on, Lieutenant, I could always escort her—"

"My job's to bring both ladies home." Not even a hint of "no, thank you, sir" or "much obliged." Devon's pleasantries had slowly fallen by the wayside the farther they'd walked between the rows of towering bales. Had he been bored, or maybe he didn't care to play second fiddle to a cotton king?

Devon turned toward Morning Fawn and offered his linked fingers for her foot.

She pressed her shoe into his callused flesh as she stepped into the saddle, smiling at the slender wisps of cotton that clung to his felt hat.

In a matter of minutes, Devon had them headed back toward the ferry, past the freight wagons. "That man's slicker than a snake oil salesman."

"A what?"

"Never mind." He unwound his canteen from his saddle horn and took a swig. "I'm trying to say he's not to be trusted."

"You don't even know him."

"I know a fox when I see one."

She rolled her eyes. "You're one to talk, Lieutenant. Going around stealing women."

He exhaled. "There's a world of light and dark between me and the likes of Moyer, Miss Logan." He pulled ahead, ramrod straight in the saddle.

Silence dropped between them. But when she thought he'd turn right toward the river, he guided them left.

"Where are we going?" She slowed her mount.

"To see a doctor about my eye."

She blinked at him. "But you said we had to get back to my aunt. She's waiting, you know."

"Since when does something like that trouble you?" He arched an eyebrow at her and moved farther right as a carriage rumbled past. "My eye's been bothering me, and I have the name of a doctor in Alleyton someone recommended."

Only the small pinkish scar on the bridge of his nose gave any clue to the injury.

What did the leather patch hide? Did he have any hope of

regaining his sight? Even she had been around society long enough to know not to ask such questions.

She scrunched up her nose at the murky water trickling along in the shallow ditch as they headed into the scruffy clapboard town. A dog trotted alongside of them. Soldiers, too many of them, meandered along the street. Men in suits walked amongst them. A handful of them gathered at a cotton factor's office and another group by the saloon. A boy laughed as he splashed himself in the horse trough before a lady hurried over to scold him.

After asking at a couple of places, Devon led them down a narrow side street of split-log cabins shoved together like cattle huddling for warmth. He stopped in front of one with a worn shingle. The word *doctor* was etched across its grain. Trimmed, weathered grass lined the path to the door, and a white flower box, its contents withered for the season, sat below the paned window, the only building with a feminine touch on the whole street.

"We'll find a place for you to wait inside." Devon swung down from the saddle and walked over to her horse.

His palm brushed her back as he helped her dismount. Only a second, but the warmth spread all the way to her cheeks.

He smacked his gauntlets against his hand. "The only question is if I need to tie you up or not."

"Tie me up?" She huffed. Was he teasing or serious?

"I'd take your shoes and the saddle, but I figure that wouldn't stop you if you had a mind to run off." He held the gate open. Maybe there was a trace of a twinkle in his eye, but the firm set of his mouth said otherwise.

She pressed her hat to her head as the breeze ruffled it. "And why would I take off when I have a dinner guest coming Saturday evening?" No need to plot an escape until she'd sorted out the whole land-for-marriage scheme.

The odor of pig drifted her way as they walked down the path. Of course, these hovels would have animals in the back.

He scoffed under his breath and knocked on the door. "The expectation of Moyer's company would be enough to make anyone flee."

"You're free to eat in your room, Mr. Reynolds," she whispered.

The door opened before he could answer.

A brown-haired young woman, with a long braid coiled at the back of her head, stepped into view. "May I help you?" Dimples graced her smooth cheeks as her lips rose in a tentative smile.

Suddenly the pinnacle of manners, Devon swept his hat from his head. "Good afternoon, miss. I'm looking for Dr. Schramm."

"My father's in the back. Please come in vhile I alert him to your presence." A foreign accent clipped her words.

"Much obliged." He motioned for Morning Fawn to go first. "Please tell him Mr. Carson sent me. About my eye."

Their petite hostess startled, then regained her composure. "Yes, of course, sir. Is the lady—"

"My employer's niece. Not here to see the doctor."

Employer's niece? Just one of his work duties? Morning Fawn frowned as he watched the brown-eyed beauty retreat down the hall. Obviously, Miss Schramm didn't need a land scheme to gain his attention. "I hope you're being paid well."

"Excuse me?" Devon crinkled his brow.

"Nothing." Morning Fawn rolled her eyes and picked up a leather-bound book from the doily-covered table. It looked like a Bible, but the letters were strung together in words that didn't make any sense.

Steps in the hallway. A stout man with a gray beard and spectacles entered the room. Crinkles ringed his eyes. Tuffs of grayish hair, not quite tamed, protruded from his head. His daughter trailed behind him.

"I'm Dr. Schramm, and you must be—"

"Lieutenant Devon Reynolds, sir." Devon shook the man's hand heartily.

The doctor smiled. "And the young lady?"

"Miss Beth Logan. I'm in her uncle's employ. I was hoping she could wait in the parlor here with your daughter."

So that the doctor's daughter could keep an eye on her?

"Certainly." Dr. Schramm warmly pressed Morning Fawn's hand. "You're velcome here, Miss Logan. Frieda vill be happy to keep you company as I examine your friend."

Friend? Guard. And company wasn't exactly what she wanted. She'd prefer to look at one of their books than try to make polite feminine conversation.

Devon shot her a warning glance before he disappeared down the hall.

Frieda motioned to a wooden chair with a well-padded cushion. "Have a seat, Miss Logan. Vould you like some refreshments?"

"I wouldn't want to put you to any trouble." Morning Fawn settled onto the edge of the seat. She really needed to get herself a reticule. Give her something to do with her hands. This felt too much like a social call, something she'd had very little practice at and avoided at all costs, especially since it usually entailed sitting around a parlor chatting beside Aunt Judith or Thea and both of them critiquing her every move.

"No trouble." Frieda beamed. "I'll be right back."

Such a docile creature wouldn't survive more than a week on the prairie.

Morning Fawn fumbled with her fingers and glanced around the room. The logs showed through, no plaster like the painted and papered walls of her uncle's mansion. A faded carpet covered the floor with a rag rug at the entrance. The tick-tock of a mantel clock, the fanciest thing in the room with its bronze-leafed casing, broke the silence.

Not even a murmur from down the hall. Did Devon's eye hurt him much? What had happened? When he kidnapped her, he'd had two piercing blue eyes, hard as flint. His callused hands had jerked her wrists behind her back and tightened the ropes. That was after he'd stuffed a gag in her mouth, preventing her from crying out for help.

At the time, she'd regarded him as no better than the dirt on her moccasins. But later, on the trail to the settlements, he'd protected her against every insult and hint of mistreatment. Why? Did he get more money for bringing her back safe? Or was there a streak of honor buried beneath his ruffian exterior?

Not to mention his visit to her room a few nights ago after she'd been given the laudanum...that had nothing to do with money.

"I hope you like lemonade." Frieda strolled in with a tray and smiled as she set it on the doily on the table just shy of the Bible. "Though I must apologize. Ve're a little short on sugar. Mixed it with honey instead."

Morning Fawn thanked her and sipped. A bit tart but sweet. Probably like the girl across from her. Clean white apron, not a hair out of place, pert, and polite. Nothing like Morning Fawn. She accepted a piece of buttered bread and answered her hostess's questions with as few words as possible.

"It must be lovely to live by the river." Frieda beamed after Morning Fawn had responded to her inquiry about the plantation. "This town is a bit rough, as you may have noticed. Pa and I moved down from Friesburg after the railroad came. People flocked here after the depot vas built, and Pa knew they'd need a doctor."

A door down the hall opened. Footsteps followed. Morning Fawn stood, and a crumb flittered to the floor before she could catch it.

Frieda dabbed her mouth with a napkin, then stood without a speck of bread on her.

"Take care of yourself, Lieutenant." Schramm patted Devon on the back. "And use the ointment."

"Thank you, sir." Devon shoved something into his trouser pocket and started to don his hat. A glimpse in Frieda's direction, and he paused the latter action. "Thank you kindly for your hospitality, Miss Schramm." He glanced at the tray.

"Surely, you von't leave without taking a bit of refreshment, sir." She pressed her hands against her apron and practically stood on her tiptoes in eagerness. "I have two glasses vaiting in the kitchen for you and Papa."

"I'm afraid we'd best be going, miss." But he turned toward her and away from the door.

"Stay for a bit of lemonade, son." Dr. Schramm adjusted his spectacles.

"I'll go get the glasses." Frieda moved around Devon, her skirt coming within inches of his boots.

Morning Fawn wasn't going to stand around and watch him have a parlor chat with this too-perfect girl. "We don't have time. I'm sorry." She picked up a slice of bread without butter and stuck it in Devon's hand as he gaped at her. "Thank you kindly for the offer, Miss Schramm, but my aunt is waiting." She marched out the door.

If Devon didn't follow double-quick, he could find her in the next county. She was already mounted by the time he made it down the path.

Hat on his head, he glared at her as he hurried to his horse. "Wait up." Was there a blush on his cheeks, or was it just the heat of exasperation? "You're not the one in charge here."

A frigid smile trickled across her lips. "I wouldn't want to keep you from your lemonade."

"Miss Frieda is bringing me a cup." He reached for her reins.

Miss Frieda? The girl had gone from Miss Schramm to Miss Frieda in the two minutes since Morning Fawn had walked out? She whipped the reins from his almost-grip and pressed her knees into horse flesh, pulling the mare's head hard to the right.

He reached, his hand landing on her skirt, but not quick enough.

She spurred the horse toward a gallop, almost colliding with a carriage.

Behind her, Devon scrambled into his saddle, his harsh words a mere rumble as she neared the intersection.

A teamster cursed and yanked his team to a halt. Dust flew as she swerved in front of him.

A girl in the middle of crossing the street dropped her basket of eggs.

"Hey, lady, slow down," a man yelled behind her, but she pounded past a carriage, goading the mare toward the edge of town and beyond.

Slow-poke cotton wagons clogged the rutted road outside town. Tents lay ahead to the south and east. Too many soldiers. She veered into the other lane, bypassing the cotton freight and cutting ahead between the front two wagons to avoid another rider. The road was too crowded. She steered the mare off the path and into the brush. Hoots and hollers echoed behind her. Wind smacked her face as she inhaled fresh air.

Buffalo grass swooshed against her ankles in a field beyond the bushes. She slowed a bit. Was that horse hooves behind her? She headed the mare toward a patch of trees. The river gurgled nearby.

Her mare was at a walk by the time Devon pulled up alongside of her. His hat askew and out of breath, he reached over and snatched her reins. "I ought to hogtie you and throw you across my horse for pulling a stunt like that."

She lifted her chin. "I saved you the trouble of having to wrestle me to the ground this time."

He muttered and swiped his forearm across his brow. His knee brushed her skirt as he tightened his grip on her reins. "Why in the devil did you run off like that? Where in the world were you headed?"

She shrugged and ran her hand over her hair. No hat. When had she lost that? Her aunt would have a fit for her going about with her head uncovered. "I felt like a ride by the river before I head back to prison."

"You help put yourself there, pulling stunts like this." He smacked his hat against his thigh.

She nailed him with a glare. "I'm sorry I spoiled your lemonade." Had she really just said that to him? That and about half a dozen other things that had blurted out of her mouth in the last hour. What in the world had come over her?

~

*D*evon blinked wide. Morning Fawn was jealous? Ridiculous. No. Impossible. She couldn't care less. But what if she did? He leaned back in his saddle and scrubbed his hand across his jaw.

She put her hand on her hip. "What's that look about?"

"Nothing."

"It doesn't look like nothing."

He fought against the smile that threatened to erupt. "Don't you think we should head back? Your aunt will be worried."

She dropped the reins and glared at him. "I'm not moving until you tell me what you're thinking."

He chuckled and grabbed the reins. "I reckon I'll have to do it for you, then. I wouldn't want both of us to be banished from coming near a horse again."

She held the saddle horn as her horse shifted into motion beside his, passing through the field and back toward the ferry. "Are you going to tell them what I did?

"Of course not." He tossed her reins into her lap. "See if you can keep up and behave yourself all at the same time." His glance trailed over the fading pink in her cheeks. What if he was right? What if her remark in the harness shop about bits had to do with more than just the land?

Couldn't be. But it felt as if his world had tilted.

CHAPTER 13

*W*as it Morning Fawn's imagination, or was the whalebone corset squeezing the breath out of her? Obviously, *civilized* society hadn't figured out that there were better uses for animal bones than suffocating women.

Piano music drifted up from the parlor—Thea's attempt at charming their guests.

Morning Fawn frowned in the mirror and twirled a ringlet of hair around her finger. "I don't like the idea of getting all fancied up for Mr. Moyer—or any man, for that matter."

"Not even for Lieutenant Reynolds?" Lucy stood behind her, tugging the back of Morning Fawn's hair into a loose coil.

Morning Fawn narrowed her eyes at her friend's reflection in the mirror. "I'd probably have to march downstairs in a buckskin dress and buffalo robe before that man would notice."

Devon had been polite but distant since they'd returned from Columbus three days ago. Maybe his guilty conscience was absolved now that he'd rescued her from the laudanum and permanent confinement in the attic.

"I think he notices plenty, especially when it comes to you."

Lucy smiled and nudged the lace neckline a couple of inches below Morning Fawn's collarbone.

"You have a wild imagination." At least he managed not to go weak-kneed over Thea's constant flirtations. But maybe that was because he preferred Miss Perfect Hostess in Alleyton.

"I sees what I sees." Clothed in green plaid instead of her usual black, Lucy jabbed a hand to her slender waist.

Morning Fawn stepped away. Curls bounced against the back of her neck. Why she'd consented to the curling tongs, she had no idea. A faint smell of burnt hair wafted to her nose. A lot of trouble to get a man's attention. Lace trim scratched against her shoulders. And the crinoline hoop? She swayed her hips, and the violet silk taffeta skirt swished side to side.

"Don't you go stepping close to any fires." Lucy chuckled, picking up the discarded curling papers which fluttered around their feet like snowflakes. "I might have to help you down the stairs."

"I know nothing about any of this." Morning Fawn spread her arms wide. "Where I grew up, a warrior would linger by the creek in the evenings to catch the eye of a maiden who'd gained his interest. Maybe he'd drop a gift of meat at her family's tipi or seek her out at a dance by the fire. And the way to a man's heart had more to do with how well she could handle a horse than extra fringe or beads on a doeskin dress."

"I bet you could ride mighty fine." Lucy stepped forward, her rough hands clasped in front of her dull white apron. "Speaking of love...I'm wondering if you could see fit not to need me tonight after dinner? I knows it's a lot to ask, but if you could get out of the fancy things without my help and maybe pretend like I was up here helping, I'd be much obliged."

"Your Ned is coming to see you?"

Lucy beamed. "Mr. Dooley allows him one night a month."

"But why all the sneaking if Mr. Dooley allows it? He could come courting."

"Mr. LeBeau won't hear of such a thing. Says he'll marry me off to one of the fellows at Sweet Briar when the time comes. Thank goodness, he's in no hurry to do that." She crossed her arms. "He'd whip Ned if he caught him here. And me..."

"What?"

Lucy shivered. "He's threatened to give in to his son's pestering and send me to Louisiana with the army. To be Arthur's cook."

Morning Fawn swallowed. She didn't have to grow up on a plantation to understand that her cousin's desire to see Lucy had little to do with cooking. "Someday, I'll help you get away from here."

Lucy frowned. "You go marrying that Mr. Moyer, and you won't have any say so over anything. Mark my word. Don't matter what he promises you."

"You've only met the man once. And it was more like waiting on him than meeting."

"It don't take meeting. Takes watching. I knows men." She reached forward and nudged the neckline of the day-dress-converted-to-an-evening-gown another inch from Morning Fawn's collarbone.

"Then, why help me catch his eye?" Morning Fawn shifted her neckline back into place.

"Mr. Moyer ain't the one I'm getting you all gussied up for." Lucy smiled and pushed her toward the door.

Warmth spread upward from Morning Fawn's chest.

"Ignore the man," Lucy whispered behind her.

"Which one?"

"The one you want."

"What if I don't want either?"

"I don't believe that."

"I know which one I'd like to make miserable." She smoothed her hands against her skirt. It'd suit her just fine to show Devon Reynolds what he was missing and that she had no interest whatsoever in him.

~

Sweat dampened Morning Fawn's palms as she made her way down to the second floor and the landing. She should have accepted Lucy's offer to help, but she wasn't going to be guided like a three-year-old. Holding onto the banister, she attempted to tame the hoop with her free hand and maneuvered down the final flight of stairs, chin high.

Two men waited at the bottom.

"We thought we might have to eat without you, cousin." Thea sidled up to Devon and latched onto his elbow, like the snake in the grass she was.

Hands stuffed into his trouser pockets, his gaze locked onto Morning Fawn.

Her pulse quickened. *Ignore him.* Easier said than done.

Devon's lips twitched upward. He'd cleaned himself up. His uniform had been replaced with a dark frock coat and trousers. A charcoal silk waistcoat and a finely tailored shirt finished his ensemble. He'd combed his hair back and trimmed his beard to a thin covering. If only he was the one there to court her. Foolish thought. Scrub it from her mind.

The blue of his eye sharpened as he drank her in.

Morning Fawn pressed her lips together, forbidding herself even a trace of a smile. She had no intention of letting him know his opinion mattered.

"Be careful not to trip, dear." Thea unfurled her fan.

Moyer slipped in front of Devon and offered his hand to Morning Fawn as her foot touched the ground floor. His red silk cravat shone like a banner. "Please allow me to escort you, my lady. I am but a pauper compared to your beauty."

Behind him, Devon snorted.

Good. Let the man simmer a bit. "Thank you, Mr. Moyer. I'm not used to such compliments." She placed her fingers in his palm, wishing for the hand of another.

~

*D*evon glowered as he followed behind Morning Fawn, her deep-violet gown swishing against the carpet. If he had any sense at all, he would have elbowed that buffoon out of the way and taken Morning Fawn's hand. She wasn't used to the shoes or the crinoline, but he could get mighty used to seeing her in such dresses. But her hair? He preferred it long, flowing over her shoulders as it had on the return from Alleyton, instead of being drawn back in a bundle of fancy curls.

From the moment they sat down to dinner, Moyer dominated the conversation. The table might as well have been a stage. LeBeau soaked up the braggart's stories and financial details, leaving little doubt this new guest had supplanted Devon as the favored beau for his niece.

Just as well. Devon didn't have time for courting, fake or otherwise. He had a mission to focus on. He had a chance to make a significant difference for the North, and he wasn't about to blow it by getting distracted by a pair of hazel eyes and a fiery demeanor.

He had enough to do making sure he didn't end up swinging from a rope. And it wasn't just his life on the line. It was the Schramms' too. Unionists, they'd volunteered to help with the spying and the planning. If he could get his hands on the gunpowder in the quarter master's depot, not even half a block from the cotton warehouse, his task would be much simpler.

Thea's hand brushed his sleeve as she retrieved her butter knife.

He startled, but she seemed to hardly notice.

Her wide gaze flickered toward Moyer in response to his latest brag. She batted her eyelashes while she lavished butter on her roll. "You're in a partnership with Richard King of King's Ranch?"

Moyer settled back in his chair. "A partner in twenty thousand acres in Nueces County. But that's nothing. King has another seventy thousand, at least. We're raising a good herd of cattle there."

Morning Fawn's gaze jerked from her spoon laden with rice to her dinner partner at the mention of acres. Half of the grain spilled onto her plate.

Devon stabbed his beefsteak. If Morning Fawn was after land, she was courting the right fellow. But land didn't guarantee a home—at least, not a real one. He'd seen that all too well when his mother married his stepfather.

LeBeau leaned forward. "Any chance King will allow you a stake in his cotton contracts? From what I've heard, he's the head rooster when it comes to cotton. Got himself situated as the middleman between the European cotton brokers and the Confederate government."

"I'm counting on it, sir." Moyer reached for his brandy snifter. "Thought it best to get in on the land deal first. I don't aim to sit by while fortunes are made."

Devon blew out a breath. Men were giving their lives, and this man cared more about lining his pockets. He couldn't stomach profiteers on either side of the Mason-Dixon Line. "There *is* a war going on, Mr. Moyer."

Moyer arched an eyebrow. "That's why I've made my services available to the Cotton Bureau. My job is to safeguard the lifeblood of the Confederacy. Some of us do our part by utilizing our business skills and intellect."

Devon glowered at him. The man's head was as big as a cotton bale and just as thick. "You don't believe it requires intellect to take men into battle and bring them out alive and perhaps victorious?"

"I wholeheartedly support our boys in gray. If the Confederacy wasn't in such dire need of my services here, I'd be out there in the field."

Right. Hiding behind a tree. Talking loud enough that the enemy could hear him a mile away.

"Same here." LeBeau sliced another bite. "If I was a few years younger and didn't have more than a hundred slaves dependent upon me. Besides, if it wasn't for us planters, the men on the front wouldn't have anything but sticks and stones to throw at the enemy."

Morning Fawn flickered a glance Devon's way and traced a circular design on the tablecloth. The glow from the chandelier danced on her face. "Lieutenant Reynolds comes from a well-to-do family, but he prefers to fight for his way in the world."

Devon blinked wide. She was defending him?

"For once, you're right, cousin." Thea slipped her fingers around his upper arm. "The lieutenant told us about his battles the other night at dinner when you weren't here." She shifted in her chair as if she needed to be another inch closer to him. The yellow folds of her skirt lapped against his knee-high boots. "But I would love to hear more. Especially about his missions fighting against wild Indians."

She spouted enough tangy venom with the sugar-sweet tone to curdle his wine in his glass.

His arm itched beneath her hold. "As I mentioned the other evening, Miss Thea, I'd rather talk of more pleasant things—"

"I couldn't agree more, Reynolds." Moyer smiled. "Why dwell on the fact that you were the one to capture Miss Logan?"

"Kind of you to mention that." Devon gritted his teeth.

"Reynolds did us a fine service." LeBeau tugged on his waistcoat stretching over a slight bulge. "Best scout I could find.

He got the job done and did it right. Brought her back without a scratch."

Morning Fawn skewered Devon with her gaze.

"Lieutenant Reynolds has my eternal gratitude." Moyer smoothed his fingers over his waxed mustache. "But I'd love to hear of Miss Beth's life in the West."

Morning Fawn blinked wide.

"Her life is right here in East Texas." LeBeau cleared his throat. "And Tennessee before that."

"Oh, but sir, I wish to hear of the natural wonders she beheld in her journeys. I have longed to travel to the western frontier and beyond. Of course, I wouldn't want to cause her undue pain if the memories are too fresh."

The man was like an overflowing rainspout of words.

"I would like to hear also if Beth wouldn't mind." Mrs. LeBeau dabbed her napkin to her lips.

They'd never asked her details about her life before?

Thea's nails pressed deep into his sleeve, her proximity filling his nostrils with a scent much more potent than rosewater and not half as pleasant. "I'm sure it's all desert, cacti, and thistles, a wasteland."

Morning Fawn narrowed her eyes at her cousin and maybe him too. "Only for those who don't know what to look for." She swatted at a curl away from the smooth, bare skin of her upper shoulder. "There's the Red-Capped Canyons. But Palo Duro, as the Spanish call it, is the best. Miles and miles of mesas dressed in orange and red like Spanish skirts and trimmed in gray and white, with puffs of green dotting the valley floor..."

Her eyes lit as she talked. Her love for the lands of endless sun shone through. Enough to make him want to crawl under the table. He'd taken her from the land of her heart.

The servants cleared the plates and served a lemon tart dessert. The conversation moved on to the war. Further progress by the Yankees on Matagorda Island and Peninsula, even rumors that Fort Espenanza would fall. A silent hurrah echoed in his head. And the most significant news—orders had come through for the cotton shipments to be halted temporarily until it could be determined that the road between Columbus and San Antonio was secure. The cotton would pile up in Alleyton for now. Suited him just fine.

Just when they'd almost made it through dinner without open conflict, Moyer turned the conversation to talk of horses and asked Morning Fawn her favorite.

She stirred her peas, eyes downcast, as if she might not answer. "My favorite was a sleek black mustang. Full of spirit. My pia gave her to me—"

"What's a pia?" Thea brushed her napkin against the lace that decorated her gown's low neckline.

Morning Fawn glowered at her.

Trouble, if Devon's recollection of the Comanche word proved accurate.

Morning Fawn jutted her chin. "Moth—"

"I think we should go riding." Devon laid his fork down. Her uncle would go through the roof if she finished the word.

LeBeau sat up straight, his voice rigid. "I'd like to hear what Beth was going say."

Morning Fawn lifted her head. She met his concerned gaze with wall-like obstinacy. "I honor my mother. But my Comanche pia took me in and treated me as her own. Her, too, I honor and love."

"A filthy Indian." LeBeau spit out the words.

Morning Fawn flinched. "A woman who loved me and cared for me as a daughter, and who'd go hungry so I could eat, who nursed me in illness—"

"I've heard enough." LeBeau's lip curled. "Feeding you was the least they could do after what they did to your entire family, your sister included." He threw down his napkin.

"Robert, we have guests." Mrs. LeBeau clasped the table edge.

"And I have a sister who was murdered and likely died defending her children. I'll not have her attackers glorified."

"My pia had nothing to do with that." Morning Fawn clenched her hands. Moisture glistened in her eyes.

"They weakened your mind, young lady, turned you against your own—"

"Sir." Devon raised his voice and pressed his palms on the table. He couldn't allow him to tear into Morning Fawn like that. "Before the war, we were in the same tribe, so to speak, as Lincoln and the abolitionists. But that didn't mean we saw eye to eye or followed their ways. Can't we give Morn—Beth's adopted family the benefit of the doubt?"

LeBeau's glare bore into him. "Don't play word games with me, Lieutenant, to win her favor. And her name is Miss Logan."

Morning Fawn pushed out of her chair and stood, pale and shaking. "If I hear another word, I'm going to be sick."

"Ladyhood and decorum at its finest," Thea mumbled.

Morning Fawn strode out of the room, hand pressed to her mouth.

Devon followed, double-quick. He'd deal with LeBeau's disfavor in the morning.

Sniffling, she paused at the bottom of the stairs and swiped away tears with her knuckles.

He'd tried to save her from the fight, but he swallowed back any thought of telling her so. "I'm sorry."

She pivoted toward him. Red-rimmed eyes pierced him. "Leave me alone."

"I know you're upset and have every right to be. But if there's anything I can—"

"Allow me to take you out for a breath of air, Miss Logan." Moyer stepped between them. When had he come into the hall?

"I've had enough visiting tonight." She hugged herself tight. Moisture ran from her nose.

Devon dug in his trouser pocket. Where was his blasted handkerchief?

"I understand completely." Moyer's voice smoothed like a snake charmer as he handed her a square of white silk from his waistcoat pocket, its perfect triangular fold snapping open. "But surely, you don't want to retreat to some stuffy room. Let me escort you outside, give you a chance to settle down."

"She said she wants to be left alone." Devon moved in front of the man.

"By you." He smirked.

Jaw clenched, Devon's fingers curled into his palms. "The lady—"

"The lady wants you two to be quiet." Morning Fawn grabbed Moyer's sleeve. "Let's go."

Devon crumpled his belated handkerchief in his hand.

She paused at the threshold to the porch and glanced over her shoulder at him. In a flurry of movement, she stepped back to him, snatched the linen from his hand, and then returned to Moyer's elbow.

What in the world?

CHAPTER 14

*M*orning Fawn stuffed Devon Reynold's handkerchief in her pocket as she walked down the steps onto the pebbled lane. She should have left it in his hand. But the way he'd looked at her when she'd taken Moyer's arm...as if she'd wounded him.

It couldn't be anything more than his pride. Besides, he hadn't given her any thought when he was busy taking his hat off for Miss Perfect.

Turmoil ruled in Morning Fawn's stomach. She should know better than to allow Uncle Robert, Thea, and the rest to get to her. Foolishness. And the lamp-lit path offered no shelter from Moyer's intrusive gaze.

She shivered. The wind rustled through the branches, drying the tears on her cheeks but leaving the raw places in her heart exposed.

"You're cold, Miss Beth." Moyer stopped walking. "Let me give you my coat."

"No, I'm fine." She rubbed her hands over her arms and started ahead.

"I insist you stay close to me to keep warm." He caught up and jutted his elbow toward her.

Even she knew enough about manners to realize she couldn't refuse without insulting the man. After all, she'd been the one to invite him to dinner. Feigning interest was one thing. Living it out was another. The wool of his frock coat scratched against her stiff fingers.

Moyer's muscles flexed beneath his sleeve. His cologne and lingering cigar residue filled her nostrils. Too much. Like everything about him. Couldn't the man let her breathe? What she wouldn't give to be out here alone.

"I'm sorry you had to sit through all of that. I apologize if anything I said brought you pain, my lovely lady." Moyer placed his gloved hand over hers.

She fought the urge to cringe. "Nothing a walk in the fresh air won't cure." Couldn't he hush with that lovely lady line? Even *Miss Logan* or *Miss Beth* was preferable to that overwrought polish.

The waning moon, so much smaller here than on the open prairie, lit the nearly barren branches as they strode toward the orchard. If it wasn't for Reynolds, she'd be far from here, perhaps camped on the Arkansas River for the winter. Gathered around the fire to hear stories. Home. No, not quite home. By now, she'd have become the wife of Stands-His-Ground and perhaps have a baby on her back. For better or worse, Reynolds had saved her from that.

"It must be difficult to sit politely at the same table as the man who stole you from the only home you remember."

Difficult? Not exactly. Somehow it seemed that dinner would be more palatable with just him...and her.

"You disagree?" Moyer cocked an eyebrow.

She shrugged. "I was thinking that Mr. Reynolds's presence is no surprise. After all, my uncle *is* the one who paid him to kidnap me."

"It might be hard to believe, but your uncle only wants what he believes is best for you."

"My uncle doesn't know anything about me."

"He knows you remind him of his sister."

"He said that to you?"

He puffed out his chest. "I arrived early this evening. He and I had a cigar and brandy in his office."

She rolled her eyes and withdrew her hand. Just like her uncle to discuss her life and affairs with a man who barely qualified as an acquaintance. "Did Lieutenant Reynolds join you?"

He chuckled. "Your uncle doesn't share his confidences with the help."

"Lieutenant Reynolds is the one who came up with the marriage-for-land deal." The half truth gushed out before her better sense could hush it. She clamped her mouth shut and awaited the damage. Too much information for this fox.

"Reynolds's idea?" He cocked an eyebrow and scrubbed his hand over his jaw.

"Mostly." So her uncle had informed Moyer about the offer. Probably figured she needed all the help she could get in landing a husband. She clasped her hands in front of her. "My uncle made a couple additions to Lieutenant Reynolds's suggestion." She might as well have a deed or a price tag stuck to her forehead. *Land for sale. Price equal to one marriage.*

Moyer stuck his hand in his pocket. "Reynolds is bolder than I gave him credit for. But of course, he's overreaching."

Blast her uncle and her mouth. The man would be working on some plot next. Morning Fawn blew out a breath and stomped ahead. A raccoon scurried off the path and into the bushes.

Moyer caught up to her and took her arm. The watch fob hanging out of his waistcoat pocket jingled. "A lady has to choose carefully."

"Excuse me?"

The breeze ruffled his tonic-smooth hair. "A lady's whole life is determined by whom she marries. That one decision sets her course. What family she'll belong to. Whom she'll associate with and befriend. Her status and place in the world are all determined by the man she chooses and the weight of his billfold and his amount of acreage." His voice rang with authority as if he were addressing a row of workers at the cotton warehouse. "You want the right man. Not a dirt farmer or a ruffian who lives from one scouting job to the next. You want someone with the means to give you the life you deserve. Money offers privilege and freedom, freedom to travel, and freedom to buy the dresses you want. Or the horse you love, land, freedom. Wealth is the surest way to security."

"We're talking marriage here, not shopping at the local mercantile." She lifted her chin. "And for your information, Devon Reynolds isn't a dirt farmer or a ruffian."

A smirk darkened his face. "So you're defending him? You prefer a man who throws you over his shoulder and ties you to a horse to a gentleman who treats you like a lady?"

The nerve of the man. Before she knew what she was doing, she slapped him. The smack of her palm to his cheek rang in her ears.

He rubbed his hand across the wounded area, his eyes shooting sparks at her.

A bird took flight from a branch overhead. Wonderful. She'd managed to disturb the whole orchard.

"I'm sorry." She exhaled. "I shouldn't have done that." *Even if you deserved it.*

He straightened. "I beg your pardon, Miss Beth. I was out of line with that last remark."

Why did he have to turn into the perfect gentleman now?

She pivoted toward the house. "It's been a long evening, sir, for both of us."

"Please understand." He stepped beside her. His ring glistened in the moonlight as he scrubbed his hand over his jaw. "I was taken aback to discover I have competition for your hand."

She crossed her arms. "There isn't any competition. I'm not ready to make a decision. At the moment, I'm thinking about the benefits of being a spinster."

He chuckled. "My fair lady, we could not have that." He'd recovered quickly, his fox-like instincts sharp once more.

Skirts gathered, she headed for the house.

Once again, his hand slipped around her arm. "It'd be a shame for a lady of your beauty, spunk, and character to be shuttered away, living at your uncle's mercy and provision for the rest of your life."

Did he know about the attic? Was this a veiled threat or just flowery talk? How much had her uncle said to him? Her shoulders tensed.

"Beth." He stopped her at the bottom of the steps.

It was *Beth* now? "There's a *Miss* part there, Mr. Moyer."

He clicked his tongue. "Forgive my presumption, but my thoughts dwell on you so often, I feel as if we've known each other for ages." He stepped in front of her. "My heart cannot bear the thought of losing you."

You never had me.

He held out his hand to her. "May I?"

Reluctantly, she edged her stiff fingers toward his.

"You must give me the opportunity to win your affection." He rubbed his thumb across her knuckles.

Should she come out and say it? "There are easier ways to get land, Mr. Moyer. And you already have plenty."

His eyebrows shot up. "Miss Beth, if you think it's the land I care about, you're greatly mistaken. You can have the parcel in Parker County to do with as you please. Set up a refugee for your beloved Comanche if you wish." He brought her hand to his lips, his eyes glistening. "It is you my heart desires. I want you to reign by my side."

Everything, or almost everything, she could ask for, offered to her on the silver platter of his tongue.

A tingle ran up her arm as his lips brushed her fingers in a lingering kiss.

~

With Lucy nowhere in sight, Morning Fawn struggled out of the crinoline, dropping it to her feet on the attic floor.

Her head still spun with Moyer's lavish promises. She could have the land to do with as she pleased. Bring her pia there, and maybe others, as well. Reign? She'd seen that word in books, like a king or queen. Goodness knows that man thought enough of himself to imagine himself a king. Probably try to rule her like one as well.

She didn't want to be bought. Was it too much to ask for love?

The moon shone through the window. Stepping over the heap of clothes, she drifted to and pressed her nose to the pane, rubbing her hands over her arms. Where was this God her mother had told her about? Her mother had prayed and read the Bible to her and sang songs like "Amazing Grace."

What was that? Grace? Her mother and the preacher—her pa, too—talked about Jesus and how Jesus loved her and died for her and had forgiven her. It hardly seemed like anything more than a story. But her mother had believed it. With all of her heart. And so had Eyes-Like-Sky, at least she had before. Who knew what she believed now.

Where was this God? And what did He mean to Morning Fawn? If she prayed, would He answer? She used to pray.

At meals, the LeBeaus prayed the Lord's Prayer and other

prayers written down in a book. The same words at every meal, repeated at the right time. That wasn't how her mother prayed. Tonight at dinner, she'd opened her eyes. Devon wasn't looking around. He wasn't fiddling with his fork, anxious for the prayers to be done, the memorized words to be said. Instead, his hands were clasped and his head bowed. He stayed that way moments longer, even after the *amen* was said and everyone else opened their eyes. As if he was really praying, as if it meant something to him.

She turned from the window and picked her dress up off the floor. Devon's handkerchief tumbled halfway out of the pocket. Warmth flowed through her as she brought the clean white linen to her nose and inhaled. Bay rum, soap, a tinge of horse. Her cheeks heated. The way he'd looked at her as she'd come down the stairs... The set of his jaw had been hard, but his lake-blue eye...sparks of fire.

Nonsense. She had no business giving that man a second thought. Better get her head on straight.

~

*S*omewhere down below, a clock chimed three in the afternoon. Morning Fawn knelt by the far side of her bed, peeked under the overhanging covers, and tugged the leather pouch free from its hiding place between the ropes and the mattress. She should have a couple of hours to write in her journal before Lucy came to help her dress for the evening meal—another Saturday supper with Moyer at the table. Only this time, Reynolds wouldn't be waiting at the bottom of the stairs. On Monday, her uncle had sent him off to San Antonio on cotton business, and she hadn't seen him since.

Flipping open the flap on the pouch, she carefully pulled out the yarn-bound book with the rough brown pages she'd cut from the package wrapping stolen by Lucy. With the blockade, every scrap of paper was treasured. Too bad Morning Fawn couldn't just ask for the wrapping, but then Uncle Robert would want to see what she'd been writing. And from the way he'd reacted when that newspaperman came by a few months ago wanting to write the story of her captivity, she knew exactly where her narrative would wind up if her uncle got ahold of it. The fireplace.

As she set the pouch aside, a corner of Devon's handkerchief slipped out. Foolish of her to keep it. She fingered the initialed edge. Did it still smell of bay rum a week later?

Steps on the stairs.

She sucked in a breath and stuffed everything back inside the leather, crumpling a sheet in the process.

A knock.

"Who is it?" She shoved the pouch under the bed, no time to wiggle it into place.

"Me." Lucy bounded in with a boldness unknown to the rest of the house. "And you're never going to guess what."

Morning Fawn stood, dusting her hands on her skirt, her heart pounding from the scare. "What? Come in and close the door."

Lucy shut it and hurried over. "Moyer's here, and he's got a horse."

"Doesn't he usually have a horse? After all, he has to ride here. But what's he doing here so early?"

"That's just it." Lucy peeked out the side of the forest-green curtain. "He has an extra horse. A black mustang, and he says it's for you."

Morning Fawn gaped. "You can't be serious. Did he—I mean, I mentioned a mustang last Saturday. You don't think he went out and bought—"

"Well, I think he did." Lucy jabbed a hand to her hip. "That man is pursuing you like there's no tomorrow."

Morning Fawn braced herself on the bedpost. He was unbelievable. "I couldn't possibly accept such a gift."

"Your uncle already has but says you can only ride it when Mr. Moyer or someone else is around to watch over you. As a matter of fact, Massar wants you to come right down and go for a ride."

"I might have known." She glanced out the window.

Gussied up in a dark-blue cutaway morning coat, tan trousers, and shiny riding boots, Moyer stood at the corner of the porch talking with her uncle. Digging his hand in his pocket, Moyer fished out an apple and held it up to the black beauty's lips.

The animal chomped down on the offering.

The apple wasn't the only thing Nicholas Moyer was fishing for. She had obviously underestimated the man.

~

In need of a good bath and a decent bed, Devon nudged his bay mare through Sweet Briar's gate and down the tree-lined lane at dusk. Red dust from the trail clung to every inch of him. But maybe if he cleaned up in a hurry, he could join the family for the last half of supper. He hadn't seen Morning Fawn since Monday.

The trip had been profitable, however, and not just for LeBeau. Under the guise of being LeBeau's cotton factor, he'd gained information on the new planned cotton routes to Mexico via Laredo and Eagle Pass. He'd stuffed so many encrypted notes into the heel of his sock, he'd gotten a blister.

Voices, male and female, carried down the lane. Laughter rang out too. Why would they be gathered outside at supper time?

His stomach soured as he rode into the clearing. Off to the side of the porch, Morning Fawn stood next to a black mustang, stroking the animal's mane. Moyer waited beside her, one hand on the saddle horn, the other on his hip. Mr. and Mrs. LeBeau hovered nearby, faces lit up like someone had won a prize. Above them, Thea leaned against a white porch column, arms folded, face disgruntled.

Decked out like a fancy English gentleman, Moyer dug in his trouser pocket and brought something out. Whatever it was, he had the nerve to take Morning Fawn's hand, unfold her fingers, and place the object in it. She smiled and slipped her palm beneath the horse's lips.

Devon's muscles tensed like a drawn-back hammer on a Colt revolver, ready to explode at the flick of a finger on the trigger.

They were so engrossed that he was almost upon them before anyone—other than the blue tick hound at LeBeau's feet—turned to notice him.

LeBeau tapped his silver-tipped walking stick to the ground. "Reynolds, you're just in time to admire the newest member of our stable."

Morning Fawn's gaze shot up. Her hand fell away from the horse, her smile gone. But there was a flush in her cheeks she couldn't erase.

Devon gave his reins a light tug, drawing his bay to a halt. "I wouldn't want to interrupt anything." His voice sounded as if he'd swallowed a handful of gravel.

"Reynolds." Moyer grinned and threw back his shoulders. "So glad you made it in time to join us for supper."

LeBeau strutted forth and slapped his hand on the mustang's withers. "This little beauty is a gift from Nicholas to my niece. Fine animal. What did you say you named him, Beth?"

Morning Fawn glanced at her feet. "Ebony." She brought her hand up to Ebony's searching lips. "And I'm only accepting her as a loan, not a gift."

Right. *And you've already named her.* A mustang. The exact breed of horse she'd expressed a love for last week at supper. Devon's jaw clenched. LeBeau had probably sent him to San Antonio on purpose, to keep him out of the way of the new suitor. New? The only suitor. And now Morning Fawn couldn't look Devon in the eyes. Dandy. Just dandy.

Moyer patted the tooled saddle. Was that a gift too? "Maybe next week you can go riding with us, Reynolds. We've already had her out for a couple of hours today. We could plan a race. I bet Miss Beth and Ebony will outdo the both of us."

Devon glanced at the stable, the nodes in his throat like rocks. "I don't have time for races. I have work to do. I won't be joining you for supper." With a click, he started his bay moving again. He had no use for a woman whose head could be turned by a horse.

CHAPTER 15

*D*evon mashed his pillow. The blasted thing had too much goose down. A man's head could sink into it like a pinched valley between two smothering mountains.

After supper, Morning Fawn had spent a whole hour with Moyer, walking through the orchard. All within sight of the house as was proper. But had there been any chaperone on that two-hour ride of theirs? LeBeau was likely so giddy from the prospect of acquiring a wealthy son-in-law, he'd be willing to overlook more than a couple steps of impropriety.

Besides, one would think Morning Fawn had had enough of that Moyer's bragging without enduring it for another hour.

Devon needed his sleep. Tomorrow night, he'd get little. He had to be at Feye's landing by midnight. Should he sneak off after everyone went to bed, or make up a story about a gambling game in town?

He rolled onto his back and stared at the ceiling. Surely, Morning Fawn had enough sense to not fall for that smooth-talking dandy. Cut from the same cloth as his stepfather. His mother was a wise, caring, good-hearted woman, but none of that protected her from falling for a man whose heart was tied to his purse and who felt the color of man's skin determined his worth.

Devon blew out a breath and sat up. It was no use. He might as well make good use of the night if he wasn't going to sleep. Grabbing his trousers, he stuck his legs in. He'd head out to the stables and figure out the best way to slip off tomorrow evening unnoticed.

An hour later, Devon's feet crunched on the fresh straw as he returned the dapple grey to her stall. Working with horses was usually a balm to his mind, but not tonight. Even the familiar smells of fresh hay, oats, and horse did little to unwind the tense cords of his muscles. At least, the extra brushing hadn't done the animal any harm.

The elderly stable hand slept on a cot in the corner stall, seemingly content with Devon's excuse of wanting a late-night ride, his silence purchased with a pouch of tobacco. Hopefully, the excuse would work as well tomorrow night.

Little Ebony snorted in the back stall, restless like him, not asleep. Innocent animal, but her presence would weasel its way into Morning Fawn's heart. Making room for the biggest braggart this side of the Red River, as well? It'd be mighty convenient if someone left her stall door open, and she wandered off. He smacked his gauntlets. He wouldn't stoop to underhanded met—

A scream rent the air.

A chill ran up Devon's spine. The old man stirred, as did all of the horses up and down the line. What if it was Morning Fawn? Devon dropped the curry comb and ran for the house.

Lights came on in LeBeau's second-floor bedroom. Moments later, the downstairs glowed, as well.

Devon climbed up the front porch steps two at a time and grabbed the doorknob. Locked. Curtains covered the narrow windows that flanked the door. Raised voices sounded inside. He reached for his holster. Of course, no holster, no gun, nothing. He'd go in the back way. Down and around the corner, he hurried, almost tripping on a washboard. Grabbing a small log from the woodpile, he entered the back door of the house and crept down the hall.

A hard smack, flesh to flesh, resonated in the foyer.

"Please, master, there weren't no man." Lucy knelt on the floor near the coat rack, dressed in nothing but her chemise, arms curled over her face and head. LeBeau stood over her.

Devon's stomach dropped to his knees. His fingers hardened on the log as he moved along the shadows close to the wall.

Mrs. LeBeau stood off to the side of the stairs by the engraved sideboard, the hem of her nightgown showing beneath her wrap, her back to Devon.

Flora, the cook, huddled by the front door, her face contorted in a mass of worry. She caught sight of Devon without acknowledgment.

Revolver in his left hand, LeBeau raised his right, as if he would strike again. "Don't call my daughter a liar, you little wench. Thea said she saw a man in your room. You think she goes screaming in middle of the night for the fun of it?"

"I's not calling her liar, master." Lucy's voice shook. Her dark hair hung down loose about her face. "Maybe's she was dreaming or seeing shadows."

"You're the liar." *Smack*. LeBeau struck her on the side of the head.

She wobbled.

"Stop." Morning Fawn charged down the steps to the first floor. "Leave her alone.

"No." Mrs. LeBeau grabbed Morning Fawn with one hand, clutching her shawl across her chest with the other. "We can't interfere."

"But we can't—"

"Keep your mouth shut, niece, or you'll be hauled up to the

attic and bolted in until you forget what the sun looks like." LeBeau jabbed his finger at her.

Thea leaned over the banister. Had she been hovering there all along? Auburn curls spilled from her nightcap and down her back. "I knew Beth was too cozy with that slave girl. Defending her over her own kind."

Devon clenched his jaw. Maybe Miss Thea and her father would have a change of heart if someone took a whip to their backs. But it wasn't his place. Confronting LeBeau wouldn't help anyone. Devon set the log down on the sideboard.

A slight clunk. They all pivoted toward him.

Devon moved into the lamp-lit foyer.

Lucy lifted her face, tears streaming down her cheeks. What did he see there? Pleading? Fear?

"What are you doing there, Reynolds?" LeBeau's brow furrowed. "Did you see a man run out the back?"

"No. I heard the scream—"

The front door rattled. Flora opened it.

The overseer, Owens burst in, hair awry and rifle in hand, as ready as ever to enforce his employer's orders. His shirttails hung over his trousers, and one suspender looped loosely over his arm. "What's wrong?"

LeBeau swore. "Thea went down to ask Lucy for a warm compress for her headache and found her in bed with a man. Get out back and look for him. Get the hounds if you have to. I'll not have any whoring in my house."

Lucy raised her hands in supplication. "No, master, please. Weren't no one."

Owens sneered and stomped out the door.

What would happen if there was someone, a slave, and Owens found him?

LeBeau shoved his revolver into his wife's hand and grabbed Lucy by the hair, dragging her up to a stand.

"No," Morning Fawn cried out.

"Get upstairs." LeBeau bellowed at her.

Acid crept up Devon's throat. He had to do something. "It was me."

"What?" LeBeau pivoted toward him, mouth agape, his fingers still locked in Lucy's hair. She stumbled against her master, and he shoved her to the ground. "What did you say?"

The three ladies at the foot of the stairs stared at him wide-eyed.

"I said, it was me." The lie soured in his mouth. God forgive him. But he couldn't let this girl be beaten and her lover possibly killed.

Thea scrunched up her face like a prune.

Mrs. LeBeau paled and crossed her arms over her bosom. "We'll not have such goings on in our home, Mr. Reynolds."

But on her hands and knees, Lucy gazed up at him. New light shone in her eyes. She mouthed two words. *Thank you.* A new round of crying shook her.

Devon flinched beneath Morning Fawn's stare.

Flora swung the door open. "Mr. Owens, we found the man." She threw her lungs into it. "We's found the man." Her voice probably echoed all the way to the slave quarters.

"Stop your hollering and get back in here." LeBeau scowled.

Somewhere, a clock chimed one.

LeBeau flexed his hands at his sides, curling and uncurling his fingers into fists. "You ladies get upstairs."

"Gladly." Thea spat out the words. "I wouldn't want to soil my feet with the dirt from his boots. Maybe that's how he got his eye poked out."

Morning Fawn stood immobile, her long red shawl covering most of her nightgown and her honey hair falling over her shoulders, while the other two pushed past. Her gaze flittered between him and Lucy. Her brow furrowed deep as she turned to follow her aunt.

Great. She'd probably think of him lower than scum. Ruin any hope—

Hope of what?

"It's my fault." Lucy sniffled. "I lured him to my room. Weren't Lieutenant Reynolds doing."

"Shut up and get out of here." LeBeau scuffed his slippered foot across the floor, stopping just short of kicking her.

She scurried to her feet, shooting Devon a quick glance before she hurried down the hall, swiping her cheeks.

"You." LeBeau stormed over, toe to toe with Devon. "You have no right to my slave girls. Not without permission. You have a need? There's plenty down in the slave quarter I could give you to warm your bed, but not Lucy. Do what you like on your own plantation, but this and them are my property."

Devon walled his face and met the man's glare. "Yes, sir. Sorry, sir."

Owens thundered in, rifle still in hand. Chaw bulged in his jaw. "What happened?"

"Reynolds had himself a little visit." LeBeau tugged on the shawl collar of his silk dressing gown. "Finally owned up to it."

Owens snickered and aimed his lips toward a spittoon. Black tobacco juice spewed toward the tarnished brass container. "Should have spoken up and saved me the trouble of heading halfway to the kennel."

How many little visits had that man had? Devon swallowed back the retort and turned to LeBeau. "I apologize, sir. It won't happen again." He slunk up the stairs to the second floor. It didn't matter that he had never gone anywhere near Lucy or any slave for that purpose, ever. Shame hung over his head like a millstone.

CHAPTER 16

The next morning, Devon trudged into the back row of the small clapboard church and dropped onto the worn pew. Dr. Arthur LeBeau's borrowed black wool frock coat stretched tight across his shoulders.

The scents of lamp oil, fresh-cut cedar boughs, and wood smoke drifted his way. He couldn't recall the last time he was in a church. His visits to a formal house of worship had been few and far between since Isabelle's death. By the time he'd enlisted in the Federal Army over two years later, he was so hollowed out, he'd dropped to his knees before the Lord when he heard the circuit rider preach at the camp meeting in New Orleans.

Up front, a plump lady dressed in mourning black played "The Church Is One Foundation" on the piano.

The congregants, mostly women tugging their children, filed past. Their stares lingered on Devon as they walked to their seats. Because he was new or because of his eye...or perhaps because he was one of the few men under fifty? His fingers twitched to adjust his eyepatch. He crumpled his hat instead. They couldn't possibly know what he'd confessed to last night. At least not this quickly.

Would Morning Fawn come to church? He'd grabbed a roll from Flora in the kitchen and hurried out the door. When he'd passed Mrs. LeBeau in the hall, she'd gathered her skirts and scooted close to the wall as if being in his shadow might contaminate her.

In the stables this morning, George had gone out of his way to help him. That man knew the truth. Maybe he was even the one who'd paid Lucy a visit.

Morning Fawn wouldn't understand. She'd see him as lower than a dog. The way she'd gotten her feathers in a ruffle for him calling Miss Schramm *Frieda*, she'd be ready to skewer him for this. Could he trust her enough to tell her the truth? And why should he bother, especially now that Moyer all but had a lasso around her?

"That's him."

He glanced up as Thea trailed by on the arm of a middle-aged man with a paunch and receding hairline.

Two ladies who followed in her wake scowled at him as well, then fell to whispering as they hurried past and entered an engraved pew. The whole town would be aware of his supposed sin by the time Thea was done.

The bites of roll felt like lead in his stomach. He leaned forward, elbows on his knees, and exhaled.

What did God think of what he'd done last night? Surely, it was right to save Lucy and her lover, but maybe there could have been a better way.

A step and a green skirt moved his way. He glanced up and blinked wide. Morning Fawn.

Rosy-cheeked, with her honey-colored hair caught up in a loose knot at the back of her head, she made her way down the row, dangling her bonnet by its strings.

Goosebumps ran up his arms. Words escaped him.

Mrs. LeBeau stopped in the aisle, her tone sharp. "This isn't where we're sitting, Beth, dear." She looked down her nose at Devon as if he were a smudge to be wiped away.

Morning Fawn sat down beside him with hardly more than a glance in her aunt's direction. "This is where I'm sitting."

Mrs. LeBeau bristled. "Elizabeth."

Chin jutted, Morning Fawn tossed her bonnet on the pew beside her. Whatever look she gave her aunt must have been more than enough. Mrs. LeBeau pressed her lips tight and strutted to the front without another word.

More than a few heads turned their way.

Morning Fawn smoothed her skirt. "They're looking at me. Probably still thinking about that commotion I caused a couple weeks ago."

He blinked at her. She was doing him the courtesy of acting like the stares were all about her. "So I heard." One corner of his mouth managed to curl upward before it drooped. "That's where I came in. For better or for worse."

"I thought I'd best sit in the back in case it happens again."

It? Panic? A memory?

Morning Fawn fiddled with a fold in her green wool skirt, avoiding his gaze. Several silky locks looked ready to spill to her shoulders at any moment. He'd never seen a blush so deep on her cheeks.

Maybe there was hope of unraveling Moyer's lasso.

The congregation faded. She'd chosen to sit beside him. Would she have made the same choice if Moyer was here? Best not to question the blessing. "Please don't steal any horses today. I'm too beaten down to come after you."

Hazel eyes, with golden specks, met his. "Perfect time to escape." She smiled. At him. First time ever, except for the night of the laudanum. She whispered, "Don't worry. I won't today."

Warmth stirred within him, siphoning off the tension. Did

she know the truth about last night? He wanted to be certain. "I didn't do it." His cheeks heated.

"I know."

The millstone cracked. His shoulders lifted.

Up front, the minister moved toward the pulpit.

Devon lowered his voice to hardly more than a breath. "I can't stomach everyone thinking I did. But poor Lucy—"

"You saved her from blame and a whipping. I'd hate to guess what you saved her Ned from." Her lover.

His pulse throbbed in his neck as their gazes lingered.

The pianist struck a key, and the congregation stood. The notes of "Come Thou Fount of Every Blessing" sounded throughout the small sanctuary. Devon rose beside Morning Fawn and picked up the hymnal. He knew the first verse, not the rest. Palms sweaty, he fumbled through the pages to the correct one and held the book out for Morning Fawn. His swallow stuck in his throat as her fingers slipped around the right bottom corner to hold the hymnal with him.

"'Prone to wander Lord, I feel it. Take my heart Lord, take and seal it, seal it for thy courts above....'" Morning Fawn's voice blended with his.

A hum of awakening swelled within his chest. The first rays of dawn peeked over the horizon of his heart.

~

*C*louds moved across the midnight moon as Devon tied his horse and made his way through the brush. The wispy buffalo grass parted like wheat beneath his step. Hopefully, his knee-high cavalry boots would protect him against any snakes that had yet to slither off into hibernation. Tiny bits of paper pricked his heel.

His brain had been full of sap ever since church. Morning

Fawn had strolled along on his arm as he'd walked her to her carriage after the service, in no hurry to depart. The warmth of her touch flowed through him like hot maple syrup. She'd made no mention of Ebony or Moyer.

She also hadn't said a word about Devon's handkerchief from a week ago. Was it in a heap of dirty laundry, or was it something she didn't want to let go of? But what was a handkerchief compared to a horse?

Maybe he should agree to race the man, put him in his place.

Gurgling drifted on the breeze as Devon neared the river. An owl hooted. He hooted back. A man, equal to his height, stepped from the far side of an ancient cottonwood, its trunk wide as a table. Captain Jeremy Carson. In the year they'd served together, they'd become fast friends, and as equal as a captain and a lieutenant could be despite the fact that Jeremy was a West Point man. A man who loved Texas as much as Devon and wanted to see her free. Worn trousers, a patched coat, and a beaten-down slouch hat had replaced his usual neat uniform.

"You weren't followed, were you?" Jeremy stepped forward, his usually clean-shaven face deep in whiskers.

"No, I made certain. And if anyone asks, I was in Alleyton playing cards."

Jeremy clamped a hand on his shoulder. "Good to see you. I wanted to come in person to see what you've been about."

"And what are you supposed to be? From the looks of you, the provost marshal might arrest you and ship you off with the rest of the dregs of the Confederacy to the front lines."

"No, I have me a card." Jeremy pulled a piece of paper from his pocket. "Signed by the governor's deputy—or at least, it looks like his signature—saying I'm exempt from conscription because I'm a teamster hauling cotton. As a matter of fact, I'm supposed to be off the day after tomorrow with a load headed for Eagle's Pass."

"Only, your load isn't going to make it to Mexico?"

Jeremy grinned. "I'm sorry to say, the whole cotton train, ten wagons strong, will be hit by a squad of Yankees if I can help it. It's about time we started setting things right in this state."

Devon punched his friend's arm. "With such good work, you won't need me. I was coming to tell you about the new routes to Laredo and Eagle Pass."

"I'm hungry for all of the information you have. I don't know much beyond where my mules are told to go." Jeremy dug a piece of dried beef out of his pocket, broke it in half, and handed Devon a portion. "Besides, you're the one sitting within striking distance of the mother lode."

"I've information for you." Devon sat on a gnarled root. His boot heels dug into the soft mud. A month from now, it'd likely be frozen. He worked his foot free of boot and sock. "Numbers of troops, sketches of fortifications, routes and more. I didn't know if you'd be here in person."

The dampness of the night descended around them. Jeremy sat down beside him, undid his top trouser buttons, and tucked the rolled notes into a secret slit in his waistband.

Devon leaned forward, forearms on his knees. "There's two encampments in the Columbus and Alleyton area. A regiment of cavalry and one of infantry. Probably more coming. The Rebs are mighty nervous about their cotton. They've added an extra train engine at the depot, in case they need to get the troops somewhere in a hurry. And don't expect any more cotton to be coming your way down in San Antonio after what's already on the road gets there. Confederate headquarters sent orders in the last week to shut down the shipments until further notice."

Jeremy finished off his beef. "You're in the perfect place. All you have to do is wait for the right time."

"Yeah, I figure there's still bales on the way to Alleyton, already on the road before the order went out. Not all of it comes by train. Some planters from Arkansas and western Louisiana haul it by wagon."

"Let the bales stack up for a while. The best time to hit would be if you could get word of when they plan to start the shipments south again and strike right before they move it out."

That *would* be the best time. And befriending Moyer or encouraging his courtship of Morning Fawn would be the perfect way to learn such information. Right. About as likely as Lincoln calling the troops home and letting Jeff Davis have his way. "We'll see."

Jeremy quirked his eyebrows. "I'm counting on you. For every bale that doesn't make it to market, it's hundreds of dollars the Rebs don't have. Wagon loads of guns and ammunition the enemy can't afford to purchase." Jeremy met Devon's gaze. "How are things going with your accomplices?"

"Good." Devon shifted on the log, striving for a spot that didn't bore into his backside. A late-season tree frog chirped nearby. "Dr. Schramm and his daughter are capable and eager to help. They've had experience in hiding escaped slaves and helping to move them to Indian Country. They even have a secret hold beneath the floor in his office. Hid a slave there for two weeks one time."

"Excellent. What's the plan?"

"I used the excuse of my eye to visit the doctor. That'll work for a couple of times, but then to avoid suspicion, the plan is for me to call on Miss Frieda. Take her strolling down by the depot end of town. A couple so distracted by each other they couldn't possibly notice anything else around them." He groaned within. How in the devil was he going to keep Morning Fawn from hearing rumors of the alleged courtship? If it came to it, he'd have to make his affection for Frieda look real. He raked his fingers through his hair.

Jeremy leaned back against the tree. "What's wrong?"

"Nothing."

"Is there a problem?"

"Nothing I can't take care of." A mosquito buzzed near Devon's ear. He swatted at the creature. "An added bonus is that a couple months back, the Rebs unloaded twenty wagonloads of gunpowder in Brownsville. Sent it up to Alleyton by way of the Cotton Road. Much of it has already passed through to the army in Louisiana, but there's enough still there to make the prettiest firework show you ever laid eyes on, courtesy of the cotton warehouse."

"Make sure you get out before the show starts. You owe me another card game back in New Orleans."

"That's the goal." Devon slapped him on the shoulder. "But I've had enough of cards and New Orleans. No use retreating to our old encampment. Why don't we plan on meeting up for a beefsteak dinner after our men take Galveston?"

"Sounds good to me." Jeremy smiled. "But I want to hear about that girl before I go."

"Which girl?"

"That spunky captive you rescued. Is she still living with her uncle?" Jeremy rubbed the back of his neck. "Did I tell you my friend from West Point married a captive he rescued? Though from what I've heard of it, *rescued* isn't a word his wife would agree with."

"What's his wife's name?"

"One you won't forget." Jeremy smiled. "Eyes-Like-Sky."

Morning Fawn's sister had married a Federal officer and gone east. But LeBeau had only called her by her English name, Margaret Logan. "The girl I rescued? She's so thankful, she could wring my neck. But she has a sister who was a captive. Reclaimed a couple of years earlier than Morning Fawn. Maybe when you get back to Federal territory, you can write to your friend and see if his wife has a sister." It could be what he'd been looking for, a safe place to send Morning Fawn where she wouldn't have to marry for her freedom. Get her away from the likes of LeBeau and Moyer.

Only, he had a cotton warehouse to blow up and a German girl to faux court first. He had no business getting himself entangled with honey hair and a pair of hazel eyes. No business making promises.

$\mathcal{M}$orning Fawn wiped her damp palms on her skirt as she headed for the stables. The last of the late fall's red and yellow canopy of leaves lay scattered on the ground. She had been waiting all afternoon for Devon to return. He'd ridden out early this morning before breakfast. She hadn't dared ask where he'd headed off to. Ever since the incident with Lucy, Aunt Julia and Thea had acted like Devon was the worst sinner in the world. Let them think what they liked. She knew better.

Was their disapproval the reason he'd avoided joining the family in the dining room for meals since the incident? Or was it because he was disgusted with her over Ebony? She had accepted the mustang as a loan, not a gift. But the clarification had seemed to bounce off his ears the night he'd seen the horse. He'd looked as if she deserved to be strung up on the council pole in her village.

Church Sunday morning had been a whole different story. But she hadn't had a moment alone with him since.

Chickens clucked from the hen house. A couple of slave women stood in the shed near the smokehouse stirring two massive iron kettles over smoldering fires, singing as they worked. The soap-making had started in earnest this morning. Several days ago, they'd placed wood ash in straw-lined barrels. A field hand had dumped gallons of water into the mix every few hours. He'd poured the run-off from that into the kettles, mixed it with lime, and left the concoction to set. Today, they'd added pounds of tallow and more water. She would have gladly joined in the work in hopes of being able to add flowers or honey to the mixture, but Aunt Judith had given a definite no.

Murmurs carried on the breeze from the stables. Low, rich notes. Devon's voice. Was he talking to a horse or a stable hand?

A twig crunched beneath her foot. She bent down and wrestled her shoes off. Hard cow leather and bothersome lacings. If she'd worn such troublesome blocks on her feet during her time with the Comanche, she would have starved. Maybe if she asked, Devon would agree to take her hunting. What she wouldn't give to have a pair of moccasins. But she had more important things to ask today.

Shoes in hand, she lifted her skirts and stepped quietly across the ground. Maybe she could catch a glimpse of Devon before he saw her. Holding her breath, she reached the half-open door and peeked in.

The smells of hay, horse, and manure greeted her nostrils. Shadows draped the stalls. Kneeling by a Morgan, George wedged a pick in the cracks of a hoof. Devon stood in the foreground with his back to the door. A beam of sunlight from the upper window danced on his scuffed cavalry boots.

"Good girl." Devon wove the curry comb in circles across the mare's shoulder, loosening dust and mud from the animal's reddish-brown hide. Smooth, strong strokes, yet as gentle as a hair brushing, he took his time, care evident in his every movement.

His muscles flexed beneath the light blue work shirt. The ends of his thick dark-brown hair scraped against his collar.

Morning Fawn's pulse quickened.

"Mays I help you, Miss Logan?" George dropped the Morgan's hoof and straightened.

She startled and bumped the creaky door. Her shoes fell onto the dirt floor.

My goodness. How clumsy could she be? She knelt to pick them up.

Quick to the draw, Devon reached the second shoe before she did. "You're barefoot?"

She tucked a loose strand of hair behind her ear. "No, I have my stockings."

"In the dirt, with all the pebbles and prickly grasses?" His gaze fell into hers as he handed her the shoe, the depth of his lake-blue eye drawing her in.

Speak. Why couldn't she get her mouth to move? "I need to talk to you alone," she whispered.

His eyebrows shot up.

Why couldn't she say anything right? No telling what she'd have him thinking. "About Lucy."

"Oh." He exhaled. "George, please leave us for a bit."

"Yes, sir." Swiping his sleeve across his forehead, he took the Morgan by the lead rope and ambled out the back to the corral.

Ebony poked her head over her stall door, her big brown eyes calling.

Shoes in hand, Morning Fawn ignored her horse and stood still. She wasn't about to lift her skirts and put her shoes on in front of Devon. When had that happened? Eighteen months ago, she would have thought nothing of showing a man her bare feet, and she would have worn leggings and a short skirt.

"What about Lucy?" Devon frowned and returned to combing his horse, except he moved around to the other side of the mare, facing her with the horse between them.

Direct and to the point. No "how have you been," almost as if he wanted to put distance between them. She might have known she was being too forward on Sunday, sitting beside him uninvited. But how else was she supposed to show him she understood and respected him for what he'd done? And prove to him she wasn't at Nicholas's beck and call.

A couple stalls down, LeBeau's quarter horse, Lightning, kicked against a board, acting as though he owned the place just like his owner. Ebony nickered.

Devon shot the mustang a glare that could freeze steam.

Morning Fawn's tongue scraped against the roof of her mouth. She'd better get herself talking before he ordered her and the horse out of the stable. "I think we should help Lucy get married."

"What?" Devon looked at her as if she were out of her mind. The comb stopped.

"It isn't right, them... being together not married." She fiddled with the shoelaces and dropped her gaze. A mouse scurried into a far corner. "She loves Ned, and he loves her."

Devon swiped his brow with his neckerchief. "Morning Fawn, it's not that simple. It's not even up to them. And who is Ned, anyhow?"

"A slave on a neighboring plantation. Works as a carpenter. And it *should* be up to them. We could do it secretly." She bit her lip and stepped closer to the mare.

Devon blew out a breath and tossed the comb on the tack shelf, rattling the other tools. A piece of straw clung to his sleeve. "From what I can tell, LeBeau would never agree to it."

"If you noticed, I said 'secret.' I bet Ned's master would be willing. He allows Ned to sneak over here occasionally."

Devon laid his arms on the mare's back. "LeBeau has the authority to marry her off to whomever he pleases, to whatever field hand or house servant he favors. It doesn't matter how many 'I do's' Lucy says in the dark. There wouldn't be anything legal about it."

A lock of rich brown hair dipped down to his eyepatch.

Morning Fawn exhaled. The hard-soled shoes clunked together as she moved her arms about. "I reckon we'd have to deal with that if the time came."

He shook his head and lowered his voice to a mere breath. "Helping could land us all in a heap of trouble."

"I'm willing to take that risk."

His brow furrowed. "What does Lucy say about all of this?"

She shrugged. "She likes the idea, but she's afraid. For all the reasons you said and then some."

He shoved his fingers through his errant hair, sweeping it back off of his forehead. "Just between you and me, LeBeau is mighty protective of her. Called me into his office Monday and berated me again for overstepping boundaries. Said I was welcome to avail myself of any of his other female slaves, but not her."

She gaped at him.

A blush spread across his tanned cheeks. "I'd never 'avail myself' of anyone."

"I don't even want to know what that word means, but I can guess."

"I just want you to know he's not likely to tolerate her being married to anyone. Ned would be better off if he stayed away."

She jabbed a hand to her hip. "Would you?"

"Would I what?"

"Stay away from the woman you loved because it was safer?"

"Maybe safer is better."

"I don't believe that."

"You've been reading too many novels."

"You never answered my question. What would you do if it was the woman you loved?" She winced. How could she dare such boldness?

His arms slipped from the back of the mare. A muscle twitched beneath his light layer of beard. He turned away.

"Isabelle, my wife, was the daughter of our cook on our plantation. A hired Mexican. You don't fall in love with the help."

Morning Fawn bit her lip, then whispered, "What happened?"

The bay mare nickered.

Devon stuffed his hands in his pockets. "I didn't stay away." His voice trailed off. So did his gaze.

Morning Fawn shivered. He'd loved his wife. Still did. "I'm sorry you lost her."

Devon startled as if he'd forgotten her presence. "Long time ago." He cleared his throat and stepped away, leading the mare to the feed sack. A sigh rattled through him. "If Lucy is serious about this, I'll help." His back still to her, he picked up the curry comb he'd tossed aside and hung it on a nail. "Only, she should know, and probably already does, that it could bring her a world of heartache. We'd all face your uncle's and the community's wrath. All she has to do is end up with child for LeBeau to get wise."

Morning Fawn clapped. "I'll work with her and figure it out. Set it for Ned's next visit if we can."

He pivoted, a deep crease between his eyebrows. "I don't know how much time I have here. Sooner or later, I need to head out to look for my regiment in Louisiana."

Her hands dropped to her sides. "There's no need to hurry to the frontline again and get yourself shot at."

"I recall a conversation where you insinuated any warrior worth his snuff would return to the battle lines as soon as he could."

"I don't know what *insinuated* means, but I do know a warrior can take an extra month or two to heal and rest up." Why did her stupid voice wobble?

He shot her a look, then grabbed a hoof pick. "I can't give you any guarantees, Morning Fawn. Only that if I leave, I'll be back eventually."

They were in the middle of a war. No one could guarantee anything. "I'm going to go tell Lucy." She jutted out her chin. "Don't you forget what you promised me the night you came to my room. I'm going to hold you to it."

Shoes in tow, she hurried to the door before he could object.

"I won't forget. As long as you don't have a stall of horses at your beck and call by then." His voice trailed after her.

∽

Someone ought to sew her mouth shut. Morning Fawn dug her nails into her palms and stomped up the back steps to the main house. The scent of freshly baked bread wafted from the detached kitchen. Why in the world had she said all of that? Holding him to his promises? What kind of forward talk was that? Trying to tell him he needed to stay around? She might as well throw herself at the man.

Aunt Judith called from the library office. "Is that you, Beth?"

"Heading out for a walk." Morning Fawn quickly stepped down the tiled hall to the front, blocking her ears to whatever words followed. The last thing she wanted was to be dragged into conversation. She'd only come into the house to avoid Devon's gaze from the stables. Or was it a glare? And that comment he'd made about horses... Did he think she was someone whose hand could be purchased?

"Beth?" Her aunt's voice rang down the hall.

Morning Fawn skedaddled down the front steps and around the corner, away from the stables and toward the barren apple orchard. Gnarled limbs stretched toward the sky. Farther down the lane and to the right, two slave children ran about with buckets gathering pecans, searching the trampled grass beneath the trees.

"Ouch." Something sharp poked her toe. She sat down on a flat rock and rubbed her foot. Thistles and wisps of grass clung to her torn stocking.

Devon had loved his wife deeply. How long did it take to get over a love and loss like that?

Morning Fawn swiped her nose. He'd probably felt sorry for her that night in the attic. His promises had likely been nothing more than an attempt to settle down someone half out of their head on laudanum. Guilt over his role in bringing her here. And goodness knows he had plenty to feel guilty about. But guilt had nothing to do with love or even affection.

Horse hooves clomped toward her, followed by a jingle. She shoved her feet into her shoes and stood.

Thea. Of all people. Atop a palomino quarter horse and wearing a black satin riding habit, her cousin wove her way down the narrow path toward her. Morning Fawn stiffened. She could scurry back to the house, but she wasn't about to give Thea the satisfaction of seeing her flee.

Sitting tall and proud on her sidesaddle, Thea drew rein. "I've had quite a day." She fanned herself with her hand. The wind fluttered the ostrich feather in her hat and jingled the tiny bells that decorated her horse's bridle.

"I won't keep you, then." Morning Fawn gathered her skirts and pivoted toward a path between the apple trees.

"I've been visiting the sick." Thea nudged her mount forward. "You should try it sometime. Helping others is a balm to the soul."

As if Thea knew anything about the soul or genuinely caring for anyone other than herself. Morning Fawn halted. "Exactly how did you help?"

Thea beamed. "I went with Beulah Larson and Eva Brown, other members of the Confederate Ladies of Colorado County. Not just anyone can join, you know." She looked down her nose as if Morning Fawn was one of the anyones.

"We took baskets of baked goods to the poorer soldier families. Their farms look like mud pits. You should see what pitiful hovels they live in. I'm sure our slaves are better provided for. I shall have to bathe when I return to the house." She scrunched up her nose as if she could smell the odor now.

Morning Fawn crossed her arms. "Have you ever been?"

"To where?"

"The slave cabins?"

Thea swatted the dangling ostrich feather away from her cheek. "You know my constitution is too delicate for the air in those places."

Morning Fawn rolled her eyes. She had better things to do than listen to Thea's fluff. "Your mother's in the house if you're looking for her."

A crow cawed from a nearby branch.

"I'll go in soon enough. I wanted to enjoy the fresh air." She flicked her riding crop at a fly. "Speaking of fresh air, I'm surprised Lieutenant Reynolds didn't invite you to ride to Alleyton with him today, seeing that neither of you cares about what is proper."

Morning Fawn stilled. "Dev—the lieutenant went to Alleyton this morning?" Her voice wavered. A mistake.

"Devon?" Thea's face glowed with an impish grin like the old woman who had lured Hansel and Gretel into her gingerbread house. "He didn't tell you? Weren't you talking to him in the stables a few minutes ago? When I rode up in the yard, I saw you hurrying out of there, and him standing at the door."

"It's none of my concern where he goes." She might as well have bared her neck to Thea's claws for the kill.

"I don't know. You seem a little concerned. Do you think he went to see the doctor again? Or someone else?" If Thea had a tail, it would have switched back and forth like a cat's while eyeing its prey. "By the way, just how many men are you on a given-name basis with? First Mr. Moyer, and now the lieutenant?"

Morning Fawn jutted out her chin and pivoted toward the house. "I don't waste words on busy bodies."

Thea's laugh scraped across her nerves all the way back to the house.

~

"*L*ieutenant Reynolds says he'll help." Morning Fawn ran a brush through her shoulder-blade-length hair. *If he's not too busy having lemonade with Miss Frieda.*

The dinner bell rang outside, calling the work day to an end. Newly lit oil lamps flickered, supplementing the gray dusk from the attic window.

Lucy hugged the petticoat she'd dug out of Morning Fawn's trunk. "But what if Ned ain't willing? You expecting me to ask him? That ain't the way it's supposed to be."

"How is Ned supposed to ask you if he doesn't know it's possible?" Morning Fawn pivoted on the stool where she sat in front of the mirror. "You can tell him how the lieutenant helped save both of you—"

"I'm sure he's heard. Us slaves know how to get the word around."

"So it shouldn't come as a surprise to him that the lieutenant and I are offering to help with a wedding."

Lucy bit her lip. A raised welt stretched along her jawline, a raw reminder of LeBeau's blows. How many more marks were on her body? "I don't know about this whole scheme."

"You love Ned, don't you?"

"With all my heart. I'd give anything to be free and have my own little cabin with him. Only, it don't matter how many times we jump over the broom, it ain't going to be like that." Clouds filled Lucy's usually cheerful expression.

"Someday maybe it will be." Morning Fawn touched her arm. "All I know is, if you're going to willingly have Ned in your bed, you got to marry him. That way, you know you're doing right, regardless of what happens. And you'll know he's made his commitment to you. Control what you can."

Lucy pulled away. "I've got little say so about who's in my bed."

Morning Fawn shuddered. Were Devon's suspicions about her uncle correct? One more reason to despise her uncle. An image of the way Old Owl looked at Eyes-Like-Sky back in the village before Dancing Eagle had claimed her flickered through Morning Fawn's mind. She fumbled for words, her voice barely more than a whisper. "But Ned gives you a choice?"

Lucy nodded.

"Then that's what you can control." Morning Fawn hugged herself. "Maybe things will change if the Yankees win this war."

"I'll believe that when I sees it." Lucy exhaled and handed the petticoat to Morning Fawn. "But I believes you're right. Why wait for someone else to fix things?" She threw back her shoulders. "I'll pass on word to Ned. I'm not going to let Massar LeBeau or no one else tell me who I can marry. I'm willing if Ned is."

What about herself, rushing to marry for a piece of land? Just like her uncle to think he could control every inch of a person's life.

Lucy picked up a corset. "Let's get you ready for dinner, or folks will be wondering what happened to you."

"I don't need that thing." Morning Fawn turned her nose up at the contraption. "Not unless Mr. Moyer decided to pay us an unexpected visit."

"Mr. Moyer don't need nothing. You're wearing this for the lieutenant. The cook tells me he'll be joining you all for dinner tonight."

Morning Fawn folded her arms across her chemise. "I don't care what the lieutenant does."

"Whys, you was just telling me how he going to help us, and how I should be pleased."

"Helping you is one thing, and I'm grateful for that if he manages to keep his word."

"You think he might change his mind?" Lucy's voice faltered.

"No. I was just shooting my mouth off." Morning Fawn touched Lucy's faded sleeve. "Forgive me. I'm sure he'll help you, regardless of what else he may or may not do."

Lucy scrunched up her brow. "Why you acting like he done spoiled your cream?"

"He went to Alleyton this morning. Spent the day there and didn't mention a word of it to me."

"And why should he?" Lucy urged Morning Fawn to her feet, facing her. "He inspected the cotton gin yesterday and didn't say a word then, did he?"

"I told you what's in Alleyton." Morning Fawn sucked in a breath as Lucy hooked up the corset front and the whale baleen tightened around her ribs.

"So you goin' yell at him or have a conniption fit? Give him a piece of your mind? You think that will win him over? You think that's what this Miss Frieda did when he showed up at her house today?"

"I don't want to think about what that woman did. I'd like to throw her cookies to the pigs."

Lucy chuckled. "You don't own that man, girl. Not yet. He make any promises to you? Come calling yet?"

Well, he had made a promise—just not the kind Lucy meant. "I don't care if that man ever comes calling. And he'd better get it straight in his head that I'm not the cookie-and-lemonade type of girl. I don't crochet doilies either."

Lucy laughed. "Maybe he don't want no doilies. Maybe he

wants him a woman who can ride a horse as fast as he can or better. A woman who loves adventure and who has fire in her eyes and cheeks, not cream." She shook her finger at Morning Fawn. "Just don't go chasin' him away with your temper."

How in the world did she get into this conversation? "You're just all sunshine and rainbows over him because he saved you and Ned the other night, and you have every right to be, but that doesn't have anything to do with his opinion of me. And you should see the way he looks at Ebony, as if he'd like to sell her for horse meat. As if I'm stupid enough to believe every line that comes out of Nicholas Moyer's mouth."

Lucy clicked her tongue. "Now here I thought you'd gone and done wrong by accepting that horse."

"I've told you and everyone else—I'm only borrowing Ebony."

"If you say so. Just don't get tangled in that net Moyers is throwing out for you. But if you've got the lieutenant riled up about it, then maybe good will come of it." Standing on tiptoe, Lucy lifted the royal-blue dress, an updated hand-me-down wrenched from Thea's trunk, and draped it over Morning Fawn's head. "That man has eyes for you. So when you's goes down to dinner, don't let that Miss Thea get you all caught up in throwing words at each other, like fists."

"Doesn't your temper ever get the best of you?"

"I simmer something terrible at times. Except I've learned to hold my tongue until I'm out of earshot of those who think they have power over me. I remind myself that the Good Lord is the real massar, and the LeBeaus are going to figure that out someday."

Morning Fawn smoothed the folds of her skirt. The fancy lace trim on the bodice scratched against her collarbone. If the Lord cared about Lucy, why didn't he rescue her from slavery? For that matter, why had he allowed Morning Fawn's parents to die? Her life held a bucket of *whys* so deep, she could drown in it.

~

*D*evon sipped his wine and glanced across the table at Morning Fawn. The royal-blue silk suited her well. The pagoda sleeves and lace trim added an air of elegance. Her hair had been drawn away from the front of her face and woven into a loose knot, but the rest spilled onto her shoulders like spun honey.

A slight blush glowed on her cheeks. Because of his gaze? He'd like to think so. Stupid of him. She likely had no interest other than having him help Lucy. He should have figured that out the moment she walked into the barn today. That black mustang had made enough noise to remind him of it. But still—

"Papa, it was wise of you to have Adela wait on us tonight." Kitty-corner across from him instead of at her usual seat by his side, Thea nodded toward the middle-aged servant who usually aided Flora in the kitchen.

Devon sawed into his pork. They'd gone out of their way to remove Lucy from the dining room. Afraid he'd be tempted by her proximity? Leave it to Thea to rub his face in his supposed wrongs.

LeBeau cleared his throat. "Adela needs to get out of the kitchen now and then." He settled back in his chair and hooked a thumb in his waistcoat pocket. "Reynolds, what do you know about horse racing? I'm not talking about Moyer's offer. Mr. Franklin of Pryor Place is aiming to throw a real race together."

Devon lifted his fork. "If he's planning on racing that beauty I saw three weeks ago, I think everyone else will be left in the dust."

"That Thoroughbred isn't as fast as she looks." LeBeau puffed out his chest.

"Especially after Beth finished with her." Thea twirled an auburn curl around her finger.

Morning Fawn straightened. "I think Lieutenant Reynold's horse would have a chance of winning."

"Of course, you do." Thea rolled her eyes.

"I was thinking more of my Lightning." LeBeau frowned. "Finest quarter horse in Colorado County."

"Perhaps you can challenge Franklin to a sprint?" That'd be the only hope of winning against a Thoroughbred.

"Excellent idea, Reynolds. I'll propose that to Franklin next time I see him."

Thea swirled her wine in her glass. "How was your trip to Alleyton today, Lieutenant Reynolds? I heard you went to the doctor."

Obviously, she hadn't caused enough trouble yet. Maybe she was the one who should be locked in the attic. Devon glared at her, then shot a glance at Morning Fawn, bracing himself. "It went well enough. He wanted to check on how his treatment was working." He lifted a finger toward his eyepatch.

Morning Fawn crumpled her napkin. She wouldn't believe he'd gone there to just see Dr. Schramm. Her gaze darted away from his. Jealous? As she had been in Alleyton? The steady pump of his heart thrummed harder. She wasn't indifferent to him, despite Moyer's elaborate gift.

"I suppose you'll have to go back for more treatments." Thea smirked.

Could he strangle the woman here and now? Did she know about Frieda, or had she merely picked up on Morning Fawn's displeasure? "I prefer not to discuss my wound at dinner, Miss LeBeau." His voice cut sharp. "I believe your father and I were discussing horses."

"Of course. Please pardon my daughter, sir." LeBeau dabbed

his mustache with a napkin. "Now where were we? Lightning..."

Devon stirred his fork in his sweet potatoes as he half listened. He'd steered clear of Morning Fawn ever since she'd sat beside him at church four days ago. But he'd relived those moments beside her in the pew at least a dozen times since Sunday. Then, today in the barn, he started digging memories out of the dungeon of his heart. Getting all googly-eyed because Morning Fawn showed him a scrap of attention. He had no business stirring up feelings there wasn't time or place for.

A wise man would snuff out the sparks.

He touched a hand to his sternum where beneath layers of linen Isabelle's locket pressed against his flesh. Would the day come when it would be time to tuck the treasure away in a trunk instead of wearing it on his person?

Devon excused himself before dessert, but instead of heading upstairs where he should work on details for his mission, he drifted to the front door. A starlit night greeted him as he stood in the open doorway. A slight chill shimmered the leaves. A perfect evening for a walk. He lingered on the threshold. He didn't want to think about why. But when Morning Fawn's step sounded in the hall, he sucked in a breath, and when her foot struck the bottom stair to go up, he turned. "We could get some fresh air." Stupid line.

She halted. "I suppose so. I'd have to fetch my shawl."

"I don't know about that. What if you don't make it back down?"

A smile tugged at her lips. "Well, I guess you'll have to wait and see." She tossed her hair back and sashayed up the stairs as if she knew he was going to watch the minute detail of her every move.

And he did.

CHAPTER 18

Morning Fawn slowed her steps on the bottom flight of stairs. Her red shawl hung over her arm. Per instructions of Lucy, she was to have Devon drape it over her shoulders.

Devon looked up at her as he had the night Nicholas came to dinner. However, this time, she was coming down just for him. But had any other audience mattered since he showed up at the house?

He sucked in a breath and tugged on the lapels of his frock coat. A wide smile crossed his lips.

"I need help." She pushed the shawl toward him and turned her back to him.

"I can't leave a lady in distress." His fingers skimmed her shoulders as he draped the red spun wool around her, slipping the material beneath her hair. Goosebumps.

The dining room door clicked.

"Come on." He touched her elbow and hurried her out before they could be accosted by the LeBeaus.

As they stepped off the porch, she curled her fingers around his steady arm, his muscles firm beneath his coat sleeve. A tingle wove its way through her.

Just like— No. She wasn't going to think of *Pride and Prejudice* or *Jane Eyre*. This wasn't a romance novel. Devon had no vast estate, and thank goodness, he didn't have a wife hidden in the attic. They were merely going on a walk. But the way her pulse pounded in her ears, her heart hadn't gotten the message.

Down the moonlit path, they strolled. Banjo music drifted up from the slave quarter. The scent of soap and bay rum caught her nostrils, with only a touch of horse. Devon had washed up before dinner. For her?

A whip-poor-will called from a branch as they drifted through the grove of pecan trees making small talk.

On the porch, a door swung shut. Morning Fawn resisted the urge to turn and look. Why couldn't those people leave her be?

Devon whispered, "We'd best not wander any farther from the path, or someone might come join us."

"Last thing I'd want." Pecan shells crunched beneath her shoes.

In a shadowed area next to the main lane, Devon stopped and gazed upward. "So many stars."

A twinkling canopy of lights lit the heavens.

"You can see even more in Palo Duro or the Llano Escatado." She clutched her shawl. The memory hitched her heart. The closest thing she had to a real home, and here she was half smitten with the man who'd taken her away from it all.

He dropped his gaze, his voice thick with emotion. "I'm sorry."

So much gentler now than the first time he'd spoken to her. "About what?" How could this be the same man who'd stuck a gag in her mouth and jerked her hands behind her back?

"Taking you from your home. The rough treatment. Everything." He shifted his arm from her touch and stuffed his hands into his pockets.

She had sworn at him. Called him a weasel warrior, a dog, and worse. Now, different words came out of her mouth. "You had your reasons." She glanced down at his boots. He'd protected her from the others. Given her as much kindness as he could without allowing her to escape. And goodness knows, she'd tried several times. Almost got them killed.

"Land and avoiding conscription." He exhaled and shoved his fingers through his hair. "Plus, I figured I was helping you."

Helping her? Yes, most people would see it that way. The truth bubbled out. "I was so angry at first, I could have put a knife in you if I'd had one. Later, I decided my uncle was the real devil, and you were just a hired bandit."

He winced. "And now? Or do I even want to know?"

Now? Her heart swelled with admiration and respect. "I think differently." She pulled her shawl snug and swayed a step closer. "I saw what you did for Lucy. And I haven't forgotten those two empty nail holes in my window sill." Her voice lilted.

"So you do remember." The tension drained from his face.

She'd best change the subject before every thought spilled from her head. Land. "You said you needed money for land? Did your stepfather take away your inheritance?" The question was out before she could stop it.

His eyebrows arched. "You'd better watch out, or Pinkerton will come draft you into his service."

"Who's Pinkerton?"

"Runs a detective agency up North. I hear he's the best."

She blinked wide. Interesting that he'd come up with such an example.

"What?" He shot her a puzzled look.

She scrambled for a reply. "I was wondering... You considered paying for a substitute to avoid conscription yet volunteered in the end? Even though you disapprove of slavery?"

"Shhhh." He placed his finger to his lips. "Not a sentiment to spread far and wide."

"I'd never say anything to endanger you," she whispered. There she went again, sounding like some maiden who'd never been out of a tipi before.

He scuffed his boot against the dirt. "I enlisted because I care about Texas. I figured it wasn't right of me to avoid the fight while so many were giving their all." He cleared his throat. "And after I'd hauled you to Fort Belknap against your will, you fighting me every mile of the way, I decided I'd had enough of hiring out as a scout."

"You quit because of me?"

He shrugged.

"Maybe I was too tough to handle?"

The corners of his mouth lifted. "I don't shy away from challenges." His tone lightened, but his eye spoke something different. Regret? Guilt? Was that the reason he was here walking with her now? Was he merely making amends?

Silence dropped around them. She fiddled with the fringe on her shawl, softer but similar to the fringe of the doeskin blouse she used to wear.

Devon scrubbed his hand over his bearded jaw. "I didn't intend to bring all of this up tonight. But I want you to know that sooner or later, I'll get you out of here if that's what you want. You don't have to put up with Moyer for a piece of land."

"But what if I like the idea of owning land?"

He bristled. "I reckon you already have won a horse. The land shouldn't be far behind."

Her stupid mouth, only speaking half a thought. "The way menfolk behave, I'd almost rather be a spinster and have the land all to myself to do as I please."

He kicked a pecan. "Mighty lonely sitting on a piece of dirt all by yourself, but that'd be better than sitting on it a lifetime with someone you don't care for." He turned as if he would leave.

Moisture sprang to her eyes. She grabbed his sleeve. "Don't go."

He glanced at her hand.

Cheeks aflame, she withdrew her touch. Why couldn't she do anything right?

"Maybe we should talk about something else." He offered his arm to her.

She slipped her fingers around his elbow. Why couldn't she have the land *and* the man she wanted? The rules didn't say it had to be Moyer. She gazed at the sky. "What do you know about stars?"

His arm relaxed beneath her hold. "I used to study them as a boy." His voice took on a whimsical note. "When I was seven, my pa acquired a piece of land just west of Dallas. Barely inside the settlement line at the time. I had a friend, more like an uncle. He was Kiowa. Worked for my pa. Taught me how to hunt and track, how to go through the woods without a sound. He was better than kin. But you probably know as much as I do about the stars."

"I do not. I used to love to lie out on the grass outside the tipi on hot summer nights and study them, but I know nothing of what *you* call them."

He pointed overhead. "I'm sure you know the North Star. Part of the Little Dipper."

She nodded.

"And then the Big Dipper closer to the horizon. And you see those three there." He leaned closer. The folds of her skirt lapped against his trouser leg. "That's Orion's belt."

Who was Orion? She didn't care.

He stopped talking as they gazed heavenward, his breathing punctuating the darkness. "Would you like to sit?" He nodded to the low stone wall next to an ancient oak, its weathered trunk witness to the days when no white foot had touched the soil above its roots.

"Yes." Her heart thudded.

He guided her to the wall, but she pushed herself up on it before he could assist. Cool stone met her palms as she gathered her skirts beneath her. He settled down beside her and removed his slouch hat. A canopy of leaves sheltered them from prying eyes on the porch.

Across the fields, a cow mooed. Such a minor creature compared to a buffalo, the lifeblood of her people. Her people? Where did she really belong in this vast universe?

"Tell me about your Kiowa friend. What was his name?" She leaned her head against the tree, mere inches from his.

"*Sate. Bear* in English." His voice wrapped around her like a blanket as he told her of his childhood adventures—treeing a coon, his first deer, a narrow escape from a bear, the anticipation of his first buffalo hunt...

"You never got to go?"

"No." He exhaled. "Things changed."

How? Why? His father's death? She pressed her lips together.

He shifted his weight on the wall. "Enough about me."

His next words might be that it was time to go in. She wasn't about to let that happen. "Maybe you can take me hunting sometime."

"Hunting?"

"Yes." She kicked her feet from beneath her skirt. "I'm tired of wrenching my feet into these hard-soled traps. I'd love to have a pair of moccasins."

"That would go over well with your uncle."

"I don't care. Besides, how much attention does he pay to what's on my feet?"

"I could hunt and bring you back a hide."

"No. I want to go." She snuggled closer to his arm. "I'm

pretty good at it, at least with a bow and arrow. And it'd give me a chance to get away from Sweet Briar. To be free—"

"Can't have you running off." His tone took on a hint of a scold.

"I wouldn't think of it. It would be a pleasure to escape the plantation for a little while." And to be with him.

"I took you to Columbus a couple weeks ago with your aunt." Thank goodness, he had the grace to not mention the ride she'd had with Nicholas on Saturday.

"Scruffy little clapboard towns don't compare to the prairies. And I've never been hunting in the woods, or a swamp. There's all kinds of places to explore." She shifted toward him. Her knee bumped his thigh. She startled and moved to scoot back, half slipping off the wall. A couple of loose crumbles of rock broke off.

He grabbed her shoulder. "Wouldn't want you to fall."

A whole foot to the ground from where her feet dangled? But he could leave his hand there as long as he wanted.

Their gazes met. Moonlight shimmered in his eye. Steady jaw. Firm lips.

His hand dropped away, and he settled back against the tree. "I could teach you how to shoot a rifle."

She pressed her heels against the stone to keep from sliding down. "I don't know. I'd have a better chance at beating you with a bow and arrow."

He chuckled. "So it's a competition?"

She bit her lip and clasped her hands in her lap. "You can teach me to shoot." Much cozier.

The breeze caught a strand of hair and dangled it across her eyes. She blinked and lifted her hand, but Devon was quicker. With the slightest touch of a knuckle, he nudged it from her face.

Her lips parted.

His gaze dipped to them before quickly darting away. "A rifle it will be, then, but there's also the matter of your uncle."

"My uncle."

"After my confession about Lucy, he's convinced I'm a scoundrel. He might not allow me to take you away from the perimeter of the house without a chaperone."

"I could sneak out. Make up a story."

"I don't want to get you in trouble."

"You've caused me trouble ever since I met you." But she couldn't hide the warmth that crept into her voice. "Some things are worth trouble." Oh, my goodness. She might as well just lay herself at his feet, the way she was talking. She'd done so well at dinner with holding her tongue, but now...

"I think you're plenty trouble too." He smiled. "*Taa Aruka.*" *Morning Fawn.*

Her heart fluttered. "How do you know how to say my name in Comanche?"

"I'd rather not remind you of how I know."

The kidnapping. Her stomach knotted, at war with her heart. But he regretted his actions and changed his life. Volunteered to fight. Probably lost sight in his eye because of it.

He exhaled and fumbled with his hat in his lap.

She bit her lip. "I still like it when you say it." Oh my goodness. She squeezed her eyes shut. Couldn't she shut her mouth as well? She shivered.

"Are you cold?" He reached for her hand and tucked it inside the crook of his arm once more, pressing it to his side and laying his hand over hers.

She should have worn gloves. Her aunt had scolded her many times about that. But the feel of Devon's rough, callused palm suited her just fine.

She leaned against the oak and looked to the heavens. If only she could freeze this moment in time. She'd searched so long for the place where she belonged. What if it was at the side of this man? "Tell me more about the stars."

Devon leaned back as well. "'He healeth those that are broken in heart, and bindeth up their sores. He counteth the number of the stars, *and* calleth them all by their names. Great *is* our Lord, and great *is his* power: his wisdom is infinite.'"

"What is that?"

"It's from the Bible. Psalms 147. Talks about how the Lord heals the brokenhearted."

Was she the brokenhearted, or was he?

The warmth of his hand penetrated hers. "It also talks about how He knows each star, like jewels from his hands scattered across the sky."

"Sounds like poetry."

"I suppose so. And that's what Psalms is. But it's more than that. It's truth. From the God who created the universe."

Goosebumps prickled her arms. She bit her lip, then whispered, "I've seen you at the dinner table. You really pray, don't you?"

He tilted his face toward her. "Yes. Don't you?"

She shrugged. "Sometimes, I guess. I mean, it's kind of like seeing someone you know for the first time in a long while. You don't quite know what to say to them."

"The Lord wants you to talk to Him, Morning Fawn. Tell Him what's on your heart."

That's what her mother had spoken about as she'd brushed Morning Fawn's hair and tucked her in. Morning Fawn couldn't remember her face, only the portrait in LeBeau's office, but her voice still rang in Morning Fawn's ears, so comforting, so sweet. Gone forever from this world.

Morning Fawn shivered. "Please, let's not talk about my mother anymore."

"I didn't know that we were." His eyebrows quirked upward.

"Yes, in a roundabout way." Sweat broke out on the back of her neck. "Please."

"Of course." He turned back to the stars, speaking of the wonders of the sky as his thumb moved back and forth across her hand, sending tingles up and down her arms.

Her heart settled onto a certainty. This was the man she wanted to marry. *God of the heavens, if You hear me, please let it be so.*

CHAPTER 19

The moon had passed its meridian, and wispy fingers of clouds covered some of the stars by the time Devon walked Morning Fawn to the porch steps. Her scent of rosewater and citrus filled his nostrils and permeated his thoughts. Sitting so close to her on the wall that a wave of her hair lapped against his shoulder, and her hand lying supple beneath his, warming him to his core, he'd lost track of time. It'd been all he could do to not touch his lips to her brow.

His legs, everything about him, wobbled. How could the lady at his side be the same woman he'd yanked off a horse and wrestled to the ground only three weeks before? He was in trouble in more ways than he could count. If they were in Brownsville, within the Yankee lines and his mission done, and no scoundrel trying to weasel in on his girl with black mustangs, that'd be a different story, but...

The front door swung open as they stepped onto the porch. LeBeau stood in the entryway, against the glow of the hallway lamps. Light bled through the tall curtained windows that flanked the door on either side, like sentinels.

Morning Fawn tensed.

Devon lowered his mouth close to her ear. "Whatever he says, leave it to me. You go to your room, and I'll see you tomorrow."

She frowned and slipped her hand from Devon's arm.

LeBeau snapped his pocket watch shut. He'd discarded his frock coat and cravat. His Adam's apple bulged above his loosened collar. "Get up to your room, young lady." His voice came out a tired grumble.

She skirted past him and headed for the stairs.

Devon removed his slouch hat and stepped inside. He braced himself against the onslaught of LeBeau's scowl. Seconds ticked away.

Morning Fawn's footfalls reached the landing and proceeded up the second flight.

Devon exhaled. "I apologize for the late hour, sir. We were only talking. In the view of the house the whole time."

"I know what you were doing. I've been watching." LeBeau tugged on his half-buttoned waistcoat. The tail ends flapped against the slight paunch of his belly. "Only, there's a good amount of trouble that can be hatched beyond the purview of the naked eye."

How was he supposed to answer that? Devon crumpled his hat brim. "My intentions are honorable, sir."

Lebeau sputtered out a half laugh. "We saw how honorable your intentions were last Saturday night, Reynolds."

Devon ground his teeth. Mighty fine how this man sought to blacken him with crimes he, himself, was likely guilty of. But he couldn't dispute the remark without stirring up a heap of trouble for Ned and Lucy.

LeBeau threw back his shoulders. "My niece is a whole different matter than one of my slaves. I don't care how many savages she tramped around with, I expect you to treat Beth as a lady."

Devon narrowed his eye. "I don't believe Mor—Miss Beth

has ever tramped around with anyone." His fingers curled into fists at his sides. "She is a lady of honor, and I have the utmost respect for her."

LeBeau quirked his eyebrows. "Is that so?" He smoothed his fingers over his straight handlebar mustache and long-whiskered chin. His gaze scoured Devon from head to toe. "We'll finish this discussion in the library."

What now? The man had better not dredge up anything to impugn Morning Fawn's character. Devon trailed behind him, leaving the door to the room open until LeBeau lit the lamp. The flame leaped to life within the glass globe, casting shadows against the drawn curtains and wallpaper.

LeBeau moved behind his desk and plucked a cigar from his cedar humidor. "Care for one?"

"No, thank you, sir." Devon closed the door and settled onto the edge of the cushioned high-back chair in front of the desk, not certain whether he was in for an interrogation, a negotiation, or something in between.

LeBeau removed the lamp globe and lit his cigar before taking a seat in his leather-padded chair. The framed image of his sister, Morning Fawn's mother, hung on the wall behind him. Dark-haired and pretty, she appeared to be mild-mannered, but there must be spunk that lurked somewhere in those pale eyes. She'd defied the LeBeau family and set an example for her daughters, choosing her heart over tradition, protocol, and wealth, or so Devon had heard.

The mantel clock chimed once. Twelve-thirty or one o'clock? It had to be somewhere in there. No wonder the man was so displeased. Devon held his fingers stiff on his hat, resisting the urge to crumple the brim.

LeBeau inhaled, then blew out a ring of smoke as he withdrew the cigar. The woody aroma wafted across the desk. "Tell me, Reynolds. What are your intentions toward my niece?"

Devon blinked at him. How was he supposed to answer that when he had no clue? "To treat her with respect and honor."

"Beyond that. We already covered that ground." LeBeau drew hard on the cigar.

"I'm still figuring out my intentions, sir."

LeBeau's gaze measured him as if he were some accounting ledger to be deciphered. "Let me know when you do. Until then, I'll continue to allow Nicholas to call."

Devon sat up straight. "That man—"

"That man has declared his intentions."

Devon gripped the chair arms. "That man doesn't care about her."

"And you do?"

Devon's jaw clenched. He couldn't declare intentions toward Morning Fawn, not when he was supposed to maintain a pretense of courting Frieda. "There's a place in this world for friendship, Mr. LeBeau. I very much care for your niece's well-being."

"What I saw in the shadows from the porch this evening didn't look like friendship to me."

"I was every bit the gentleman this evening."

"Didn't say you weren't. I'm concerned about what comes next."

Devon leaned forward. "I'll continue to be a gentleman where Morning Fawn is concerned—tomorrow, next week, next month, as long as she is in my acquaintance."

"Morning Fawn?" LeBeau's lip curled. "You can't even remember her correct name. And my niece doesn't have a year or two to spend in friendships and acquaintances. She needs a husband this season. I don't intend to stand by and allow her to jeopardize a serious courtship for someone who can't make up his mind."

"Your niece deserves an opportunity to wait and find the man she wants to spend the rest of her life with."

"Are you offering a proposal, Reynolds? Or at least a courtship?"

Devon blew out a breath. "I told you before about my wife. I'm not ready to marry again."

"Suit yourself." LeBeau clumped his forearms on the desktop. "When you're ready to declare your plans toward Beth, let me know. And when that day comes, I'll ask you to send for references and proof that you can adequately support her."

"References? You know me. You hired me. Twice. And I've done fine work for you."

"That's true. You have, but hiring a man to do a job and considering that man as a potential husband for my niece are two different things."

"A couple of weeks ago, you practically invited me to court your niece."

"Yes. But you declined. Other contenders entered into the picture, one with thousands of acres and a bright future."

How bright could a man's future be if he was so puffed up his head might float away? "Your niece needs a man of honor who will love her and care for her as she deserves. Moyer's first love is himself."

LeBeau snorted. "We'll see who crosses the finish line, Lieutenant."

Devon's hands clenched and unclenched as he marched up the stairs. If it wasn't for Morning Fawn, he'd grab his gear and sleep in the stables rather than spend another night under this man's roof. No, the stables wouldn't be far enough. He'd clear off the man's property completely.

In the privacy of his own room, Devon threw his hat on the floor and drove his fingers through his hair. The nerve of that man, questioning whether he was good enough for Morning Fawn. Asking for references. References from his home county. That'd be enough to get him treed as a spy. His stepfather and others were not ignorant of his Unionist views.

Even if it wasn't for the sham courtship with Frieda, he couldn't declare intentions toward Morning Fawn. Couldn't risk LeBeau having him investigated. Not until the mission was over. Not until the whole war had been won, unless he could get Morning Fawn out of here.

Would there ever be a time and place for a courtship with her?

He'd never be able to compete with Moyer in LeBeau's eyes. He didn't own an inch of land at the moment. In regard to Morning Fawn's dreams of those acres in Parker County? Devon was about as far as she could get from finding a loyal Confederate.

No more evening strolls. LeBeau had made that clear. No more unaccompanied anything, not until he petitioned to court her. If Devon violated the rule, the man would likely bolt her door shut or kick him off the premises.

~

Two days of silence. Morning Fawn couldn't tolerate another morning of it. She threw off the covers and shuffled over to the window. The gray of dawn hovered across the sky. A trickle of orange edged above the horizon, blurred by a curtain of light mist that enveloped the yard and beyond. This was her chance. Devon was an early riser. Her relatives were not—at least, not in winter.

She grabbed her green wool dress and tugged it over her head, thankful for the protection against the chill that pervaded her room. Devon would be at the stables. Grabbing her shoes, she slipped out of her room, tiptoed down the stairs, and headed for the back door.

Pans clanked, and the sweet scent of freshly baked bread wafted from the detached kitchen, but she didn't dare stop for a bite.

The light frost stung her stockinged feet as she pattered across dried grass and pebbles. The soap vats lay idle. She sat down on an upturned barrel by the smokehouse and wiggled on her shoes. The warmth of two days ago had vanished. She shivered. She should have grabbed a coat or at least a shawl, but she wasn't about to turn back now.

Morning Fawn entered the stables through the side, out of view of the house, in case someone was watching. The worn wooden door creaked as she opened it. Voices hushed. Dressed in his lieutenant's uniform, Devon squatted in the open grooming area, giving Ginger's cinch belt one last tug. His eye widened as he pivoted. "Morning Fawn?" He lost his balance, dropping to one knee.

George paused in the middle of mucking out a stall, and the boy Oliver swayed from the weight of two feed buckets, one in each hand.

Devon nodded to George. "Could you give us a few minutes?"

"Yes, sir. We'll take a couple of these beauties out for some fresh air." He leaned his pitchfork against a pole and slipped a halter over a quarter horse's head. "Come on, Ollie. Set one of those buckets down and bring Prince out for a walk."

Benson, the hound dog, loped out of an empty stall and followed along after them.

Ebony lifted her head over the stall door and stared. Morning Fawn's fingers twitched to stroke the beauty's mane. Instead, she clasped her hands and waited.

Cavalry boots hugging his lower legs, Devon looped the strap through the saddle ring and then slowly pivoted toward her when the back stable door swung closed. His cartridge belt and holster hung low on his hips. He was going somewhere.

Where?

His hands dropped to his sides as his gaze drank her in. A smile vanquished his frown. "You were in a hurry?"

Morning Fawn touched a hand to her hair. My goodness, she hadn't even brushed it. It hung loose over her shoulders and down her back. "I didn't want to wait around for my relatives to crawl out of bed." She smoothed her hand over her waves.

"Don't worry about it." He drifted a step closer. A red linen shirt showed beneath his unbuttoned shell jacket. "You look mighty fine."

She crossed her arms, but that didn't stop the flutter in her stomach or the wobble in her knees. "Where have you been?"

The crinkles at the corner of his eye deepened as he glanced at her shoulders. "Is your dress buttoned all of the way?"

"What?" Her face heated like a kettle on a stovetop. She reached up and around. Her collar dropped away from her neck. How in the world could she have forgotten the last three buttons?

"Turn around. I'll see what I can do."

"I don't need your help."

He cocked his eyebrows as if to say differently. "Should I close my eyes while you take care of the problem?"

Her hands were shaking so much, she'd never manage the buttons. "No. Fix it. And behave yourself." She turned her back to him.

Her breath caught as he lifted waves of hair and gently laid them on her shoulder. His hand paused ever so lightly there before continuing with the task. He tugged the two sides of the dress together and buttoned the garment.

The collar tightened snugly around her throat. Did she imagine it, or did his fingers tremble? Her thoughts scattered.

"I'm sorry I've made myself scarce these last couple of days." He stepped back toward Ginger.

"Why have you?" She bit her lip.

"Your uncle thought it best." He picked up the loose end of the strap and looped it through the ring two more times.

"I figured he had something to do with it. What did he say?"

Devon flipped the left stirrup down from atop the saddle. Bits of straw clung to his trouser knees.

Ginger shifted her head toward Morning Fawn and nuzzled. Morning Fawn rubbed the mare's forehead before moving on to stroke her neck. "What did he say?"

Devon snagged a bridle from a hook and walked over. "He ordered me to stay away from you."

Her mouth dropped. "Why? Surely, he doesn't think you did anything ungentlemanly on our walk. I could talk to him. I could tell him."

"It's not that."

"Then what is it? He's the one who wanted me to find—" She pressed her lips shut. A husband. For land. But land had nothing to do with their walk or the tremble in her voice now.

"A potential groom?" He finished her sentence for her. The bridle dangled in his hand.

She blinked at him. "Yes. But that's not why..."

He studied her face as if he wasn't convinced. Why did her uncle have to invent the whole land deal?

"What does that have to do with us going for a stroll?" she asked.

He shifted into motion, drawing the mare's muzzle through the noseband and laying the headstall against her forehead as he situated the bit.

Morning Fawn bit her lip. Wasn't he going to answer?

The crinkles at the corners of his eyes deepened as he poked Ginger's ears inside the top of the bridle. "Your uncle wants me to either declare my intentions to court you or to stay away from you." His words rang with finality.

"Oh."

"I'm not ready to consider marrying, Morning Fawn."

"I never suggested it."

A loose lock of hair slipped to Devon's forehead, and he shoved it back. "Your uncle did."

Why couldn't her uncle keep his mouth shut?

Devon secured the latch beneath the horse's throat, paying more attention to the animal than her. "I can't make any commitments at the present."

"I'm not asking you to. It doesn't matter what my uncle said." For goodness' sakes, she wasn't going to beg the man. Hadn't she told him she'd just as soon be a spinster? Her gaze fell on the back stall. Ebony waited there, neglected. "What's wrong with two friends or acquaintances going on a walk together?" Best use the word *friends* rather than those going through her heart. No need to scare him clear back to Dallas.

"I said the same thing to your uncle."

"And?"

"He said no."

"You're going to take no as an answer?" If the other evening meant something to him, why wasn't he willing to fight for it? "We don't have to listen to my uncle. I could sneak out for a stroll now and then."

Devon scrubbed a hand over his face. "My goal is to find a way to get you out of here eventually. Crossing your uncle now will only make that more difficult."

"And what happens when you do rescue me?"

His brow furrowed. "I'll get you to some friends of mine. They'll hide you, give you a place to stay, until you figure out what you want to do."

"And what about you?"

"I'm a soldier. I have commitments until the war ends."

Why should she expect anything different? He'd help her escape because he felt guilty, but he wouldn't be with her. She jabbed a hand to her hip. "So the stroll the other night ...was just another Saturday evening? After you've done your duty by me, you'll find another girl to walk with?" Probably wouldn't even wait that long.

He scuffed his boot against the straw-peppered dirt. "You're the most contrary girl I ever met, and the most forward."

"I am not forward." She snatched his slouch hat from a railing and aimed it toward a pile of manure. Blowing out a breath, she tossed it at his feet instead. "Forget I said anything. I don't want to take up your time, and I don't want any more of your help." Her gaze settled on Ebony. "It's Saturday. Nicholas is coming to dinner again tonight."

He picked up his hat and dusted it off. "Thanks for the warning. I'll make sure not to hurry back."

"You're going to Alleyton again, aren't you?"

"I'm sure you'll be too busy with Nicholas to care. Before you know it, it'll be Nick."

"Fit right in with Frieda." She hadn't come out here to fight. How had this conversation gone so wrong?

"Well, a glass of lemonade hardly equals a horse."

"Speaking of horses, I've been neglecting mine." She pushed past him, grabbed a curry brush, and headed to the back of the stable.

"At least you're finally ending the charade that the mustang is only on loan."

Halfway down the aisle, she pivoted toward her accuser. "I don't know what *charade* means."

"Ask Nick. I'm sure he's master of them." He gripped the saddle horn, stuck his left foot in the stirrup, and swung his right leg over. "And if you don't watch it, he'll try to be master of you."

"No one's going to be master of me."

He blew out a breath. "We'll see about that." He gathered his reins. "If the cook asks, I may not be back until morning."

"Morning?" Her hands dropped to her sides. He was going to be gone all night?

"I've got business in town, then a card game. Might go late."

"I didn't know Frieda played cards."

"It's nothing to do with Frieda."

"I could care less." She jutted out her chin. "If you show up at church tomorrow, I'll walk by as if I don't even know you."

"That's fine by me." He flicked the reins. "I bet Nick Moyer doesn't even know what the inside of a church looks like."

Air whistled through her clenched teeth like a tea kettle as he rode out of the stable. Infuriating man. He could stay gone as far as she was concerned.

CHAPTER 20

$\mathcal{A}$ late-afternoon rain spoiled any hope for a ride. Not that Morning Fawn wanted to spend an hour trotting around the countryside with Nicholas, but she would have endured it for the sake of getting away from the house. At least she wouldn't have had to worry about doing any of the talking.

Nicholas. The word didn't sit right on her tongue even though he insisted she drop the formality of *Mr. Moyer.*

Dinner was a miserable affair. She picked at her food and ignored her aunt's prodding to join in the conversation. No matter—Thea reigned supreme. She flirted with Mr. Howard and Nicholas and still managed to take more stabs at Devon's absence than she did at her beefsteak.

After the meal, Morning Fawn rose and headed for the hall. She was in no mood for a walk even if the rain had stopped. How had she and Devon gotten into such a terrible argument this morning? She'd gone to the stable with good intentions, and he'd seemed genuinely glad to see her. He said she was forward. But she wasn't the one who brought up marriage. That was her uncle, and goodness knows, she couldn't control that man. Besides, if Devon Reynolds was so set on nothing but friendship, why did he look like he'd swallowed a lemon every time he saw her even glance at Ebony?

As Morning Fawn neared the stairs, she slipped her finger beneath the lace fichu that covered her cleavage and shoulders. When she got to her room, she would yank the itchy thing off and stuff it in the bottom of her trunk.

"My lady." Nicholas stepped up behind her and touched her elbow. "Why don't we take a stroll through the garden? It's a little chilly out, but I'm sure a heavy shawl would suffice."

Did *suffice* mean be enough? It didn't matter. She clasped her hands tight against her waist. "I'm sorry. Another evening. I have a headache." She'd heard that excuse plenty of times from Thea when there was work to be done.

"I wager fresh air would go a long way toward helping you feel better."

"I'm afraid I'm not up to it this evening." Couldn't the man take no for an answer? "Perhaps you and Mr. Howard could both accompany my cousin."

Nicholas's mustache twitched as he moved in closer. The coconut scent of his hair tonic flooded her nostrils. "No offense to your cousin, Miss Beth, but you are the lady I ride two hours to visit." He took her hand. "It's your presence I covet."

"Please let go of my hand, sir." She tugged herself free.

"I beg your pardon, Beth." His brown eyes simmered like coffee. Annoyance or desire? He was unreadable beneath his polished front. "I apologize for my forwardness."

Forwardness. Like her this morning? Definitely not the same.

"If you're not up for a walk, we could join your family in the parlor. Or if you prefer, we could check on Ebony. I stopped by there when I first arrived, and she whispered she felt neglected this week and is in need of a gentle hand."

She narrowed her eyes at him. "I never neglect a horse."

"I'm sure you do not, but perhaps you haven't doted on her

as you might..." He traced the engraved knob on the bannister. "If it weren't for the scowls from a particular plantation hand."

The nerve of the man. Was the whole house full of spies? "I have a headache. If you're worried about how I care for Ebony, you're welcome to take her ba—"

"Beth will be happy to join us in the parlor." Her uncle tapped his walking stick to the floor as he sauntered past with Aunt Julia on his arm. How long had he been hovering?

Shoulders back, she marched ahead into the parlor, not about to give Moyer a chance to scoop her hand to his elbow. She headed for the velvet parlor chair, but...her step slowed. Devon had been preparing to leave for Alleyton *even before* they'd argued. Not just a little visit, but an all-day-long, into the evening, and possibly the next morning visit. Did he really expect her to believe it had nothing to do with Frieda?

She turned toward the low-back wine-colored sofa. It was time for Devon Reynolds to hear a different story. Thea could be counted on to spill the juicy details of the whole evening to anyone who would listen

"Pardon me." When she barely missed his toe, Nicholas stepped aside and opened his arms wide, offering her first choice of where to sit.

She planted herself next to the end. That'd save her from being pinned in on the other side by Mr. Howard.

Nicholas smiled and sat beside her.

She scooped her red plaid skirt hard against her side lest an article of her clothing lap against his finely tailored gray wool suit.

He leaned back and hooked his thumb in his watch pocket. His voice purred like the river. "I meant no insult there in the hallway. You did a masterful job of handling Ebony last Saturday. You have a way with horses, Beth, a firm but gentle touch."

She crossed her arms. "Thank you. You may call me 'Miss Beth.'"

"But surely, at this point in our courtship—"

"Acquaintanceship."

"Hmmm." He leaned closer and whispered, "You should know, *Miss Beth*, that I am a man greatly smitten, and I plan to lay siege against all fortifications."

She rolled her eyes. The smell of coconut and cigar filled her nostrils once more. Couldn't he stay on his section of the sofa? She shifted closer to the side. "*You* should know, I'm skilled at archery."

"We shall see." He chuckled and leaned back. "Before dinner, I spoke with your uncle about me taking you on a real ride next Saturday, not a little trot around the plantation. I have an American saddlebred I'd like to try out, and it'd give you a perfect opportunity to see what Ebony is made of. We'd make an afternoon of it."

"I have no idea whether I'll be available next Saturday or not." She'd be more than happy to ride as far as she could from Sweet Briar, if only it didn't come at the price of his company.

"I pray you'll be able to spare a couple of hours for Cinnamon's sake. I'm quite lost when it comes to her willful spirit."

Were they still talking about the horse?

Thea sat down on the piano stool and opened the music sheets. "I'll start with...."

Morning Fawn shifted in her seat and, for once, gave Thea at least the appearance of her undivided attention.

Nicholas stretched his hand across the back of the sofa and whispered, "We'd make a race of it if—"

Morning Fawn waved her hand to hush him and pointed to the piano. Music flowed from the instrument as Thea's fingers alternately pounded and swept the keys. Eight o'clock and Devon wasn't home yet. A lonesome wind rattled the windows. Was he headed back in the dark—or sitting on Frieda's sofa? Or was he playing cards in some smoky saloon? Drinking and gambling all night long, too drunk to travel home? That didn't sound like the man she knew. But how much did she really know?

Too many questions.

As soon as the music ended, she excused herself and headed for the stairs, but Nicholas, quick on the draw, caught her by the elbow. "A word, Miss Beth." He motioned toward the front door. "We'll only step out onto the porch for a moment or two. I promise not to keep you."

Tension knotted her shoulders, but she followed him into the damp night air. Lights from the hallway flowed onto the porch through the tall, narrow windows that flanked the door.

As soon as it closed, Nicholas turned to face her. "I was right about one thing I said in the hallway. It's that lieutenant, isn't it?" He tugged on the lapels of his frock coat. "Your kidnapper has become your hero?"

The nerve of the man. She crossed her arms. "The lieutenant is none of your concern."

He hooked his thumbs around his suspenders, beneath the straight bottom edge of his waistcoat. "I've got half a mind to investigate him."

She gaped. "And what would you investigate? I'm sure my uncle checked his references before he hired him to look for me. And as for his character—"

"To be frank with you, Beth, I question why he's here. He's in no hurry to return to his regiment, taking the long way around to do it, coming all the way back here to Texas from Mississippi where he was supposedly captured."

"I'm sure he gave his word to the Yankees he wouldn't return to fighting—at least, not right away. I've heard that's how prisoner exchanges work. And as for the rest, he's been waiting for his eye to heal."

"You're certainly ready to defend him, aren't you?" A cool smile crept across his lips.

"I don't like to see anyone bad-mouthed unless they deserve it."

"Well, that's the question, isn't it?"

"What?"

"Does he deserve it?"

She narrowed her eyes. "Investigate all you like. But something written on a piece of paper about how many days he's been absent from his regiment won't win you any gratitude from me, or strolls either." She gathered her skirts and pivoted toward the heavy oak door.

"What would win your gratitude, Miss Beth?"

She turned and nailed him with a glare. "Nothing I can think of at the moment."

"Think about that piece of empty land in Parker County. If that man is a shirker, a deserter, what does that say about his character? And the fact that he was so desperate for money that he hired out to kidnap you and tear you from your home? One might wonder if he had to kill anyone to get in and out of Comanche territory alive. What else might he do for money? And what makes you think he has the wherewithal to build you a house or a ranch on that land, or anything else, for that matter? A drifter is a drifter. No settling down."

"You've given it so much thought, Mr. Moyer, why don't you talk with Reynolds and ask him yourself? As for my part, just because I turned you down for a walk doesn't mean I'm ready to beg another man for a proposal."

"I'm glad to hear it, Miss Beth. The man isn't worthy of you." He stuck out his chest. "I'd love to have another opportunity to deepen our acquaintance. There's a ball coming up at Robson's castle Christmas Eve. I'd enjoy the pleasure of your company."

Her brow furrowed. "I don't care for balls." Not that she'd ever been to one, but if it meant hanging on his arm for the whole evening, she wanted nothing to do with it. She grabbed the door and hurried in.

Was there any truth to Nicholas's accusations? What else had Devon done?

She wouldn't think on it. She'd seen the man pray. She knew his character. Didn't she?

Cold and stiff, Devon made his way through the back alleyways and side streets to the Schramms' home. A sleepless night spent watching the shift changes of the troops guarding the quartermaster depot and the cotton warehouse had taken its toll.

How could he have left things in such a mess with Morning Fawn? As soon as she'd glanced at that mustang, his temper had snapped. She'd hurried out to the stables to see him, hair unbrushed, dress not quite buttoned all the way. Maybe she'd done that on purpose. No, absolutely not. Thea or some other woman might do that to get a man's interest and hands on them, but not Morning Fawn.

Couldn't she tell by the way he looked at her that he'd love to take her on a walk every evening, go riding with her, hunting... He scrubbed his hand over his jaw. He'd outright court her if it wasn't for his mission. But that was the problem. He had no business losing himself in her eyes and her company when lives were depending upon him. Not when his deception hung between them like a blade ready to sever any tendrils of affection and attraction that dared spring up between them.

She had the patience of a matchstick. What if his actions drove her right into Moyer's arms? He shuddered.

His boots crunched on the ground as he approached the Schrams's two-horse stable. He'd tethered his horse in there to give the illusion he'd spent the night at their place. Trudging onto their backyard, he passed their chicken house and pig pen. The Brahma hens clucked in the pre-dawn gray, but the sow only gave a half-hearted snort. A low light glowed in the small kitchen window. Frieda would be up to greet him. It'd be better if she wasn't.

The door opened as he stepped onto the cracked stone stoop of the white wood-framed house.

"Come in and get varm." Frieda wiped sleep from her eyes. Her dark ringlets hung down her back. "I have half a braid of bread from last night's supper, and I'll heat some Mettvurst sausage. Maybe boil you an egg too."

"I wouldn't want to put you to any trouble." He removed his hat and hung it on a hook. "I'm worn out. A slice of bread would do me fine, then I'll try to grab a couple hours of sleep—"

"No trouble at all." She tied her apron behind her. "Give me your coat, and I'll hang it by the fire, get it dried off.

He sighed and shrugged out of the wool frock coat he'd borrowed from her father. Briars and leaves clung to the fabric. It was unwise to let her do too much for him. The pretense of courtship was for public eyes, not for the privacy of her home. "I'll brush it off outside first."

"I could—"

He stepped out the door before she finished. Her actions were likely nothing more than kindness and the camaraderie of being joined in a cause. His gut told him otherwise.

By the time he stepped back inside, she had lit the fire in the cast-iron stove. The delicious smell of coffee wafted from a pot.

"Real coffee?" He cocked his eyebrows and draped the damp coat over the back of a chair close to the heat.

Frieda smiled. "Yes, Papa traded an officer for it, for treatment. Some of the soldiers manage to confiscate a portion of vhat comes up from Mexico for themselves."

"Much obliged for you sharing it with me." He glanced at his hands. "Mind if I go wash up?"

"Go ahead. I left vater for you in the pitcher in my father's office."

"Thank you." He ducked into the hallway and the second door on the left.

Hands and face scrubbed and hair combed, he returned to the kitchen and sat at the small table. Steam wafted up from a white china cup, the finest one in the house from what he could tell, when tin would have sufficed.

Her hair was now drawn back in a loose knot, and an apron covered her green plaid dress. She set a plate in front of him with a hearty portion of bread chunked full of nuts and dried fruit.

"A real treat." His mouth watered. "Would you care for a piece?" He picked up a knife from the embroidered tablecloth.

"You go ahead. All of that is for you. You're the one out in the chill all night."

He slathered on the butter and ate as sausage sizzled in the pan on the stove. In between bites, he answered Frieda's questions and savored the coffee.

"Best breakfast I've had in years." Careful to avoid any touch, he sat back when she added the sausage to his plate. A hint of lavender muted the pervasive odors of wood smoke and pork which permeated the rest of the kitchen.

Returning to the stove, she hummed.

Not good. He tensed. This was too homey. "As soon as I finish up, I'll take a quick nap and then hit the trail."

"But you vere up all night." She ladled an egg out of a pan of boiling water. "You can use the cot in my father's examining room and sleep until ve return from church."

"I would." He swallowed a bite of sausage. "Only, I promised Morning Fawn I'd try to make it to our church in the village by Sweet Briar." It'd been more of a threat than a promise, but he needed to get there and check on her.

Her smile dimmed. "Morning Fawn? You mean Miss Logan?"

"Yes." He sliced another bite of sausage. "She tends to get nervous in churches, not used to crowds." This was the right thing to do. Bring Morning Fawn into the picture and put distance between him and Frieda.

She fished out a second egg and placed both in a bowl. "I didn't realize it vhen I met her the first day you came here, but she's the captive girl vho stole the Thoroughbred, isn't she?" Cautious concern laced her tone.

He swallowed another bite. "That's the reason her uncle asked me to look after her. Make sure she doesn't try to run off again." Wrong choice of words. There was a lot more to it than her uncle's request. "We have no idea what she's been through."

"True." Brow furrowed, she placed a boiled egg on his plate. It rolled across the pink flower print and came to rest against the chunk of bread. "I've heard that sometimes captives aren't ever right in the head again after they're rescued from the Indi-ans." She sat down across from him.

"Mor—Miss Logan is fine in the head, just a little high strung, and prone to panic on occasion. Unfortunately, her uncle and his family don't understand. She needs a friend." The last part slipped out of its own accord, but it was the truth regardless of what else had happened between them.

"A female friend?"

"That would be good too. There's a slave girl she talks to a lot."

"You are her friend?" Frieda pursed her lips. "Vhat vill become of her once your mission is complete, and you have to leave? Vill her uncle hire someone else to look after her?"

Leave? Flee for his life, if he still had one. He gnawed a piece of bread and chewed. Frieda didn't need to know every-thing. "Hopefully, I'll figure that out by the time we blow up the warehouse."

She tapped an egg on the table edge and began to peel off the shell. "You'll figure it out? Instead of leaving it up to her uncle?" Blue eyes blinked wide in question.

Should he ask the Schramms to help Morning Fawn if he didn't survive? He chomped down half his egg. A full mouth couldn't be expected to speak. He didn't want to leave her fate up to anyone else, but if he helped her escape before he concluded the mission, it could stir up a whirlwind of suspicion. "What I have to figure out right now is the duty changes of the guards at the depot." He dabbed his mouth with a napkin. "Last night, they changed guards at eleven, two a.m., and five a.m. just before I left. Two guards at the warehouse and two at the depot, and that was just in the back. I'm sure they have as many if not more in the front."

Frieda cut her egg with a fork and knife, precisely in easily manageable bites. "That's not so many guards. Papa vill be pleased to hear that. There are others in the Unionist German League who vill be happy to help us. Ve could take care of the guards."

"Not 'we.'" He pointed his fork in her direction. "Me and they. You're only helping with the spying. The night of the explosion, you're staying put right here in this house. Ready to get in the hideout if needed. And you should keep your papa here with you."

A dimple dented each cheek. "Your concern is much appreciated. I know you'll do everything in your power to keep us safe." Determination filled her eyes. "But ve must help. It is our country now. Ve must help save it."

"You and your papa have already done much and will continue to do so right up until the last night." He firmed his tone. "But I'm in charge here. My orders are to be obeyed. You will keep your father safe in this house and stay here in case I need to flee here for help."

She clasped her hands under her chin. "I vill listen, Devon."

Her voice a soft murmur. "I know you vish to do vhat is best for us. I respect your courage and honor."

He wiggled his finger between his collar and his neck. How should he respond to such a compliment? "It is you and your father who show courage. This is your home. You're risking everything."

"You're modest." She blushed.

Time to finish the conversation before his sleep-deprived brain miscalculated a word and led him into trouble. He yawned.

She stood. "Now you must go rest. I'll vake you. My father vill vant to know more of vhat you saw last night."

He pushed up out of the chair. "Yes, I need to ask your father to find out if someone in the Unionist German league knows about steam engines. I thought of another idea while I was sitting out freezing last night."

~

The preacher had already started with his sermon by the time Devon eased the door open and crept into the church, hat in hand. A few heads turned from the rear rows. A little boy facing backwards in the pew waved before his mother poked him and made him turn around.

The back seat was empty. True to her word, Morning Fawn sat next to her aunt in the family pew, second row from the front. No Nick Moyer. That was the fox's loss. The bench contained Thea, a balding fellow he'd seen before, Morning Fawn, her aunt, and a couple of others. But Morning Fawn was on the aisle end.

The corners of Devon's mouth curved upward as he tapped his hat to his leg. What he should do was sit in the back and try to grab a couple of minutes with her on the way out. But that wouldn't make an impression.

The wide-plank floor creaked beneath his muddy boots as he moved toward the front. The kind-faced preacher raised an eyebrow but kept reading from the Bible about Samuel going to anoint David. A lady in a bluebird bonnet shot him a scowl. Two of the gossips from last week took to whispering. Had it only been a week?

Morning Fawn glanced over her shoulder, then turned halfway around, her straw hat almost swatting the man behind her who sat too far forward. Her eyes lit, not with warmth, but something harder. Her lips twitched. Maybe there was a momentary shadow of an almost-smile, but it was quickly vanquished and replaced by another look that made him feel as if he were a puppy dog begging for entrance at her back door.

He threw back his shoulders and proceeded. He would not beg.

On the other side of Mrs. LeBeau, Thea glared over at him when he reached the pew opening, her countenance as welcoming as a petrified tree. Her mother's startled expression wasn't any better. The balding man glanced around as if he had no clue of what to do.

A few murmurs rippled through the rows.

Devon nodded to the preacher, mouthed "Sorry, sir," and stepped in, his boot brushing Morning Fawn's hem. She rolled her eyes and turned back to the front. Ruffled up like some chicken in a barnyard, Mrs. LeBeau looked as if she didn't know whether to peck or squawk.

He wedged himself into the too-small opening between Morning Fawn and the solid oak pew arm. She snapped her skirts tight against her thigh, scooting no more than five or six inches toward her aunt, forcing him to choose between having his hip pressed against the wood or her. For propriety's sake, he chose the former.

Devon puffed his cheeks out in a slow exhale as he settled in. He might as well have sat down in a cactus patch.

The preacher adjusted his spectacles. "Now that we're all seated, let us continue." He picked up his Bible and began to read about David's years on the run from King Saul.

Devon closed his eyes for a moment and willed the rope-tight tension from his muscles. He was here now, next to her. He'd better make it count.

As welcoming as a block of ice in sawdust, Morning Fawn sat forward, with her hands clasped around her knees, and stared at the preacher as if she hung on every word.

Devon leaned her way an inch and whispered, "I'm sorry about yesterday."

Ice.

He dug his finger between his neck and his too-tight collar. Another few minutes of sweating, and he tried again. "I was stupid."

She slung her hair back, almost whapping his nose with her hat, but her gaze remained fixed on the pulpit.

Mrs. LeBeau scorched him with glare that said her husband would hear of this.

So be it. Devon pressed his lips together and tried to listen to the sermon. He didn't dare rest against the back of the pew lest he nod off.

If he didn't do something before the end of the service, Morning Fawn would be faster than Mr. Franklin's Thoroughbred exiting the church. His shoulder brushed hers. He dug out his heart and mouthed a statement a scratch above silence. "I was jealous."

Slowly, she tilted her face, her gaze meeting his before she peered down her nose at him, as if she were at a livestock auction giving him a good lookover to see if he were worthy of consideration. "You look as if you haven't slept."

He couldn't tell the truth, but he didn't want to out and out lie. "I was helping Dr. Schramm."

She snorted.

In front of them, a lady dressed in full mourning scooted forward as if to escape their whispers.

He leaned toward Morning Fawn, lips close to her ear, and inhaled the scent of rose in her hair. "Dr. Schramm, not Miss Schramm."

"Miss Schramm now? It's none of my concern what you do in Alleyton. I had my own evening with Mr. Moyer."

The mere mention of the name clenched his jaw. He settled back and folded his arms.

The preacher talked about David as king. How he'd loved the Lord, followed the Lord, and yet had fallen so badly in the case of Bathsheba and Uriah.

Good message, but Devon was ready for a hymn. The room grew warm. His eyes drifted closed.

Morning Fawn elbowed him, and he jerked awake.

She narrowed her eyes at him. "You better listen. You might learn something about women and being led astray."

He shot her a glance and moved within the shadow of her hat, his lips close to her hair. "I'm sitting next to the only woman who has any hope of distracting me." The words were out of his mouth before he could think better of it.

She swung her face toward him, her nose almost colliding with his chin before he pulled his head back.

"Shhh." Her aunt jabbed a finger in his direction.

His eyepatch scratched against his heated cheek.

Morning Fawn scooted away a couple of inches before refocusing her gaze on the preacher.

Devon leaned forward, elbows on knees, and listened. King David repented. Prostrated himself, begging the Lord's forgiveness. It was later after this that the Lord called David a man after his own heart.

Forgiveness. The balm of complete forgiveness. The weight of the past sank onto Devon's shoulders. How could the Lord give him such a gift if he himself wasn't willing to accept it? His sin had been nothing like King David's. He had simply failed to be at his wife's side when she needed him most. His shoulders drooped. His presence might not have saved Isabelle or their newborn child, but at least she would not have gone through the agony alone.

And here he was feeling like he was seventeen again in the presence of this impetuous, determined, fiery-tempered woman who was nothing like Isabelle.

The last song came. They stood, and Devon opened the hymnal to share with Morning Fawn, his heart heavy.

The left half of the book hung in the air until her hand slowly came up to hold the other side. She flicked a glance his way, questions in her eyes.

He nudged his pinky to hers beneath the hardcover of the hymnal. His sore heart thirsted for a drop of affection. She shuffled her finger out of reach but held the hymnal firm.

The pianist plunked the last note, and the preacher pronounced the benediction.

Devon latched onto Morning Fawn's arm and stepped into the aisle, drawing her toward the exit. His only hope for a couple of minutes of private conversation was to get her out that door before her aunt could catch her.

"Excuse us." He shouldered his way past the lady with the little boy and the other congregants. The sanctuary buzzed behind him. He and Morning Fawn would be the talk of the town by dinner.

Morning Fawn shook free of his hold as they pattered down the steps. "Here I thought I was the only one who knew how to create a scandal during a church service. Do you plan to steal a horse too?"

Clouds covered the sun. Patches of mud pock-marked the churchyard as they moved away from the building.

"You're the expert on that." The corners of his mouth edged upward. "I want to speak with you before your aunt swoops in." Touching her elbow, he steered her away from the waiting carriages.

She lifted her skirts. "Thea's the one you should be talking to. I'm sure she'd love to share with you about the lovely evening we had last night."

Gravel rumbled in Devon's craw and his belly. "Dallying with that man is like sticking your head in a fox's mouth."

She halted. "Maybe I'd consider your advice if you weren't so busy with the doctor's daughter."

They didn't have time to fight. Mrs. LeBeau stood at the top of the stairs trying to escape the preacher's hand clasp.

He pivoted, front and center, his boot toes to the edge of Morning Fawn's skirt. "What did I tell you in there, Miss Trouble? You're the girl. The only girl who has my head in a spin."

Her breath caught. Those hazel irises locked on to him. Beautiful eyes. His heartbeat drummed in his ears.

"Is that so?" The breeze lifted the brim on her straw hat and flopped the ends of the blue checkered ribbon that encircled the crown against her hair. "I'd like to hear where you've been all night."

"Helping Dr. Schramm. It had nothing to do with Frieda."

"Hmmm. Who won the game?"

"What game?"

"The card game you supposedly stayed up all night playing." She swung into motion, stomping ahead.

How was he supposed to answer that? Give her an excuse such as Dr. Schramm didn't want his daughter knowing he gambled, so Devon was covering for him? He'd never earn Morning Fawn's trust if he kept lying to her, but the truth wasn't an option. He caught up to her. "It's a secret. We're helping a friend of Dr. Schramm's who is in bad shape. It's not my secret to tell."

"Sounds pretty fishy to me." She quirked her mouth to the side.

Mrs. LeBeau barreled toward them, reticule whapping against her leg.

"I've got to go." He flicked the blue hat ribbon away from her face. An idea popped into his head. "I'll send a note through Lucy."

"A note?" Her eyes widened.

"What do you think you're doing?" Mrs. LeBeau bustled up.

He hurried off without reply. Writing to Morning Fawn? Where had that idea come from? On the way to the Schramms this morning, he'd come up with almost half a dozen reasons why he should distance himself from her. And here he was throwing logic out the window. He had to be insane.

CHAPTER 21

*D*evon splashed his face with water from the basin on the small washstand in his room. He'd thought the evening would never end. Mr. Clement and Mr. Snodgrass from nearby plantations had joined them for supper and then an evening of brandy, cigars, and cards in the library for the men. And even though he didn't care for the latter two, he'd endured all three for the sake of listening in on their discussion of the cotton trade. Two shots of watered-down brandy and one cigar. His head was cloudy and his throat irritated.

He was good at cards—too many nights of playing by Ranger campfires and in the officer quarters and the saloons in New Orleans while he waited to ship out to retake Texas—but he'd lost badly tonight. Every time his mind had a moment to drift, it'd spun circles around moments with Morning Fawn. If only he could blame it on the brandy, but it was more than that, much more.

Exhaling, he dried his face, loosened his shirt buttons close to his neck, and sat down at his writing desk. Not really his. Borrowed from the absent Dr. Arthur Lebeau. Devon didn't own a stick of furniture of his own. Not good husband material. He'd better not forget that.

The oil lamp flickered, and shadows danced on the wall. What would it be like to dance with Morning Fawn, to hold her for a waltz? She'd probably step on his toes, but he could teach her, her hand in his, him leading her...

He shook himself and picked up a pencil. To start, he could try to spell out Morning Fawn's Comanche name in English. He touched the graphite to the paper—paper intended for mission notes. What was he doing creating expectations and starting a romance he could not finish? How much time did he have? Two or three weeks before he struck the cotton warehouse. There was no guarantee of anything after that. He scrubbed his hand over his eyes. He didn't need a love note, just a few simple words. Maybe a question. He knew so little about her past life, the years with the Comanche.

He couldn't ask the question that came foremost to his mind. Had she ever been in love? It fractured into several.

After he'd located her Comanche village, he'd paid a trader to go in and find out as much as he could about her. The man had reported that Morning Fawn didn't have a husband yet, but she was intended to soon be joined with one of the lead warriors, a man maybe two decades older than her. Devon and his men had captured her three days later. Was she in love with the man? Most young Comanche women would have been married by her age. For all he knew, she could have been married and widowed before. He couldn't imagine her married to a warrior. If he hadn't rescued her, she might be a mother by now. He couldn't imagine her married to anyone but—

The thought froze his finger.

A knock sounded somewhere down the hall. Voices murmured and then a door closed. No retreating steps. Perhaps Mr. LeBeau had chosen to visit his wife's chambers. Never in his life would Devon have a separate bedroom from his wife. If he ever married again...when he married again, he and his wife would share a bed every night. Any disagreements, they'd settle before slumber overtook them. *Let not the sun go down upon your wrath.* That's what the Bible said, and that's what he'd practiced...with Isabelle.

He blew out a breath and rested his forehead on his interlaced fingers, the pencil still in his grip. Isabelle. He'd written her love letters.

The thought shuddered through him. How could he have forgotten? Not forgotten. Buried the memory deep. After he'd left home at seventeen to make his own way, he'd written her from the trails, the prairies, dirt-hole towns, the light of a campfire when the Rangers allowed a fire, even from a saloon or two. He'd written, and she had replied, keeping their love alive during their six years of separation.

He laid down the pencil and sank against the back of the chair. Would Isabelle have been better off if he had never written? No, he couldn't, wouldn't believe that. They'd been happy, so head over heels in love.

His heart drooped. He had no business stirring up feelings and hopes between him and Morning Fawn. If his mission failed, he'd be on the run, in prison, or dead. If he succeeded, he'd only survive by outrunning any pursuers. He needed to make arrangements with the Schramms for the German League to get Morning Fawn out of the county after he was gone. He couldn't leave her here. He'd promised. But it would put her life in jeopardy if he took her with him.

The lamp flickered, casting shadows on the page.

His stomach felt as if it were filled with lead. He'd send his Bible to her, but he'd squash any hint of romance.

Sometimes the most loving thing to do was to walk away.

~

$\mathcal{S}$unlight filtered in through the rough panes of the textile cabin. A concoction of smells—onion, beet, and others—from the shed out back where Aunt Mamie stood stirring her vats of dyes drifted in through the cracks in the chinking.

Morning Fawn angled the awl into the supple buckskin and twisted it until the sharp point poked through the other side. One hole after another, she worked her way around the foot-shaped pattern. Devon had passed the hide to her through Lucy on his return from his two-day trip to Columbus and Alleyton. It wasn't as if he'd gone there of his own choice. Her uncle sent him there on cotton business, but cotton wasn't the only thing in Alleyton.

When she'd mentioned to her uncle that she needed more material for dresses and asked to go along, bringing her aunt as chaperone, not only had LeBeau said no, but Devon had agreed with him. Was it for show, or had Devon meant it? And as for his promise to write her? The clerk at the general store could have sent a better note.

> *I'm sending my Bible for your use.* The marked verses have been invaluable to me in my life.

Devon had handed off the Bible through Lucy the next day, but he hadn't bothered to reply to her thank you. Why? She rammed the point through the leather, going deep this time and nicking her finger.

"Ow." She shook her hand and sucked on the drip of blood that trickled from the top of her forefinger.

"The deer's already dead. Don't have to kill it again." Lucy chuckled as she wove the shuttle through the warp threads on the loom.

The rhythmic pattern of the weaving usually fascinated

Morning Fawn, and she'd worked at learning the terms related to weaving, but not today.

"So you going to talk to me, girl?" Lucy glanced over from her work.

Morning Fawn punctured the last hole and tossed the awl into her sewing basket. "I'm thankful to have the buckskin, but Lieutenant Reynolds promised to take me hunting and teach me how to shoot a rifle, not bring me back a piece of store-brought hide."

"Mighty fine piece of leather. Said he bought it off a trader."

"And he couldn't take two minutes to come tell me that or at least send a note? I thought he was a man of his word."

Lucy stepped on the first treadle, shot the shuttle through again, and drew the beater bar down hard against the weave. "He did ask me how you liked it. And maybe the hunting will come later."

"The man has a mouth. He can talk to me. Especially with my uncle off in Houston for the week buying a horse." LeBeau could stay gone two weeks as far as she was concerned. "Lieutenant Reynolds has another thought coming if he thinks he can be all smiles on Sunday morning, then run off to Alleyton anytime he pleases the rest of the week without me." She picked up an arm's length of sinew Aunt Mamie had secretly secured for her and poked it through the needle eye. "I've come up with a plan."

"That doesn't sound good."

"I'm going to Alleyton next time Devon goes, and I need your and George's help."

Lucy's eyebrows shot up. "What kind of help?"

"I'll get permission for you and me to go on a long walk and a picnic, a day-long adventure. No horses. In return, I'll agree to go riding with Mr. Moyer again on Saturday." Last Saturday had been tolerable. During the afternoon on Ebony, testing the horse's stride and inhaling freedom, she'd stayed as far ahead of the man as possible, keeping the chatter to a minimum, and later excused herself from dinner due to a headache.

"A walk? No horses?" Lucy shifted the treadle and sailed the shuttle through again. "You plan on walking to Alleyton? Ain't that near fifteen miles?"

"My uncle won't let me ride unless I'm accompanied by Mr. Moyer or himself. But I figure George can take Ebony along when he goes to the outer pasture that morning. Then he can leave her at a pre-arranged spot for me. Along with a set of clothes."

"You must be out of your head, girl. There's an awful lot of pieces in this puzzle. Just one of them gets out of place, and we're all in trouble. Liable to be whipped."

"Then we'll have to make sure it goes as planned." Morning Fawn threaded the sinew through the first hole, joining the sole to the top of the moccasin. "If we get caught, I'll tell them I ordered you to do it."

"That won't save us none. They'll figure we should have better sense than to listen to you."

"Well, forget it, then." Morning Fawn cast the moccasin pieces into her basket and stood. "I'll sneak out of my room before dawn. You come to get me dressed like always and tell them I'm sick in bed having a hard time with my monthly and want to be left alone. That'll scare them all away." She crossed the rough-hewn planks to the loom. "But I'll still need the set of clothes. Men's clothes. George's or someone else's. I could steal Devon's, for that matter. Those would fit me better anyhow."

"Men's clothes? What the devil for?" Lucy gaped at her as if she'd lost her mind. "You're going to get yourself locked in the attic and laudenumed."

"I'll take my chances. I've had enough sitting around here while my uncle and Nick Moyer plan out my life and the man I care about gallivants off to Alleyton every chance he gets. I want them to get their sticky fingers off my life, and I want

Devon Reynolds to look me in the eye and tell the truth about what he's up to."

"You got a lot of wants."

Morning Fawn threw her arms open wide. "If I had any sense, I'd grabbed one of those horses in the stable some night and ride out of here and never come back."

"But you ain't going to do that." Lucy's voice dipped. "You're going to stay here and win that man of yours."

"I'm done with sitting around parlors. I'm going to sneak into Alleyton, dressed as a man, and spy on him."

"You're what?"

"You heard me."

"So you're determined to get yourself in trouble?"

"My uncle won't be back for a few days."

"You don't think your aunt and Thea will tattle?"

Morning Fawn lifted her chin. "Sometimes trouble is worth the cost. But if everything goes well, no one will know. Only you, me, and George.""

Lucy sputtered and pumped away at the treadles, ramming the beater bar after every shot of the shuttle.

Aunt Mamie's singing voice carried in from the shed.

Morning Fawn rubbed her hands over her arms. "I understand if your answer's no."

Lucy blew out a breath. "You is risking yourself for me and Ned. I reckon I can do the same for you."

Morning Fawn touched her shoulder. "Only, we should do it the second way, with you pretending I'm in my room in bed."

"And what if you're discovered missing...or get dragged back here by the sheriff or somebody?"

"You can tell them I was there the first time you looked, but the other times, you figured I was sleeping under the covers, and you didn't want to disturb me."

Lucy mumbled and halted her work. "No, we'll do it the first way." She swatted at a fly. "We'll go on the picnic. I'll act likes I was all innocent. That you ordered me to stay with the food while you went on a walk alone. And I waited and waited 'cause I do what I'm told. And I had no idea you had done sneaked yourself a horse during the night and left it there with plans to ride off to Alleyton to visit Mr. Moyer. I'll say 'Mr. Moyer' 'cause that'll make them more pleased."

"Bravo." Morning Fawn clapped.

Lucy jabbed her hand to her hip. "If yous get yourself laudanumed, it ain't my fault. Just make sure you're allowed out of the attic in time to help with my weddin' on Christmas Eve."

Morning Fawn gave her a quick hug, then jumped back as footsteps sounded outside the door.

Thea sashayed in with her nose scrunched up so tight, it was a wonder she could breathe. "Might have known I would find you down here, cousin, dear, mingling with the help." She hunched her shoulders inward as if the very air might contain a contaminant.

"Working on my sewing. Learning about weaving." Morning Fawn crossed her arms and cast a glimpse toward her sewing basket. If LeBeau got wind she was working on moccasins, he'd probably confiscate the leather. "I'm surprised you even know the way here."

Thea smirked. "I know plenty. Know your prince charming is headed up to Alleyton tomorrow to visit his girl. I might have him drop me by Bealah Brown's on the way."

Morning Fawn's jaw clenched so tight her words came out muffled. "Fine by me. I reckon you've forgotten it's Mr. Moyer who is set on courting me."

"It's amazing what greed for land can motivate a man to do." Skirts lifted high, Thea strutted over the loom.

Let the remark pass. Morning Fawn pressed her lips shut and stepped between Thea and Lucy lest her friend be the next victim of the venom.

Thea poked her finger at a thread. "You messed up, girl. The pattern doesn't call for purple there. I knew I should have someone else working on my shawl."

"Sorry, miss. Won't happen again." Lucy lowered her head and curtseyed.

"I distracted her." Morning Fawn crossed her arms.

"That's what comes of being friendly with the servants." Thea marched over to the table, picked up a pair of shears, and returned.

"Don't you dare." Fawn's shoulders arched toward her ears.

Lucy shuffled her foot beneath Morning Fawn's skirt and stepped on her toe. A warning to let it be.

Thea lowered the sheers and snipped through a length of waft. Frayed threads fluttered down as the shuttle tumbled against a treadle. "Maybe next time, you'll get it right."

Morning Fawn clenched her hands, but Lucy's foot mashed harder.

Thea hummed as she exited. "See you at supper, cousin."

Steam practically hissed through Morning Fawn's teeth as the door shut. "I could have stopped her."

"Maybe you could have." Lucy sighed. "But then she would have gotten at me a half a dozen ways when you weren't looking. Best not to show her how much you care."

"We can't go through with the plan. I can't put you at risk."

Lucy grabbed Morning Fawn's arm. Her lip trembled. "We're going through with the plan, all right. My life would be like this even if you had never showed up on this plantation. My only hope of it being different is you and Lieutenant Reynolds. We're both going to show Miss Thea her bossin' only goes so far. And when you have that man of yours, you and he sees if you can help me and mine."

When. As in, it really could happen. For all she knew, she'd already lost Devon. But she wouldn't fail Lucy. "When I get away from here, I'll find a way to help you escape as well."

Dear Lord in heaven, please let it be so.

CHAPTER 22

iar. Morning Fawn swiped the back of her hand across her nose and whittled another shaving off the point of the stick. At the rate she was going, it'd be a spike, not a cane. "Two-faced weasel," she muttered as she glanced from beneath the brim of the floppy-brimmed work hat. It smelled of sweat, George's sweat, but that was all right. Better than that pig-smelling Miss Perfect who sashayed down the street on Devon's arm.

A snood confined Frieda's dark waves beneath a burgundy bonnet. Decked out in a flattering green plaid dress trimmed in black velvet, Frieda practically skipped with delight. She might as well have angel wings.

Morning Fawn's stomach sank to the bottom of her rough boots. She shouldn't have come. Why put herself through this torture? How could she ever have been fool enough to believe that Devon might prefer her?

Last night at dinner, Devon hadn't mentioned anything about the trip. Instead, he'd snuck out of the house before breakfast and ridden off. George had been the one to end up taking Thea an hour later. Morning Fawn had waited until her cousin was out of sight before announcing plans for the picnic. Her aunt had only commented on the weather being a bit chilly for an outing but had let the matter pass upon Morning Fawn's promise to go riding with Mr. Moyer on Saturday. And thankfully, George had fulfilled his part of the plan before he'd left. Ebony and the clothes were at the designated spot.

Near the end of the street, Devon glanced over his shoulder.

Morning Fawn jerked her gaze back to the stick, driving the knife's blade against the pecan wood. The cracked stone stoop bit into her backside. George's patched brown coat hung loose on her frame, all the better to hide her bound chest. And the trousers? She'd had to tighten the suspenders so high that the waistline struck the bottom of her ribs. she'd even taken care to smudge dirt on her face and hands.

A gray-haired slave lumbered down the street with a wheelbarrow full of wood. Two doors down, a lady leaned out the window and emptied a bucket of liquid. Water or worse? And they called this civilization?

Morning Fawn should find her way back to her real home and throw herself at Stands-His-Ground's feet.

She glanced up as the two lovers disappeared around the corner. No, she wasn't leaving yet. Not until she'd witnessed the full extent of Devon's betrayal. With a quick pat to her hat, she stood and jogged toward the intersection.

A ball rolled toward her. She dodged it, ignoring the two boys playing in the dirt street, and smacked a tear from her cheek. Crying was completely unacceptable.

She slowed down as she reached the main street and tugged her flop hat lower, her hair pinned tight to her head.

Devon and Miss Perfect crossed the street, hurrying out of the way of an army wagon laden with food stuffs and supplies. Once they reached the plank sidewalk, they strolled westward, his hand over hers on his arm, her skirts lapping against his trouser leg, just as he'd walked with Morning Fawn. Traitor.

Her hands clenched. She'd never be able to return home and sit across the dinner table from him or pass him in the hall and say nothing of this. And what about all of those prayers of his? The man might as well have horns.

The couple paused at the mercantile window. Glass. Reflection. Best blend in. Morning Fawn stuck the knife in its sheath strapped to her waist and plodded down the street, tapping the stick against her leg, head lowered.

An elderly man rattled past in a buggy.

Two soldiers jawing and elbowing each other dipped their hats to the lady walking in front of her.

A spittoon and a stoop. A good spot for observing. Morning Fawn stopped to let the soldiers pass.

"Watch what you're doing, boy." An oversized man in a checkered suit clipped her shoulder as he hurried by.

Morning Fawn dropped down on the stoop, puffed out her cheek, and spit into the tin spittoon. Rubbing her grimy hands on her trousers, she chanced a glance across the street.

Devon and Frieda were on the move again, strolling toward the end of town which contained the depot and warehouse, and beyond that, the train station. Walking as if they had all the time in the world, they leaned their heads toward one another, Devon's mouth close to Frieda's hair. Whispering? Lost in each other. How had she ever dreamed that could be him and herself?

Because he'd led her to believe it might so.

Morning Fawn glowered. Served her right for believing him and for thinking she might actually have a home amongst these people.

And Nick Moyer? Could she endure him for the sake of the land?

She didn't belong here. She rubbed her palm on her scratchy wool trousers. The clothes were perfect. And she had a saddlebag of picnic food. She could stretch it out for a few days.

Now would be the perfect time to escape. Her best chance ever. Once they realized she was missing, they'd look for her in Alleyton, and they'd be looking for a girl in a dress.

A hard smile wormed its way across her lips. She could get to Dallas or Fort Worth, but eventually, she'd need money for food and a gun. She'd need work. The clothes would help with that. Maybe she'd even chop off her hair. Safer, traveling in disguise as a boy.

She glanced at the western horizon, or at least where it should be if it weren't blocked by a cluster of wooden hovels trying to pass themselves off as a town. She'd traveled on the plains alone for a day and a night. She could hunt and track, and she'd even fought to help protect the children when her band had been attacked by Apaches. Better to risk the unknown than to be turned into a parlor princess or chase after a man who didn't appreciate her.

But her stupid heart tugged her gaze back to the man with the forked tongue. Devon and Frieda blended with the passersby, almost out of sight at the far end of the plank walkway.

Morning Fawn stood and ran across the street.

A carriage driver yanked on his reins and yelled at her. Thankfully, Devon and Frieda didn't turn around. She half stumbled in the too-big boots that scraped against her heels and jammed her toes into the wads of cotton stuffed in the ends.

Hitching her trousers, Morning Fawn made her way down the boardwalk. She smacked another tear from her cheek. She couldn't leave East Texas without Devon knowing his skunky ways had been discovered. She wouldn't confront him in these clothes. No, she'd dress in her fanciest gown, flirt openly with Moyer, and put that weasel lieutenant in his place. There'd be time enough for running off later, when the LeBeaus least expected it. She'd procured the horse and clothes once. She could do it again.

A passing soldier frowned at her. She coughed and spit on the sidewalk for good measure.

Two blocks ahead, Devon and Miss Perfect turned the corner at the warehouse toward the train station. Morning Fawn headed between the warehouse and the quartermaster's depot.

"Boy, where do you think you're going?" A corporal marched over, chest puffed out.

She scuffed her feet and lowered her voice. "Fetching river stones. My pa's working on Mr. Moyer's place. Said I'd better have them back quick, or I'd be whipped." She tipped her head upward but not enough to show her face beneath the shadow of her hat. "You got a wheelbarrow I can borrow?"

"I don't have time for your sorry story or to be doing your work for you." A cigar stump wiggled between his teeth. "Get on out of here and fetch your own rocks. Be quick about it."

"Yes, sir." She saluted and hauled off between the buildings.

"Fool kid," he called behind her.

Not a kid. Just a foolish girl in love with a man who couldn't be trusted.

~

*D*evon's stomach felt as if he were still crossing the Gulf of Mexico from New Orleans to Brownsville. No rolling waves today, just the turmoil in his heart. He couldn't wait for this mission to be over, and to be done with pretense.

Frieda bit her lip. "Perhaps, we should stop somevhere and act like you're fixing my shoe. That'd give us a chance to take a more thorough look."

"Good idea." The corners of his mouth edged upward. She had a knack for subterfuge. But he wasn't dull enough to believe the glow in her cheeks had anything to do with cotton and sabotage.

A mosquito buzzed near his ear. He slapped at it. The weather hadn't gotten cold enough yet to kill them off for the winter.

Devon guided Frieda beyond the platform and over a set of tracks, then another, mindful of her slower step. "Let's wait till we get past the roundhouse. We'll find a stump or discarded rail to sit on."

A freight worker, in his shirt sleeves and scruffy trousers, took a gander at them.

Devon nodded to the man, then gave Frieda a playful bump with his shoulder. "Best play it up a little more, sweetheart."

"Of course, darling." Frieda twirled her fringed reticule on her arm. "You always know best." She cuddled closer, teetering in the process.

A handful of workers hustled between tasks at the roundhouse. The spare steam engine towered in its domain like a sleeping dragon ready to spring to life if given a meal of coal in its belly. At the loading docks, men hauled crates from the quartermaster's depot, fresh supplies for the troops back east in western Louisiana. Devon had memorized the train schedule. One should arrive in less than an hour, bringing more cotton to the bulging warehouse and carrying away goods.

He'd seen the layout back here at night from a distance with only the stars for a guide. Daylight added clarity and much more detail. If he was lucky, they'd throw the depot doors wide open as they transferred supplies, giving him a good look at what lay inside.

He needed to strike before the order came from Confederate headquarters to load the cotton onto wagons headed for San Antonio and beyond to Mexico. He'd selected five men from the German League to help. Hopefully, New Year's Eve would be soon enough.

He led Frieda past the hoists and crates into crumpled grass. About a quarter of a mile farther, they stopped in the shade of a pin oak. Devon spread his neckerchief over the top of a rotting stump, and Frieda sat with her back to the warehouse.

Blushing, she stuck her dainty foot out from beneath her skirt. "I've never had a beau before. You'll have to forgive me if my act isn't polished."

"You're doing fine." Devon knelt in front of her. "I can't believe you've never courted." He snapped his lips shut, but not before the words slipped through. The last thing he needed to do was make this personal.

"Oh, there was a fellow or two. Bought my pies at the fairs, but no one I fancied. Besides, I vas too busy helping my father."

Frowning, he tugged off her shoe, avoiding the touch of his fingers to her stocking. He needed to get this conversation back on track. "A few fellows glanced our way, but they don't seem overly concerned." He turned her shoe in his hand, one way and the other, supposedly examining it while his gaze scoured their surroundings.

A hawk sailed overhead. White clouds with gray undersides loomed on the western horizon. The weather had been unusually warm lately. A storm could be brewing. He needed to finish his surveillance, get Frieda home, and head back to Sweet Briar before evening.

The hair spiked on the back of his neck, just as it had on occasion when he traveled through Comancheria, half expecting an arrow in his back at any moment. He rocked on to his heels. A shiver coursed down his spine.

He directed his gaze at the buildings. Nothing unusual. No one seemed to be looking his way. The front of the roundhouse was out of view now, and only the east side of the loading dock was visible from here. Men moved between the dock and the quartermaster's depot. The half-open door revealed a stack of crates.

Beyond all of that, some slight fellow, dressed in a rough brown coat and a flop hat, sat on a log working on something with his hands. Maybe a slave, maybe not. Hadn't there been someone dressed like that on the street outside Frieda's house?

Could it be possible that someone was following them, watching them? Probably just his imagination. He wouldn't give it another thought if it wasn't for the hair prickling on the back of his neck. After all, if the Rebs suspected something serious, they wouldn't send a fellow in full uniform to march up and ask questions. The smarter move would be for them to wait and watch, catch the whole network.

Wiggling Frieda's shoe back on, he stood and held his hand out to her. "Let's go for a walk. There's a fellow I want a better look at." He patted her hand to his arm.

A furrow creased the space between her eyebrows. "Something wrong?"

"Probably nothing. But just in case, let's put on a show when we get closer. Follow my lead."

She nodded. The breeze ruffled the lace on her bonnet. "Yes, of course."

Forsaking the path which meandered toward the river, they made their way parallel to the buildings. Hip-high buffalo grass swiped at his cavalry boots and clung to her skirt.

As they neared the spot, he drew her closer to his side. One of her errant curls caught on his beard. "Tell me something fun from your childhood, a happy memory. It'll show on your face." He inhaled lilac. Lilac wasn't required for a pretend courtship.

She batted her lashes and smiled until her cheeks dimpled. "There was the time my brother Clem was chased by an armadillo. He was only six, and he swore it was a monster...." Her voice lilted as she wove the tale, only a slight quaver now and then, easily attributed to the excitement of a young lady walking with her beau.

Devon chuckled as he wove them closer to the whittling youth, not a direct path but a casual drift that brought them within earshot.

The young man wore a patched brown coat and rough trousers rolled a good three or four inches at the cuff above scuffed boots. A battered hat with the world's floppiest brim shadowed the fellow's face, revealing just enough to show he was white, not black, not a slave. Maybe a drifter. Nothing unusual, not even a glance their way. The boy whittled away at the spike as if he weren't aware of their proximity. But that's what didn't fit. Wouldn't someone glance up to see who was passing?

But would the Rebs really hire a boy to spy? He'd seen worse—dead boys on the field of battle not even old enough to shave.

Air leaked out of Devon's lungs.

"I can't vait for you to see what I've fixed you for dinner tonight." Frieda squeezed his arm.

"Let me guess." He refocused and nudged his elbow to hers. "A pie?"

"No, silly, you can't have dessert first. I'm talking dinner."

"Everything that comes from your hands tastes like dessert."

"I bet you say that to all the ladies."

"None compare to you." He lifted her hand and brushed his lips to her gloved fingers.

Frieda sucked in a breath. Her face went dead serious.

Don't fall for the act. He returned her hand to his elbow. "I'll expound more on your charms this evening in your parlor."

"You shall?" Her voice fluttered.

"Dinner?" He whispered. "We were talking about dinner."

"Oh, yes." She blushed. "Vhat do you think about

dumplings? Papa butchered a chicken last night since you vere coming. Chicken and dumplings, and blackberry pie?"

"Best meal of my life." He turned their steps to the beaten trail that led back to the street and shot a side-glimpse toward the youth.

The boy jerked his head down. He'd been looking.

Devon squared his shoulders. Time to give their observer something else to goggle at. "Frieda," he whispered. "Forgive me." He pivoted to her front and inhaled. Hand trembling and stomach contorting, he lifted her chin.

Her eyes widened.

This was not who he should be kissing.

His arid tongue cleaved to the roof of his mouth as he bent his head and brushed his lips to her cheek.

She fluttered like a chickadee fluffing its wings. Her lips skimmed his beard before he could withdraw. He fought against the wince that threatened to squeeze his eyes. Their lives might depend upon this deception.

He gazed into her sparkling blue irises and spawned a smile as if he considered her the most beautiful woman in the world. He should say something, but what?

She squeezed his hand and whispered. "I know ve're only pretending." But the tremor in her voice said otherwise.

He nodded. She deserved to have a beau. But not him. "Slowly, let your reticule slip to the ground between us. Out of sight of the fellow behind us."

Her eyebrows arched. "Vhat?"

"I need an excuse to return and see what he's up to."

She frowned. The reticule plopped lightly on his boot toe.

"Thank you." He tucked her hand around his elbow and strode down the path to the street. Once they returned to the hubbub of people and wagons, he stopped. "I want you to head straight home. I'll be along later."

"No. I'll vait." She clung to his arm. "I mean, I'm fine going back on my own, but vhat if the fellow's dangerous?"

"Don't worry. I can handle him." He tapped the revolver beneath his coat. "But I don't think it'll come to that. I'll ask him if he's seen your reticule. It'll give me a chance to take a good look at him and get a better sense of what he's up to."

"Be careful." Worry filled her eyes. Her dimples faded.

"I'm sure it's nothing." The foolish notion of kissing her forehead in reassurance flittered through his brain. This mission was getting to him. He touched her sleeve. "If we're being watched, it's best to find out now. Head home. I'll be there soon as I can."

He stood watching for a moment or two as she headed down the plank sidewalk toward the mercantile.

Should he tell her she and her father needed to leave town if he wasn't at their place by dinner? No, it couldn't be anything that serious. Yet.

Devon rubbed his neck. The chill was still there. Stuffing his hands in his pockets, he passed in front of the quartermaster's depot and started down the other side. A sergeant looked up from the bench out front where he sat. A cigar stub wobbled between his teeth.

"My girl lost her reticule." Devon nodded to the man.

"Maybe you distracted her." The sergeant chuckled.

"Probably did." Devon smirked.

"Happy hunting." The sergeant settled back on the bench.

"Thanks." Devon shuffled off around the building, muscles tense.

He stepped from between the buildings, passed a couple of soldiers lugging a crate toward the loading dock, and walked toward the far end. The whittling fellow had left his perch. Devon's step quickened.

There he was. He hovered near the side path Devon and Frieda had taken to the street a few minutes before. His trousers sagged, as did the coat, as though he'd borrowed his papa's clothes or was too poor to buy his own. The fellow turned, his face shadowed. Their gazes locked across the distance. Something familiar...

The youth pivoted and hiked toward the tree line.

Devon followed, keeping parallel to the buildings, not heading directly for the youth but closing the distance. By the time Devon passed the depot and path, the fellow was almost to the woods, slugging through waves of buffalo grass.

The reticule forgotten, Devon turned toward the trees. His longer, stronger legs gained ground through the silvery-green waves.

The flop-hatted fellow glanced over his shoulder, reached down, and yanked off a boot.

"I didn't mean to scare you. Just wanted to talk," Devon called out. Best to maintain an air of normalcy, but his hand hovered near his coat flap where the solid metal of his revolver pressed the holster to his thigh.

The youth tossed a second boot aside and broke into a run. Devon took off after him. Into the trees, they flew. The boy plowed through brush and undergrowth, low-lying branches tearing at his flapping coat.

Devon's hat snagged on an outstretched limb. He kept going, pumping his arms and crashing through the thistles and brush, his feet and lower legs protected by his thick cavalry boots.

A murder of crows took flight. Their caws echoed overhead.

The boy stumbled, caught himself, and drove on.

The ground sloped. Water rumbled to the left. They were coming upon the river. The boy vaulted over a downed tree trunk and ran on. Sunlight poured into the clearing ahead.

A branch scratched at Devon's face. He backhanded it out of the way, closing quickly. Suddenly, the boy's feet flew out from beneath him. He shot down the hill on his side, hit a bump, and rolled. Devon pivoted and skittered down the slope on the sides of his boots. Bending his knees, he struggled to slow his descent and keep upright. Pebbles and soil scattered in his wake.

The Colorado River gurgled beyond a strip of cattails and grasses. Cottonwoods loomed along the banks.

The fellow gained his feet. Devon lunged. The youth landed with a grunt, Devon atop him. A sheathed knife swung from the stranger's side. Devon scrambled to pin him down, slamming the scoundrel's wrists to the leaf-strewn moss.

The youth's hat tumbled off. Long honey-blond hair spewed from beneath. Goosebumps swept over Devon's limbs. The face. Her face. Morning Fawn. *Dear God*. It was as if someone had dumped a bucket of spring water over his head on a sweat-dripping day. Every droplet of air evaporated from his lungs.

He rocked backward. "What the devil..." Words failed him. He waved his hand over her. "Dressed like..."

Hazel eyes bore into him with fiery venom. "Get off me." She shoved him with more force than he'd imagined her capable of.

Mouth agape, he landed on his backside.

She scrambled to her bloodied feet. "What are *you* doing here? That's the question. You two-faced liar." She picked up her hat and swung it at him.

He leaped to his feet before she started kicking. "Who sent you?"

"What do you mean?"

"Who told you to follow me?"

"No one. Why would they? None of the rest of the world cares if you have your fancy set on Frieda Schramm. You weasel. You said it wasn't about her." She swung at him again.

He dodged. That's what this was about? Morning Fawn... was jealous?

"What does that look mean?" She jabbed both hands to her hips. Hips covered in *trousers*.

"Nothing."

"It means something. And I want a real answer." She brandished her slouch hat in his direction. "You and Frieda deserve each other." She scowled at him. "Nick Moyer could lose more land by dinner time than you'll ever own in your life."

How dare she? "So that's the measure of a man, huh? How much land he owns? If that's what you think matters in a marriage, then you go ahead and wrangle a proposal out of that man."

"Couldn't be any worse than you chasing after Miss Perfect. I can see you now, all settled down, mucking out the pigs every evening, then scrubbing up to come sit by the fireside, read the newspaper, and watch her make doilies. Maybe if you're lucky, you'll get a good night peck on the cheek."

He snorted. Him marrying Frieda. Doilies. Kiss on the cheek.

She glowered at him. Moisture glistened in her eyes. "You can wallow with the pigs as far as I'm concerned." She pivoted from him.

"Morning Fawn." He touched her shoulder.

She jerked away and punched at his arm.

He blocked her fist, the impact landing solidly in his palm. She raised her other hand, and he latched onto her wrists. "If you try to hit me again, I'm going to pin you to the ground until you're ready to listen."

Golden sparks flared at him from the hazel depths of her eyes. "Get your hands off me and never touch me again. I'm done with you. If I ever see you again, it'll be too soon."

Tears streamed down her cheeks, turning his knees to pond scum. Realization dawned. She was in love with him.

And he'd hurt her.

She scrubbed the heels of her palms across her cheeks. "I couldn't care less about you."

"It's not what you think, Taa Aruka."

She startled at the last two words. "You told me that one before."

Words rasped out of his throat. "I'm a spy."

"A what?"

Dear Lord, should he do this? But how could he not? Mouth dry, he stepped toe to toe with her. "A spy." His voice was hardly more than a breath. She needed to understand the possible consequences. "I could be killed if I'm discovered."

Her mouth slackened. "You're serious?"

He pointed to his face. "Do I look like I'm lying?"

She teetered. "No."

He steadied her with his hand on her shoulder. His palm sank deep against the twig and leaf-speckled wool coat. "What you saw between me and Frieda was an act."

"You two practically melted all over each other."

He winced. Obviously, he'd been too good at acting. Anything short of honesty would deem his credibility worth about as much as the leavings from a morning bedpan. "I'm on a secret mission. The Schramms are my contacts. The courtship with Frieda is part of my cover to avoid suspicion." Dare he tell her everything? There were more lives than his at stake.

She swiped her nose. "What kind of secret mission? What kind of spy?"

He should release her shoulder, but it was all he could do to not draw her closer.

A strand of her hair brushed against his callused fingers.

He swallowed. "It wouldn't be a secret if I told you."

"But Frieda knows."

"Frieda's part of the operation. My contact set up the meeting with her and her father."

"Did your contact say you had to pretend to be in love with Frieda and kiss her?"

She could have been an attorney. He grunted and dropped his hands to his sides.

"I take that as a no."

"There are bigger concerns at stake here than you or me."

"Then tell me."

He had his orders and his backup lie. Her tears had stopped, but the residue of their tracks still lined the dirt on her cheeks. She had come all this way for him. The coat, the trousers, all of it for him. How had she managed to sneak off the plantation and find her way here? The lady was a fireball.

Risk the truth? Or lose her with a lie? She was an abolitionist at heart. The problem was that quick mouth of hers. He rubbed his hand over his jaw.

"You're not going to tell me, are you?" Her voice faltered. "I should have figured as much. Better not to say anything than make promises you don't intend to keep. Like saying you'll take me on walks or write me notes and then avoiding me instead." She narrowed her eyes. "Your actions have made your true intentions painfully clear. A couple hours of sweet talk followed by a week of silence and disappearing. Don't tell me that's part of the mission too. Nicholas is a lot of things, but at least he's not inconsistent. You fancy Frieda?" She scooped her hat from the ground. "She can have you." Morning Fawn coiled her hair in a knot and stuffed it beneath her hat.

"My staying away and not writing has nothing to do with Frieda."

She rolled her eyes and tucked her shirt tails back into her trousers, which hung loose despite the suspenders.

He ground his teeth. "Has anyone ever told you that you're impetuous and quick-tempered?"

"Has anyone ever told you that you have a forked tongue?" She jutted out her chin. "And I suppose Miss Perfect is calm as glass, never a hair out of place, never a ruffled feather."

"'Miss Perfect'?" He scowled. "That's what you think of her?"

"That's what *you* think of her." She jabbed her finger in his direction. "And I've had enough of it."

"You're wrong."

"Why don't you write that in a note sometime? See if I'm around to read it." She pivoted and started up the embankment, gripping an exposed root to pull herself up. Loose dirt slid beneath her torn, bloodied stockings. "Don't bother to look for me."

He scuffed his boot. Morning Fawn was the most exasperating woman who had ever lived. And if he didn't speak up, he was going to lose her. "It's Isabelle."

She half slid back down the hill and jabbed her hands to her hips. "What?"

He marched over and snatched the hat off her head. She wouldn't run off without it, not dressed in trousers. A bitter taste rose up in the back of his throat. Was he really going to start this conversation now? "Isabelle is the reason I didn't write." He could almost hear the suture rip in his heart.

She blinked at him. "Because you still love her?" Her voice wobbled.

He swallowed. "I will always love her."

She inhaled sharply. New moisture pooled in her eyes.

His arms twitched toward her, but he held them steady. "However, I've recently discovered my heart is bigger than I realized. It has a chamber for Isabelle. But..." What in the world was he doing? He reached for Morning Fawn's hand and lifted her fingers to his left breast. "It also has a huge chamber for someone else, a girl who has more courage, strength, determination, and spunk than anyone I've ever known."

She sniffled. Her fingers pressed against his shell jacket as if a magnet drew them toward the flesh beneath. "If you mean

that, why didn't you write? Why do you make yourself scarce?"
Her bottom lip trembled.

A red-winged blackbird landed on a nearby tree branch and
trilled.

Devon ripped another suture. "I failed Isabelle. I don't want
to end up hurting you too."

"I'm sure you never meant to hurt her."

He dropped her hand and stepped away. Sweat broke out
beneath his hairline. His stomach churned. "A body can do a
bushel of harm without ever meaning to."

"Tell me." She touched his side.

Tell this girl the darkest moment of his life? They didn't
have time for this here. One of the men from the docks might
have seen them head into the woods. Might eventually come to
investigate.

He turned to her. "Meet me tomorrow. In the center of the
garden by the sundial at sunrise. If one of us can't make it, we'll
meet at midnight, same place. I'll tell you then."

Her expression clouded. He could see her thoughts.
Another put-off, another promise he wouldn't keep.

He had to give her something. Heart pounding, he took her
in his arms. Not the right thing to do. His head spun. The feel
of her robbed him of his breath. He pressed his mouth to her
ear, fighting for clarity. "I'm a Yankee spy."

She shuddered and leaned back to meet his gaze. Silence
for a full moment. She paled and mouthed, "A Yankee?"

"Hanging offense in these parts." The nodes in his throat
hardened, barely letting the words past. Saying it made it more
real.

She latched on to the front of his jacket. "LeBeau would
string you up if he knew. So would Nicholas."

He nodded.

"Were you a spy when you kidnapped me?"

"No." A dry laugh rattled through him. "I planned to use the three hundred dollar reward to pay for a substitute and stay out of the war. Just like I told you before."

"But you didn't."

"After I delivered you to your uncle's men, I traveled to Louisiana, joined Grant's army, then transferred to the First U.S. Texas Cavalry, Texans fighting to redeem the state from the Rebs."

"I know you hate slavery. But I had no idea you were...You told me you enlisted in the Confederate cavalry to protect Texas."

"I meant what I said. Only, I figured the best way to help Texas was to fight to free her from the Reb stranglehold." His gaze dropped into gold-speckled irises. "I'm trusting you with my life."

"I'd never do anything to harm you." Her voice little more than a breath.

A splash resonated from the water beyond the trees.

Devon tensed and touched a finger to his lips. They held still as a deer bounded through the brush and up the hill. Only a deer...but something had spooked it. "We should go."

Her eyes widened. "I have something else to tell you. Nicholas suspects something."

"What?"

"Saturday before last, he talked about having you investigated."

He shifted her to elbow distance. "What did he say? Tell me exactly."

"He doesn't suspect the Yankee part, just that maybe you're a deserter or slacker. He talked about having one of his agents look into it."

Devon scrubbed his hand over his face. "If he sends inquiries to my stepfather or any of his associates, he'll learn soon enough where my sympathies lie."

"But they don't know you joined the Yankees?"

"No, but once Moyer learns I'm a Unionist, he'll dig further." He needed to throw the man off the trail and move up the timetable for the mission.

"What are you going to do?"

He released her. "I'll figure something out. I have a backup cover—that I'm here from the Confederate government investigating the quartermaster." He exhaled. "I'll give it more thought. But right now, you need to get back to your horse, change, and ride home." Her horse? She'd probably ridden that blasted mustang. He prayed to God he wasn't a fool for trusting her.

"I want to help. I can spy. You see that I can." Morning Fawn waved her hand over her clothes. "Should I make up something to say to Nicholas?"

"Absolutely not. I want you to get home and act like nothing has changed. If they notice you were missing, tell them you went for a long ride. If they lock you in the attic, I'll work to get you out."

She folded her arms. "I'll do that for now, but I'm a better spy than Frieda."

Men's voices sounded in the distance. A disagreement at the loading docks or something else?

He jabbed a finger toward the hill. "I don't have time to argue with you. We'll discuss it later. Go. We'll talk tomorrow morning, sunrise. And remember what I told you."

She nodded and scurried up, pawing dirt as she climbed. Her poor stockinged feet.

He'd better speed up this mission while he had any brains left. There'd be no way to keep Morning Fawn uninvolved now that she knew. It'd be like shooting off the starting pistol at a race and telling a Thoroughbred not to gallop. Although the Schramms were not going to understand, and neither would Captain Carson, he had to figure out a way for Morning Fawn

to help and keep her and everyone else safe all at the same
time.

CHAPTER 24

*M*orning Fawn trembled as she plunged through the buffalo grass, the wispy heads of grain parting like waves. Devon was a Yankee. And a spy. A warrior taking a terrible risk.

He said he had feelings for her. Why, he'd almost looked as if he could kiss her today. He *had* kissed Frieda. Not on the lips, but still, the thought scraped over her nerves like the sharp edge of a shell. And goodness knows, he'd said plenty of pretty words before without them translating to faithful actions.

But today, he'd told her his secret. At least one of them. He was trusting her with his life. She wouldn't give up until she found a way to assist him and prove herself. For the first time since her arrival in this society, she had a real purpose—two, to be exact. She'd help Devon spy on the Rebs, and together, they'd help Lucy and Ned. For eighteen months, she'd had nothing to wake up in the morning for except the hope of escaping. And she'd failed at that, though she had only put half her heart into it. The distance was too great on her own with no certainty of what awaited on the other end. But this was different.

If only she hadn't made such a spectacle of herself today. Clearly, she'd demonstrated she didn't have a clue about behaving in a ladylike manner. The man probably thought she was better suited for jawing over a spittoon than dancing at a ball.

Gnats hovered around her head. She swatted at them.

Frieda Schramm had better keep her hands off Devon.

She hitched her trousers as she neared the buildings. A couple of the soldiers behind the depot paused in their work and stared her way.

Best get back to the main street and blend in, then she could cut through the alleys to the other side of town where she left her horse. She lowered her hat over her eyes and hurried onto the pebbled path. Pain pricked the soles of her injured feet. A sign of softness. They'd once been as tough as hide.

"Hey, boy, what you been up to down there?" A soldier with a scraggly beard hollered at her.

"Doing my business. Couldn't find an outhouse." She shoved her hands in her pockets and hurried faster.

"Hope you didn't leave anything for me to step in."

The redheaded man beside him straightened. "Didn't I see you being chased?"

"Didn't want a whipping," Should she hurry by them or head for the other side of the building? Her feet weren't up for another chase. "Fellow said I stared too much at his girl."

The one with the beard chuckled. "How old are you, anyhow?"

"Old enough." She hastened past. "Gotta get home. Ma'll have a fit."

The redhead's silence didn't bode well. Morning Fawn picked her speed up to a jog. The street, safety—a lady with a baby carriage, a slave woman walking behind her mistress, another solider, two men in suits. She bolted through onto the planked walkway and ran smack dab into a man's hard muscular chest.

She stumbled backward and landed on her rear end with her legs splayed wide. A few strands of hair fell from beneath her hat.

Nicholas gaped down at her.

Her face flamed. She jabbed her hat down and scrambled to her feet. A sinkhole would come in mighty handy right about now. "Excuse me, sir." Her voice warbled instead of dipping low.

The lady with the baby carriage stopped to stare, but the two businessmen mumbled and strode past.

Morning Fawn pivoted to the street, ready to dash.

Nicholas locked onto her arm and turned her toward him. He reached for her hat.

"Please don't. Not here." Panic laced her whisper, her voice undisguised.

"Miss Beth?" His eyebrows shot up to his hairline.

She tugged her coat across her front and nodded.

"You said *miss*?" The lady's brow furrowed.

"Miss Beth's servant boy. Good day, ma'am." Moyer glared at the woman until she continued on her way, servant in tow. He stood back to take Morning Fawn in. "What the devil?"

She mumbled under her breath. "Spying. Trying to find out if Reynolds was a lying snake."

Nicholas scoured Morning Fawn with his gaze. "Spying on Reynolds?" A grin erupted across his face. "You'll have to tell me more. But not here." He tucked the loose strand beneath her hat rim. "Come along, boy. I'll teach you to run into me."

He didn't release her until they were behind his closed office door. As soon as his hand fell away, she dusted off the spot where it had rested on the coat. She should have kept her mouth shut. But she had to say something, and the truth had popped out. Lies took more time. She'd better be prepared to spin a skein full.

Hair slicked back, mustache waxed, and his fine wool trousers and frock coat spotless, the man belonged with Miss Perfect. Only, he'd never take a second look at Frieda, and if he did, his fox-like nature would probably spook her back into her chicken coop of a life.

Nicholas pointed to the high-back chair across from his desk. Morning Fawn practically dove in it. A single chair, much better than a sofa for distancing herself from him. Her hat slipped, and she yanked it off. Hair cascaded across her shoulders and onto her back.

Grin still wide, Nicholas shoved his cigar box aside and leaned back against the front of his desk, half resting on the beveled edge. He shook his head as he gave her another look over. "What happened to your feet?"

She tucked them under the chair. "Reynolds caught a glimpse of me spying on him. I took off running. Didn't want to be caught. Discarded my boots along the way. I left him wandering in the woods, with no clue. That's…when I bumped into you. That's why I was in a hurry." She shrugged, but her heart felt as if it'd pound out of her chest. Devon's life was at stake here. *Dear God, help me.* Did the Lord help people lie? She couldn't afford to mess up.

"Obviously, you're not the girl I thought you were." A fire burned in his eyes. Was that good or bad?

She rubbed her hands on her scuffed trouser legs. "I reckon I'm not. Too many years on the frontier with the Comanche. I should go—"

"Go? I'm dying to hear what you discovered about our lieutenant. Less than two weeks ago, you told me he was the epitome of virtue, and now I see you…" He waved his hand toward her. "And now you're playing detective and dressed like Sally Skull."

"Sally who?"

"Toughest cotton teamster this side of the Rio Grande. And a good shot. A wise man doesn't touch her cotton or get in her way." He unbuttoned his coat, revealing a charcoal-colored waistcoat. "But you're a much finer lady than she could ever hope to be."

Fine lady? Morning Fawn smothered a sputter as she glanced down at her attire.

"I can see you still underestimate yourself." The words flowed smoother than milk. "But I digress. I'm dying to hear about Reynolds."

She swallowed. *Keep it close to truth. Throw this man off the trail.* "I was tired of his lying, sneaking ways. You...you were right about me having an interest in him. He'd be sweet as pie on some moonlight walk or sharing hymnals in church, but then he'd disappear off to Alleyton and not have a word for me. I knew there was someone else. A doctor's daughter. Frieda. 'Miss Perfect,' that's what I call her. Always after him to have some lemonade or cookies. But I've seen the way they looked at each other, and the way he went to calling her by her given name ten minutes after they met."

She curled her fingers inward at the thought of it. "And then him telling me he was going to Alleyton on business and that I was his one and only. Well, I got tired of being taken for a fool. I snuck off the plantation, got me some clothes and a horse, and came to find out for myself."

"Amazing." He gnawed his lip. His expression faded to dead serious. "What did you discover?"

"I caught them hanging all over each other...and kissing. More than I could stomach." She flipped her hair behind her shoulder. "I'm finished with that man. Miss Lemonade and Cookies can have him."

Nicholas stroked his thin mustache, pressing the curled ends against his short beard and then releasing them.

Had she said too much? Would he read more than Frieda into why Devon was coming to Alleyton? Sweat slicked her palms, but she willed her hands to be still. She needed to appear angry, not nervous.

"Have you found out anything else about him?" He arched his eyebrows. "I've sent inquiries—"

Her heart sank. "Inquiries? Any word back yet? I'm sorry I didn't listen to you a couple weeks ago."

"Too bad you wasted your affection when you had another beau faithfully seeking it."

She squirmed in her seat. What was she supposed to say to that? "I reckon I got what I deserved."

"I reckon you did." He withdrew a cigar from the box at his side. "There was something about the man that didn't set right with me from the first day I laid eyes on him. I'm still waiting to hear from my agent, but I'm sure he'll dig—"

"There was one more thing." Her chest tightened. She had to steer this weasel off course. This was her chance. What to say? Devon was depending on her to get it right. "I wouldn't necessarily trust your agent."

"You don't know anything about my agent."

"I know what I overheard Dev—Reynolds saying to Miss Perfect."

"What?" He leaned forward.

"That he has men inside your circle. That he's here from Confederate headquarters. Spying on you."

He shot up off the desk. "Spying on me?"

She shrugged. "I wasn't sure if I should tell you."

"And why the devil not?"

"He made it sound as if you weren't to be trusted. Which is rather funny coming from Mr. Two-Timing Liar." She bit her lip. *Please let this be the right thing to do, Lord. For Devon's sake.* "They...Confederate headquarters suspect you of keeping some of the cotton for yourself. Selling it off and using it to buy all those acres you've been snatching up. They sent him to investigate."

"What?" His hands clenched. "How dare they? Did he mention any names?"

"Not that I heard."

"And to use a scum like him!" He paced, strangling his unlit cigar between his fingers. "You heard him say all of this to her? Why would he tell that stupid girl his business?" He jerked to a halt right in front of her. Legs wide and hands on his hips, he towered over her.

Morning Fawn scooted against the chair back and gazed into his razor glare. This was the moment that counted—she had to sell the story. For Devon's sake. "He was bragging to her. Pressing for more than kisses, from what I could tell. Maybe also wanting her to help with digging up information."

"What did she say?"

"She put off the helping part, but things got kind of quiet and muffled. I couldn't see. But I was ready to leap through the bushes and scratch her face off. Then I accidentally stepped on a stick. Reynolds jumped up. I took off running because I didn't want him to see me in this get-up and know I'd gone to all of this trouble for him." She sniffled. The lie and half truths sat rotten in her belly.

He worked his jaw as if trying to puzzle it all out in his head.

"I didn't know if I should tell you." She fiddled with her worn cuff. "If you were really stealing from the Confederates... Not that I care that much for the war, but people worked hard to harvest that cotton." She squirmed. The binding around her chest bit into her flesh. "But then again, the warriors from my village stole from the whites, and it was counted as honorable."

"I can assure you, I'm not stealing."

"I figured Reynolds and those higher-ups were probably wrong." She cast a glance his way and stood. "I need to get headed home. I snuck off. I've got to get back before they discover I'm missing."

"No."

"No?" Was he going to try and hold her? He didn't believe her?

He eyed her appraisingly. "You're nothing like I thought you were. I have been mistaken in how I've attempted to court you."

"I understand I have broken your trust." She coiled her hair and inched toward the door. "I'll make up an excuse to my uncle about why you stopped calling, and I'll ask them to return Ebony to you."

"My dear Beth, you greatly misunderstand." He stepped toward her. "You're exactly the woman I want to court. Only, I have been going about it as if you were a light-headed damsel in need of a man's protection and catering to your every whim." He puffed out his chest. "I see now that you're more of an equal."

A compliment she actually cared about. "Flattery will get you nowhere, Mr. Moyer."

"Honest praise, and it's Nick." He might as well have had fox ears, the way he eyed her. "I'll personally escort you home after I've procured you decent clothing and had a servant girl look after your feet. I'll tell your uncle you came to see me. That I'd invited you but hadn't realized you'd attempt the journey without an escort. I'll apologize profusely and assure him we had a proper chaperone at all times. As proof to him, I'll have one of my servants ride back with us."

She blinked at him and took a step back. "I have my own clothes and Ebony. I just need to get back to them. Maybe your servant could give me a ride. Then I could find my own way home."

"And get in trouble? Or risk danger on the return trip? I wouldn't hear of it."

She touched the leather sheath which swung at her side. "I

have a knife, and I know how to use it, Nicholas." She forced the mettle into her too-quivery voice.

He chuckled. "Is that for me or a ruffian along the road?"

"Whoever needs it."

"I wouldn't dream of being ungentlemanly. I don't believe in a man forcing his affections upon a lady." He motioned to the chair. "Have a seat. I'll send to my house for my maid to come look after your feet and bandage them up. And then, if it's your wish, I'll have my servant take you in my carriage to your horse, and I'll see you at Sweet Briar for dinner. If your uncle gives you trouble, tell them I'm on my way, and I'll explain everything."

Was this an elaborate trick? Or a sincere effort to gain her affection? But it'd be foolish to refuse. "Thank you." She fumbled with her hat in her hands. "I'd rather not be seen like this any more than I have to."

"Do you think Reynolds will be at dinner?"

"I have no idea. He might be busy eating Miss Perfect's cooking."

"I hope not." He tossed the unlit cigar on his desk and checked his pocket watch. "I'd love to see his face when you put him in his place."

She inwardly grimaced. Not a sight she wanted to see. Obviously, the show wasn't over yet.

$\mathcal{D}$ark had fallen by the time Devon strode across the ground between the stables and the house. A chorus of coyotes sang in the distance. Dinner would be over, and that suited him just fine. His thoughts were too jumbled to sit across from Morning Fawn at a table after everything that had happened.

Images flooded his mind. Her tear-streaked face. Her hair tumbling out from beneath that battered hat. Trousers. Her poor feet. Why had she run from him?

He'd ridden back from Alleyton in a daze. Morning Fawn was beautiful. Unpredictable. More clever and brave and determined than he'd ever imagined. And potentially, unintentionally dangerous. He'd lost his head. How else could he explain why he'd told her everything? Or almost everything.

Of course, Frieda and Dr. Schramm hadn't understood why he'd done it. Frieda's silent brooding and Schramm's deep worry had echoed across the room. He couldn't tell them it was because he couldn't bear to hurt Morning Fawn or lie to her again. He'd told them he trusted her with his life, that her not knowing was more dangerous than her knowing. Otherwise, she'd continue to poke around until she was in the middle of everything, and it'd be safer to give her a minor task where she could be a part of helping but not in a place of consequence.

His stomach rumbled. He should have asked Morning Fawn to meet him in the kitchen after everyone else turned in for the night. Even one day was too long to leave her stewing over what he'd told her. Besides, he needed to hear she'd returned safely. Hopefully, she'd made it back without detection and wasn't locked in the attic.

At least the house wasn't lit up in alarm with search parties waiting to be sent out. No, everything was quiet. Almost.

The porch swing creaked. A low light glowed against the columns. Would Morning Fawn have dared wait up for him?

He stepped quickly through the damp grass to the front of the house and stopped dead in his tracks.

Creak. Creak. Back and forth, Nick Moyer pumped the swing with his legs, a brandy snifter in his hand and Morning Fawn at his side, her feet tucked beneath the seat, both hands curled around the scumbag's arm.

Devon froze, his mind in full stutter.

The couple glanced his way, Moyer looking as if he were a cat who'd swallowed a mouse.

Morning Fawn had acted as if she had no interest in Moyer. Had it all been subterfuge? She wouldn't dare reveal his secret to Moyer. Would she? He couldn't have been that wrong about her.

Devon rocked backward on his heels. What if it had all been a ploy to get him to talk?

"Evening, Lieutenant." She straightened. "You missed supper."

How in the devil was he to play this? Her syrupy, taunting voice grated against his nerves.

"I'll scrounge up something in the kitchen." The words

tasted like gravel. For all he knew, they could have men waiting in the house or yard to arrest him.

Morning Fawn swatted at a mosquito. "I figure you were too busy taking care of business. Black wavy curls and sweet-talking type of business. Sugar lips too."

Devon's jaw clenched. She'd told Moyer about Frieda. What else?

Moyer's smirk was so wide, it was a wonder his brandy didn't drool out of his mouth.

"Cat got your tongue?" Morning Fawn smoothed her hand over her skirt. "I want you to know, I've heard about your double-dealing, and Miss Perfect can have you. I also wanted to inform you that I've accepted Nicholas's request to court me." She cuddled up close to the rat and waved her hand toward Devon. "That's all. You can run along now. Unless you want to stay and watch us star gaze. I've had enough of your snaky ways."

He'd be happy to run along after he'd pummeled that popinjay's face to a pulp. "You're sitting next to the real snake." How could this be the same woman he held close today? He ground his teeth.

His feet thundered as he went up the steps and into the house. Should he keep on going down the hall and out the back door? He had no clue what she was up to or how much she'd told. Did she somehow think she could get Frieda in trouble and spare him?

Who was he kidding? She had every reason to strike at him. He'd been the one to steal her from her home and Comanche family. What had he been thinking, trusting her? The safest bet would be to head to the stables, grab his horse, and be shed of this place.

He glanced up the stairs.

Lucy leaned over the banister and put a finger to her lips. Her purple hand-me-down dress hung limp around her as she crept down a few stairs. She glanced over her shoulder with every step, a deep frown crinkling her forehead. "Miss Beth says to meet her later tonight, in the spot you talked about."

"Did she say anything el—"

A door opened somewhere on the second floor. Lucy flew up the stairs, and Devon moved out of view of the banister.

"What are you doing sneaking around, girl?" Mrs. LeBeau asked.

"Nothing, ma'am. Just going down to see if Miss Beth was coming in soon so I could help her get ready for bed."

"What was all that stomping about?"

"Lieutenant Reynolds, ma'am."

A grumble, and the voices faded.

Meet Morning Fawn in the garden. That had to be what the message meant. So she could explain herself, gloat over her revenge, or have him arrested as a Yankee?

Murmurs echoed in from the front porch. What he wouldn't give to drag that man off that swing and wring his neck.

His muscles hardening like gun barrels, Devon headed for the back door. He'd meet her, all right.

~

*A*n hour. Devon had paced enough to dig a trench halfway around Vicksburg by now.

Trimmed to green conical shapes, Leland cypress trees lined the center rows of Mrs. LeBeau's garden, blocking Devon's view of the discarded leavings in the vegetable plots and hiding him from sight of anyone at the house.

Was Morning Fawn still in that porch swing with Moyer, or had he gone home? Devon didn't even want to think about how much a man like that would try to get away with in an hour, especially after a brandy or two. Was she letting him?

Devon kicked a fallen stake out of his path. A sliver of a

moon hovered in the sky—all that remained of the globe that lit his path with Morning Fawn a few weeks before. A Great-Horned owl hooted, *who-who-who*. Its voice echoed across the garden. Golden eyes peered at Devon from a gnarled Osage orange tree in a corner.

He had half a mind to head for the stables and —

Leaves crunched behind him.

He swung around, hand on his holster.

Morning Fawn halted beneath a vined arch. A shawl flowed over her shoulders and the bodice of the shimmering gown she'd worn on the porch. Her hair hung loose. A beautiful deceiver.

She tugged her shawl tighter. "Please forgive me for having to say—"

"Should I hold my hands out for the ropes now or later?" He strode toward her.

"What ropes?"

"The ones they'll tie my hands with after you finish spilling everything I told you to that snake."

"I didn't tell him any—"

"He knows about Frieda. And the way you were cozied up to him on the porch, probably couldn't get a feather between you." He flexed his hands at his sides. "I trusted you."

"I'm trying to save your life."

"By betraying me?" He ground a withered vine beneath his boot. "I hope he comes down here to confront me. I'd like nothing better than to lay into him."

"Now who has the temper?"

He narrowed his eyes. "Is that what this is about? Revenge."

"Of course not. I'm trying to throw him off your trail." She latched onto his arm. "I ran into him when I hurried back to the street, and he recognized me. I had to do something. I had to come up with an excuse for why I was dressed like a man."

He shrugged off her hold. "What did you tell him?"

"That I was jealous and spying on you. That I thought there was a doctor's daughter who'd caught your eye. I figured the closer it was to the truth, the better the lie."

If she'd stayed put on the plantation today, there'd be no need for thinking up lies, but he swallowed the rebuke before it left his lips. "Did he believe you?"

"Yes. But then he said he'd sent an agent to your home county to investigate you. That he was waiting to hear back." She gestured toward him, palms up. "I had to do something to throw him off track."

He stilled, almost afraid to ask. "And what was that?"

Her voice sank. "I didn't know what to say." She fiddled with the fringe on her shawl. "All I wanted to do was to protect you, keep you safe. I remembered what you'd said about a backup lie. I told him you were here from Confederate headquarters and that you were investigating him."

Devon blew out his cheeks and slid his hand down his face. "That wasn't yours to tell." Leave it to Morning Fawn to turn this mission into a wild horse with no reins. Maybe they'd win the race, or maybe they'd fall off and get trampled.

"You're upset with me?"

"Not exactly."

"I was afraid for you." Her voice wobbled.

"You've upended so many parts of the plan, I don't even know where to start."

"I'm sorry." Big, wet eyes gazed into his, penetrating his defenses.

His heart rolled over. He gulped a steadying breath and exhaled. "You did help." In a wild horse type of way that would probably give him gray hairs before she was finished. "Hopefully, your story will divert his attention from the worst possibility and buy us time."

"You don't sound certain." She swished her hand against her skirt folds.

"There aren't any guarantees in this kind of work." He caught her hand. His fingers curled around hers. She'd thrown herself right in the mix with him, putting her life in danger when he would have done everything he could, except for sacrificing the mission, in order to keep her safe. "It's like a game of cards where the stakes are lives instead of money. You study your opponent, calculate, and take risks. Only today, while I was in the middle of a game with a good hand, you walked in after I'd made my bets, and you threw all the cards in the middle and said. 'Let's re-deal.'"

"Maybe your opponent had an even better hand and was about to take everything you had?" She bit her lip.

Or maybe she'd handed his opponent means to wipe him out. But as he gazed into her face, his shoulders unlocked. There'd be no scolding her. His rebuke would bounce off her like raindrops on a rubberized blanket. Either that, or she'd take it so much to heart she'd be wounded beyond hope. "We...I will have to revise the plan. Moyer is going to watch me like a hawk. And he'll have men keep an eye on the Schramms too."

"But he'll be afraid to do anything or say much to anyone. Because he thinks he's under suspicion. And the way he acted when I said it...maybe he really is a thief."

"I hope he is. That would keep him looking over his shoulder." The slime had put his hands on...his girl. Devon's girl. "I've got to know. Did you let that man kiss you? Because I'd rather take my chances of being hung than for you to allow him such liberties."

"No kisses." She smiled. "I told him I'd let you kiss me before I found out about your skunky ways and that I wasn't going to allow another man to kiss me until I was engaged."

"I've *never* had the pleasure of kissing you."

"I had to say something to make him keep his lips to himself."

He ground his molars. "I don't want that man anywhere near you."

"Then we'd better work on finishing your mission."

"'We'?" The change he'd agreed to was still a bit hard to swallow, but he didn't want to talk about that right now. Didn't want to talk about anything. He touched her cheek. Lightning sizzled up his arm. In the wake of it, every clear thought in his head evaporated. "It's not just the mission. You've turned my whole world upside down."

"Is that good or bad?"

"Both." He drew her into his arms. His heart thundered in his ears.

Wide-eyed, she sucked in a breath. Her hands slipped over his chest, weaving a web of sweetness.

"Morning Fawn." He breathed her name.

He lowered his gaze to her lips. The only woman he wanted to kiss. He dipped his head.

Her lips parted like a morning glory opening to the sun... then closed.

Her nimble fingers squeezed between his lips and hers. "You promised to tell me about Isabelle. I can't bear to be in your arms tonight, and then tomorrow, maybe you don't even speak to me."

The way her body melted against his, he'd be willing to bet he could shove those fingers aside and kiss her half the night. His chest rose and fell hard. But she deserved an answer to her question. With a groan, he loosened his hold on her. "All right. Come."

He led her to a wrought-iron bench, one of four that faced the starlit cupid statue at the center of the garden where the arched walkways converged. Flanked by two cypresses, the seat would provide a measure of privacy.

Morning Fawn didn't bother tucking her skirt beneath her. It splayed across the bench. He nudged the cream-soft satin out of the way.

"I snuck off and spied on you today because I couldn't stand another moment of waiting in the shadows like some useless, worn-out doily that no one had any use for." Her voice hardly more than a whisper, she traced a strip of lace on her cuff.

"Nothing could be further from the truth." He touched a finger to the hard spot beneath his shirt where the locket lingered. He had no business trying to kiss Morning Fawn while he still wore the keepsake.

"How could I know that?"

"I never meant to hurt you. I thought staying away was the most caring thing I could do."

"How could you think that?"

A breath slid between his teeth like a cracked steam valve. He lowered his elbows to his knees and shifted forward. "For one, I'm on a dangerous mission and didn't want to drag you into it. But there was more to it than that. I didn't write you because I started thinking about how I used to write Isabelle."

"Oh." Her chest deflated.

A sharp breeze rustled the branches of the trees around them as mounting puffs of clouds shadowed the moon.

Morning Fawn shivered. "You...you said you hurt her somehow?"

Devon took her hand in his, weaving their fingers together. What if she wanted nothing to do with him once she heard what he had to say?

Morning Fawn squeezed his hand.

Where to begin? "I left home when I was seventeen. Isabelle and I were apart for six years. I wrote every chance I could, and so did she, sending our letters through a third party. Her father was a Mexican working as a cook on a neighboring plantation. A Mexican and a servant. Two boundaries not to be crossed in high-class planter society."

"If you loved her, why didn't you marry her and take her with you?"

"We were young. I didn't have a way to support her. I lived rough. Worked as a teamster, then joined the Texas Rangers. My only home was the next campfire."

"I see."

His tongue felt like sandpaper. "Eventually, I joined the cavalry as a scout. Worked myself up to a corporal. Then, when I saved my colonel from a scalping, they made me a brevet second lieutenant. That's when I went for Isabelle. I'd waited until I could bring her to the fort as an officer's wife." He squeezed his eyes shut. All those years of waiting and planning. Their time together had been so short. Memories washed over him. The joy on her face when he knelt and asked her to marry him, the days and nights as a young married couple at the fort, the love in her eyes and her hands...the hand that had turned cold in his the day she died. He shuddered and stood.

The coyotes picked up their song, one mournful cry echoed by five or six more.

"I wasn't there when she needed me most." Sweat dampened his jacket collar and under his arms. "We'd been married two years. She was with child and living at the fort with me. My colonel needed me to track a raiding party. Stop them before they struck deeper into the frontier and took more lives. The baby wasn't due for another month. The colonel mentioned that if I felt I really needed to stay, he'd send someone else. But...I knew they needed me. I was the best tracker. Settler lives were at stake. I thought Isabelle would be fine. We were supposed to be back in a week...." How many times had he wished to God he could relive that day, take back that decision?

"It took two weeks. Isabelle went into labor the eleventh day. Three days of terrible pain. The baby was breech. By the time they were able to get the baby turned, it was too late. Isabelle was hemorrhaging. When I got there, our baby was dead, and Isabelle was slipping away." His voice broke. He sank onto the bench, his gaze plastered on the ground. The memories tore into his heart like wolf teeth.

"It wasn't your fault. You couldn't have known. The baby was weeks early."

"It was careless and reckless of me. Babies can come early. She needed me, and I wasn't there." He rubbed the moisture beneath his eyepatch. "The fort's doctor looked after her, but he had more experience with wounds than birthing babies. If I had been there...I could have ridden north across the Red River. I'd heard of a Comanche midwife on a reservation a day's ride away. I would have found her and brought her back."

"There's no way of knowing if that would have changed anything."

"But at least I would have known I'd done everything possible. Or at least been there to comfort her through the worst hours of her life." His chest burned. So did his eyes. He needed to get away. Go for a ride until both he and the horse were totally exhausted. "I've got to go."

CHAPTER 26

orning Fawn's mouth dropped open. "What?"

Devon jumped to his feet. "I can't talk about this anymore."

"No. Wait."

But he'd already started through the arch and down the path toward the back garden gate.

She stood. What could she say? She'd never been good at comforting others. She had failed miserably when her adopted brother died five years ago. She'd hidden her tears and kept silent. Her pia and her ahpu must have thought she didn't care. It'd created a wall that had been slow in coming down. She could not let the man she loved go off with his raw hurt now. "Devon."

She ran. The hard leather of her shoes gritted into her wounds like a saw.

He reached for the gate latch.

She slapped her hand on top of it first, half stumbling against the stone wall.

He glared at her in the dark. Not even the shrouded moon could fail to reveal the pain raging in his moisture-laden eye.

"It's not your fault." Her voice shook. Words pushed themselves out of her heart. "Isabelle loved you. She wouldn't want you carrying this burden. I'm certain of it."

He swiped his nose and stared at her in stony silence.

She touched his sleeve. "I know what it's like to hurt someone you love and feel like you don't deserve anything."

"You do?" His voice dipped.

"More than I want to know." Her throat clogged. Dare she say more? But the words, locked away for so long, spilled out. "In the months after I was captured by the Comanche, I watched my sister...be beaten and starved. And said nothing. I...I tried to sneak her food a couple of times. But I was afraid they'd see I belonged with her and treat me the same. I deserted her..." She wadded the wool of his jacket in her fist.

"You were a child."

"I could have done more. I was a coward." Laid bare, she longed to lower her head. Instead, she looked into the face of the man who needed her. "I didn't mean to start talking about me. I just want you to know I understand."

He slipped his palm beneath her jaw, his gaze piercing deep within her soul. "Maybe you were a scared little girl once, but the woman I see before me is a warrior who'd risk her life for her sister or anyone else she cares about. She'd take on the whole tribe to do so."

Tears trickled down her cheeks. "And I see a man of courage and honor who loved his wife with everything he had."

A breath shuddered through him. He yanked off his patch.

She gasped. His eye appeared whole, not injured.

His arms locked around her, sweeping her away from the precipice of the past and bathing her in warmth. She buried her face in the crook of his neck and tightened her arms around him as he pressed his cheek to her head, his grief dampening her hair, even as hers wet his jacket.

Cradling her close, he nudged her to sit against the ancient

Osage orange tree and held her. For how long? It didn't matter. She never wanted to uncurl from the cocoon of his side. She had never felt so loved.

He whispered against her hair, "I haven't looked at a woman in three years. Then I came here, and from day one, I could hardly think of anything or anyone but you..." He stroked her cheek. "I'm afraid I've... fallen for you. And the last thing in this world I want to do is hurt you. My mission is dangerous. I might not—"

She pressed her fingers to his lips. "Hush. You're going to come out fine. You're going to complete your mission and take me away." She smiled. "And I'm so thankful your eye is all right."

"Part of my cover. An excuse for not returning to my regiment and a reason to seek out Dr. Schramm." He brushed his thumb over her shoulder. "I'll do everything in my power to look after you and protect you. I'm going to get you out of here."

She nuzzled deeper and squeezed his side where her arm rested across his chest. "I want to be with you, wherever that is." She was in love, and she was loved. Nothing else mattered, not even the land her uncle had promised.

He cuddled her closer. "My intention, Warrior Girl, is to get you and me to Brownsville. We probably won't go together or even at the same time. I have the mission to complete first. But when we get there, I plan to court you."

Court? She'd marry him next week if he asked her. But she pressed her lips tight. Best keep her mouth shut. There was no guarantee he was ready to hear he was the man she wanted to spend the rest of her life with.

"I don't know what your mission is yet."

"It's best you don't. That way, if you're caught—"

"I'd never breathe a word to them. I grew up Comanche. I know what torture is."

He stiffened and nudged her gaze up to his. "I don't plan to give them a reason to torture you." His brow furrowed deep. "Besides, they wouldn't torture a woman. Might let her go hungry and put her in filthy quarters." His Adam's apple dipped.. "You'd best know what you've gotten yourself into. If they think you're part of it, you could go to prison, even face the...gallows."

"Same as you."

"Unacceptable." He sat up straight. "I'm going to speak with my contact. I have a meeting in a few days. I'll see about arranging for you to be smuggled to the coast as soon as possible."

"You can talk to your contact all you want, but I'm not leaving until you do."

No more embrace. His hands dropped away. "After everything I told you about Isabelle, you think I'm going to allow you to stay in harm's way?"

"I notice that Isabelle wasn't back in some town or plantation waiting for you. She loved you. She was there at the fort, with you as much as she could be. And I bet if you could ask her, she wouldn't have done it any differently. I'm not some parlor maiden sitting around worrying about which color of flowers to put in my garden or what pattern to embroider for my hope chest. You said it yourself. I'm a fighter."

A chuckle. "That much is true."

"Besides, do you think I'm going to cower down in Brownsville, wherever that might be, while Miss Perfect is here risking her life with you?" The very thought had her off the ground and her hand on her hip.

He scowled. "Have you ever heard of the word *obstinate*? It's you. Stubborn, hard-headed, in woeful need of learning to accept orders and direction."

She folded her arms.

He shoved his fingers through his hair. "And for your information, Frieda is risking her life for the Union, not for me. This mission is about saving the lives of soldiers. Impeding the cotton trade so the Rebs have less money for ammunition, guns, and other supplies."

"I'm guessing *impeding* means to stop or slow down. If that's the case, I'm volunteering. The Rebs haven't done me any favors. And I think about as much of slavery as I do manure."

He shook his head. "I knew you'd be like this. You'd either stomp off and want nothing to do with it or insist on being right there in the middle." He jabbed his finger at her. "Let me tell you something, Miss Warrior Girl. You're having no part of anything until you can convince me you know how to follow orders. This is a military operation."

A smile broke across her face. She latched onto his sleeve. "I'll listen. I promise. Just as long as you let me have a part and don't send me away."

His gaze fell into hers. "It'll take more than words, Taa Aruka." His voice dipped low. "And the first time you don't listen, you're going to be on the road to the coast even if I have to hog-tie you and gag you like I did back on the Brazos."

"If I don't listen, you have my permission to send me off." She clasped her hands behind her. Her shawl slipped to her elbows, the ends dragging against the exposed tree roots.

"You can count on it." He tugged the finely woven garment upward. His fingertips slid along her arms, spreading goose-bumps over her limbs as he returned the shawl to its rightful place.

"And let's get one thing straight." He planted his hands on her shoulders. "You're not coming with me the night we strike. And *we* doesn't mean Frieda. She's under orders to be at her home, ready to flee if needed. Your assignment, as much as it sours my stomach, will be to distract Moyer." As tolerable as sticking cactus needles in his eyes. "If you care about my life and our future, you'll listen. I can't think of anything that would put me in jeopardy more than having you there at the depot or warehouse because my attention would be split between carrying out the mission and keeping you safe."

His hands fell away. "And I don't know how you think courting works, but it usually involves listening and waiting. You waiting for me to call on you to take you for a walk, or visit in a parlor, maybe go riding, come pick you up for church, come by your place for dinner."

She quirked her mouth and gazed up at him. "I don't know if I see that."

"What?"

"Me waiting around like that." She swung her arms at her sides. "Besides, what are *you* going to wait for?"

His eyes glistened in the dark. "To kiss you."

"You're going to wait for that?"

A smile lit his lips. "No." He reached inside his collar, yanked a chain over his head, a locket in tow, and stuffed it in his pocket. His eyes shone as he took her in his arms.

Her heart thudded.

His mouth lowered to hers. His breath tickled her lips. "I'm allowed an impetuous streak now and then too."

Her eyes fluttered closed, and her lips parted. *Please. Please. Please.*

She melted against him as his lips brushed hers. Her hands swept over his shoulders, and her fingers locked around the back of his neck.

His arms tightened, and he cradled her head as he deepened the kiss, flooding her with a wave of warmth that washed past hurts beyond the horizon.

CHAPTER 27

*L*amplight flickered across the Schramms' oil-cloth-covered table. Devon had come to clarify Morning Fawn's role in the mission and to later rendezvous with the recruits from the German League. From his perch next to the flower-print curtains, Devon wrapped his fingers around a steaming mug of coffee. Frieda sat at the end, as far from Devon as she could while still being at the table. A frown, deeper than he'd imagined her capable of, furrowed her brow, adding years to her face.

She seemed to have the ability to see through every valid reason he'd come up with for why he'd allowed Morning Fawn a part, and she'd taken it personally. But there was nothing he could say, short of a lie, that would fix matters between him and Frieda. He hadn't intended to hurt her. The first day he'd visited this house, he'd had Morning Fawn at his side, and he'd reminded Frieda on several occasions that the courtship was only pretense.

Thank goodness, he'd had sense enough to make Morning Fawn stay at home today, under threat he'd send her off with Captain Jeremy Carson three days from now if she didn't prove her ability to listen and obey orders. Her presence here would have been like a matchstick to kindling.

Across from him, Dr. Schramm laced his worn fingers across his paunch. "You have feelings for this captive girl."

Devon startled, splashing a wave of coffee out of the cup and onto his finger. He winced at the sting. "Sir?" He flashed a glance at Frieda, who'd stiffened like a statue of some martyr.

Dr. Schramm held up his hand. "My daughter must hear this too. It is all of our lives at stake." A sigh rattled through him. "It's a statement, not a question. There is no need to expound upon the fact. I see it in your face and in your actions. Even in the reticule I had to go looking for last time you vere here."

"I apologize for that. As I explained before, I didn't willingly bring Morn—Miss Logan in. She followed me—"

"I understand the situation, Lieutenant Reynolds." The doctor returned his hands to his belly. "I vould have no problem with the girl if she came to my house for dinner or called as a patient, but as far as the mission goes, ve must acknowledge that she is a volatile element. After all, she is the girl who stole the Thoroughbred in the middle of a church service. She does not possess the calm, thoughtful, practical demeanor of my daughter."

Devon settled back in his chair. A seepage of breath eked out between his teeth. The man's assessment was too close to the facts to dispute. "I won't argue with you. Frieda is an exceptional assistant, and her character is above reproach." He glanced away from the end of the table where she fluttered at his words. "I have greatly appreciated her help and would welcome her continued assistance. However, Miss Logan is now part of this mission, and if it wasn't for her quick thinking in planting suspicion in Moyer's mind regarding his superiors and agents, I might be in danger of arrest at any moment."

Dr. Schramm pushed his glasses back upon his nose. "It vill only be a matter of time before the danger returns."

"Yes, but I don't plan to wait around for it." Devon leaned forward, elbows on the table. "But precious time that Morning Fawn bought gives us a window of opportunity to strike. I'm moving up the date to Christmas night. I've instructed Miss Logan to accept Moyer's invitation to the Christmas Ball at Robson's Castle. She'll keep him away from the warehouse. I believe the quartermaster will be attending the ball, as well. For the soldiers on guard, we'll see if we can get them some liquor as a Christmas present."

"I...I could do that." Frieda shifted forward in her seat.

Devon jerked his head toward her, eyebrows raised. "I don't want you anywhere near the warehouse or depot on Christmas."

She clasped her hands on the table, no trace of a dimple on her smooth, pale skin. "I'd be out of there hours before anything happens. I'll go after the changing of the guard. Some of the fellows come to my father seeking remedies they've heard about from snake oil salesmen, basically alcohol. I'll tell them my father got in a special batch for Christmas."

"I don't like it." Dr. Schramm ran a hand over his untamed tuft of gray hair.

"I'll not allow you to go alone amongst the men after dark." Devon firmed his voice.

"You could go with me, Lieutenant." She flattened her lips.

He rubbed his hand over the back of his neck. It could work, but he still didn't like it. He shoved his coffee aside. "If you do something such as that, your father and you would need to leave town immediately afterward." He glanced around at the morning-glory-print wallpaper, the hand-painted porcelain cups, the beautifully carved cupboard. "You'd have to leave it all behind."

"Frieda and I have discussed it." Dr. Schramm heaved a

sigh. "Considering all of the developments, ve do not feel safe staying. Even if the only connection to Frieda was her pretend courtship vith you, it vould be a risk. Ve are Germans. Ve're not well-liked. Too many of our people have already been hunted down as Unionists. I've told you of the young men vho sought to leave Texas in order to join the Union and vere slaughtered. Ve cannot count on reasonable treatment. I'll allow Frieda to go vith you to deliver the gifts of remedy to the guards, then she and I vill head out of town. Hours before the explosion. We'll pack a few things and send them off ahead of time."

"I'm villing to sacrifice the comforts of home for a cause I believe in." Frieda tilted her chin. "There are men dying on the battlefields, giving their all. I only seek to do my little part. For me, this isn't some grand, flirtatious adventure. It's a commitment." A self-satisfied smile lifted her lips, revealing the tarnish on her halo.

Devon stared at her for a moment. "Morning Fawn is willing to risk her life, and if I'd allowed her, she'd have been right here with me tonight."

"Vith *you*. If she took a fancy to some Reb, vould she be vith him and their cause?" Frieda pressed her lips together and stood, dismissing the subject. "You've hardly touched your coffee. I'll pour a little more and varm it up before you and papa head to the meeting."

He glared at her. She was jealous. A wise man would ignore the barbs. "My coffee is fine." He covered his cup with his hand.

"Very vell." She clanked the pot back down on the stove. "It is *you* Papa and I are most concerned about. I just hate to see..." She held up her hands. "Never mind. I need to go milk the cow."

He shifted in his seat. The cow? Was it a ploy to get him to speak to her alone? Should he go try to explain things more?

"I might need help carrying the bucket." She glared at him with bloodshot eyes.

He shook himself. She wanted to talk privately. The gentlemanly thing to do would be to accompany her outside and apologize. But he'd already said everything he could. He exhaled and stayed in his seat. They needed distance, not privacy.

She yanked off her apron and shouldered her way out the door like a steam engine ready to run over anything in her path.

Devon sank down in his chair a notch.

Dr. Schramm tapped his coffee cup. "Ve should go soon. I told the league eight p.m."

"All right. I want to finalize the details of the attack. I assume tonight it'll only be those who have volunteered to help?"

"Frederic, Gunter, Jarvis and his brothers."

"Good men. I spoke with them during my initial meeting with the league." Devon nodded. "Tomorrow night, I'm rendezvousing with Captain Carson and digging up the supply of guns I buried when I first arrived in the area. My recommendation is that you and Frieda don't leave town on Christmas. We can ask the league if someone could volunteer to hide you for a few weeks until everything settles down. The Rebs will scour the roads after the attack. I don't have confidence you could outrun them."

"Sound plan." Schramm leaned forward. "I have a request. I know it's a lot to ask. But I'll ask it, anyvay, because my daughter is all I have left in this vorld except for my practice and my faith, and I'm getting ready to give up my practice, at least for now."

Devon braced himself.

Schramm fingered the rim of his coffee cup. "If anything happens to me, or if for some reason Frieda is in danger, I'm asking you to look after her and do vhat you can to protect her."

Devon's lungs deflated in a stream that emptied out his

stamina in addition to the air. Just how long of a commitment was her father asking him for?

~

*M*orning Fawn pressed her sweaty palms to her skirt as she stood in front of her uncle's desk. Cigar odor stung her nose. Nick had called on her uncle earlier in the day without a word to her. She'd been relieved to have not spent the afternoon acting, but why had he come? Did it have something to do with Devon? Her uncle's summons had jolted her further.

"Have a seat." LeBeau motioned to the high-back, cushioned chair on her left. His crimson cravat covered his neck in a flourish all the way to the pointed beard on his chin.

A fire crackled in the fireplace. The weather had taken a turn.

She settled on the edge and clasped her hands in her lap. "You asked to see me?"

"I've been pleased with recent developments." He pushed his ledgers with their pages of pencil scratches and numbers aside. "Especially your courtship with Nick. Wise decision. That man may end up owning a tenth of the state someday."

Suited her just fine if the Yankees put Nick in his place someday. Confiscated all his property. "It's only a courtship, an opportunity to become better acquainted."

His ice-blue eyes glistened. "It's much more than that, my dear. You've succeeded beyond my dreams. Nick made you an offer of marriage today."

"He what?" She teetered on the edge of her seat.

"Proposed marriage. We plan to announce the engagement at the Christmas Ball."

"He...he never said a word to me. I mean...not an outright proposal. Not since we started courting."

Her uncle leaned back in his padded leather chair. "He showed me the particulars of his holdings, even provided references—not that I would have asked for them. It's a matter best decided between men."

"I'm the one he wants to marry. It's my life. My decision."

Her uncle glowered. "There can only be one possible answer when a staunchly loyal Confederate of means and character with a brilliant future proposes to my niece." He shifted forward, elbows on his desk. "Any other answer would be completely unacceptable and risk my wrath."

"I can't—"

Her uncle stood, his brow as contorted as a bull preparing to charge.

"We've only officially courted for three days."

"What were you doing when he gave you the horse? You've been courting for weeks. I'm not about to give you a month or two to disillusion the man. He's ready to marry you. All I have to do is name the time and place." LeBeau slapped his palms onto the desk surface. "The first few weeks of marriage will be a perfect time to get to know each other better." A sliver of his slicked hair dared inch toward his forehead. He swept it back with a force that could have laid a regiment low. "As for Reynolds, put him out of your head. I have questions about that man's character and his means. You'll never have my permission to court him, let alone be his wife. I'm dismissing him from my services by the end of the month."

She pressed her lips together. If she said much more, she'd get herself locked in the attic until further notice. The proposal, the engagement,—none of it mattered. She'd be leaving here Christmas night. With such a fate hanging over her head, Devon would surely take her away with him the night of the attack. They'd rendezvous somewhere—

"Beth." LeBeau puffed out his chest. "I expect your full cooperation with this, and since I'm a man of my word, I'll sign the deed to the land in Parker County over to you on your wedding day."

She glanced up at the portrait of her mother hanging over his head. Is this what they'd done to her? Found some suited planter with a load of acres, a wad of cash, and a wooden heart to be her future husband? No wonder her mother had run, forsaking wealth and everything she'd known. So would she.

Only, her parents' lack of means had eventually led them to the wagon trail across the Texas frontier and their deaths. She would not follow their fate. "I will comply with the engagement."

CHAPTER 28

*D*evon stepped back into the dark corner between the cupboard and the door, his heart pounding. He'd slipped Morning Fawn a message to meet him here in the stone-walled kitchen out back of the main house at midnight.

Bundles of sage, mint, and other herbs swung from the ceiling, mixing with the aroma of the glowing coals which lingered on the hearth beneath the iron kettle. Ladles dangled from hooks. Crockery of various sizes filled the work table. In the corner by the cavernous fireplace, moonlight trickled in through the east windows and the small window used for passing wood in to the cook.

Footsteps. The latch clicked, and the door opened. Devon held his breath as Morning Fawn stepped inside. Her hair flowed down. She closed the door behind her and peered into the almost dark.

Devon sprung, clasping a hand over her mouth smothering her gasp, and drew her back against him. "Caught you."

She tensed momentarily, then relaxed against his chest, flooding him with warmth. His hand dropped to her shoulder.

"What if I had screamed?" She leaned her head against his chin.

"I was betting you wouldn't." He inhaled the fresh-washed scent of her hair and rosewater. Hiding? Surprising her? He felt like a kid again. Only, this was no time for play. Four days until Christmas. He needed to go over plans and make sure she was ready. So little time. He wrapped his arms around her waist. "I missed you yesterday."

She placed her hands over his.

What if these few days were all they had? *Please God, don't let it be so.* He lingered there with her, swaying in the shadows.

Something scurried in the corner. A mouse?

"I was worried about you last night," she whispered. "You met with your contact?"

"Everything went fine. I got supplies, filled in Jer—Captain Carson—and finalized our plans."

"Are you going to tell me?"

"I'll tell you everything about the escape plans. The rest as needed." He loosened his hold and turned her to face him.

She touched his eyepatch.

He tugged it off and tucked it in his pocket.

Her fingers fluttered over his lashes.

He captured her hand and pressed his lips to her palm. He could sit right down on the work bench and cuddle all night long. But there was much to discuss. Five days from now, their lives could depend upon his clear thinking.

He nuzzled his chin against the palm of her hand, then stepped back. "I was worried too. About Moyer." The name stuck like tar on his tongue. "Did he call this evening? LeBeau sent me to Patterson's late this afternoon to check on a horse. I get the feeling your uncle is trying to keep me as far away from you as possible."

"There's a problem." She tucked a strand of hair behind her ear. "Two problems."

"Moyer?" The word came out as a growl. "Has he gotten out of line?"

"No. Nothing like that... He asked my uncle for my hand in marriage."

Devon exhaled. "What did your uncle say?"

She lowered her gaze. "It doesn't matter what he said because I'm going to be leaving here Christmas night."

The implications of her avoidance sank onto his shoulders. "Your uncle said yes without even asking you?"

She shuddered. "My opinion wasn't required. They're going to announce the engagement at the Christmas Ball. If I'd refused, I would have ended up locked in the attic. But as I said, it doesn't matter. I won't be here for the wedding."

"I don't like it one bit." There were no guarantees. He'd said it himself a dozen times. What if somehow he couldn't get Morning Fawn away from here? He should've insisted Jeremy work with him to get her out before Christmas Eve, but a disruption like that could throw the plan off in ways they couldn't calculate. "Captain Carson and I decided the best option would be for you to leave after Christmas...when they have a posse out looking for me."

"I want to leave when you do." Her voice took on an edge, like the neigh of a wild mare preparing to buck. "You said you'd have a horse ready for me."

"I'll still do that. Two horses. One here in the woods beyond the stables, and one near the river close to the castle. I want you to have a way out in case suspicion falls on you, but if we play it right, no one has to know you had any clue of what I was up to. You can tell them I must have seen you spying on me the day behind the depot and made up a story to mislead you." His throat tightened. What if Morning Fawn didn't get away? "Moyer will pursue me with a vengeance. I bet your uncle will too. The fewer people around to notice your departure, the safer you'll be. You can head for Houston, the opposite of where they'd think you'd go, then cut over for the coast. I'll have a boat waiting for you. I'll give you directions and wait for you there three days after the attack, and every day after that until you show."

"Don't put yourself at risk for me."

"I'll be careful, but if for some reason I can't make it, Captain Carson or one of his men will be at the rendezvous point."

"What do you mean if you don't make it?" She latched onto his arms.

His swallow stuck in his throat. "If they're pursuing me too closely, I'll have to head directly to Matagorda Bay or the nearest Yankee stronghold, then rendezvous with you later in Brownsville."

"You're going to make it. You're going to escape and be fine." Was there a tremor in her voice?

He wrapped her in his arms. "I'd wait for you outside of town Christmas night and ride with you if I didn't think it'd put you in further danger. I hate the idea of not being there to protect you."

"Don't you dare wait for anything. I'll find you on the coast."

Outside the snug walls of the kitchen, a dog howled.

He'd do whatever he had to do to protect her. Why did it feel as if he were abandoning her? "I'll get word to Lucy before I go, without giving her any details, to let you out if they lock you in the attic."

"That's the second problem." She withdrew from his hold.

"What?"

She wound the fringe from her shawl around her finger and drifted over to the workbench next to the butter churn. "Lucy."

"What about her? Is Ned having trouble getting leave of his master for Christmas Eve?" He shoved a couple buckets over to make room on the bench and dropped down beside her.

"Not that." She puffed out her cheeks and exhaled. She

clutched a handful of the shawl. "I promised her weeks ago that if...not *if*, *when* I left here, I'd find a way to help her escape too."

"Why would you do such a thing? You didn't say anything about the mission, did you?"

"Of course not. I didn't say a word about it. She has no idea we're leaving in a few days."

"Good. It needs to stay that way." He shoved his fingers through his hair. "But why in the world would you make such a promise to her?"

"She's been my only friend here. Until you. The only one who has showed me any kindness. I can't bear the thought of doing nothing to help her."

"We *are* helping her. We're arranging a wedding for her and the man she loves."

"It's not enough." She laid her hand on his arm. "I can't abandon her. And now there's Ned."

"What do you mean, now there's Ned?" He almost shot off the bench. "You're wanting him to escape too?"

She turned those puppy-dog eyes on him.

"We can't free them all on our own, Morning Fawn. Why do you think I'm risking my life to destroy the cotton? Slavery is evil, and if the Confederacy wins, that evil will keep on going."

She blinked at him. "Lucy can't wait for the Yankees to win. She needs our help now. Especially after what you and she have implied about my uncle's interest in her."

He pinched the bridge of his nose. "She's likely been dealing with your uncle for weeks or even months. Ned will have to accept that reality."

"It sounds like you don't care."

He glared at her. "I humiliated and shamed myself in front of the entire family by acting like I'd been the man to visit Lucy's bedroom because I didn't want to see her whipped or her lover beaten or worse. I've found a preacher willing to marry them, and I'm committed to getting her out of her room Christmas Eve night and to her wedding. I've done plenty."

"I know." She dropped her gaze. "I'm sorry I said that."

A noise sounded in the corner by the broom—the mouse again.

He blew out a breath. "I have all that I can handle, leading half a dozen men on a mission to strike the quartermaster's depot and the cotton warehouse without getting any of us killed. And on top of that, I have to protect you and Fr—the Schramms."

"Frieda?"

"She is part of this mission, and so is her father. They have orders to vacate their house before the attack. Just like you have your orders to stay put a couple extra days and then come."

"Is she travelling with you?"

"No. Of course not." He rolled his eyes. "They are hiding out and then leaving on their own. They'll be assisted by their people."

"But how can I leave Lucy? I promised her."

He arched his eyebrows. "You had no business promising, especially not if you did so on my behalf. I'm only one man. There's only so many people I can handle looking after."

"Lucy reminds me of my sister."

"Your sister?"

"Eyes-Like-Sky. The first few years after our capture, she belonged to a warrior named Old Owl. I'd hate to think of what she suffered at his hands. I couldn't do anything to help her. I have to do something to help Lucy." Her mournful voice wrapped its tentacles around him.

Eyes closed, he leaned against the cool, rough stone, the edges biting through his jacket. He ran both his hands over his hair. As much as he believed in and hoped for it, there was no guarantee the war would end slavery in Texas. If he did nothing, Lucy might never gain her freedom. Could he live with that?

His lungs deflated. "I'll find her the address of a house. Someone who could hide her and help her get north. The Schramms have friends who've helped smuggle escaped slaves to safety. But just like with us, there aren't any guarantees. Christmas is going to stir up a hornet's nest. I'll get her the name, without any of the particulars of our plans, but she needs to wait until after Christmas to tell Ned. It'll be their responsibility to find a way there."

"Thank you." Morning Fawn beamed and hugged him tight. "Thank you. I know you have much to do. Too much. If we give them the name, we're giving them a chance, and not adding any risk for us. More than anything, I want you to be safe." She bubbled like a gushing brook. Gratitude sparkled in her eyes.

How could a man say no when his lady made him feel as if he'd righted the world?

He touched her cheek. Words spilled forth from his tongue that he never thought he'd say to anyone again. "I love you."

Wide-eyed, she hushed. Her lips parted.

Heat pulsed through him. He lowered his head and took the kiss he'd waited two days for. Heaven. If only they were already on a long, slow boat ride to Brownsville, with the danger behind them and their courting days ahead. He was quickly becoming a believer in a short courtship.

~

*M*orning Fawn crept through the back door of the house. Down the hall in the parlor, the mantel clock chimed twice. She hugged herself and leaned against the closed door.

Devon. Her heart soared. She could have sat on that bench cuddling with him all night long. His lips and his arms. His steadfastness and strength. His courage. He wanted a future for them. He hadn't said marriage yet, but he would. Is this how things had been between Eyes-Like-Sky and Dancing Eagle?

She shuddered. Eyes-Like-Sky had lost the man of her heart. Morning Fawn glanced at the ceiling, imagining the stars beyond. Did the God of the universe listen to prayers, especially ones from someone like her who knew so little about Him? Devon would—

A creak on the stairs.

Morning Fawn held her breath. Another creak. She straightened. There was no need to flee. Her story would be that she'd been to the outhouse.

Head held high, she tightened her shawl around her and headed for the foyer.

Thea waited on the bottom step. An open silk dressing gown half covered her nightgown. A cluster of curling papers fluttered around her head, no doubt dampened with Senegal gum.

Morning Fawn tensed.

"Where have you been?" Thea arched her eyebrows and flitted her gaze over Morning Fawn from head to toe. A smirk hovered across her lips.

"To the outhouse." Why the smirk? Did Thea suspect something?

"You got all dressed up just for that? A chamber pot wouldn't do?"

"Hate to dump it out. As for my dress, I don't believe in strolling around the house half clothed." She squinted at Thea's untied gown.

Thea's eyes glistened in the dark. "By all means. You wouldn't want the lieutenant to see anything."

"I'm sure the lieutenant sleeps through the night. I was thinking more of your father."

"Of course you were." A sing-songy note rang in her voice as if she were giving a three-year-old a pat on the head.

"What are you doing up?" Morning Fawn crossed her arms.

"On my way to the outhouse just like you were." She strutted past as if she were a queen.

Morning Fawn held onto the banister and stared after her. What did it matter if Thea suspected she'd slipped out to meet with Devon? There was no proof. And no need to bother Devon with it. He'd probably be over-cautious and determined they shouldn't meet anymore.

She bit her lip and proceeded up the stairs, the magical cocoon of his arms fading into memory.

CHAPTER 29

Morning Fawn clutched Devon's hand as they made their way along the path through the woods. A small, hooded lantern swung in his other hand, emitting a narrow beam of light only wide enough to keep them from tripping over roots and other obstacles. Lucy walked behind them, humming softly to herself. The wedding had been a success. Ned's owner had given him a travel pass as a Christmas present, either out of kindness or to spite LeBeau, but it didn't matter. There'd been a wedding. The Unionist-leaning preacher Devon had procured backed out earlier in the day, probably afraid for his life. In his stead, Pastor Combs, a circuit rider who traveled the state secretly preaching to slaves, performed the ceremony.

Morning Fawn had never seen the likes of such singing and dancing. They'd gathered on the back edge of the property near the creek where they could celebrate without fear of overseers or masters. The songs had spoken of a faith so deep that chains couldn't bind it nor slavery smother it. And the dancing? Her heart had soared free to the stars as Devon swung her around the bare ground. What would her own wedding be like?

"Watch your step." Devon ducked under a branch, and she did likewise.

Lucy caught up to them. "Maybe we'd best stop here so I can go behind one of these bushes and change."

"No." Morning Fawn squinted at the white floral-print gown showing beneath Lucy's dark cloak. "I want you to keep the dress. If anyone asks, I'll tell them I gave it to you as a Christmas present. Even my uncle plans to give out gifts tomorrow to all the hands."

"Slaves, you mean." Lucy corrected her. "But I owe you two the world." She squeezed Morning Fawn's hand, her smile gleaming in the dark. "Me and Ned won't forget. If you need anything, you just say so. And that house you told us about—"

"I'm thankful we could help. Just keep it quiet for now." Devon slipped his arm around Morning Fawn's shoulders. "You didn't tell Ned the house number yet, did you?"

"No, sir. I just told him we was working on a plan." A few tendrils of hair escaped from Lucy's chignon and bounced on her shoulders. "I'll wait until Miss Morning Fawn up and disappears before we sneak off."

"Thank you." Devon rubbed the back of his neck. "Morning Fawn and I could use your prayers. As she mentioned, I can't share details, but I have some important work to take care of in the next few days. I won't be back, and neither will she after she leaves."

"The Lord bless you." Lucy touched Morning Fawn's sleeve.

The tree limbs rustled as a burst of wind rattled through the grove, stinging Morning Fawn's cheeks and earlobes.

"Storm coming." Devon tugged his collar up to his chin. "We best get back. I'll keep to the tree line while you two go ahead. But after the fine dinner they had this evening and the drinks, I imagine they're all as fast asleep as when we snuck out."

"And tomorrow Massar will sit on his front steps giving out

hand-me-downs and fresh meat, acting like he's Santi Claus." Lucy kept pace. "But everybody knows New Year's is just 'round the corner. Heartbreak Day. Thank the Lord Ned and me don't have to worry about being sold or rented out this year."

Leaves and twigs, coated in frost, crunched beneath their feet as they moved along the path. An owl hooted.

Morning Fawn's heart chilled. Tomorrow night was the ball and Nicholas. Tomorrow night was life or death. She'd faced danger for herself and loved ones countless times with the Comanche. Had she gone soft in this settler world? Or was it that she'd never so completely given her heart away? Tomorrow could destroy her.

They came to the clearing. To the left, music rang out from the slave quarters. Some had already returned from the wedding, ready to celebrate the beginning of five days off. All was quiet at the blacksmith shop and the other work buildings. Across the fields, glimmers of light peeked through the cotton-woods that flanked the main house.

It should be dark, and had been so when they left at ten.

Devon tensed and halted, his hold on her hand tightening. "Something's wrong."

He retreated into the shadows of the trees. Morning Fawn followed suit, with Lucy at her side.

"Maybe one of them came looking for me." Lucy hung her head. "I...I can tell 'em I came down to the quarter to celebrate Christmas."

"Might be more than that." A hard breath swooshed between Devon's teeth.

A bitter taste rose in the back of Morning Fawn's throat. What if Thea had seen or heard something? Or maybe Nick had received word from his agents and decided to believe them? "It might be nothing more than Christmas visitors come to stay the night, or maybe one of the slaves got in trouble." Her voice sounded about as solid as an uncooked egg.

Devon clicked the lantern hood shut. Darkness dropped around them except for the glow from the quarters and the muted moonlight peaking from behind a fist of clouds. Silence reigned, except for the wind, and a pig snorting from the pen by the barn.

Devon turned to Morning Fawn. "I feel like it's real trouble." He gripped her shoulders. "I can't take a chance that it's not. I've put too much work into this mission to let it come to nothing." He glanced past her, frowned, and led her several feet away from Lucy, dropping his voice to a whisper. "People have risked their freedom and their lives. My captain and my colonel are counting on me. I have a chance to make a genuine difference in this war."

"You...you're not thinking of striking tonight, are you?" She pressed her palms to his chest, a solid wall of warmth to steady her trembling soul. "You're not ready. You could hide out in the woods and let Lucy and me go on to the house—"

"It might be tonight or never."

"No." She bunched his frock coat lapels in her hands. "What if something happens to you?"

He enveloped her in his arms and pressed his cheek to her hair. "The Lord will watch over us."

"The Lord lets people die." The words burst forth, shaking her to her core. "He let my mother die. She loved Him and served Him all of her life, and He let her die."

Devon braced her shoulders. "I don't have all the answers. I spent a year being angry with God over Isabelle's and the baby's deaths. And two years of hating myself for not doing my part. But I know deep in my heart that God's will and doings are beyond our comprehension. I don't understand why He allowed your mother or Isabelle to die—"

"He could have stepped in, but He didn't."

"I don't know why He didn't, and probably won't know this side of Heaven. But His Word tells us that He will work everything out for good for those who love Him and follow Him. I've decided to put my trust in Him even though my stubborn heart doesn't always understand. And I know you're right about Isabelle—"

"I want you to live. Here. With me. I don't mean right here. But alive on this earth and not taking foolish chances. You stay, hide in the woods, and I'll send you word—"

"Morning Fawn." His firm tone hushed her. "I can't wait. I'm counting on you. Do everything you can to delay them. Buy me time without implicating yourself. As far as they're concerned, you don't know I'm a Yankee. You believed the story about me spying on Moyer for the Rebs. I was with you and Lucy at a church meeting tonight, but I left alone. Told you I was headed home for Christmas."

She clung to him. "I'm not a warrior. I'm a girl who has lost too many people, and I don't know if I trust the God of the heavens to bring you back."

"You are strong. You can do this," he whispered in her ear. "I need you to do this."

She inhaled.

"The Lord will be with us. Keep telling your mind and your heart that until it takes root."

She swallowed back her doubts. "I'll do as you say."

His arms loosened, enough for him to tip her face to his. He tugged his eyepatch off, both of his eyes drinking her in. "I love you."

"I love you too." *So much that losing you would rip my heart out.*

His gaze dropped to her lips. She swept her hand around his neck, shoving her fingers into his hair, and drew his mouth to hers.

His lips overtook hers with a hunger that dropped her stomach into her toes. Liquid warmth surged through her limbs as she melted against him. A kiss she never wanted to end. The world swirled. She dug her fingers into his back. *Let this be tomorrow and every day afterwards—*

Swoosh. He withdrew his lips, and the dream evaporated, landing her back into the not-dark-enough night, with the comfort of his arms slipping away.

"I've got to go. George will have a horse in the woods for you." He stepped back, his chest heaving as if he'd run a great race. He dug in his pocket and shoved a few bills into Morning Fawn's hand. "I'll see you at the coast. The spot I told you about last night. I'll wait every night for you."

"Don't worry about me. Just make sure you get there." Morning Fawn sniffled and lifted her chin. She would protect Devon at all costs. She would not, could not fail.

~

*M*orning Fawn blinked in the too-brilliant light of the porch. A muscular man in a gray slouch hat and buckskin coat eyed her from the hitching post where he stood. Two horses, one a fine American saddlebred, the match for Cinnamon, munched from feed sacks. Nick was here. Why? It couldn't be good.

She dragged her feet as she neared the door and lifted the latch. *Lord, help me.*

LeBeau's manservant, Jim, met her at the threshold. "Miss Beth, they's been looking for ya." He bobbed his gray-haired head.

She handed him her red wool cloak. "Who are *they*?"

A door clicked down the hall. Silver-tipped walking stick in hand, LeBeau stepped out of his office, his eyes puffy as if he'd missed his sleep. Nick followed, dressed in his shirt-sleeves and waistcoat. A cigar dangled from his fingers. His boots clicked on the tiled floor like a drum signaling a call to war.

LeBeau's glare scorched. He thundered toward her. "Where have you been?"

"At a camp meeting."

"A camp meeting at this hour? With Lucy and Lieutenant Reynolds?"

They must have checked the whole house to see who was missing. "I've bothered Lucy for months to take me to one. Not one in town, but a slave gathering where they sing all of the spirituals. I love to listen to them sing while they work, and I wanted to see—"

"I don't believe you." LeBeau cut her short.

Nick drew on the cigar. "Spin us another fable."

A simmering laugh rang out from the top of the stairs. Thea slithered down, in full day dress as if she'd been up for a while. *Plop, plop, plop,* she eased down one step at a time as if she were an actress on a stage. "I told them about how you sneaked off to the kitchen with the lieutenant the other night. Getting mighty cozy, from what I could tell."

A tendon in Morning Fawn's neck twitched. Thea had seen them. Had she overheard? How much could one hear through kitchen windows? What if she'd told them about the mission? Morning Fawn should have warned Devon that Thea had been up that night.

Nick shouldered past LeBeau. His hands curled into fists at his side, the cigar wedged between two fingers. "You met that pauper in secret after you telling me he betrayed you and you wanted nothing to do with him? Not to mention that tale about him investigating me?"

"Where is Reynolds?" LeBeau marched up to the edge of her skirt hem.

Morning Fawn glanced at Thea, then pivoted toward Nick. "She's right. I was with Devon in the kitchen two nights ago. Kissing." Her tongue tripped over the word. She should have told them Thea was lying, but it would've been her word against her cousin's. "My courting you was eating him up. He told me how sorry he was for chasing after Frieda. He begged for forgiveness. I know it was wrong to betray you like that." She'd say whatever she had to. Even destroy her reputation if it helped Devon. "I fell for his charms—"

"Meeting men alone at night." *Whap.* Her uncle's hand stung her face like a whip. "You have disgraced this family."

She covered her cheek. "I'm sorry." Another lie.

"You're going to be." A second slap, this one on the other side. "I opened my home to you. Gave you everything you needed. Even offered you land, and this is how you repay me."

Thea tittered.

"Get upstairs." A vein in LeBeau's forehead bulged. He pivoted and jutted his finger toward his daughter. "You've said enough."

"Father, I can't help it if my cousin's a harlot."

"Hush." Aunt Judith stood at the railing drawing her robe around her, her frown so deep, it bordered on tears as if she actually cared. "Come up here this instant."

Thea trounced up to her room, her curls bobbing.

Morning Fawn's heart pounded. Thea had said *harlot,* not *traitor.* Maybe they didn't—

The back door opened. Hair topsy-turvy and shirt half tucked into his trousers, Owens strode down the hall with Lucy in tow. "Caught this one sneaking to her room as if she'd never gone anywhere."

Lucy stumbled along at his side, her arm locked in his vice-like grip.

LeBeau narrowed his eyes. "What is she doing in that dress?"

"I gave it to her as a Christmas present." Morning Fawn took a half step toward her.

Lucy dropped her gaze to the floor, almost bumping into

Owens as he came to a halt. "I's take it off you's don't like it, Massar."

"Get her out of here." LeBeau grumbled. "Take her into the parlor for now. Don't let her sit on the furniture."

"I won't let her dirty anything." Owens chuckled and jerked Lucy toward the parlor. A thump and a female groan resonated as he closed the door behind them.

Surely, LeBeau cared for Lucy, even if he forced her to be his mistress. He wouldn't allow Owens to go too far, would he?

Nick placed a hand on her uncle's shoulder. "We should talk to Beth in your office. More privacy."

"I'd be happy to." Morning Fawn threw back her shoulders and headed for the office before either man could drag her. Every minute they talked to her was one more minute they weren't on Devon's trail.

Lamplight and cigar odor filled the room. They'd probably sat in here plotting, waiting for her return. Her legs in danger of giving out, she plopped down in the straight-back chair before they closed the door.

Nick ambled over and leaned his backside against the desk. His dark eyes bored into her. "I've had word back from my agent. You know what he said?"

"I have no idea, but I'm sure you're about to tell me and show me how wrong I've been about Reynolds."

"Reynolds is a Unionist." His lip curled.

Best play dumb. "A what?"

"See, I told you she doesn't have the brains to be a traitor." Her uncle stomped over to the side of the desk.

Nick held up his hand. A man who could shush her uncle? "A Yankee sympathizer. A worm who'd turn on his own people."

She blinked at him. "As I said before, I don't know much about the war and don't care one way or the other, but if your agent told you this, are you sure you can trust him?" She glanced in her uncle's direction. "I assume you told him what I overheard Reynolds say?"

"I did." A slick smile spread across Nick's lips. "I've been thinking about what you said. And it occurred to me that if my agent was working for Reynolds and Confederate headquarters, why would he want to discredit Reynolds? It doesn't make any sense. If he was working with the man, he'd bring back word that the lieutenant was an angel and a flag-waving Confederate."

She shrugged. "I have no idea why your agent would or wouldn't say anything. All I know is what I heard Reynolds say when I snuck up on him and Frieda. But it occurred to me that maybe he knew I was there all along."

Nick smashed the end of his cigar in the ashtray. "If that were the case, why would he make up such a story?"

"Where is he?" LeBeau's handlebar mustache twitched like a rat tail. "You tell us before we send the dogs out."

She flinched. Could the animals discern a fresh scent? Devon had been all over the yard and stables in the last few days. She smoothed her voice. "I don't know where he is."

"Don't know or won't say?" LeBeau grabbed the back of her chair and jutted his face within inches of hers. His unsettled dinner hung on his breath. "We know you were with him tonight. We checked all of the rooms and the stables looking for the three of you."

Nick tapped his fingers on the desk.

She pressed her hands on her lap. "We...he was with us at the meeting. Lieutenant Reynolds heard I was going with Lucy and wanted to follow along. Not that he cared about the singing and all. I think it was more of a chance to get me alone in the dark, sneak another kiss."

"I bet that wasn't all he snuck." LeBeau grabbed her chin. His fingers bit into her flesh.

She glared deep into his ice-blue eyes. "I never let any man have more than a kiss."

LeBeau flung her head to the side.

Her nose collided with the chair's wooden trim, pushing her teeth in her lip. A metallic taste lingered on her tongue. "I don't care what you believe. It's the truth. And Reynolds didn't walk us back. Said he had a friend to visit back home"—they'd never believe he'd visit family—"and planned to use the days you gave him off for Christmas."

Both men sat back against the desk, studying her.

Nick smoothed his fingers over his bearded chin. "We need to look for Reynolds. Question the slave and see how her story lines up with Beth's."

"I'll do better than that. I'll have Owens bring a handful of them in one by one. If there was a meeting, Lucy and my niece wouldn't have been the only ones at it."

"We'll need men to search—"

"What do you need a bunch of men for? I told you where he went, or at least where he said he was going." Morning Fawn sat straight.

Nick smirked. "I know what you said. I also know you're the smartest and quickest little darling I ever met. In need of a man to tame you. More woman than a scrawny fellow like Reynolds can handle."

She narrowed her eyes at the man. *He's more man than you could ever dream of being.* "Personally, I'd rather turn into a withered spinster and never own an inch of land than to have anything to do with either of you."

"You brat." LeBeau shoved off the desk, ready to strike again.

She ducked.

Nick grabbed his arm, then released it. "Let her sauce off. I can take it. Maybe we'll get some truth out of her, sooner or later."

LeBeau tugged down his sleeve where Nick had touched him, splitting his glare between him and her.

"I don't care what you believe." She jutted out her chin, her cheek still throbbing from the previous blows. "I'll let you and Reynolds work it out amongst yourselves when he returns. I'd just as soon go to my room and forget the whole night."

Nick bent close, bracing himself on the chair arms until the pampered flesh of his face was only a few inches from hers.

What did he see in her eyes? She pressed her lips shut and steeled herself against the onslaught of his prying stare.

"Maybe I'll still marry you." He chuckled mirthlessly and stood.

"You'd still consider marrying her?" Lebeau almost tripped over himself.

She half choked. "I'm not volunteering."

"We'll see about that." Nick reached behind her and grabbed his frock coat which hung from the chair back. He might as well have had fox ears and a tail. "Meanwhile, Robert, we need to look for that yellow-bellied, Yankee-loving scoundrel. Question whatever slaves you see fit, starting with that Lucy girl. I'll send a couple men on the road to his home county, and a couple more to pay a visit to Miss Frieda Schramm."

The last word raked up her spine like a claw. Surely, Devon wouldn't linger there any longer than to give a brief warning? She clasped her hands in her lap and glanced downward, feeling like prey in grass, uncertain of whether to say something to try to divert them or remain silent.

The fox leaned in until his breath heated her ear. A whiff of brandy stung her nose even as her heart curdled. "I think you care about him even though he's been two-timing you with Miss Schramm. But I also think you're a liar. As a matter of fact, I believe I'll call on Miss Schramm myself."

Right now? That wouldn't give Devon enough time. Her

stomach clenched. "Think what you please. I'm done with the both of you. My uncle can fire Reynolds when he returns as far as I'm concerned."

LeBeau tugged on his waistcoat. "We're not going to get anything else from her. I'll have Owens start on Lucy."

Morning Fawn stiffened. Lucy wouldn't talk, and neither would she. No matter what.

"Excellent idea." Nick shoved his arms into his coat sleeves. "I'll ride to Alleyton, and I'll assign more men to help with the search. Send word immediately if you find out anything. I bet the scoundrel headed for his second honey pot."

LeBeau chuckled. "Good bet. The man finds an excuse to travel to Alleyton every chance he gets."

"Does he, now?" Nick's step halted. He pivoted, his brow furrowed.

"What do you expect with how googled-eyed he is over Frieda Schramm?" She stood.

Nick tugged his gloves from his pocket and exhaled. "I say we lock her in her room until we can thoroughly investigate."

LeBeau latched onto her elbow with his talon-like fingers. "Good plan."

Nick headed for the door. Hand on the knob, he paused. "You followed Reynolds and Miss Schramm to the woods behind the depot?"

Her throat constricted to a wheeze of air. "I reckon he couldn't carry on with her right under her father's nose."

"Hmmm." He opened the door, absent-mindedly slapping his gloves against his thigh.

"What are you thinking?" LeBeau pulled her along into the hall.

"I don't know yet. It's a jumble of possibilities." Nick drove his hand over his hair. A tic worked itself in his cheek.

The lackey who'd been out front on the porch now lounged

on a bench by the coatrack. He stood as they approached and donned his hat.

Owens opened the parlor door. "Ready for me, sir?"

"Yes." LeBeau released his hold. "I'll take care of Lucy. Go fetch George and a couple others."

Morning Fawn eyed the back door. The pathway was clear. Nick's horse was out front at the hitching post. If she got her hands on it and rode off in the opposite direction of Alleyton, they'd follow, probably assume she was headed to warn Devon...and end any shred of a chance she had of looking innocent. It'd buy Devon time. But it'd also turn their hot coal of suspicion into a prairie fire. A gamble, but she'd rather risk the option that'd put more distance between Devon and his enemies. Even if it landed her in jail.

"Butler," Nick called to his man. "You stay for the questioning, then ride for Alleyton double quick. I'm going to round up some men at the warehouse—"

Morning Fawn gathered her skirts and bolted for the back door.

"Stop." Her uncle swung for her and missed.

"Catch her." Nick's booted steps pounded behind her.

She grabbed the latch. It clicked, and the door swung open. She tripped on the stone step, stumbled but caught herself. A hand reached out. Fingertips grazed her shoulder. She pumped her legs and ran on. Turning the corner, skidding on a slip of mud, she leaped over a bucket.

Something clattered behind her.

"She's going for the front." Nick's voice burst forth harsh and winded.

Frost-covered grass crumpled beneath her feet. A dog howled. What if they loosed the beast on her? She rounded the second corner. Two horses at the posts. Butler bounded onto the porch and to the steps.

She dove for the saddlebred's lead rope. Tearing it from the post, she shoved her left foot into the stirrup and swung her right leg over.

Hands clawed into her waist and yanked her backward. She landed feet on the ground and swung with her fist. Butler whammed his forearm against hers, blocking the blow. He grabbed her shoulder, his meaty fingers pressing deep. She spun toward him and drove her knee into his groin.

"Uggh." His hands fell from her. He crumpled.

Nick rounded the corner.

She swung into the saddle.

Nick latched onto the bridle.

She yanked hard on the reins, rearing the stallion's front legs, forcing Nick to jump clear.

Pulse pounding in her head, she pressed her heels against the horse's sides. The animal snorted and jolted forth. His hooves thudded on the gravel path. She rose in the saddle, the breeze picking up her hair.

A sharp whistle cut through the air. The stallion reared to a stop, jolting her, but she clung to the saddle horn and reins. Nick charged toward her on the second horse. She goaded the stallion. He neighed, tossed his head, and reared again. Nick had trained his horse well. Morning Fawn leaned forward on the horse's neck and whistled softly near his ear, cooing as she'd heard her adopted brother do. The animal stirred, stepped forward. She clicked the reins. He broke into a canter.

Nick's knee jabbed into her thigh, his stirrup cutting into her ankle. His hands latched hold of her. The stallion bucked, and Nick pulled her onto his lap.

The present moment fractured into shards of memory. The Comanche warrior dragging her from beneath the wagon and away from her mother. Then the night nine years later when Devon Reynolds grabbed her from behind and stole her from the world she'd become part of.

Instinct took over. Fists, feet, legs—Morning Fawn threw

everything she had into the fight, striking blindly and with all of her might, but other hands caught her and drug her to the ground. Owens's knee leveled into her back as he wrenched her arms around behind her and snared her wrists with a raw rope that bit into her skin. Blades of frost-slicked grass pressed against her lips.

Defeated.

"Well, we know one thing." Nick stood over her, rubbing his cheek that bore the imprint of her nails. His waistcoat hung open, and his mussed-up hair looked as if it hadn't seen a comb for days. He spit on the ground. Was his lip bleeding too? "There's something with Reynolds and Alleyton worth fighting over."

Morning Fawn rolled her face into the dirt. A shiver ran through her. The night wind blew across her sweat-soaked clothing, chilling her fury-heated body.

She had failed.

CHAPTER 30

Sweat dampened Devon's shirt collar beneath his frock coat. He'd armed himself well, a revolver on each hip, a knife in his knee-high cavalry boot and another up his sleeve, a cartridge belt around his waist, and another across his chest. A flask of brandy in hand, he patted his pocket, feeling for the small rubberized pouch of Lucifer matches.

Sleet pelted his face. The storm would help with the element of surprise. They had to take care of the guards at the back of the quartermaster's depot without firing a shot. The two guards on the far end had already been knocked out and tied up.

Frieda had begged to come, insisting that having a woman along would distract the guards. But he'd refused. He'd put her at enough risk already. After tonight, the Reb authorities would hunt for her, jail her, or worse if they caught her.

Instead, he'd sent her to round up as many of the volunteers from the league as she could rouse. Not an easy task on such short notice in the middle of the night on Christmas Eve.

It was bad enough her father was down the street acting as a lookout. But with only four of the volunteers answering the call, Devon needed every man he could get. By now, Frieda should be on her way to friends who'd shelter her and her father behind a hidden compartment in their house. The same house Devon had told Lucy about.

"'God Rest Ye Merry Gentlemen...'" Devon whistled the tune as he neared the back entrance. A teamster with loose lips and a couple drinks too many had informed him the Rebs had been slow to ship out the rest of the gunpowder to the regiments in Louisiana, too afraid the ones in Texas might need it more.

"Halt." A soldier stepped from the doorframe.

A second soldier rose to his feet with the enthusiasm of a slug. Both men wore their kepis down far enough that only their noses could be seen beneath the bills. A faint light glowed from the narrow warehouse windows under the overhang.

"Gentleman, thank goodness you're here." Devon clamored as if he'd had too much to drink. He'd swished a shot of brandy in his mouth and dabbed a little on his coat for good measure. "I'm in need of reprieve from the storm. Got a little too friendly with my lady after a bit of Christmas rum, and her papa kicked me out into the cold." He swung his arm wide, barely gripping the flask between his thumb and forefinger.

"Ain't no shelter here." The first soldier tugged his collar up over his ears.

The slug reached out a hand to steady the flask. "Don't want to drop that."

Devon teetered. "Friend..." He leaned a hand on the sluggard, pressing the flask to the man's coat. "All I ask is a few minutes inside before I become an icicle. Willing to share a couple drinks."

"Can't do that, sir. Orders." The alert one rested his rifle against the jamb. "Best go make amends with the papa."

"I wouldn't mind a swig." The sluggard tapped his hand to the flask.

Wind whipped at their backs. The pace of the sleet picked up. Precious time was ticking away. Moyer or soldiers from Camp Web south of town could show up any minute. Devon stepped in closer to the narrow shelter of the jamb. All the better to block the soldiers' view of Gunter creeping along flush with the building.

Devon slipped the flask into the sluggard's hand. "Just a swig."

"Obliged." The man grinned.

"I don't know." The first one turned toward the door when another blast of wind swept by.

"It's Christmas." Sluggard swiped his mouth. His fingers stuck out the ends of his worn gloves. "The blasted officers aren't out here in the cold." He handed the flask off to the first man.

"Don't you fellows have any keys to this place? I bet they have a stove in there." Devon slipped his hand beneath his frock coat as a shadow moved on his left.

Gunter sprang, clamping his thick hand over the mouth of the first soldier, flipping him to the ground, and knocking him out.

The drinker turned. "What—"

Devon cracked the butt of his revolver against the man's head. He crumpled.

"Check for the keys." Devon riffled through his victim's pockets.

"Found them." Gunter held up a ring with three clanking keys and handed them to Devon.

The first key didn't work. He fumbled with the second one. It didn't quite fit. He jiggled it. The door clicked open. A dimly lit lantern swung from a cable strung over a rafter near the far end. Gunter came behind him, followed by Frederick.

Revolver in his hand, Devon called out, "Came in to get warm."

No answer, and no light in the office near the street side of the building. Frederick, the dark-haired baker, who'd built his muscles working in a warehouse back east before he'd immigrated to Texas, moved through the building to verify no one else was there.

Shelves of tents, boots, cooking pots, haversacks, rubberized blankets, and more lined the walls. Rows of crates stretched along the floor. Devon picked up a lantern and lit it.

Gunter found a crowbar and pried off one lid after another. Hardtack. Cartridges. Rifles. And in the center beneath a tar-covered canvas? A couple dozen stubby powder kegs stood next to fifteen larger barrels of gunpowder.

"Should we carry some to the cotton warehouse, or leave it here?" Frederick joined them. Melted sleet dripped from his coat

Devon scrubbed his hand over his jaw. He had no idea how long Morning Fawn would be able to stall whoever it was at Sweetbriar. The safest plan would be to blow everything up here and get away as fast as they could. But that would leave a goldmine of cotton in Reb hands. A month ago, Moyer bragged he had over a thousand bales. Now with the cessation of the shipments to Mexico, maybe it could be two thousand. Devon couldn't leave it untouched.

"Gunter, help me." Devon rubbed his damp hands on his dry waistcoat and picked up a keg under each arm. "Frederick, help him tip one of the barrels down. Then, Gunter, roll it outside and to the warehouse. Take your time."

"Time's vhat ve don't have." Gunter swiped his brow.

"Schramm will signal if he sees anyone approaching." Devon headed for the door and peeked out. Nothing, then a small light at the back of the cotton warehouse blinked three times. Oscar's signal. They'd taken care of the guards at the warehouse. Devon gave a short whistle, then proceeded. "I'll be back. And while we're gone, Frederick, you start pouring a line of powder."

Devon's muscles strained against the weight of the kegs. Gunter followed him. Wind whipped at Devon's coattails and pelted his back and ears. The tightly coopered wooden casks would keep the powder dry, but there'd be no option of pouring a trail of gunpowder down the hill toward the trees before he struck the match. No, in both cases, the trail would need to be lit within the shelter of the buildings. Close. Too close. Would there be enough time for a man to strike the match and get away?

Slick pebbles gritted beneath his boots. The ice was sticking to the ground now, not melting on contact. He hurried past the opening between the two buildings that led to the street, thankful for the cover of the storm.

He'd have to light one of the lines of gunpowder. He'd take a volunteer for the other. Get everyone clear if they had the time. Jeremy had agreed to come rescue Morning Fawn if anything happened to Devon and get her to Federal territory. *Please, Lord, don't let it come to that.*

The barn-door-wide entrance to the back of the warehouse sat ajar. He shoved it with his shoulder. A couple of lanterns swayed from the rafters, dimly illuminating row upon row of burlap-wrapped bales. A narrow maze of pathways separated the cotton towers, and three iron hoists hovered silently overhead.

He handed Oscar and his brother a keg each. "Start here at the door and pour a line each between the main rows, then join them at the center of the building. Take off your coats—and your boots if you have to. Can't get the powder wet."

Gunter set his barrel in the center, then followed him out the door. Two more loads. Double quick. Oscar's brother Jarvis joined them on the third trip. Sweat soaked Devon's shirt.

Kegs and barrel in the center. Two lines of powder between

the rows, meeting close to the door. Ready to light if the enemy showed up. But there weren't enough kegs here yet, not if he wanted the towers to turn into unstoppable infernos.

Devon pointed to Jarvis. "Help us carry another couple of loads over from the supply depot."

A bugle blast. Schramm's signal. The hairs on Devon's arms stood. He broke two matchsticks off the bundle and shoved them into Oscar's hand. "Light it and get out."

Devon took off at a run, followed by Gunter. He had to get to the depot. Blow those supplies sky-high.

Halfway there, he slipped on the ice. Pain coursed through his knee.

"Hey, you." Someone yelled as he pumped his legs past the opening between the buildings.

Gunter halted at the corner and shouldered his rifle.

Devon lunged for the depot. The cotton warehouse should have blown by now.

Gunfire.

Frederick swung the depot door open. "What—"

"Get to the trees." Devon flung his coat off and rubbed his hands against his shirt.

"But—"

"I'll light it." Heel against the doorjamb, Devon dug a Lucifer out of the waterproof pouch. His hand shook.

A different bugle. Shots rang through the air.

Devon struck the match, his heart pounding. *Dear God in heaven, please don't let this be the end. Take care of Morning Fawn.* He bent and dropped the flickering flame onto the black powder. A sizzle. It caught.

He spun on his heels and bolted into the storm. Ice pellets, slicked grass, blistering wind... He ran with all his might. Shots, men yelling, men coming after him. Up ahead, Frederic fell. A boom rocked the air, throwing him forward and to the ground. But not the charge he'd set—farther away. His head rang. He scrambled to his feet. Something tore into his arm. Still, he ran. No time. Not far enough away. He dove for the incline, just a small slope. Maybe it'd be enough. Landed on his belly and slid downward—

Boom! Boom. Boom. His hip slammed into a tree. Time stopped. No more men. Smoke filled the air and clogged his lungs. No more sound. Only a ringing deep in his head. He had to get up. He had to move. His life depended upon it.

He crawled to his knees. Pebbles and sleet stung his palms. A board lay in front of him. From the warehouse? He stood. Pain shot through his thigh. He'd crawl. Stay hidden that way. Hand and knee, hand and knee, he plunged forward into the brush.

Snags clawed at him as he moved toward the river. He gained his feet. The pain didn't matter. If he didn't get away, he'd never feel pain again.

The hill sloped to the water. He half tumbled and rolled. Shots. He could hear again. The water—he heard that too. He shivered, pushed to his feet, and ran.

A woman stepped out of the shadows. Morning Fawn?

No. Dark cloak and hair. Frieda. "What are you doing here?" He grabbed her arms.

"You're bleeding. You're hurt." Her voice raked the air.

"I told you to get to the safe house."

"I found someone to loan me a boat." She pointed to the water where a canoe slushed against the bank.

Fire glowed back up on the hill, despite the sleet. Bells rang. And in the mix, gunfire snapped through the air. He shoved her toward the canoe.

Frieda stepped from the bank. One foot landed in the canoe, one in the water. The canoe tipped sideward, spilling her into the river. He jumped into the frigid water, righting the boat and shoving her onto the bank. Every second was an unaffordable loss. He heaved himself over the edge, then from a squat, held out his arms and braced her as she stepped from the bank. The canoe rocked as she boarded.

"Halt." Someone crashed through the underbrush.

Devon grabbed the paddle and struck wood to water. "Lie down," he commanded Frieda.

She crouched.

A shot struck the wooden side, splintering the wood. Then another winged his sleeve.

If they wounded or killed him, they'd get her too. If he turned himself in and bought her time—

Another shot grazed the wood.

"I give up. Don't shoot." He threw the paddle down and lifted his hands. "Don't shoot."

"Don't." She stirred.

"Try anything, and I'll put a bullet in your back." Moyer's voice boomed.

"Stay still," he hissed to Frieda. "You can swim, right? When I get up, I'm going to tip the canoe. I'll swim for shore. You keep swimming with the river, underwater and in the shadows. They'll chase me—"

"No." Horror gripped her words.

"You. Do. It." He pushed his arms higher. "Standing," he called to Moyer and the noose.

Moyer thrashed through the cattails, moving closer along the shore. "Wait."

Dear God, help us. Devon stood. The canoe wobbled.

"I'll shoot—"

Devon lunged to the far side. The canoe flipped. Gunfire. A sting to his ear. He slugged toward the shore, pumping his wavering limbs, swimming with everything he had left.

He swallowed water, coughed it out, forcing himself forward. Had the shots stopped, or had he gone deaf again? His hands struck reeds, and he pulled himself up. Maybe he should just hover. No, they'd seen him. They'd be coming. He drug himself onto the bank. He had to get up, keep going, keep them coming after him and not Frieda.

He pushed up on all fours.

A fist hammered the side of his head. He dropped to the ground. A boot slammed into his ribs. He curled inward, slipping his hand inside his boot for the knife.

Moyer kicked it from his hand and dove in with his fists until all light faded.

CHAPTER 31

*L*ight poured in through the attic window. Morning Fawn never wanted to move again. Her mouth tasted like cotton. She hated cotton. That's what Devon had come here to destroy. Risked his life for. Had he died for it? Or was that still to come?

She rolled over and curled into a ball. She had failed him. The realization ricocheted through her. She should have told him about Thea being awake that night they'd been in the kitchen. She should have gotten away last night and led them on a wild goose chase south. If only she'd moved a little quicker, fought a little harder.

Her stomach clenched. She scrambled off the bare mattress, dropped to her knees, and emptied the dregs of her stomach into the chamber pot. The result of the laudanum which they'd shoved down her throat or guilt? Either way, she swiped her mouth on her torn skirt and hung her head.

Replacing the lid, she shoved the pot back under the bed and curled toward her lap. Devon had trusted her. Now he was either dead or in jail with no hope but a noose.

Flashes of memory burst through her clogged brain.

Shouts around dawn. Her uncle had returned and who else? LeBeau had thrown open her door and shook his fist. "We got him. We got him. We got the mangy-hide, bloodsucking Yankee you sold your soul to. Moyer put a bullet in him. Beat him to a pulp."

Later, he'd burst into her room again, and someone else had grabbed her. Owens? They'd torn the room apart, ripping off the bedding, overturning her chair and desk, everything a mess, scouring the place for any secrets. LeBeau had waved the journal in her face.

He'd said more. What? It didn't matter. They had Devon. Wounded and bloodied and in pain. How seriously had he been shot? If he survived, they'd execute him. Her heart had caved in.

Sobs rocked through her. Her fault. She should have never followed him that day. Stayed away. Stayed out of it. Her and her big mouth. Her and her jealousy. The hours in the garden, in his arms, sharing their hearts. The kiss that had swept her to heaven and back. The kitchen...that first night when he'd come to her room and promised her the moon...his friendship, his love...lost.

The sun had shifted to the other side of the pane by the time the door clicked. Late afternoon. Morning Fawn's tongue clung to the roof of her mouth. She stirred at the sound of steps, her body a concoction of aches too numerous to count.

"Let me help you up." Flora's rich voice broke the dull air.

Morning Fawn pushed up to her knees and rocked back onto her folded legs.

Kind eyes shone from beneath a wrinkled brow. "The missus done sent me up to get you cleaned up a bit."

"Are they going to take me to jail?"

The middle-aged servant clucked her tongue. "I's don't knows their plans. I reckon the missus doesn't either." The hefty lady dressed in a red floral dress and a white apron bent over and offered her hand. "I'll get you a wet washcloth and a change of clothes."

Flora *tsk*ed at the shards of pottery from the broken pitcher and shoved them out of the way with her shoe as she led her to the other side of the room.

Morning Fawn dropped onto the wooden seat Flora righted. The room spun.

"Least they had sense enough to not break the lamps." She heaved the desk upright and stepped over the strewn contents of Morning Fawn's trunk. "I'll be back with water. You sit tight." She exited, and the lock clicked.

Why lock it? Where would she run? What was there left to do? Morning Fawn rubbed her hands over her arms. Why couldn't she stop trembling?

Minutes later, Flora returned with a new pitcher, a glass, and the sweetest water Morning Fawn had ever tasted. She swallowed deeply and sat numbly as Flora washed her face and cleaned the scrapes on her face, hands, and limbs.

"You put up quite a fight." Flora dabbed away with water and ointment.

"Do...do you know anything else about the lieutenant?"

Flora exhaled. "He's alive, I reckon. In bad shape. They's got him in jail. Can't wait to hang him. Mister Moyer wants it done proper. Your uncle's ready to have it done today."

Morning Fawn closed her eyes. Her stomach threatened to erupt again. "And the cotton warehouse?"

Flora wriggled the filthy dress off her. "Some of the cotton burned. But they's saved most of it. Now, that quartermaster's place is a different story. Blowed most of the supplies to kingdom come. All them fancy-dressed gents and soldiers are fit to be tied. And it being on Christmas Day and all. Massar done cancelled Christmas."

A partial success? None of it was worth Devon's life.

"And Lucy?" Morning Fawn shivered.

Flora tugged a clean chemise from the pile on the floor. "They's got her locked up in the cellar."

"Did they beat her?"

"Slapped her around a bit, but when you tried to take off on that horse, that got them all scattered. All they could think of was getting to town."

At least her actions had helped somebody.

Flora nudged Morning Fawn's arms upward. "Only someone done went and told about the wedding."

"Who?" Feeling more like a marionette than a living, breathing person, Morning Fawn held her arms up while the garment shimmered downward.

"I's don't know. If we's find out, he'll done be shunned."

"What...what will happen to Lucy?"

"I's don't know. Massar had a fit. Might sell her. Right now, he's too busy with the mess in town and you." Flora had her stand and take off her pantalettes as the chemise flowed past her knees.

Tears stung her eyes once more.

Flora took her in her arms and held her. "The good Lord will watch over ya, girl."

"I'm not worried about me."

"He'll watch over your loved ones." The servant patted her back. "You pray and keep on praying."

What if He didn't watch over them? What if He let Devon die, just as He'd allowed her mother to die?

Footsteps on the stairs.

Flora started. "They's coming." She jumped back and grabbed the green wool dress from the trunk. "Don't tell 'em I told you nothing. Massar says anyone help you, they's be taken to the caboose, whipped to within an inch of their lives, and sold."

Morning Fawn swiped her nose.

A rapid knock rattled the door.

Flora worked the dress over her head. "Just a minute, Massar, Miss Beth still dressing. Just a minute." She whipped the dress into place. "Keep your courage up, girl, and keep praying," she whispered as Morning Fawn quickly buttoned up the front.

The door burst open. Her uncle marched in, his riding whip in hand. "What are you doing up here, woman?"

"Missus's orders, sir." Flora curtseyed. "Wanted me to wash her up. In case you had plans of taking her into town."

"Get out. And don't come back unless I or Owens say so." His mouth contorted like a tree burl.

Flora scurried out.

No fine suit today. LeBeau wore his hunting trousers and coat. He smacked the whip against the doorjamb. "You have disgraced this family with a deeper stain than can ever be washed out with blood. I will. Never. Forgive. You."

She shuddered and hung her head. There were no words to buffet his wrath. "I'm ready to go to jail."

He snorted, a chilling laugh that sent goosebumps up her arms like a January norther. "I'd like nothing better, but I'll not have you disgrace this family further. I'll be living down the scourge Reynolds has brought to this house for the rest of my life. He traded on my good name." LeBeau's fingers curled until his hands were white-knuckled. "As far as anyone outside this plantation is concerned, you had no prior knowledge of Reynolds's plans. You were just a silly girl fooled by that traitor scum, giving away a few moonlit kisses. If anyone says differently, they'll answer to me for it."

No threat of execution or arrest? She gaped at him. His good name? His reputation? "I'd rather be locked away in town than be your prisoner in this attic."

He scoffed. "That sounds like something you'd say. Cut off your nose to spite your face. But you aren't going to have any say about your fate. Don't worry. I have no desire to have you under this roof a minute longer than you have to be. I have no intention of leaving you around here to cause any more trouble."

"I'd say or do anything you asked if only you'd convince the authorities to spare Devon's life."

"You'll do what I say or end up in a locked room in an asylum. As for Reynolds, the only choices left regarding him are whether he'll die by hanging or a firing squad, and whether we'll have the pleasure here in Alleyton, or if that will be saved for San Antonio."

Dear God, no. Please don't let it be so. Her legs wavered. She closed her eyes.

She blinked as the door slammed. LeBeau was gone for now. If only he could stay away forever. Nick too.

Devon. She dropped to her knees by a pile of clothing. His Bible lay amongst the garments. She grabbed it and pressed it to her chest. The only thing she had of his.

Dear God, help me. Help Devon. Please. She folded over and wept. *I can't do this on my own. Please, Lord, I can't lose him. I've lost so much. I need You to scrape me off the floor and put me back together. I cannot bear this.*

A seed of comfort awoke within her chest. She was not alone.

CHAPTER 32

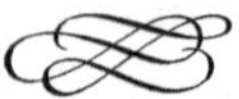

*E*yes puffy and swollen, Devon peered through a narrow slit in his right eye. Bars. He groaned and rolled over to his side. His whole body ached, and the cold stone floor didn't help. There was no good side to lie on. A bullet had passed through his left bicep's outer muscle, and his right hip throbbed, badly bruised from the impact of the tree.

They'd taken away the cot, given him two blankets—one to lie on and one to cover up with—and nothing else but a tin cup and a bucket to do his business in. He was filthy from head to toe.

He'd already be dead if it weren't for the fact that Moyer and the quartermaster wanted a public execution. That was the only reason they'd allowed a doctor to treat his wounds.

The quartermaster took pleasure in telling him that Gunter and Dr. Schramm had died at the hands of Confederate troops. No one escaped the cotton warehouse. Troops had entered, there'd been firing, then the explosion. As far as Devon knew, they hadn't caught Frieda or Frederick. Otherwise, the Rebs would have bragged about it, and the other cell wouldn't be empty.

Thank God, Frieda had escaped, but she shouldn't have been there at the river in the first place. If she hadn't shown up, would he have escaped, or would his fate have been the same?

Moyer said the explosion had hardly touched the cotton. Devon didn't believe it. When the trial came, he'd hear a different story of the horrendous damage he'd done. The truth probably lay somewhere in between.

The quartermaster's depot was another matter. They couldn't cover up that damage. The boy who swept the cells spoke of the gaping hole in the roof and the blackened walls. The only thing they could hide was the amount of supplies lost.

He shifted his foot, and a chain rattled—leg irons. As if the bars weren't enough to hold him.

Morning Fawn. Four days and so far he hadn't heard any female voices in the jail. *Dear God, please let her be all right.* Would they bring her here or take her someplace else? What did they do with female prisoners? The Federal government wasn't shy about sticking lady spies like Rosie Greenhow and Belle Boyd in prison until they figured out what to do with them. But at least the women had been imprisoned or exiled, not executed. From what he'd heard, Reb authorities under General Bragg threatened to execute Federal spy Pauline Cushman, but thankfully, her falling ill delayed the action, and U.S. cavalry rescued her.

He should have stayed away from Morning Fawn. He raked his hand over his face and drove his fingers through his disheveled hair. Stupid of him to smile at her and welcome her company. That night he went to her room to check on her after her uncle and Owens had forced poison down her throat? She'd been better off living through the poison than becoming entangled with him. He'd known his mission was dangerous. He'd tried to keep her out of it. But then she'd gone and dressed up in George's clothes and followed him. He was already too far gone by then, hopelessly in love, afraid to admit it.

In the end he'd done more harm to her than anyone else since the raid on her family's wagon train. If he'd had any sense, he'd have ignored her protest and shipped her off to the coast with Jeremy, bound and gagged if he had to, regardless of whatever effect that had on the mission. Her life was at stake.

Just as Isabelle's had been.

An hour later—or was it five? —he awakened to his stomach gnawing on itself. Four days and nothing to eat but a pan of gruel yesterday and a slice of stale bread the day before. A clank. He glanced toward the bars. His dry lips curled.

Moyer stood there dressed in a fine wool suit as if he'd never seen a fire. Unmarred, except for a bruise under one eye and four scratch marks on his other cheek. Were the marks new, or had he been too out of it to notice the first time the scum had showed up to taunt him?

Devon winced and pushed up to a seated position.

"Thought you might be hungry." Moyer jabbed his thumb, and the jailor stepped forward with a metal tray.

The grubby man with his overhung belly bent and shoved the food through a slit near the bottom of the door. A chunk of bread and a small piece of cheese.

Devon's mouth watered. But he would not dive in like a dog at the feet of this man. "Say what you got to say." His words came out thick through still-swollen lips.

Moyer smirked. "I've been to see Beth."

Devon's hand shook.

Moyer dismissed the jailor, and the man trudged down the hall toward the main door and steps.

"Not hungry?" Moyer nudged his boot toe toward the tray.

"Not with you around."

Moyer chuckled. "Might as well eat while you still have a throat that can swallow." He puffed out his chest. "I'm mighty grateful for Beth alerting us to the danger the other night and hurrying us off to Alleyton. Otherwise, we might have wasted the rest of the night whipping slaves."

"She didn't tell you a thing." Devon jumped to his feet, wobbling for a moment before gaining his balance. "She didn't have any idea what I was up to, and if she had, she'd held on to the information with her last breath."

Moyer strummed his knuckles against the bars. "I beg to differ. She hopped on a horse ready to lead us here. That's why she's not in jail and isn't going to be."

Devon ground his teeth. "You're a liar." He spit on the ground with what little spit he could muster. "What are those claw marks on your face? They didn't come from me. If you hurt her—"

"If I did hurt her, what would you do about it?" Self-satisfaction dripped from his tongue like venom. "But you don't have to worry about that. I plan to take good care of her. She and I are to be married."

"She would never touch your mangy hide." Devon's throat constricted.

"On the contrary. We'll be married within the month. I'm taking her to England with me to work on securing more cotton contracts. If you're still alive then, I'll consider getting you an armed guard and allowing you to come to the wedding."

"You're full of stories tonight." But his voice faltered. Morning Fawn would never agree to marry this man. And why would Moyer even consider her? Surely, he knew she'd played him for a fool. She wouldn't have warned them about the attack even if her life were at risk. Would she? Could she somehow have thought she was helping by telling?

Moyer laughed.

Devon picked up the tray and threw it at him.

"Your loss." Moyer shrugged and ambled toward the entrance and freedom.

The bread rolled back toward the bars. Maybe within reach

if Devon laid down and stretched to his utmost limit from chain to fingertips. He sank to his knees instead. Morning Fawn would not betray him. She would not marry this man of her own free will. Maybe they were lying to her too. But if it saved her life...

Dear God, help us. I know You can make a way where there is no way. Please deliver her from harm. Let her know that I love her. And that You do too. If there could somehow be a way in Your infinite grace and purpose, let there be a future for us. A life here on this earth. A way for me to escape this fate.

~

 $\mathcal{M}$ orning Fawn pressed her nose to her bedroom windowpane. Five days since Christmas. A roughened man in a captain's uniform dismounted from a quarter horse and sauntered to the hitching post. A stranger. Dirty, dusty, he'd come far. And there was something different about his uniform. Not standard issue. He glanced upward.

"Are you listening to me?" Her uncle rapped his cane against the floor behind her.

"I heard you." She hugged herself, trying to stave the leakage of all hope. "But I can't understand why Mr. Moyer would have any interest in marrying me. I'd think he'd never want to lay eyes on me again."

"Well, there's a pretty dollar or two at stake, let me tell you. It's costing me all of your Aunt Judith's land in Brazoria County given to her as her dowry upon our marriage." His voice ground like two stones rubbing together. "Acres of prime cotton land. But I have no choice, thanks to you. Not if I'm to keep our name from the spittoon and save any hopes of Thea marrying well. It'll cost you the land in Parker County. It'll be in his name, not yours. And he's going to ship you off to England until after the war. See if that will keep you out of trouble."

She turned back to the window. The horse hovered at the post, but the stranger wasn't in sight. Maybe he was here with news of Devon's trial.

"You will cooperate." Her uncle stomped closer. "I expect you to look at me when I talk with you."

"Or what?" She pivoted. Five days of groveling, and it'd done her no good. "If I had some assurance it'd save Devon from a death sentence, I'd marry a toad."

"You ungrateful hussy." He grabbed her jaw and forced her gaze up to his face. His fingers dug into her skin. Ice-blue eyes sizzled beneath a brow furrowed so deep he could plant cotton in it. "I'm saving you from jail, maybe even the gallows, and this is how you repay me? I've taken you in, fed you, clothed you—"

"Stole me from my home."

"You should pray to God I don't throw you back to the savages."

If only he would. A better fate than marriage to a man she detested. What happened to her didn't matter.

A knock on the door.

"What is it?" Her uncle's hand fell away from her.

"Excuse me, sir." George poked his head in. "There's an officer downstairs to see you."

"He can wait. I'm busy."

"Yes, sir." George bowed out.

Her uncle threw back his shoulders. "As I was getting ready to say, you will accept the engagement. Publicly. As if you adore Nick Moyer and have eyes for no one else. The ball at Robson's castle has been rescheduled for a week from today."

She jabbed her arms together.

"Your cooperation will buy one thing."

"What?"

"A better home for Lucy. Your actions will determine whether she's sold downriver to a sugar cane plantation or to a home in Marshall as a house servant."

"Don't lay this on my shoulders. If you care anything for her, you won't sell her."

"What are you implying?" His shoulders rose like a bull getting ready to charge. "She's a slave—a rebellious one, at that. Property. And that supposed marriage of hers had as much legality as an outhouse leaf. You and Reynolds could have saved yourselves the trouble. Maybe he'd have burned a couple more bales of cotton if he hadn't been distracted by such nonsense."

Another stone thrown into the heap, weighing her down in an ocean of despair. Would Devon have struck sooner and had more success if she hadn't burdened him with helping with the wedding and then planning Lucy and Ned's escape?

They were going to kill Devon, and she didn't know how to stop them. "Can't you leave me alone?" She picked up an unlit candle from the nearby desk. Her hand shook.

LeBeau's eyes widened.

She'd like nothing better than to smash his face. Instead, she slammed the candle on the desk, breaking off a chunk of wax.

LeBeau's eyebrows hovered low. "The day you strike me, that's the day I'll have you hauled off to the asylum. No marriage. No England. Nothing." His words struck cool and hard like iron.

No hope.

Unacceptable. She turned back to the window. If he said anything else, she didn't heed it. Instead, she stared at the windowsill with its two fresh nails. Locked tight again, enough to stifle her and break a sweat on the back of her neck. But she would, could not panic.

Tension ebbed from her shoulders as LeBeau retreated and closed the door behind him.

"'Yea though I walk through the valley of the shadow of death...'" She whispered the psalm she'd memorized. There were so many of them—David and others crying out to the

Lord, trusting Him when all seemed lost. She'd spent hours upon hours reading these last few days. Devon had marked Psalms and Luke and Romans. And she'd read of the grace her mother had often spoken of. Grace enough for her and all her shortcomings. Her untrusting heart, her words spoken too quickly, her jealousies... And what of the lies she'd told to protect Devon? How did the Lord look upon that? Maybe the Lord had not forgotten her. Maybe He'd been reaching out to her all along. Waiting for her to turn her heart to Him.

She went down on her knees, praying.

Minutes later, a thought came to her. If she agreed to the public announcement of the engagement, her uncle would let her out of the attic. They'd watch her like vultures, but she'd get to go to the ball. She'd only be two or three miles from the Colorado County Jail. What she could do with that, she had no idea. She couldn't ask Flora or any of the slaves to help her. They'd be whipped and sold if caught. Devon would be locked away and heavily guarded. But still...

Trembling with hope, she pulled herself up to stand in front of the window. The stranger was there again. He stuck his boot in the stirrup and mounted. A deep frown had settled above his scraggly brown beard. He picked up his reins, but just when she thought he'd turn the horse and ride off, he looked up, his gaze scanning the upper floors.

Did he see her staring at him through the bare branches of the cottonwood?

She waved for some foolish reason.

He paused, tipped his hat to her, and rode off.

He had seen her? But what could it possibly matter?

CHAPTER 33

Morning Fawn clasped her reticule and drew her feet in as far as she could beneath the cushioned seat of the landau carriage. Although the seat, the walls, even the roof cocooned her in royal-blue velvet, she would have rather traveled in an oxcart than sit across from Nick Moyer.

She trained her gaze on the glass window that encompassed the upper half of the carriage door. His silent stare had bored into her without relief for over an hour. She could have ridden all the way from Sweet Briar to the ball with her supposed family, but that was more than she could stomach.

The lace on her burgundy taffeta gown scratched against her lower arms and her collarbone. She'd never been to a ball. But all of the finery in the world couldn't compare to the hour she'd spent dancing in Devon's arms at Lucy's wedding.

Right now, she'd give everything she had for a future where Devon was alive and free. She'd tucked the small bottle of laudanum that Flora had stolen from the medicine cabinet into the inner pocket of her gown—safer there than risking its discovery in her reticule.

Devon's life was at stake. Morning Fawn couldn't sit by

and do nothing. Her casting aside the agreement with LeBeau wouldn't help Lucy, who was already at the slave trader's lockup in Columbus, waiting to supposedly be sold as a house servant. Morning Fawn would have to find another way to aid her. If she complied with LeBeau's plan, Devon would be dead, and Lucy would still be a slave.

If nothing else, she'd dose Nick with the laudanum and escape to the Alleyton house Devon told Lucy about. Maybe the underground network could help her figure out a plan to rescue him. Provided the members hadn't been rounded up and arrested. But it wasn't only Nick she had to worry about. He had his driver and a guard to help watch her.

Nick stirred as the rows of wedge tents outside Alleyton came into view. Campfires littered the barren hillside, more open now that the trees had been sacrificed for the sake of the soldiers' warmth.

Nick tapped the window. "Those fellows would have had a little neck-tying party for our friend Reynolds the other night if Captain Starr hadn't intervened."

"What do you mean?" Morning Fawn twisted the beaded fringes on her reticule.

Nick settled back against the cushions. "Those soldiers and many like them will go barefoot and cold the rest of the winter because of Reynolds. Hardworking men putting their lives on the line for Texas. The good citizens of Colorado County agree. I wouldn't be surprised if a mob showed up on the road to San Antonio to cut his trip short."

"San Antonio? What are you talking about?"

"Your uncle didn't mention that they're moving him tomorrow? The Confederate authorities want to make an example out of Reynolds. Hold an elaborate trial before they get on with the hanging. The only question is whether he'll make it there with his heart still beating."

Her chest tightened like a vise had just clamped its teeth into her ribs. "Surely, the army wouldn't allow that to happen."

Nick shrugged. "Some members of the military would prefer to not waste time and money on a trial. A rope around the branch of a big cottonwood along the way would serve the purpose just fine." He stroked his mustache. "Personally, I like the idea of a spectacle and the total humiliation of the man in front of the citizenry of Texas, but then a lynch mob asks fewer questions."

"Questions about what?"

"About *your* role. About your uncle. About me."

"I'd be willing to spend the rest of my life in jail if it'd save Devon."

"Very noble of you." He rolled his eyes. "But it wouldn't do him a bit of good."

Her heart dropped to her feet. Devon wouldn't make it to San Antonio. Her escaping and finding her way to the hideout house wouldn't be enough. Not unless they could organize a plan and men overnight. Enough men to take on a military escort? In the middle of Nick and her uncle scouring the area for her. *Dear God, help me. This cannot be how it ends.*

A ferryman stood at the edge of her vision talking to the carriage driver. The gurgle of the Colorado River filled the gaps as the driver clicked the reins and walked the team of four onto the ferry.

Nick fished a flask out of his fine wool frock coat pocket. "You know how Reynolds got captured, don't you?"

"By you." She folded her arms, but there wasn't enough steel in her to hide the tremor in her voice.

He took a swig and licked his lips. "I shot him in the arm, but he might have gotten away if it wasn't for the Schramm girl."

"Frieda?" She sat straight up.

The carriage jerked as the ferry started across the river, tugged by the ropes.

"He let himself get caught to save her."

Her lungs constricted. "You're lying. She wasn't anywhere near there."

"On the contrary, she was waiting at the river with a canoe. I'd shot him, but he'd run on. Probably would have made it if the fair maiden hadn't shown up and offered him a ride. He hopped in ready to paddle away with her—only, his stopping momentarily to greet her gave me time."

Acid rose in her throat.

His eyes sparkled. "I fired. Ready to put a bullet in one or both of them. He stood up, acting like he was going to surrender, then flipped the canoe. He knew I'd have to choose who to go after. Of course, I followed him. Beat him to a pulp and dragged his sorry carcass off to jail. Frieda Schramm got away. I could have killed Reynolds right then and there—miserable worm of a man he is—only, I figured that'd be too easy."

Devon had sacrificed himself to save Frieda? After he'd promised Frieda wouldn't be there. That he wouldn't allow Frieda or Morning Fawn to be part of the attack. What if he'd said that because he thought Morning Fawn was incompetent, that she'd mess up or get in the way? She sunk back against the cushions.

"You're lying." She strangled the flimsy reticule in her grip.

Nick tugged his watch from its pocket. "Ask him yourself."

"What do you mean?"

"I figured since it's the last time either of us will see the man, we'd stop for a little visit. I think it's only proper we let him know you'll be well provided for, that he needn't worry about you as he heads to San Antonio."

"You want to gloat."

"Reynolds has been a worthy opponent. No harm in saying 'good game.'"

"'Good game?'" She almost came off her seat. "The man is on his way to his death."

"He knew the consequences if he got caught. He made his decision. Obviously, his mission and the German girl meant more to him than any romance he had with you. And of course, he made the poor decision of having her be part of his squad instead of you, the more capable actress."

She closed her eyes and pressed her hands to her stomach, lest she throw up. Had Devon lied to her? Or was the addition of Frieda a last-minute decision? One that could still cost him his life.

The ferry docked, and the carriage rolled off onto dry land.

She would see the layout of the jail, and she'd see Devon. It was more than she could have asked for. But what if it wasn't enough?

What if he'd betrayed her with Frieda?

～

*L*amplight from the streets filtered into Devon's cell through the bars on the window. He shivered and pulled his blanket around him like a cape. Carriages and buggies had rolled past for the last hour. The gala at Robson's Castle had been delayed, not canceled, as if the attack never happened, as if Devon's mission had meant nothing.

The iron shackle chafed against his ankle as he sat up. He rubbed his fingers over his eyes, no longer swollen. His bruises had receded beneath the layer of dirt that covered him. A bath wasn't a luxury granted by his jailors. He was thankful if he received two or three cups of water a day and a meager meal of watery broth and weevil-laden hardtack. Vermin were available in plentiful supply.

The soreness in his hip had settled down to a dull ache whenever he moved his right leg, but he couldn't bend his left arm without gritting his teeth. It throbbed throughout his waking hours and restless nights.

Tomorrow he'd be on the road to San Antonio. Would that give Jeremy an opportunity to strike, provided he could gather enough troops in the limited amount of time? Or perhaps the German League could muster a contingent? Far-flung hopes.

He needed to be ready to attempt escape at the slightest opportunity. It'd be better to end up with a bullet in his back than face the gallows. He could try the excuse Morning Fawn pulled on the way to the fort after her kidnapping, her "I need to go behind the bushes" maneuver. It'd almost worked. She'd managed to knock out the dumb kid who should have been at home on his ranch instead of hiring on as a guard.

Morning Fawn. His heart clenched.

Footsteps trudged up the stairs, followed by lighter ones. Devon stiffened. What now?

Keys clanked. The outer door's lock turned over in the tumbler. Devon rose and dropped his blanket. Best face whatever was coming on his feet. The potbellied jailer swung a lantern and stepped to the side.

Devon blinked in the light.

Another lantern and another man. Moyer. Dressed in his finest as if he'd stopped by on the way to the ball. Someone moved from behind, also dressed for the gala. Burgundy gown, white lace, and a dark-green cape.

Morning Fawn. Devon's knees wobbled. His breath left him. He sputtered out a cough.

Her hair was drawn back from her face in a mass of waves and curls. A tiara encircled the crown of her head. Emerald earrings swung from her ears, a perfect match to the necklace which adorned her neck.

Moyer strutted forth. "I promised to bring my betrothed to say goodbye."

Devon clenched his hands at his sides. What he wouldn't

give to lay his fists into that smug snout. "You make a mockery of the word 'betrothed.' Coercing a woman is hardly something to brag about."

"I'd never force a woman to marry me."

"You must have left all of the dirty dealing to her uncle, then."

Morning Fawn said nothing to disavow the claim. Her face tight and pale, she stepped toward the bars.

Moyer waved the jailer away. "Wait outside the door."

Devon ran a trembling hand over his face and hair, beyond repair.

She wrapped her gloved fingers around the bars. He couldn't reach them. The chain rattled as he tried.

Moyer chuckled. "I've been telling Morning Fawn how you gave yourself up to save the Schramm girl."

Morning Fawn? That was his name for her, no one else's. Devon ground his molars. Of course, this devil would work every angle he could to worm dissent between him and the woman he loved. "Frieda disobeyed orders. She was supposed to flee. Instead, she showed up with a canoe. I couldn't let her be shot or hung on my account, just as I wouldn't allow any woman die for me if I could help it. I'd have done the same for a seventy-year-old grandmother."

Morning Fawn stared at him, wounded doe eyes filled with depths he couldn't fathom.

He pivoted and uncurled his chain from its post in the floor.

"Pity it didn't amount to much." Moyer hung the lantern from a hook.

The chain length or the mission? "Don't tell me it didn't mean anything. I smelled smoke for three days afterward."

"A few bales. We snuffed that one out. And then a bit of the roof of the depot. Nothing more."

"He's lying." Her words sounded as if they were poured

through sand. "You destroyed the depot. And burned countless bales of cotton."

Moyer stuck his hands in his pockets. "Fables to comfort the dying."

Morning Fawn flinched.

Devon strode forward and yanked. Three feet closer. With his arms stretched, he curled his fingers around the bars just below Morning Fawn's.

She startled as if she might withdraw.

Dear God, no. Don't let her go. Don't let her believe the devil's lies about Frieda. His breath came short as he lost himself in her hazel gaze. "You're the woman I love. You are the woman I wanted...*want* to spend the rest of my life with."

"I love you. And only you." Her words latched hold of his sinking heart and thrust it toward daylight. "Forever."

Moyer snorted. "It's time to go."

"Don't marry him." Devon slipped his hands up over hers. Couldn't she take off the gloves? What if he never saw her again on this earth? "You'd be better off scrubbing floors than to spend one day with the likes of him." *George will have a horse. Find the safe house.* He mouthed the words.

Her lips moved.

Moyer tugged on his cuffs. "I like the idea of taming a wild-cat. A few months abroad and her puppy-dog infatuation with you will be a distant memory."

"I'll do what I have to do," she said simply.

What was that supposed to mean? Where was her fighting spirit and quick temper? Maybe they'd threatened her with imprisonment if she didn't comply. But that shouldn't matter. Let her play along with the engagement announcement tonight. Tomorrow or the next evening, she should be able to slip away. That part of the escape plan should still be secure. He searched her gaze.

She trembled. "I'm sorry about Christmas Eve. I've thought

of a half-dozen things I could have done differently, and maybe you wouldn't be here—"

"It's not your fault." He squeezed her hands with all of his might. "I don't know what happened at the plantation the night of the attack, but you did not fail me. I love you." *I will escape and come for you or die trying.* This could not be the end. "If we do not meet again on this earth, we will meet in heaven." But dear God, let it be on this earth.

She dipped her head and kissed his dirty fingers. "The Lord be with you."

"Enough." Moyer grabbed her arm. "This man is going to die because he cared more for another woman than his own life." He pulled on her. "And you, Reynolds, how selfish of you. You'd ask her to be a poor, lonely spinster if you can't have her?"

"No. I only ask her to seek the Lord's guidance. And to know I'll always love her." *Find the house,* he mouthed again.

One hand fell away, but she held tight to the bar with the other. Couldn't she mouth something back? Devon strained forward. The metal cuff cut into his shin. If only he could get close enough for a kiss.

Moyer yanked her clear. She didn't resist further, other than to turn and glance over her shoulder for one more lingering look.

Her lips moved soundlessly. "Don't give up." Then Moyer had her out the door.

"Why do they have to chain him up like an animal?" Her voice retreated.

"Can't have the traitor escaping. I don't even have the key." The jailer whistled as the door clanked shut.

Don't give up. Were those really her words or a desperate imagining on his part?

CHAPTER 34

*M*orning Fawn gazed out the window as the carriage rumbled over the drawbridge, above the moat. Candlelight and lamplight bathed the limestone castle which towered three stories. It was a setting suited for *Robinhood* or *Ivanhoe*, not Texas. A billowing Confederate flag hung below the rooftop garden. Music drifted out of the windows. A sight to behold, but the only sight she cared about was three miles away in a two-story jail surrounded by a locked fence, and chained to an iron stake with no key on the grounds.

Nick said something.

She leaned forward, pressing her nose to the pane, ignoring him. He didn't matter. None of it mattered. Devon would be on the road to San Antonio tomorrow. Dear God, what was she going to do?

"I feel sick." She wrapped her arms around her middle. "I need to go to the privy."

He arched an eyebrow. "There'll be time enough for that inside. Robson actually has running water in the castle."

She stared at him. "Running water?"

"Robson pumps water from the Colorado River to the roof

and pipes it throughout the house." He tugged on his gloves. "You can go to the privy all you want. One of my men or I will be at the door waiting for you every second."

A glimmer caught her eye as they rode through the gate—his flask lying on his seat half covered by his coattail. She glanced away, chin set. She wasn't going home tonight, one way or the other.

As they disembarked, he stepped out first, spoke to the footman, and turned to offer his hand. A few seconds, but it was enough. She swiped the flask beneath her cloak. The privy would provide the perfect opportunity to access the laudanum and add a little flavoring to the man's drink for the ride home.

She stepped down.

"What are you doing?" Nick grabbed her arm.

"What do you mean?"

Without letting go, he poked his head into the carriage, then patted his coat pocket with his free hand. "What are you up to?"

"I have no idea what you're talking about."

His eyes narrowed. "Back in the carriage."

"I have to go to the pr—"

"No, you don't." He jabbed a finger at her and pushed her back.

"Well, I never."

"I never either." He climbed in across from her and slammed the door. "I've been tricked by you one too many times."

"I don't know what you're talking about. I'm sick to my stomach because the man I love is about to...die. And there's nothing I can do about it."

He rolled his eyes. "I don't believe it."

"You'll believe it when I throw up on your boot."

"I was ready to do that myself back there at the jail with all of that 'I love you forever' trash."

"That's because you don't know the first thing about love unless it's the dollars that line your pocket." She snatched up her reticule and threw it at him.

He grabbed it and tossed it aside. "You're wasting your time grieving for a man who chose the mission and Miss Perfect over you. At the very least, he should have had *you* with him spying on the warehouse, had you up in Alleyton with him the night of the attack. You're the woman who could have helped him succeed."

"I'm the woman who ended up with my face in the dirt, and the man I love is in jail about to be hung."

"You're the woman who doesn't give up." He drummed his fingers on this thigh. "So I ask again, what are you up to?"

"Nothing, other than trying not to fall apart in front of a ballroom full of people. You have bested me. I have no choice but to go along with this sham betrothal. I can't save Devon. All I can do is try to keep myself from being thrown in jail for treason and bargain for Lucy to have a decent owner."

He loosened his blue silk cravat. "I don't believe it. You're too quiet, too compliant. It's not like you. You're up to something. Do you have a knife hidden beneath your skirt? And what's that flask all about?"

"What flask?"

"The one you swiped from me." He held out his hand.

Spearing him with her eyes, she smacked the gold-plated tin into his palm.

"Should I have one of my men search you for weapons?"

"I'll scratch the face off of anyone who touches me, including you."

"Hmm." He settled back against the cushions and rapped on the door with his knuckles.

"Yes, sir?" The footman popped his head in the door, looking more like a gunman than a footman with a holster on each hip.

"We're not staying. Tell Henry to turn the coach around. We're going for a ride. West of town. Find a secluded area."

"Yes, sir." The man tipped his hat and shot Morning Fawn a glance better aimed at a tart.

She stiffened as the door closed. "I've warned you what will happen if you put your hands on me."

"Settle down." He fingered the flask lid as the carriage pulled into motion. "I want to have a real talk with you. I mean, I thought I had one a couple weeks ago in my office after I found you dressed in that ridiculous outfit. I was foolish enough to think I'd finally discovered your true self. But I was mistaken. There are layers of deception and determination I've only begun to decipher."

"I'm a stone wall as far as you're concerned." She tightened her cloak about her. "I want nothing to do with you. So you might as well take me back to the ball and have me play my part for the night." As if she could. She shifted her gaze to the far window. "I don't care what you do—there will never be anything between you and me. I bet my uncle would still give you the land you're after if you'd do him the courtesy of depositing me at the nearest monastery or asylum."

"Nunnery."

"Excuse me?"

"Monasteries are for men. Nunneries are for women."

The carriage rumbled across the drawbridge and onto the road.

"I don't care." She threw her arms open wide. "The point is, my heart isn't for sale. And there are better ways to get land than saddling yourself with a wife who wants nothing to do with you, so I'm begging you to leave me off at a street corner before we get out of town."

"Hmmm." He pursed his lips and stared at her.

She scooted to the cushioned corner. Streetlights flickered

by. Her stomach tumbled. The passing of the minutes pulsed in her head. *Dear Lord, what am I to do?*

She could bolt out of the carriage as soon as it stopped and take a gamble his men wouldn't shoot, but how far could she get on foot? She needed a horse and a key. The jailer didn't have the key to the leg irons. Maybe a strong man could bust the chain with a sledgehammer, but how was *she* to do that? The jail would be the first place Nick would look. She needed to get to Alleyton and contact the Germans. But would they have the men and the will to attack the transport before it was too late?

"I can see the gears of your mind working at full steam." His voice broke the silence.

She cinched her cloak tighter. She should have gotten her hands on a knife.

Darkness filled the windows now. She squinted at the outlines of a fence or field, an occasional far-off light from a barn or house. An outcropping of trees came up on the left.

Nick rapped on the ceiling. "Here."

The carriage pulled over.

She steeled herself for what was to come.

He tugged his gloves off and tossed them aside. "You'll never be able to save Reynolds on your own."

It was as if he'd stolen the thought from her head. She gaped at him.

His gaze bored into her. "You think there's nothing to me? That money's all I care about."

"I'm sure you love success and power, as well, and an occasional visit to a brothel."

"I'm a man who knows what he wants and finds a way to get it. I don't accept defeat, especially at the hands of a worm like Reynolds."

"Too late."

The edge of his mouth quirked upward in a smirk. "Do you know what I've been sitting here thinking?"

"I have no idea." She crossed her arms.

"Death isn't good enough for Reynolds."

She shivered. "What is that supposed to mean?"

Nick's expression hardened. "He has smeared my name and reputation. The news of his attack will spread across civilized Texas and the western division of the Confederacy."

"You stopped him. Saved most of the cotton."

"Not good enough. I should have figured him out weeks ago. At least, I'm not like that buffoon of a quartermaster who would have let the entire town burn down. However, the smear is still there, and will spread far and wide." He narrowed his eyes. "Furthermore, Reynolds stole the affection of the woman I want."

She pressed her lips together. He *didn't steal it. He won it.*

"Death isn't good enough because when he dies, it's over. He's paid his debt. No more suffering or consequences for him. How does that benefit me?"

She froze. What if she was the payment he was looking for? "You come near me, you'll live to regret it."

"I told you once before, I don't force myself upon women."

"In that case, I'm sure you'll die a lonely old bachelor. You might as well turn around, take me back to town."

"Tell me, Morning Fawn, what are you willing to do in order to save Devon Reynolds?"

Her heart clunked.

The question hung between them. The murmur of voices drifted in—the driver and the footman talking. A distant coyote let loose a howl. Devon might never hear a coyote again. Might never see the stars again.

She fought to steady her voice. "I wouldn't give you anything because there's nothing you could do. I don't care what you promise me for a night on the carriage bench or whatever you might dream up. I'm not foolish enough to imagine all those generals down in San Antonio would listen to you. Even you don't have that kind of power. And I wouldn't trust you if you did. Your word isn't worth spit."

"My word? I don't recall lying to you. But you've spun a basketful to me. " He drummed his fingers on the seat and blew out his cheeks. "What if your part of the deal wasn't payable until Reynolds was free?"

"What do you mean?"

"If I save Reynolds from the noose, you have to marry me. That would be enough. He would live the rest of his life, knowing I had you."

She blinked at him. Marry Nick? The threat of such a posh enslavement had hung over her head for weeks, easily cast aside. Until now. "I'm not going to discuss that with you because it's not going to happen. You're not going to set him free. You're a liar, a braggart, and a cheat who cares for nothing but himself and his money."

He scrubbed his hand over his well-groomed jaw. "I'll tell you what." He stretched his arms across the tops of the cushions and crossed his ankle over his knee as if he had all of the time in the world. "You know that slave friend of yours? Lucy? The one your uncle has chained up at the slave trader's shop in town? We'll fetch her. Let her carry a message to those traitors Reynolds was in league with."

She gaped at him. "You must think I'm stupid. You'd have her followed, and you'd throw every Unionist you could get your hands on in jail or worse. It'd be more notches on your scalp pole."

"You'd be with me the whole time. My two men won't go anywhere. I'd get her free. More likely, buy her and turn my back while she runs off. You'd give her the information on where to go if she already doesn't know, and you'd give her the message that Reynolds is being moved tomorrow. I'll give you the name of the spot where the escort will likely spend the night on the road. Provided they can muster enough guts and guns, the Unionists will have an opportunity to rescue their hero. It'd give Reynolds a fighting chance."

"This is a trick. You want to use me to destroy people's lives." She glowered at him, her nails slicing into her palms.

He pulled his watch out of his pocket and clicked open the lid.

The *tick, tick, tick* pounded in her temples.

He snapped the timepiece shut. "We can sit here and talk all night. It's up to you if you want to allow Reynolds a hope." He tugged on his cuffs. "But you have my word that I won't follow Lucy or try to find who she contacts. I won't alert the military. She'll have her freedom, and the men will have the opportunity to rescue Reynolds. They may or may not succeed. Reynolds might not survive the attempt, but if he doesn't, that'd be a shame. His Unionist comrades should strike as soon as possible if they want to beat the lynching crew that will likely attack before San Antonio." He cocked his eyebrows. "It's up to you."

"Why would you do this? If anyone finds out, you'll be viewed as a traitor."

He unscrewed the lid on his flask and took a swig. "A man doesn't earn a partnership with Richard King by living ordinary and limiting his risks. One doesn't hope to corner the cattle market by staying with the herd. You'd make a perfect wife for the future I envision for myself on the frontier. A life Reynolds could never provide. He's too busy throwing away his opportunities for his principles. He'd rather scrape by kidnapping women and wasting his talents trying to avoid the war and then feel guilty about it and enlist, a man blown about by the wind."

"He's willing to risk his life for what he believes in and to save others. You're only willing to risk your reputation and only to line your pocket."

He rolled his eyes for the second time this evening.

This could be her only hope of saving Devon. But what if she ended up betraying everyone who had helped with the mission, everyone who had any loyalty to Devon? She gripped her midsection. "Where would I be while we wait to see what happens? Locked up in my uncle's attic?"

"Absolutely not. Once we set this in motion, you are with me. I'd leave word that I'm eloping with you, traveling to Galveston to get married, and then setting sail for England. I'm going to win the Confederacy the largest cotton contracts they've ever seen. The cotton lost at the warehouse will be but a thimbleful compared to it."

She narrowed her eyes at him. "You said I wouldn't have to marry you until after the escape."

"You wouldn't. You'd be with me in my rooms. Your reputation would be ruined, but I wouldn't touch you against your will until we're married, and we wouldn't marry until we receive word of his escape."

"You'd let everyone think that you'd...that we'd... No one decent would have me after that. I might as well be a saloon girl."

He shrugged.

"You don't care." Of course, he didn't. It'd be another tie binding her to him.

"And I should add that if you betray me, my men and I will hunt Reynolds down, and I'll put a bullet between his eyes, and you'll be mine, wed or not." He smiled like a fox about to have dinner. "Just to be clear."

She rocked forward, her chest pressed to her knees. Nausea engulfed her, but there was no purging. She drug her fingers through her hair, pressing her nails to her skull. *Dear Lord, help me. What am I to do?*

He shifted his foot to the floor and leaned forward, elbows on knees. "I'll be a good husband to you, Morning Fawn. My mother wasn't treated right by my father. I will treat you right."

You don't know the first thing about being a husband. It will be a prison sentence, not a life.

"From the way you two talked to each other in the jail, I thought you'd be willing to do anything to save him."

She groaned down deep in her soul. She'd failed her sister. She'd not been willing to put herself at risk for Eyes-Like-Sky. "I won't betray his accomplices. I won't sacrifice Lucy."

"But?" His voice bore the strained eagerness of a racehorse at the line, eager for the starting shot.

She lifted her head, heart scraping bottom beneath fathoms of lost hopes. "I *will* sacrifice *myself*. Turn the carriage around. Head for the slave trader's place. And if you dilly-dally on any of it, I'll jump across this seat and throttle you."

He half chuckled and rapped his knuckles against the door.

CHAPTER 35

$\mathcal{M}$orning Fawn moved in a fog. None of this was real, couldn't be. Lawrence, the gunman-turned-footman, banged on the quarters at the slave compound. Three crude brick buildings connected by a high wooden fence stood in back of the small house.

A whiskered man with trousers under his nightshirt finally answered the door. As agreed, Morning Fawn accompanied Nick into the man's office, with Lawrence right behind her ready to grab her at the first hint of an escape attempt.

Her stomach knotted as Nick argued back and forth with the trader, proclaiming that he was eloping with Lebeau's niece and that Lebeau would be more than happy to sell Lucy to him for any price in gratitude for securing a decent marriage for his wayward niece.

Finally, the man swiped his forearm across his nose and hitched his trousers. The deal was struck. A thousand dollars, a bargain, and an extra commission for the trader for the rush. Nick scrawled his signature across the bill of sale, and the man woke his wife to fetch Lucy.

No, don't. Stop. I can't go through with this. Morning Fawn swallowed back her protests and pressed her lips shut.

Head lowered, Lucy trudged in through a back door, wearing a faded plaid dress and a worn cloak. Her hair was pulled back in an untidy chignon at the base of her neck. Shackles clanked around her feet.

The trader's wife followed, her rollered hair wrapped in a neckerchief. "Act lively, girl. Here's your new owners."

Lucy looked up and startled. Her glance flitted between Nick and Morning Fawn, her mouth agape.

Nick laid his arm around Morning Fawn's shoulders. "We're eloping. You're my wedding present to Miss Logan."

Morning Fawn flinched.

Lucy's eyes widened. She raised her hands in supplication. "Don't do that for me, miss. Don't do that for me."

"Hush." Nick's voice boomed.

Lucy stilled.

Nick picked up the piece of paper and tucked it into his pocket. "Take the chains off. Have her brought to the carriage. We must be on our way."

He pivoted toward the door, turning Morning Fawn with him. Her burgundy gown swiped the torn rag-rug-covered floor. What she wouldn't give for a doeskin outfit and moccasins right about now, and the fastest horse this side of the Palo Duro. But what good would they do? She was bound by her word as long as Nick Moyer kept his.

At the carriage with only Nick and his men as witnesses, Morning Fawn embraced Lucy.

Nick emitted a guttural groan as if she'd stepped into a pigsty.

Lucy stiffened and whispered, "Not in front of him. And don't you dare go taking up with that man for me."

"It's not only for you." Morning Fawn stepped back and gripped her shoulders. "It's your freedom and Devon's life."

"Freedom?" Lucy's brow furrowed like tree bark. "The lieutenant's life?"

"We don't have all night." Nick swung open the door. "Does she want to walk from here or get a ride across the river?"

"The river." Morning Fawn grabbed Lucy's wrist and hurried her into the carriage.

"You're allowing that...girl to ride inside?" Lawrence scowled.

"Unless you want her riding on back with you." Nick raised a handkerchief to his nose as he entered the compartment.

Morning Fawn ignored the odor of someone being locked away for days with no facilities to bathe. Devon hadn't smelt any better.

Lucy squeezed into the corner with Morning Fawn on the other side of her.

Nick settled down at the far end of the other bench. "I want to hear every word."

Lucy held her tongue as Morning Fawn shared the basic details of the agreement and Lucy's part.

At the end, Lucy shifted her glance to the ogre who stared out the window. She mouthed to Morning Fawn, "You and him, no. Gotta be another way."

Morning Fawn shivered. "I'll do whatever it takes to save Devon."

"He...we...the rescue might not..."

Morning Fawn squeezed her friend's hand. "You run like the wind and pour out your heart to those Unionists. Devon risked his life for their cause. Make them understand."

Lucy nodded and mouthed, "You get away when it's done."

Morning Fawn turned her head and stared at her jailer. She'd given her word.

Across the river, Nick ordered his driver to pull over in a wooded spot outside of town. "This is where you get off, girl. I'll allow Miss Beth a moment in here alone with you for her to tell you the location of the Unionist hideout. And I'll give you the route the escort will take and where they're likely to stop. Then Reynold's life is in your hands."

Lucy shuddered and lowered her gaze. "In the Lord's hands, sir."

"It's not the Lord who's going to be running and begging. Never saw Him wield a gun. You'd best stick with the Unionists, pitiful lot that they are." He puffed out his chest. "And let me give you warning. If any word of my help here reaches Confederate ears, I'll launch a manhunt for Reynolds the likes of which this state has ever seen, and Miss Logan will be my mistress, not my wife. Therefore, the Unionists don't need to know about my involvement. Telling them would be like pouring water in a bucket with a hole. As far as they're concerned, Miss Logan helped you escape from me. If you see Reynolds in person, you can tell him the whole story."

"I could write a note." Morning Fawn clutched her hands. "A short note saying I've agreed to marry you." *And that I'll love him forever.*

Nick frowned. "All right. It'd be a shame for him to not hear the news. You've got three minutes to tell her and to write the note, and I'm going to read it."

Ten minutes later, Morning Fawn braced herself on a tree as Lucy took off through the woods for Alleyton. *God go with her. Keep her safe. Please spare Devon.* For that, she'd pay whatever price she had to. What did the Lord of the universe think of the bargain she'd sold herself for? Had she been wrong? What choice did she have?

~

*D*evon woke in a cold sweat. He'd dreamed of Isabelle for the first time in months. He shivered and pulled the wool blanket up to his neck, but there'd be no returning to sleep. His future loomed in front of him like a guillotine. Today, he'd start the journey to San Antonio. If the German League or Jeremy didn't take action, it would be his last journey.

Dear God, let this not be the end. Morning Fawn. *Please, Lord, look after her.*

A knock and then voices drifted up from below. Were the Rebs coming for him before dawn? He rolled up off the rock-hard floor and rubbed his eyes.

Footsteps clunked on the stairs—not just the jailer but several men. Devon got to his feet and straightened his clothes. He grabbed his blankets and his empty tin cup. He winced as he stretched out his left arm. A pent-up breath rattled through him.

An itch crawled up the back of his skull. He plucked a louse and smashed it between his fingernails.

The outer door lock clicked. Devon braced himself.

Lantern light beamed in through the open door. The jailer trudged in.

With a gun to his back?

Half a dozen men spilled into the hall that led to the cells. A motley crew of Rebs. But why did the officer in the slouch hat have a gun pointed at the jailer?

Devon blinked in the blinding light. His muscles tightened like sinew strung in a bow. If they'd come to lynch him, he wouldn't go without a fight.

Suddenly, the officer clunked the jailer in the head. The fellow thudded to the ground. The soldier with the lantern stepped out of the way, and the bearded officer hurried forth.

Jeremy. The realization exploded in Devon's head. Laughter burst from him. His meager possessions dropped from his hands. He lunged hard against his chain. "You're here."

"You bet I am." Jeremy grabbed the keys to the cell from the man who riffled through the jailer's pockets. "We've got to hurry. The other two guards are tied up downstairs. There's a heavily armed Reb escort expected here within the hour. That slave girl of LeBeau's—"

"Lucy? Was Morning Fawn with her?" Hope jolted through Devon.

"No, but she sent Lucy with word about the move and about how flimsy this jail setup was." He stuck the key into the lock and turned. "She had information about a place on the road we could strike, but I knew our best bet was here. I'd been hiding out for several days working to figure out a rescue. Even dreamed up an excuse to visit LeBeau."

The cell door swung open.

"There's no key for this." Devon jiggled his chain.

"We're prepared." Jeremy slapped him on the shoulder.

Squeezed into a Reb uniform that was busting at the seams, Frederick stepped forward, sledgehammer in hand. Two men Devon didn't recognize hustled in with a hammer and a coal chisel to help. Oscar's brother, Henry, jerked the jailer's hands behind his back and snagged a rope around the man's wrists.

Ten minutes later, Devon was running down the stairs with his rescuers, a mix of the German League and a small squad of cavalry Jeremy had rounded up, leaving the jailer and the guards tied, gagged, and locked in the cell.

Jeremy stopped him at the door to the courtyard. "From here, we take it slow until we're out of town. As far as any passersby are concerned, we're the troop escort sent to haul you down to San Antonio."

"In that case, you'd better point your gun on me." Devon brought his hands in front of him and held them as if he were still bound.

Darkness draped the streets. Two men waited outside the fence, securing the horses for the others. A rooster crowed from behind a nearby house. The bird would have people stirring even before the sliver of dawn. Devon quickstepped with his supposed captors out through the gate. He went through the motions of having to be helped into the saddle on a mustang. As they headed out, the men rode close to him on all sides.

Wearing Confederate captain bars and a slouch hat, Jeremy led them west at a trot. Every crunch of their horse hooves raked across Devon's nerves. Any second, someone could sound the alarm, and they'd all be running for their lives. *Clip-clop. Clip-clop.*

A man staggered to his front porch and waved at them, almost falling over in the process. On another corner, a dog padded across the street. Farther down the lane, a candle burned in a shop window. A small buggy rattled by. Devon's breath caught at every movement.

Scrubs and trees. The last of the buildings. Still at a steady pace, they rounded a bend.

Jeremy moved his mount closer to Devon's. "A couple of the men are going to head back home. They have families there. They plan to act as if they had nothing to do with this. The rest of us are going to take off at a gallop and head south across the next field, cut across the Cotton Road to throw off any pursuers, and head for Matagorda."

"And Morning Fawn?"

Jeremy shifted in the saddle. "She's nowhere near here. And the best thing you can do for her is stay alive." He raised his hand, swept it downward in a sharp, swift motion, and snapped his reins, bolting forward and cutting off any opportunity for further discussion.

Two men cut sharp to the north through the shrubs. The rest followed Jeremy, picking up speed. Devon pressed his thighs to the mustang. Back straight, he lowered his elbows close to his knees and pressed the animal to a gallop.

Thump, thump, thump, he rode with the movement of the horse, his boots snug in the stirrups. Down the road, then a cut to the left, gravel and dust flying. Another road and then a field. A sliver of orange peaked above the horizon. They shifted through a wooded area, slowing their pace to a canter, driving forward, creeping to a walk when they came to a creek, splashing through the water for a couple miles before heading up the other side of the bank.

They sped up again, then galloped as they crossed to another road, the morning sun on their left. When they reached the wide, dusty trail known as the Cotton Road, they stuck to it for four or five miles, letting their hoof prints mix with the hundreds of others that marred the dirt. Wisps of cotton clung to the scattered grasses, sage, and the claw-like branches of the mesquite trees, leftover traces of the tens of thousands of bales which had made this trek since the beginning of the war.

As the afternoon sun hit their backs, they peeled off into the brush two by two. Hopefully, leaving the road in such small numbers, it wouldn't garner any tracker's attention.

Late afternoon, they stopped in a wooded spot close to the Colorado River. Devon slid out of the saddle and shook each man's hand, seven in all, thanking them heartily.

Jeremy swiped his brow with his neckerchief. "We'll give the horses a rest and then start again at dark. Travel all night."

One of the cavalry troopers Jeremy had brought along glanced up from pouring feed into a canvas bucket for his horse. "Be quicker to take the river down to Matagorda."

"Too bad the Rebs will think of that too." Jeremy grabbed his horse's lead rope. "No fires. And by the time we leave this spot, I want every trace of Confederate uniform gone. No use inviting a firing squad." He motioned for Devon to follow him to the river with his horse.

Devon limped along the way. Hours in the saddle had left his injured hip worse for the wear. Pecan, hickory, and oak lined the banks. The sluggish river swirled around a downed tree branch and cattails as the horses drank their fill.

"I had a chance to survey your work from a distance."

Jeremy swigged from his canteen and passed it to Devon. "That supply depot looks like a Gettysburg cannonade struck it—"

"I need to know about Morning Fawn. Now." Devon guzzled the sweet liquid. His sandpaper throat rejoiced. "I'm done waiting." He swiped his hand over his mouth. "Where is she? Did she find the horse in the woods? Did she get away from Moyer?"

Jeremy shifted his gaze to the river and dragged a hand down across his thick brown beard. "Morning Fawn got the information from Moyer and sent Lucy to Alleyton to deliver it. Morning Fawn was determined to save you at all costs." Jeremy's words thudded like handfuls of dirt on a grave.

"At all costs?" A chill swept over Devon. "What is that supposed to mean? If I need to turn around right now and go after her, I will."

"Don't even think about it. I'll have my men tie you up, gag you, and take you prisoner for real." Jeremy jutted his finger at him. "As far as I know, she left Colorado County last night. The way to save her is to get to Federal-held territory as quickly as you can before you end up with a bullet in your back and get all of us killed trying to protect you. Get to Matagorda Peninsula, then work on a plan."

"A plan? For what?" Devon flexed his hands at his sides. His pulse strummed in his head. "If you don't tell me the whole story right now, I swear—"

"There's a letter." Jeremy fished a note out of his shell jacket pocket.

Devon's stomach dropped to his toes. A letter wasn't good. She wasn't here in person. She'd left Colorado County. Where the devil was she, and how had she gotten the information from Moyer?

"I'll leave you to read it." Jeremy slapped his dusty slouch hat against his leg and took the canteen. "I'll wait around the bend and have some hardtack and salted beef for you when you're ready. No one else but me and Lucy know how Morning Fawn got the information and what she did to save you. I imagine the letter will explain it."

Devon sank onto a rock and unfolded the paper.

My dearest love, I can't bear to stand by and let you be executed without doing everything in my power to save you. I've agreed to marry Nick Moyer in return for his assistance. We will marry shortly before we set sail for England. If you're reading this, you escaped, and you're alive. That's what matters. It is worth the cost. I will love you forever.

Dear God. There were no other words. A flash of memory. Him tired, hungry, and eager to see his wife, eager to take her in his arms, hurrying through the care of his horse, only to be greeted at the door to his quarters by the doctor with a blood-stained apron. The end of hope. For so very long.

He crumpled the paper in his fist. He wouldn't let her throw her life away for him. Limbs shaking, he jumped to his feet, already smoothing and folding her declaration of love as he walked.

"Where is she?" He rounded the point. "What else do you know? I don't care what she agreed to. That man is slime."

Jeremy glanced up from his meal, fine lines crinkled at the corners of his eyes. "From what Lucy heard, Moyer's taking Morning Fawn to Galveston. Plans to set sail for England after he marries her. They were in his carriage. They stopped by the slaver's. He bought Lucy and then allowed Morning Fawn to send her off to Alleyton with the information and the letter. "

"I'm not going to let him have her." His jaw clenched. "A promise made under such duress isn't worth the spit it takes to speak it. She's not going to throw her life away for me." His words rang out as solid as a hammer striking an anvil. "I'm going after her."

Jeremy stood. "I figured you'd say that. But you need to get to Matagorda and then take a boat to Galveston. Quicker and more unexpected. And safer than traveling over land considering the Rebs are probably going to plaster your face on posters all over East Texas. I've been giving it some thought. Columbus to Galveston is around fifty more miles than Columbus to Matagorda. And they're traveling by coach. You've got time to get to Matagorda and recruit a few volunteers. I'll round you up a dinghy and come with you. Moyer might be expecting you."

"I hope he is, and I hope he's man enough to settle our differences between the two of us without bringing in help."

"Don't count on it." The creases deepened across Jeremy's brow.

Devon nodded. "I didn't ask, but are Lucy and Miss Schramm safe?"

"They're at the safe house. Our friends plan to help them work their way down to Brownsville after everything settles down. Miss Schramm sent you a letter too. "Jeremy reached in his jacket.

Devon stuffed his hands into his pockets. "I don't want to read it. My girl is in Galveston. She'll be somebody else's over my dead body."

CHAPTER 36

*M*orning Fawn's toes dug into the damp sand. White foam lapped at the hem of her burgundy gown. She'd be happy to shed the garment and never see it again—only, she had nothing else to wear. After they'd dropped off Lucy in Alleyton, Nick had packed a trunk of his belongings, and they'd driven through the night to Eagle Lake, caught the train there, then transferred in Houston to the Galveston train, moving toward the future she didn't want at coal-powered speed.

Upon their arrival late yesterday afternoon, Nick had ordered a tailor shop to make her two dresses double quick. She could only hope they'd take a month. Surely, something could be thought of by then. He'd purchased underclothing from a general store and ordered a pair of sturdy shoes from a cobbler, all part of filling her sea trunk. Dear God, she could not do this. How could she marry a man she didn't love, didn't even like?

She glanced back at Lawrence and Guthrie. Were those first or last names? She still wasn't sure, but when Nick wasn't present, at least one of them or both followed her everywhere she went.

Various vessels dotted the Gulf. She'd gaped in awe when she'd taken her first walk by the docks last night. Towering schooners, steamers with their angry smoke stacks, and sloops. Nick had told her all of the proper names, but she'd just stared. And that was just the wharf. Never in her life had she seen so many people, and there were hundreds of city blocks filled with more buildings and houses than she ever imagined possible. A world as foreign to her as the surface of the moon.

The wide open space of the beach was the only place she could breathe.

She glanced toward the road. Dressed in a dark suit, Nick strode toward them. Her shoulders tensed. A paper hung from his hand. News of Devon? She lifted her skirts and pattered toward him. *Dear Lord, please let it be good.* She'd lain awake, tossed between prayer and worry the past two nights, fighting for the faith of which Devon had spoken.

Nick removed his hat. His face gave no clue. He handed her the folded paper.

Her hands shook as she opened the one-page newspaper. Huge black letters blared at her. *Prison Break. Yankee Spy Escapes...*

She uttered a cry and dropped to her knees. *Thank You, Lord. Thank You.* She clutched the paper to her chest. Tears trickled down her cheeks. The Lord had heard her prayers. Devon was safe. Or almost safe. Her sacrifice had made a difference. Now he had to stay free. Stay alive.

She quickly scanned the paper. It was dated this afternoon. The escape had been yesterday morning. He and his accomplices hadn't been captured yet, although several Unionists in Alleyton had been rounded up for questioning and a few had been jailed. But the writer assured the reader that state militia and Confederate cavalry were hot on the Yankee's trail. The next edition promised a sketch of the wanted man and, very likely, his recapture.

Nick stuck his hands in his trouser pockets and studied her. "If he has any brains, he'll get out of Texas."

Swiping her cheeks, she struggled to stand.

He held out his hand to her. She took it without thinking, the band of his jeweled ring pressing against her fingers.

She pulled her hand away as soon as she gained her feet. A new idea struck her. "They rescued him before he started for San Antonio. They didn't do it your way." Hope trembled within.

He snorted. "They used the information you sent them by way of the slave girl I bought to be our messenger. Bought and set free, mind you. A thousand dollars gone. Without that, his Unionist buddies would have had no idea he was about to be moved, and no clue of how to break him out of the jail. So don't you try to weasel out of your word, Morning Fawn. I upheld my end of the deal."

The name grated on her nerves. "My name is Beth to you." She turned and walked off, back to the cool, wet sand. She had no desire to hear him rattle off the possible consequences of her breaking her word. He wouldn't be above reporting Lucy as an escaped slave or telegraphing the authorities where Devon might be. Risks she wasn't willing to take. She might have failed Eyes-Like-Sky all of those years ago, but she wouldn't fail Devon or Lucy.

Several minutes later, Nick walked up beside her. He took off his coat and tossed it on the sand. Sitting down, he yanked off his socks and shoes as if they were done with the unpleasantness. "Come. I bet you've never seen the ocean before." He reached for her hand. And maybe for the first time ever, at least in her sight, he wore a genuine smile.

She pressed her hands to her sides. "I don't want to go in."

But she did. Only, she wanted to go in by herself...and maybe never come out.

His smile faded. "All right. I'll give you time. Maybe tomorrow."

Maybe never.

If Devon were here, she'd run in with him and jump the waves. He'd hold her hand and tell her there was nothing to be afraid of, that he would protect her.

Tears stung her eyes. Devon would live to see the ocean again someday. Praise the Lord.

But he would not see it with her. Never. Not if she could help it. The very thought of her meeting him years from now after she'd married Nick and become what she would become curdled her stomach. No. Let him remember her how she had been. Not the woman who blushed from head to toe every time some hotel clerk or baggage handler looked at her. Of course, she'd be married to Nick by then, but it wouldn't matter. Nick had kept his word so far about not bedding her until after the wedding, but it was perception that counted in the eyes of others. That type of stain would never go away.

Frieda might very well win Devon's affection. Morning Fawn would rather stay in England her whole life than see such a thing.

A handful of seagulls glided overhead, hovering on the breeze. Two of their counterparts strutted on the beach looking for leavings. Farther out, a pelican skimmed along the top of the water, flapping its wings and scooping up fish.

The water called to her. She stepped forward, lifting her skirts only a few inches. Cold brown liquid swirled past her ankles. A few feet more, and it was to her mid-calves. This water would carry her from Texas, as far from her pia and the home she'd come to be part of as the moon was from earth. Devon had once promised her the moon. She could live without it. What she wanted was him in her life, every day, always.

She'd done right in making the deal, and if she had it to do over again, she'd do the same. But living the future she'd agreed to? Water splashed against her knees as a wave came in, then retreated. Sand and bits of shells rushed against her legs on their way back out into the Gulf.

"You don't look well." Nick stood in front of her.

She hadn't even seen him coming. The sun glinted in her eyes as she looked up at his frown.

"Come on." He took her by the arm and drew her toward shore. "We're going back to the hotel."

"No. I'll smother there." Smother beneath the looks, the walls, the world that wasn't hers. "Let me stay here. Leave your men to watch if you want. I'll sit on the shore."

The wind whipped his usually toniced hair over his forehead. "If that's what you want, but you'll be tired of the ocean by the time we reach England. I went down to Kuhns Wharf today. Found the captain of a blockade runner, the *Eliza Jane*, getting ready to sail in two days. I secured passage for both of us. He can marry us as well. I even stopped by the tailor's and paid him to work through the nights on your dresses."

"Two days?" She gulped. Her knees wavered.

"Yes. I have cotton contracts to secure in England. There won't be another runner out for a week."

"But I might not hear by then if Devon made it safely to the Yankee lines."

He thrust out a breath. "You'll probably never hear that, my dear. It's not like they're going to make an announcement. The only news will be if they catch him. But to be sure, I'll check the papers before we sail." He picked up his shoes. "If you're hoping he'll show up here, don't count on it. He'll be doing good to get to Matagorda or Brownsville free of bullet holes. The authorities up and down the coast will be searching for him. Besides, if he comes to Galveston, someone is going home in a casket. And it won't be you." A half smile flittered across his lips.

"I hope he doesn't show." She turned back to the water. What if he did? A wild surge of hope flowed through her before reality stopped it cold. She'd given her word to Nick. Her word. A fetter that couldn't be broken even with a sledgehammer.

CHAPTER 37

*E*very muscle taut, Devon leaned onto his mustang's foam-coated neck. Almost to Matagorda, and they'd been spotted by a squad of Reb cavalry. He gripped the reins in one hand as he goaded the animal with his knees, demanding every extra hoof beat he could get.

Hip-high brown brittle grass swished by. No tree cover, just prairie and marsh. His saddle horn pressed below his ribs as they plowed through the carpet of growth and struck the red dirt of the trail. The Federal lines couldn't be much farther. Not even Jeremy knew for certain how far. They could only pray that their troops still controlled the peninsula.

Bare-headed, Jeremy galloped alongside at breakneck speed, reins in one hand and a carbine in the other, twisting and firing. Frederick hung on for dear life while the cavalry troopers amongst the group rode and shot as best they could manage.

Bullets from their pursuers zinged by. One grazed Devon's ear. The muscles of his injured arm rebelled as he flexed his left hand tight on the reins and reached for his Colt with his right.

A biting wind kicked sand into his face. Salt air mixed with the rotten egg stink of gunpowder. A bugle sounded up ahead. He squinted and peered into the distance. Men on horseback? *Dear God. Please let it be.* He blinked again. A couple dozen soldiers rode toward them. Soldiers dressed in dusty blue. Thank God! Hope surged through him.

Another bullet whizzed by, close enough to slice his sleeve and tingle his flesh.

A loud grunt from somewhere close behind. He couldn't turn, couldn't afford to look back.

In one glorious whoosh, the cavalry filtered past toward the enemy at full charge, carbines blazing. Devon rode on, slacking the pace for his exhausted horse as the gunfire became distant, and the Federal fortifications, rows of drift-wood stacked three or four feet high in front of grass-laden sandy hills, drew near.

~

Dressed in a short kersey wool jacket and trousers, Devon swung his legs over the oyster sloop's railing and dug his boot toes into the rope ladder rungs as he descended to the waiting dinghy. A pink glow edged over the eastern horizon. Enough waiting. A norther had hit the evening Devon arrived at the Matagorda Peninsula with Jeremy and the five survivors of the seven who'd started the journey with them. The soldiers' tents had proved inadequate for the monstrous winds that pounded the canvas and plummeted the tempera-tures well below freezing. Some of the troops had shoveled holes in the sand to protect themselves.

Stiff-limbed and cold, Devon had crawled out from under the canvas the next morning ready to find a boat. Major Tucker, commanding officer of the company manning the fortifications, had argued, but Jeremy had set him straight. Jeremy was under the direct command of Colonel Davis of the 1st Texas US

Cavalry. Therefore, he and Devon could pursue their mission as they saw fit.

It'd taken most of the day to locate a conveyance with a Unionist-leaning captain willing to help. An oyster boat was the perfect cover for traveling close to the Confederate-controlled coast without drawing suspicion. But they'd had to wait until that night for the sea to settle before they could set out.

Jeremy followed after Devon on the rope ladder. The dinghy rocked as Devon stepped foot in it and sat. Hidden by the port side of the boat from view of the Reb patrols, they'd row for the grasses and walk into Galveston. Catch Moyer at breakfast if they were lucky. What if that breakfast was with Morning Fawn in a shared hotel room? What if they were already married?

Couldn't be. Devon would be in time to stop any wedding. He had to be. Coming by coach, Moyer probably hadn't arrived until yesterday or the day before. Morning Fawn couldn't be that man's wife. And if the scoundrel had done anything else to her...he would pay.

"You stay low once we get there." Jeremy picked up the oars. Ocean spray clung to his black wool wheel cap. "I'll go to the hotels. Pose as a messenger looking for Moyer."

"If you find out where he's staying, you come tell me. I'll be at the wharf. I'll smudge some dirt on my face, keep my cap down, and mingle with the workers. See if I can get word on any blockade runners preparing to leave for England. I'll act interested in hiring on." Devon reached for the oars.

Jeremy shook his head. "Save your arm for what's coming. You let the doc look at it for all of ten minutes yesterday. It's only been two-and-a-half weeks since you had a bullet slice through it."

"There'll be time enough for me to take care of myself after I have my girl safe and sound." It didn't matter what Moyer had done or not done. Morning Fawn was Devon's woman.

*C*hill shuddered through Devon despite the mid-morning sun. "Could you repeat that?"

The gray-haired slave lowered his crate to the weathered planks of the pier. "The *Eliza Jane* slipped out of here a couple hours before sunup. Painted gray, low in the water, low smoke stacks—a blockade runner, sure as my name's Frankie. I's helped load her up, sir." He tugged off his neckerchief and mopped his wrinkled brow.

Waves crashed against the pilings.

Devon swallowed. "Did you happen to catch a glimpse at the passengers? I'm looking for a young woman, honey-blond hair." His breath snagged in his throat.

The man scratched his head. "Yep, she was on it. With some fellow in a fancy suit."

Iron bands cinched Devon's chest. *No!* An inward cry blasted through him. "You...she...she departed with him? You're certain?"

The man's eyes softened. "Sorry, Massar. But I reckon she did."

"I'm not your massar." The monotone words tumbled out without thought. Morning Fawn gone. Gone. On a steamer, faster than a sloop. He scoured the horizon. How would a man even begin to find a ship out there?

The slave shuffled his boots. A stockinged toe stuck out of a worn flap. "She done looked none too pleased. The way she kept looking back, I's figured she might just run down the plank."

"But she didn't?"

"No, sir."

Why not? He scrubbed his hand down his face in a long-drawn-out pull that he wished would scrub away every day since Christmas Eve. "Do you know if they were married, her and the gentleman?"

"I's don't know." The man bent down for his crate. "I's got to get back to work before my massar catch me loafing. Sorry I couldn't be of no more help."

Devon nodded his thanks.

He had failed her. He bent over hands to his knees. *Dear God, no.*

The sun chose that moment to peek through a puff of white clouds. Its brilliance shimmered on the water. He glanced up. Seagulls circled overhead against a deep-blue sky which had churned angry black only a couple days before. Hope. The blue sky had been there all along, just temporarily covered by the storm.

A thought pulsed through him. He wouldn't give up. He had an oyster sloop at his disposal, provided he could convince the captain to go along with the wild idea of pursuing a blockade runner. The steamer was faster, but maybe it'd have to slow down or even hide out to avoid a Federal blockader. Maybe the captain of the oyster boat would have some knowledge of the routes usually taken by blockade runners.

No. He wouldn't give up. Heart pounding, he took off at a run to find Jeremy.

CHAPTER 38

The *Eliza Jane* rolled beneath Morning Fawn's feet. Sailors bustled about. Overhead, one manned the crow's nest on lookout. Painted a dull gray, the sharp, narrow frame of the side-wheel steamer glided across the water like a ramrod-straight snake slithering in the shallows to avoid its enemies. Burning smokeless coal, its short smokestacks blew clear, further enabling it to fade from sight.

Enemies. Maybe that is what Morning Fawn needed. The captain and Nick had discussed the dangers of the scattered contingents of Yankee ships monitoring the waters between Galveston and the open sea. The *Eliza Jane* had to run dark until they made it past the blockade lines. What if the Yankees found them?

Salt pricked her lips as she gazed westward, no land in sight. A burst of orange streaked from behind the fading clouds. The Gulf of Mexico's waters had settled down to a ripple, a soft hum after the norther that had torn into Galveston two evenings ago.

She gripped the rail. In a few minutes, she'd go to the master cabin with Nick. The captain would open a Bible and say a few words over them. Nick would place his signet ring on her finger, as a temporary measure, and kiss her, his lips like a king's seal, leaving no doubt of his ownership and authority.

He'd already demanded a token payment on that ownership this morning when he took her in his arms and bruised her lips with a kiss that contained all of the gentleness of a steam engine driving forward. Such fire, when she felt nothing.

After the ceremony, there'd be a dinner at the captain's table. And then what? Would Nick insist upon his full husbandly rights or give her more time? A century wouldn't be enough. But the way her stomach felt, she could claim seasickness.

Back in her Comanche village, she'd resigned herself to marrying Stands-His-Ground. Only after Devon kidnapped her and showed up at Sweet Briar a year and a half later had she dared hope to marry for love. A blessing she didn't deserve and now would never have.

Her gaze fell to a cluster of boats swinging near the stern. The captain said he was traveling just out of sight of land for now. If she managed to steal a jolly boat, would she have any hope of reaching shore or a Yankee ship? Planning a successful escape would take time. Time she didn't have.

She touched the emerald necklace beneath the collar of her blue wool dress. The earrings were in her pocket. The tiara was in her sea chest. Aunt Judith had loaned her the jewelry for the ball. A bribe to a cooperative sailor might buy her way into a rowboat quietly lowered over the side. It might even buy her an oarsman, but a word to the wrong man would earn her Nick's wrath and an end to all patience.

She'd given her word. She had to keep it, didn't she? She'd marry Nick Moyer and chain herself to him for life. But did that mean she had to be at his side? What if she found her way to shore? Became a cook, a seamstress, or even a washwoman? The emeralds would fetch a good price if she could manage to only pay the sailor a portion. Money to live on.

The wind tore through her hair, blowing spray in her face. Where was Devon? Had he made it to Brownsville or Matagorda? Was he wounded? Would he see Frieda there? Her throat constricted. A cough wracked through her.

She lowered her head. *Lord, what would you have me do? What about those women in the Bible? Had Bathsheba wanted to become David's wife?* Devon had been wise to not come for her. It would have been akin to a death sentence.

But why hadn't he come?

Maybe he'd arrived too late. Maybe that's why Nick had hurried them away from Galveston. She scrunched her eyes, clenched her hands, and bent her head to the rail.

Enemies. That's what she needed. And time. What if she managed to leave a lantern on? Would one small light make a difference?

A firm hand touched her back. "How is my bride?"

She looked up into dark eyes and shivered. "Seasick."

His cigar-laden breath drifted her way as he bent to whisper in her ear. "A man only has so much patience, and mine is running thin. You can rest after the ceremony."

She glanced at the boats. Could an emerald necklace get her back to Comancheria?

~

Bells clanged in middle of the night. Morning Fawn shot up from her protective cocoon of covers on the bunk. Dressed in his ankle-length drawers, his chest bare, Nick rolled off the thin mattress on the deck and stood.

The ship's boilers rumbled. The captain must be driving the boat full steam ahead. The constant smack of the paddles to the water even resonated in the cabin suite the first mate had given up for them. What had happened to being silent and slipping by the Yankees?

"Get dressed." Nick grabbed his trousers.

"I never got undressed." She scrambled off the bunk and smoothed her wrinkled skirt.

"Of course not." His voice dripped with sarcasm. "I've had enough of your delays. We're getting married tomorrow, seasick or not, even if you have to do it from bed."

Loud voices and shouting rang out from the main deck.

"There's trouble." Nick pulled his shirt down and shoved his arms in—

A faint flash across the skylight overhead. *Boom.* The roar jolted through Morning Fawn. *Wham.* The ship rocked. Nick's shoulder banged into the bulkhead. Morning Fawn stumbled and caught herself on the bunk.

"We've been hit." Nick threw open his trunk and lugged out his money belt and arm holster.

The Yankees had found them? *God help us.* And she hadn't even had an opportunity to light a lamp. She grabbed her cloak. Where were her shoes?

"Get a move on. We need to get out of here." He hooked the gold-laden pouches around his waist and secured his holster. "Do you have your necklace?"

"I don't know." She patted beneath her pillow. "I placed it here. But with all of the jarring..." How much damage could the ship endure? *Dear Lord, please protect us.* "We don't have time—"

He ransacked her covers and swiped his hands across the bunk. "Where the devil did you put it?"

Boom. The ship shuddered.

"Us firing back, but we don't have much firepower." He huffed like a steam engine as he dropped to his hands and knees, searching the floor.

"Forget the necklace." She grabbed at his arm.

"Found it." He jumped to his feet, stuffed it in his pocket, and threw on his coat.

She shoved her shoes on.

Boom. Wham. A curdling yell overhead. Morning Fawn rocked against Nick. He slammed his hand against the bulkhead, bracing himself.

Her whole body atremble, she gained her feet. "I'm leaving." Her voice was so garbled, it sounded like a two-year-old's. She headed for the door.

"Where's your tiara—"

Another flash across the skylight. A roar. *Wham*—the sound of a blacksmith hammer striking an anvil, except a hundred times louder. A groan shuddered through the deck.

She took off running. She had no intention of drowning for a few jewels. They had to get topside.

Nick followed.

She latched onto the ladder that led to the open hatch.

Farther down the dark passageway, someone called out. "We're taking on water."

A sailor shoved past her and hurried up the steps. "Stay here."

Above the open hold, men rushed about. The captain yelled, "Make for the shore. Run her aground before they board us."

"That man's out of his mind if he thinks I'm staying down here." Nick snagged her hand with the force of a hook. "Come on—you belong to me."

He pulled her up the ladder. His revolver was out of his holster by the time they emerged from below. "We need protection if there's not enough lifeboats."

Chaos reigned. Men ran about. A monster loomed off the port side, a steamer with every lamp lit and guns out, barreling toward them.

Suddenly, the *Eliza Jane* swung starboard. Morning Fawn's

knees hit the deck. So did Nick's. His revolver skidded across the deck's oak boards, slamming into the pilothouse.

Nick dove for it.

A thunderous roar. The foremast crashed to the deck, crushing a man beneath and flinging the sailor from the crow's nest into the water. The railing near the stern folded like sticks, its bulwark shattered.

Morning Fawn crawled for the railing midship.

"All hands!" A voice rang out. "Brace for impact."

Morning Fawn grabbed ahold of the unfurled rope ladder flapping against the inside of the railing, burrowing her hands as deep as should could into the hemp cords. *Dear Lord, help.*

CHAPTER 39

*D*evon's lips ached, cracked from the sun and wind. A layer of salted moisture covered him. From late morning to more than halfway through the night, he'd rooted himself to the forecastle of the oyster sloop, *Penny*. He'd explained to the captain how Morning Fawn had sacrificed her freedom for the sake of the striking a serious blow to the Confederate cotton supply and how they might be able to get their hands on a cotton emissary. The captain had agreed to the pursuit, ready to do what he could to help the Union.

Devon had taken a few bites of salted pork and biscuits when Jeremy shoved it his way, but he had no appetite. The only thing that mattered was the *Eliza Jane*. He could only pray that the Reb captain had taken the customary route they were now following.

Just before dawn, thunder rumbled, followed by a pinprick of light to the south. Not lightning. More thunder, followed by quick flashes. Cannon fire? Devon rubbed his sleep-deprived eyes and leaned hard against the forecastle railing. Every hair on his limbs stood on end.

"Take a look!" Standing outside his cabin, Captain Abrams

yelled at the lookout in the crow's nest through his speaking trumpet. His heavy wool frock coat tugged against his belly.

Wind whipped about the sailor as he leaned forward, palm shielding his forehead, eyeing the gunfire.

Boom. Flash. *Boom*.

Devon's breath solidified. His eyes scratched at the darkness, seeking solid form in the inky moonlit dark. The *Eliza Jane* wouldn't be the one doing the firing. Blockade runners were built for stealth and speed, not fighting.

"It's a battle, sir," the sailor called down from above. "Looks like a Federal steamer firing on a blockade runner."

"We've got to go there." Devon turned and headed for the captain. "It could be her."

"Could be." Abrams lowered his spyglass and tipped his cap back. Black whiskers lined his cheeks. "But we've no business sailing into the middle of a battle. This is an oyster boat, not a gunboat. We've got no defense but side arms."

Jeremy walked up looking as if he'd just crawled out of a hammock. "What's happening?"

Devon ignored him. "Captain, I'm begging you…just get me close enough. I'll take one of the rowboats."

"Getting yourself shot or run down by a steamer ain't going to do your girl a bit a good, son." The sea-weathered man puffed out a breath and scratched his scarred chin. "We'll head that direction but hang back until the firing's done. The blockade runner will likely try to run aground if she doesn't sink first."

"Sir, I didn't come this far to do nothing while the woman I love is in danger." Devon jutted his finger to the south.

Abrams spit tobacco juice onto the deck. "Convincing me to let you use my ship to chase her halfway across the Gulf ain't nothing. But I'm still the captain, and my word goes. You'd best ready yourself for what's coming when we arrive."

"He's right." Jeremy put a hand on Devon's back.

Devon shoved it aside and marched back to the bow. Pent-up steam flowed through his veins, enough to blow a boiler. He pulled his revolver from his holster and spun the chamber. Six loads. He was going to be ready, all right.

Did Morning Fawn know how to swim? Even if she did, knowing how to swim wasn't any guarantee of survival. If the ship went down, it could suck her right down with it. His thoughts spun off in a circle of what-ifs.

No. He gripped the railing and lifted his gaze to the stars. *Lord of the universe, she's in Your hands.*

~

Devon strained at his post as they neared the wreck. Dawn's misty web coated the world in a haze. Abrams furled the sails, taking it slow through the debris. The signaler stood in the crow's nest whipping the flag this way and that, alerting the officers of the well-armed Federal steamer that the oyster boat *Penny* was friendly. Thankfully, the captain had worked with Yankees previously and knew their codes.

Boards, a cap, even an umbrella lapped back and forth on the waves. A man's body floated close by. Three rowboat loads of blue-clad troops from the Federal ship struck for shore.

The bow of a gray-clad steamer lay buried halfway up in the sand. The silent hull listed to its starboard side. One iron panel lay peeled back like an onion. The stern rocked with the waves.

Sweat broke out along his brow. An image of the doctor greeting him at his doorway when he rode into Fort Belknap eager to see his wife shivered through him.

Jeremy nudged his shoulder and handed him a cavalry kepi, part of the two Federal uniforms they'd hidden below deck. "Maybe it's not even Morning Fawn's ship. But we'll find her if it is."

Dead or alive or still on her way to England? Devon stuffed

the hat on his head, lest he be mistaken as the enemy. "I'm rowing ashore. We're close enough." His step shifted to a run.

Jeremy and two armed sailors followed as he descended the rope ladder.

Devon grabbed the oars. "I'm rowing." He struck the water like a grist mill, pouring himself into the motion, propelling them forward with all his might.

On the shore, two Confederate sailors crawled over the side of the wreck and dropped to the ground as smoke rose from the belly of the dilapidated vessel. They ran for the woods where a handful of crewmembers were already disappearing into the trees. A couple of others on the beach, wounded and dirty, struggled to stand.

The first group of Federal troopers landed. A private hopped out of the boat to pull it in.

Kaboom. A blast rent the air. The Federal private tumbled backward. Devon ducked and covered his head. A piece of iron sheeting flew by. The sailor behind him swore. The belly of the steamer belched fire and smoke.

Raising his head, Devon drove the oars through the water.

The sailor sitting in front of him nodded to the shore. "They blow it to destroy the cotton and keep it out of Yankee hands."

The oars struck sand. Devon jumped over the side, leaving the securing of the boat to the rest. Water soaked his boots as he plowed through the knee-deep water. He slushed onto the beach and beyond. What if Morning Fawn was on the ship?

Still moving forward, he scanned the debris-filled shore. Poles, pieces of metal, tangled sails, and more. A body here and there. No one in a suit, all of them male. Morning Fawn couldn't be aboard there. The men would have gotten her out. Wouldn't they?

He squatted beside a soaking-wet fellow. Seaweed dangled from the man's hair. Devon grabbed him by the collar. "Was this the *Eliza Jane*? Was there a lady on board?"

Dazed, the young sailor blinked up at him. "Yeah. Pretty lady. Getting married."

Devon's mind stuttered for a heartbeat. "Where is she?" He ratcheted his hold tighter.

The fellow shook his head. "Don't know. She was on deck when...some of us were thrown."

Devon released him. On deck, not in the hold. Thank God.

A dozen or so soldiers clamored toward the wreck, grabbing whatever they could to carry water to the blaze.

Devon moved toward the brush, farther from the shore. Something moved up ahead. Near the tree line, a man in a fancy suit stood up in a flattened swath of grass.

The devil himself. Moyer.

A chill shuddered through Devon. Moyer would know where she was. Devon ran across the sand at full charge.

Suit rumpled, Moyer turned toward him. Blood trickled down his forehead.

Hands clenched, Devon closed the distance, jumping over driftwood and tearing through the brush.

Moyer reached beneath his coat. Drew a revolver and aimed.

Devon slammed to halt, reached to his holster. Flap closed—

Moyer shot. Nothing.

Revolver in hand, Devon charged.

Moyer spun out his cylinder. Checked the chambers. Swore—

Devon plowed into him, knocking the weapon from his hand and throwing him to the ground. Devon's fists collided with Moyer's jaw, first on the right and then on the left. Moyer socked him a punch to his gut. Devon flinched. Moyer shoved him off and lunged for his gun. Devon tackled him to the ground and slammed his knee into the man's back, clamping his hand on Moyer's outstretched arm.

An audible gasp followed by a smothered squeal resonated from the left. A blur of blue snagged Devon's gaze on the peripheral. Devon turned his head. Morning Fawn. Dress torn, hair disheveled, she stumbled up from a patch of sea oats. Alive. The rope-tight tension in his heart slacked a notch.

Moyer jerked his arm free and nailed Devon with an elbow jab to the ribs. Thrown to the ground as Moyer gained his feet, Devon rolled away from the brunt of the man's boot. On his feet, Devon lunged, taking his enemy down again, wincing beneath a blow to his injured arm, but locking his grip on the man's throat and driving a knee into his gut.

As Moyer gasped for air, Devon grabbed his revolver and pointed the end of the barrel against the man's temple. "Move, and I'll put a bullet in your brain." He backed off his hold on the man's throat a hair.

He'd killed men in this war and before that as a Ranger, but he usually didn't see their faces. Moyer's eyes bugged.

Morning Fawn dropped to her knees off to the side, her voice a hushed whisper. "Devon." She touched his arm.

He locked his glare onto Moyer's face. No distractions. Unspent rage surged through him. "My powder isn't wet." Devon gritted out the statement through clenched teeth. "I want to know, what you have done to my girl?"

Moyer's lips curled upward in a crooked smile, his glare searing into Devon's gut. "She's mine." His voice rasped. "Gave her word. I rescued you. She's my wife."

"I don't think so." Devon bored the barrel into Moyer's flesh, just below where fresh blood from a cut pooled at his hairline.

Morning Fawn's trembling hand retreated to her lap. "I gave him my word..." Her voice shook.

A chill deeper than frostbite sunk muscle deep. "Are you his wife?"

"Not yet, but—"

"Then you aren't his wife. And you're not going to be."

Moyer's Adam's apple moved beneath Devon's palm. "I saved you. She's ruined. She's mine—"

"I didn't give *my* word." Devon jabbed the barrel against Moyer's skull. He coughed back saliva. The way Morning Fawn withdrew her touch. Her pale, worn face and underscored eyes... He caught it all in a glimpse. Her pain, her shame. "You deserve to die."

"Devon." Morning Fawn latched onto his sleeve. "If you kill him, you'll regret it the rest of your life."

Bloodshot eyes, one already half-swollen shut, glared into his. "I saved you." Moyer's voice bordered on a plea.

God forgive me, I want to pull the trigger.

"Please," Morning Fawn whispered. "Please, for your own sake."

A cool breeze swept through the furnace of his fury.

His heart shifted. He wouldn't mar his future with Morning Fawn by adding blood to his hands. "I'll tell you what, Nick Moyer. You rescued me from an execution. For your own selfish reasons." Devon's wounded arm throbbed. The vein in his hand on Moyer's throat bulged. "I'll repay you. I'll give you your life. Morning Fawn's word, the deal you had with her, is done. It's my life for your life. That's the trade. You saved me. I'll save you. I won't pull this trigger. And I'll let you get up and drag your miserable hide into these woods here. I won't tell the Federal troops on the beach who you are. I'm sure they'd love to throw you in the hold of their ship and leave you there until you rot. You want to live? You want to walk again? Your arrangement with Morning Fawn is done. You get that?"

Voices trailed near.

Sweat beaded on Moyer's forehead. He gritted his teeth and shuddered, then at last gave a nod.

Hammer cocked, finger on the trigger, Devon eased his hand from the scum's neck and backed off slowly, drawing Morning Fawn with him.

Moyer rubbed his throat and scooted out of reach.

Devin jutted the gun barrel at him. "Get out of here before they notice you."

Collar and waistcoat wrecked, a gaping hole beneath his coat arm, and his whole face beginning to swell, Moyer gained his feet. Twigs, grass leavings, and sand clung to his clothing. "You'll regret this."

Devon moved between Morning Fawn and Moyer. "If I ever see your sorry behind again, I'll put a bullet in you."

~

*M*orning Fawn shuddered.

Nick cast a last look at her. "Your loss." He tugged on the money belt at his waist and disappeared into the trees.

Numb, she stared after him. At least he had what really mattered to him. It was over. The battle. The shipwreck. The days of suffocating in Nick's presence with no future she wanted. Over. Waves of shivers overtook her. The world spun. She misstepped—right into Devon's arms.

He scooped an arm beneath her knees and fastened another around her back.

Voices, soldiers talking to him, he answered, and then he was carrying her away from them all. She buried her face in the crook of his neck. Breathing in, breathing out, trying to settle her stomach and steady her head. The same stomach that had led her to throw up in the captain's quarters as he'd opened the Bible to start the ceremony. She'd begged off for one more day. God in His mercy had spared her from the "I do" that would have fettered her for life.

She inhaled the sea and sweat, mixed with a tinge of blood. Devon. Safe. Here. His muscles flexing and straining beneath his dark wool jacket, his pulse throbbing against her forehead.

He'd come for her. A thousand sunrises burst within her. *Dear God, don't let this be a dream.*

A sob worked its way up her throat.

"You're safe now." His voice wrapped around her as he dropped to a knee by a rock and lowered her down. "Safe."

She latched on to him, arms around his neck, and threaded her fingers through his thick brown hair. "Thank God you're alive. I was afraid I'd never see you again. Never..." Another sob.

He settled onto the sand and pulled her securely onto his lap, into his hold. "I'm here. Thanks to you, my beautiful girl," he whispered against her hair as tears streamed down her cheeks. "I love you so much. I was afraid I'd lost you." He pressed her to his chest. His voice cracked. He swallowed hard once and then again. "I love you so much, my precious Taa Aruka."

Loved. Thankful he hadn't lost her. But shame clogged her throat. Thank God, her virtue was intact, but Nick had compromised her reputation from Columbus to Galveston and beyond. Her fingers slipped from Devon's hair. She pulled back, half out of the circle of his arms. "But you don't know how things were. He kept me—"

"It doesn't matter what happened or what that scum did." Devon's voice rang with the certainty of iron forged in a furnace. "I love you. And you are my girl."

Her heart trembled. "I've got to say it. He forced me to share a hotel room with him, and quarters on the ship, at times even his bed..." Her stomach clenched. Her hands fell into her lap. The memory of the stares seared the scarlet into her soul.

Lake-blue eyes pierced her to the depths of her being. "Whatever he did, it wasn't of your choice. There is nothing in this world Nick Moyer could do to stop me from loving you."

She bit back a sob and touched her fingers to his parched lips. "He did everything he could to ruin my reputation. But he didn't touch me in the way of a husband and a wife. Everyone up and down the coast thinks I'm his mistress. But he kept his word about waiting until the wedding night. I delayed. It was never going to happen—"

"I thank God for that." A smile tugged at his lips.

"Everyone will look at me—"

"You and I know the truth, and so does the Lord. That's what matters, my dear, precious girl." He cradled her cheek.

The tenderness of his touch, the love in his eyes...a healing salve to her heart.

He kissed her forehead, her cheeks, her parted lips, his kiss there like the fluttering of butterfly wings. She slipped her arms back around his neck, settled in his embrace, and met the butterfly wing for wing until a fire better suited for a wedding night stirred within her.

Trembling, he withdrew his lips and tucked her head beneath his chin, his chest rising and falling hard against hers. "I do have one very important question for my girl."

Farther down the beach, soldiers moved, loading rowboats with what they'd salvaged. Smoke still streamed from what had been the *Eliza Jane*. A seagull strutted on a rock nearby.

"What kind of question?" She stroked Devon's bearded jaw.

"When should we get married?"

She half laughed.

He tipped her chin up to his. "I'm serious. But I'm a reasonable man. I'll give you until we dock to think about it, and that might be a while. I imagine we'll go with the Federal steamer if the captain will have us. I need to get clear of Texas, or at least to Brownsville, and the oyster boat captain didn't sign up for a jaunt like that."

She touched the bruise beneath his eye, and another at his temple, and frowned at the warm, wet spot on his jacket sleeve. His blood. She swallowed. "It looks like you need a doctor right now, not a wife."

He settled her deeper into his lap. "A wife would suit me just fine. Nothing a little loving care and time can't remedy."

"Well, you'd better get one thing straight, Mr. Trouble." She ran her finger along his jawline and down to his collarbone, her heart throwing the curtains of hope open and basking in the sun. "I'm not going to be the type of wife who sits around the plantation waiting for her soldier boy to come home. Where you go, I go, except for the battlefields. If you're at an outpost or a camp, or in some big, smothering city, it doesn't matter. I'm with you."

"The colonel or my captain might have something to say about that." His eyes twinkled.

"I'd be happy to try to set both of them straight."

"I don't doubt it." He chuckled. "It's a good thing you don't plan to sit around the plantation because I don't have one."

"I'm not marrying you for your acres."

"So it's a yes, then? You *are* marrying me?"

"Just as soon as it's decently possible."

He kissed her once more, then held her close and nuzzled his cheek to her hair. "After this war, I'll work hard and get us some land. A ranch, unless you decide you want to become a city girl."

"No city for me." She smoothed her palm over his chest.

"It won't matter what these folks in this little corner of Texas think of us. We'll have the horizon to ourselves."

"Being here in your arms, planning *our* future, it's more than I dared hope for."

"I've heard that God has a way of doing that sometimes, especially when you least expect it."

"God had been so good," she whispered. "I couldn't do it on my own. I couldn't get away from Nick. I couldn't break my word. I couldn't fix anything. There was no way to make every-thing right."

He drew her deeper into the circle of his arms. "I was in a

hole so deep, there was nothing left for me but a firing squad or the gallows. But even before that, before I met you, I was in a different type of hole. But God made a way where there was no way. And somehow, He even used Moyer to do it, and the most courageous and determined woman I've ever met...she was willing to sacrifice herself for me. I love her and want to spend the rest of my life with her."

The man with the brown beard tromped up to them, the same one who'd called on her uncle a few days after the explosion. "Are you two going to sit here all day, or are you going to catch a ride?"

Devon slipped her off his lap and jumped to his feet, pulling her up with him. "We've got a wedding to plan."

THE END

~

*T*urn the page for a sneak peek of Texas Reclaimed, the next book in the Lone Star Redemption series!

SNEAK PEEK: TEXAS RECLAIMED

Don't miss the next book in the Lone Star Redemption series!

Texas Reclaimed
(Coming February 2026)

Chapter 1

MARCH 1866
PHILADELPHIA, PA

Ben MacIntyre gripped the edges of the oak bureau and stared at himself in the beveled mirror. A bead of sweat glistened on his brow. Perpetual dark circles underscored his eyes.

Piano music drifted up from the parlor he'd vacated minutes before. Dressed in yellow silk like the first flower of spring, Olivia Edmondson would likely be surrounded by admirers as her nimble fingers slid across the keys. But surely, she'd notice his absence all the same. After all, they'd agreed their fathers would announce their engagement this evening.

He shouldn't have allowed himself to be nudged into a

proposal. Not yet. He had no business making a promise when he had another promise long overdue.

Ben loosened his royal-blue cravat from its tight bind on his throat. His head throbbed. Stupid of him to think today would be the time to cut back on his medicine. Medicine? That's what the doctor called it, and so did Olivia and his family. He knew better.

His bones seemed to grate against one another like nails on a chalkboard. Twenty-two hours since his last dose. Maybe if he only had a few drops, half a teaspoon full of laudanum, it would be enough to make it through the evening.

His hand shook as he picked up the small bottle from the lace doily.

Every pore in his body stretched forth in anticipation of the sweet taste of the brown liquid on his tongue. No. He flung the bottle to the floor. The glass clunked on the tightly woven carpet and rolled against the desk leg. His breath caught as he waited to see if the stopper would hold or if the liquid would ooze out. When it held, the crest of his tension eased back a notch.

Curse the doctor who'd ever given him the first dose of the tincture of alcohol and opium.

Lying there exhausted beyond endurance in that hospital cot in Wilmington, with his legs knotted with scurvy and curled beneath him and his stomach as useless as a shriveled prune, Ben had been willing to swallow any concoction the nurses offered. He'd been deaf to the hiss of the serpent which slithered its way into his veins.

Ben's fingers curled into a fist atop the bureau. A whole year he'd been home. Regaining his health. Working for his father. Courting Olivia. But falling short of everything he'd vowed to do when he'd hobbled out of the hell on earth that had been Andersonville.

How could he expect to get a grip on his need for laudanum

and bring an end to the war in his soul if he didn't show himself a man by keeping his promises?

His chest squeezed as if someone had tightened a vise around it. He strode over to the window and threw up the sash, desperate for fresh air. Beyond the barren maples and winter-dead lawn, the western sky glowed orange above the tree-topped ridges. Maybe freedom lay somewhere out there. He had to get out of the house and away from Philadelphia. He couldn't marry. Not yet. Not until he set things right.

He stared down at the bottle still lying on the carpet. Surely, half a teaspoon wouldn't hurt. Just enough to abate his symptoms until after he went downstairs and set matters straight with Olivia.

With leaden feet, he walked over to the desk, bent down, and picked up the bottle. His palm tingled against the cool glass. He could almost hear the hiss of the serpent eating away at everything he had been. This is how it'd been last time he'd abstained. Except he'd made it for a whole week. Then he'd given in for one sip, followed by another, and another...until the fetter was fully fastened again. *Dear God, no. Don't let it be so.*

He marched back to the window, opened the bottle stopper, and drained the contents onto the bushes below. *Lord, help me to be the man You've called me to be.* He slung the bottle as hard as he could.

"I've got to talk to you." Ben pressed his hand to Olivia's arm and guided her away from a circle of ladies clothed in a colorful array of silk, satin, and taffeta.

Olivia's tiered silk skirt swished against the floor as she moved beside him. "I thought you'd gotten lost, my love," she whispered from behind her fan. A web of lace daisies confined her carefully coiffured hair. "I played Chopin, and you missed it."

"I heard every note." He nodded to her mother as they passed.

"You two hurry back, now." Cheeks rosy, Mrs. Myrtle Edmondson beamed at them. Scattered streaks of gray highlighted her curls. A woman willing to feed any stranger at her door, but likely to throw anyone who disappointed her daughter into a social dungeon. "Mr. Edmonson is warming up for his speech."

Across the room, Ben's father glanced up from his highback leather chair where he sat amongst a cluster of business associates. The war had aged him—gray at his temples, deeper creases at the corners of his eyes, and a paunch above his trouser waist—yet still he poured himself into his newspaper company, from dawn to dusk, determined to leave a legacy to his only remaining son and the grandchildren to come. An unlit cigar wiggled beneath his heavy mustache as he tapped his silver pocket watch and shot Ben a knowing look. To him, the engagement was another step toward installing Ben as a full partner in his *Philadelphia Sentinel.*

"Can't this wait until after dinner?" Olivia followed Ben through the French doors. "I was ready to tell Mrs. Palmer about my plans for my wedding dress. Hers last year looked like a hand-me-down."

"It can't wait."

Cool evening air drifted in as he led her onto the white-columned side porch. The sunset was now a rosy pink capping the western ridges. From the yard, crickets and katydids chirped their melodies, while someone's fiddle rendition of "Lorena" floated out from the parlor above the hum of chatter.

Romantic. Only, that was the opposite of what he was looking for.

Carrying herself with perfect poise, Olivia inhaled and

curled her gloved hand around his bicep. "You impatient boy. If you wanted a moment alone with me, all you had to do was ask. No need to make it sound so serious." She pivoted in front of him. Her lips parted in expectation.

He stuttered to a halt. Three years ago on this very porch, he'd kissed her for the first time. A young officer home on furlough from war, under the spell of spring and the most charming belle he'd ever met. He didn't even know that man anymore. "It's not that." He took a step back. There was no easy way to say it. "I...I need to postpone the engagement."

"You *what*?" She gaped at him. Her face paled. "My father's getting ready to make the announcement."

"I know." A sigh rattled through him. "That's why I had to speak with you." Sweat dampened his linen shirt sleeves. He didn't want to hurt her.

Her hazel eyes flashed at him. She jabbed a hand to her hip. "You spoke to me the other night when you proposed. You asked and I said yes."

More like, he'd asked after a thousand hints. With her curled up beside him on the horsehair sofa, practically in his lap. "I'm not reneging on the proposal, but I need to delay the official betrothal."

The mournful notes of "Lorena" carried on the breeze.

"Why?" She lifted her chin. "Not ready to give up bachelorhood?" A slippery smile wove its way across her lips. "Well, I can fix that." She slid her hands inside his black wool frock coat and smoothed them over the gray silk of his waistcoat, scattering his heartbeat. "Just like I did the other night."

Thank goodness, he'd cut their sofa time short, or she'd be here telling him he was obligated to marry her. "I have to go to Texas."

Her hands fell away. "You've got to be joking."

He stepped back. Best stay clear of her skirt folds and every other part of her. "No. I've told you many times—"

"Have you had your medicine?" Her brow deepened into a ridge above her slender nose.

She might as well have slapped him.

"What is that supposed to mean?"

"Just that you're sometimes a bit disagreeable when you've been too long between doses." She shrugged her bare shoulders.

If only he could throw that despicable bottle on the floor at her feet and shatter it with his boot. "My medicine has nothing to do with this. I have unfulfilled obligations. I promised Jeb—"

She snorted. Her pearl earrings jiggled. "Not Jeb Scott again. We've been over this. I'm sorry your friend didn't survive the prison camp, and I'm thankful he helped you come back to us alive. But I'm not going to let a dead man hold up my wedding. The war is over. You did everything you could—"

"All I've done is post a few flimsy pieces of paper."

"Two letters. And never a word back from that man's kin. Even after you offered to send a bank draft. It's not your fault if they're dead, illiterate, or too rebellious to communicate with a Yankee."

"Lieutenant Scott saved my life." He stuffed his hands in his trouser pockets. "And I'm going to honor my word to him. I'm going to make sure his mother and sister are taken care of."

"Hire a Pinkerton man, for goodness' sakes. Your father has the money. Send a couple hundred with the man in case he finds the family in great need, and tell him to convey to them it's all they'll get. You don't want them trying to weasel more out of you a year down the road."

He glared at her.

"What?" She arched her eyebrows and tugged her white cotton gloves on tighter. "It's taken a year for you to regain your health. I won't have you throwing it away on some foolhardy trip you can hire someone else to make. Personally, in my humble opinion, you've done more than enough."

Humble? Not hardly. She could be kind, going to visit the soldiers' hospital with baskets as part of her weekly routine. She could be spontaneous and unpredictable, ready to go for a ride in the country, or a row on the Delaware River at a moment's notice, then spend the next day dragging him on a day-long shopping trip to find just the right hat. She was many things, but humble was not one of them. "It's not your call, Olivia. And I'm not an invalid. I'm perfectly capable of fulfilling my commitments."

Her gaze hardened to a glare. "Doesn't sound like it to me. You're talking about postponing our engagement. Our wedding..." She sputtered. "I've waited for you. Three years. Don't you think I had other fine officers home on furlough, chomping at the bit to court me?" She thudded her fingers against his chest. "You've got another thought coming, Ben Morgan, if you think I'm going to allow you to wiggle out of your promise to me. Everyone in that room is expecting the announcement tonight. And you're not going to disappoint them."

That defiant set of her chin drove into him like a needle. His voice hardened. "I'm going to Texas. I'm not taking back my proposal. Just delaying the announcement. Three months. Six months at the most."

Fiery hazel eyes glared into his. "My father makes the announcement tonight, or there is no engagement. Period."

He scrubbed his hand over his jaw.

"And in case you've forgotten what you'd be missing..." She grabbed his lapels and jerked him close, her bosom pressed against his chest. "Let me remind you." She wrapped her hands around the back of his neck and drew his head down to hers.

A heavy floral scent, some fine French perfume he couldn't name, overwhelmed his senses as their lips met in a hot, angry kiss. Desire sparked and entwined with the gnawing need for his medicine. His arms tightened around her as a groan escaped his throat. But love? He could barely remember what that felt like. Maybe the laudanum had dulled his heart, or was it Andersonville that had done the trick?

His silk waistcoat wadded in her fingers, she broke the kiss. "See?" Her eyes glistened with victory. "You're not going anywhere."

He pushed free and swallowed hard. It'd be so easy to stay. Walk in there. Please her family and his. Send another letter or a Pinkerton man. The path of least resistance. There were no guarantees anyone in Texas needed his help. How many weeks of travel was that, anyway? Train, stagecoach, and even horseback to reach western Texas. Maybe even hostile Indians.

Olivia grabbed his sleeve. "You ready to come back inside? We'll finish our discussion later after the guests leave. Go on a stroll beneath the full moon." She practically purred.

He touched his finger to his thumb, where a trace of stickiness from the brown bottle he'd thrown out lingered.

If he stayed, the liquid serpent would engulf him. "I'm sorry."

Did you enjoy this book? We hope so!
**Would you take a quick minute to leave a review where you
purchased the book?**
It doesn't have to be long. Just a sentence or two telling what
you liked about the story!

Love Christian Historical Romance?
Looking for your next favorite book?
Become a Wild Heart Books insider and receive a FREE ebook
and get exclusive updates on new releases before anyone else.
Sign up for our newsletter now.
https://wildheartbooks.org/newsletter

ABOUT THE AUTHOR

Originally from Tennessee and the Shenandoah Valley, **Sherry Shindelar** is a romantic at heart and loves to take her readers into the past. She is an avid student of the Civil War and the Old West. When she is not busy writing, she is an English professor working to pass on her love of writing to her students. Sherry is an award winning writer: 2020 ACFW First Impressions winner, 2023 Maggie finalist, 2022 Crown finalist and 2023 Genesis finalist. She currently resides in Minnesota with her husband of forty years. She has three grown children and three grandchildren. Visit her website and subscribe to her monthly newsletter at sherryshindelar.com

AUTHOR'S NOTE

I love weaving my love stories around a real historical framework. My first novel in the Lone Star Redemption series, *Texas Forsaken*, was inspired by the life of the most famous nineteenth-century captive, Cynthia Ann Parker, who was captured by the Comanche at age nine and lived with them twenty-four years, married, and had three children before she was "rescued" by U.S. Cavalry and Texas Rangers. Torn from the people she'd come to love, Cynthia Ann eventually died of a broken heart. My story of Eyes-Like-Sky and Garret reimagined a different, happier ending for a woman forced to reintegrate into settler society, a woman torn between cultures. It is a story of forgiveness, redemption, and second chances.

Texas Divided is the story of Eyes-Like-Sky's sister, Morning Fawn. All of the characters in *Texas Divided* are fictional, with the exception of the mention of Confederate generals and Richard King (a Texas entrepreneur and land baron).

Texas Divided is set in the middle of the Civil War. Until I started researching for this book, I had no clue that the Yankees ever invaded Texas. But they did in November 1863. Why? It was because of cotton. By 1863, the Federal blockade of the Confederate coastline was fairly secure, and Texas became the golden gateway for funding the Confederacy. Cotton from Arkansas, western Louisiana, and East Texas traveled the Cotton Road. This dusty trail ran from the railroad terminus in Alleyton, Texas (about seventy miles west of Houston), by way of King's Ranch near Corpus Christi to Brownsville and across the Rio Grande to Matamoros, Mexico, the largest cotton market in the world during the war.

At some points, the trail was almost a mile wide due to traffic, and more than one hundred miles of it was desert with no water. Puffs of cotton clung to the sagebrush and cacti along the way.

When the cotton reached Matamoros, it was loaded onto steamboats and/or wagons owned by Mexicans and transported to the mouth of the Rio Grande at the Gulf of Mexico. International ships from Britain, France, and other countries hovered there, sometimes hundreds at a time, waiting to fill their hulls with cotton. And the Yankees couldn't stop them. If a Federal ship fired on a British, French, Mexican, or ship of another nationality, it could have been considered an act of war.

By 1863, cotton, which had sold for .10 cents a pound in 1860, now sold for $1.89 a pound, and one bale averaged 440–500 pounds. The money made on the sale of cotton was the financial bloodline of the Confederacy. For example, in just one week in August, twenty thousand pounds of gunpowder arrived in Brownsville, purchased with proceeds from the sale of cotton.

That's why the Federal army invaded Brownsville in early November 1863. Their mission was to stop or at least seriously hinder the cotton trade. Doing so could save lives on the battlefield and perhaps bring an earlier end to the war.

In my story, Lieutenant Devon Reynolds is part of that mission.

The Yankee invasion, the hatred toward Unionists, and the towns of Alleyton and Columbus are accurately portrayed in *Texas Divided* according to historical research. Amazingly, Robson's castle was also real (including the moat, indoor plumbing, and rooftop garden). However, to my knowledge, no one attempted to blow up the cotton warehouse or the quartermaster's depot.

I am grateful to Susan Chandler, the director of the Nesbitt Memorial Library in Columbus, Texas, for her extensive help in my research of the Columbus and Alleyton areas in Colorado County, Texas. Her help was invaluable. The staff at the Texas State Library and Archives Commission were also helpful. Tours of the National Cowboy Museum, the Plains-Panhandle Historical Museum, Carnton House, Ramsey House, and Belle Meade, amongst other historical sites, also complemented my research.

I want to thank my editor, Denise Weimer, for her belief in my writing. I also deeply appreciate my writing critique partners, Erma Ullrey, Jack Cunningham, Shannon Dunlap, Becky Vleet, Patti Shene, and Kathy McKinsey, who have faithfully given me feedback on my story week after week, chapter after chapter, helping my writing to be the best it can be. I'm grateful to my other writing friends (John Tipper, Mary Pat Johns, Sarah Hanks, Jamie Ogle, and Kristine Delano), as well, for their encouragement and input.

To my husband, who is my biggest fan and who continues to encourage and support me in pursuing my dreams, and to my mother, who knew I could do it.

Writing this book was a marathon full of twists and turns, but every time I came to a juncture with no idea where to go next, I prayed, and the Lord opened up paths I hadn't imagined, clearing the way to the finish line.

And to you my reader—I greatly appreciate you reading my story. If you have a chance, please leave an online review. If you're part of a book club, check out my website for extra resources for book clubs.

I'd love to connect with all of you:

Newsletter: https://sherryshindelar.com/follow/

Website: https://sherryshindelar.com/

Instagram: https://www.instagram.com/sherryshindelarauthor/

FB Author: https://www.facebook.com/historylitgirl/

Goodreads: https://www.goodreads.com/user/show/134972322-sherry-shindelar

Bookbub: https://www.bookbub.com/profile/527022753

If you love historical romance, check out the other Wild Heart books!

Love's Winding Road by Susan F. Craft

They were forced into this marriage of convenience, but there's more at stake than their hearts on this wagon train through the mountain wilderness.

When Rose Jackson and her Irish immigrant family join a wagon train headed for a new life in South Carolina, the last thing she expects is to fall for the half-Cherokee wagon scout along the way. But their journey takes a life-changing turn when Rose is kidnapped by Indians. Daniel comes to her rescue, but the effects mean their lives will be forever intertwined.

Daniel prides himself on his self-control—inner and outer—but can't seem to get a handle on either when Rose is near. Now his life is bound to hers when the consequences of her rescue force them to marry. Now it's even more critical he maintain that self-control to keep her safe.

When tragedy strikes at the heart of their strained marriage, they leave for Daniel's home in the Blue Ridge Mountains. As they face the perils of the journey, Rose can't help but wonder why her new husband guards his heart so strongly. Why does he resist his obvious attraction for her? And what life awaits them at the end of love's winding road?

~

A Counterfeit Betrothal by Denise Weimer

A frontier scout, a healing widow, and a desperate fight for peace.

At the farthest Georgia outpost this side of hostile Creek Territory in 1813, Jared Lockridge serves his country as a scout to redeem his father's botched heritage. If he can help secure peace against Indians allied to the British, he can bring his betrothed to the home he's building and open his cabinetry shop. Then he comes across a burning cabin and a traumatized woman just widowed by a fatal shot.

Freed from a cruel marriage, Esther Andrews agrees to winter at the Lockridge homestead to help Jared's pregnant sister-in-law. Lame in one foot, Esther has always known she is second-hand goods, but the gentle carpenter-turned-scout draws her heart with as much skill as he creates furniture from wood. His family's love offers hope even as violence erupts along the frontier—and Jared's investigation into local incidents brings danger to their doorstep. Yet how could Esther ever hope a loyal man like Jared would choose her over a fine lady?

Lone Star Ranger by Renae Brumbaugh Green

Elizabeth Covington will get her man.

And she has just a week to prove her brother isn't the murderer Texas Ranger Rett Smith accuses him of being. She'll show the good-looking lawman he's wrong, even if it means setting out on a risky race across Texas to catch the real killer.

Rett doesn't want to convict an innocent man. But he can't let the Boston beauty sway his senses to set a guilty man free. When Elizabeth follows him on a dangerous trek, the Ranger vows to keep her safe. But who will protect him from the woman whose conviction and courage leave him doubting everything—even his heart?

9 781963 212136